The SECRET of REDEMPTION

JEFFREY GALE

Copyright © 2023 Jeffrey Gale
All rights reserved
First Edition

PAGE PUBLISHING
Conneaut Lake, PA

First originally published by Page Publishing 2023

ISBN 979-8-88793-759-5 (pbk)
ISBN 979-8-88793-760-1 (digital)

Printed in the United States of America

In memory of Sir Basil Henriques, the founder of the Settlement Synagogue in London, and Rabbi Robert Samuels, the late general manager of the Leo Baeck Education Center in Haifa.

Their ideas were far ahead of their times, and their contribution to humanity was immeasurable.

Dedicated to my eclectic group of colleagues and friends in Northern Manhattan, whose noble deeds I greatly respect. My interactions with them and my experiences in Washington Heights have inspired this book.

The Secret of Redemption

Forgetfulness leads to exile while
remembrance is the secret of redemption.

—Baal Shem Tov

When a stranger sojourns with you in your
land, you shall not do him wrong. You shall
treat the stranger who sojourns with you as
the native among you, and you shall love
him as yourself, for you were strangers in the
land of Egypt: I am the Lord your God.

—Leviticus 19:33–34

Part One

Rendezvous with Yesterday

> Without memory, there is no culture. Without memory, there would be no civilization, no society, no future.
>
> —Elie Wiesel

Chapter I
Lest We Forget

> Only take care, and keep your soul diligently, lest you forget the things that your eyes have seen, and lest they depart from your heart all the days of your life. Make them known to your children and to your children's children.
>
> —Deuteronomy 4:9

I

New York
November 2013

Kristallnacht, a pogrom orchestrated by the Nazis on November 9 to 10, 1938, marked the beginning of the end of European Jewry. It paved the way for further curtailment of civil rights, the loss of German citizenship for the Jewish population, the formation of ghettos, the establishment of concentration camps, and ultimately the murder of the six million. From Kristallnacht onward, the status of the European Jew rapidly degenerated from "You have no right to live among us as Jews" to "You have no right to live among us" to "You have no right to live."

The toxic state of race relations in America formed the backdrop of my congregation's observance of *Kristallnacht* in northern Manhattan. The ghosts of 1938 have reappeared on the synagogue's doorstep. Inequality, discrimination, segregation, violence against racial minorities, anti-Semitic incidents, and anti-immigrant violence were in full force. ICE was bearing down hard upon illegal immigrants. Many have taken refuge in religious institutions to avoid deportation and family separation. Hatred of "the other" was the order of the day.

In the 1980s, I was a pulpit rabbi and a Soviet Jewry activist in London. I visited the Soviet Union twice and directly witnessed the tribulations and emotional pain of refuseniks, clandestine Hebrew teachers, and prisoners of conscience. I presided over the "twinning" of my bat mitzvah student, Simone Da Costa, with Sanna Tsivkin of Leningrad.

Thirty years later, I am now the rabbi of Congregation *Rodef Tzedek*, a synagogue whose membership decades ago consisted primarily of Holocaust survivors. In the 1940s, Washington Heights was once known as Frankfort on the Hudson. Most of these survivors have passed on, but a critical remnant remains. As a spiritual leader confronting the grim realities of 2013, both Kristallnacht and its aftermath and the plight of Soviet Jewry seem as if they had only happened yesterday.

The upcoming observance of Kristallnacht set off a chain of events which would lead to both communal challenges and would move my rabbinate in an unpredictable direction. At the end of the day, all of us in northern Manhattan had a much better understanding of *rodef tzedek*, the pursuit of justice.

II

Long Island, New York
November 5, 2013

Shortly after my family moved to suburban New York, our residence became a social hub. Between Shabbat and festival meals, Pesach *sederim*, Chanukah celebrations, play dates, birthday parties, sleepovers, and the regular entertainment of out-of-town relatives, swarms of people regularly walked through our doors. Our rooms were put to good use, and there were times when we had difficulty accommodating all our guests.

Thirteen years later, empty-nest syndrome hit the Levin home with a vengeance. The boisterous house became sedate and now seemed much roomier. Our children, Bracha and Greg, were now adults and living their own lives. At present, they were both out of the country.

As I was putting the finishing touches on the seventy-fifth anniversary Kristallnacht service, I felt like I was working in a mausoleum. My wife was currently at a conference in St. Petersburg, Russia, and was making a major presentation. After the conference concluded, she also planned to break up her trip by spending two or three extra days in her favorite European city, Paris!

As I was thinking about my kids, I remembered a conversation I had with their former pediatrician, Dr. Yosef Sugarman. Last May, we met at the ice cream stand after we had both participated in a Salute to Israel Parade in Midtown, New York. As he had dutifully looked after both Bracha and Greg during their formative years, he naturally asked how they were getting along.

Knowing that Dr. Sugarman was a modern Orthodox Jew and a strong Zionist, I considered sticking to generalities but decided to state the whole truth. I had nothing to be ashamed of. I said, "Bracha is quite an ambitious young lady. A couple of summers ago, she spent two months in Morocco and immersed herself in the Arabic language. At present, she is taking some graduate classes at Hebrew University and will be learning colloquial Arabic. It will be of great use to her in her human rights work. As for Greg, he is taking advanced German and business courses in Berlin."

Dr. Sugarman shook his head. "As a rabbi, you must be distraught. Instead of strengthening their Hebrew, they are studying the languages of our enemies. German was the language of the Nazis. Arabic is the language of terrorists."

I replied, "German may have been the language of Hitler's *Mein Kampf*, but it is also the language of Goethe's *Faust*. Many Jewish academics know German. For Greg, it's a tool so that he can understand the lectures at his school. He marches to the beat of his own drum, but it doesn't hurt that he has a mind of his own.

"As for my daughter, Arabic may be the language of those who wish to seek Israel's destruction, but it's also the language of some first-rate poetry. For Bracha, it's a valuable tool for her part-time internship at *Ir Amim*."

"What's Ir Amim?"

"As you know, it means 'city of the peoples.' It's a human rights organization that addresses a variety of civil rights abuses in Israel, works for a pluralistic society, and tries to give the Arab population a fair shake."

"I am shocked! After all the terrorist attacks perpetrated against our Israeli brothers and sisters from 1948 to the present, are you allowing your daughter to work with Palestinians? Israel is a Jewish state created for the benefit of homeless Jews. She should be more concerned with her own people."

"I'm afraid that Bracha doesn't see Israel that way. She sees Palestinians and Israelis as equals. She believes that if you strip away the self-serving politicians on both sides, the average Palestinian and the average Israeli want the same things—food, shelter, a good education for their children, some creature comforts, and a hopeful future. She must serve Israel in her own way.

"Bracha takes *tikkun olam*, repairing the world, very seriously. Her burning ambition is to turn darkness into light and to create a world that is at peace. In fact, her Hebrew name is Bracha Shulamit, the blessing of peace. When she goes to law school, she plans to focus on human rights and acquire the tools for following her passions.

"Bracha inspires me in my own communal work every day of the week. To quote the last verse from a popular song performed by Martina McBride, 'In my daughter's eyes, I can see the future, a reflection of who I am and what will be. And though she'll grow and someday leave, maybe raise a family, when I'm gone I hope she'll see, how happy she made me, for I'll be there, in my daughter's eyes.'"

Having known for years that I was no traditional rabbi and that he wasn't going to change my mind, Dr. Sugarman did not respond further. He gave a deep sigh, shook his head, and rejoined his own family at the kosher hot dog stand.

III

As my thoughts shifted from Dr. Sugarman to my rabbinic tasks, Bracha contacted me from Israel on Facetime. I was just beginning to get used to this form of communication. Thirty years ago, cell phones were nonexistent. The United States and the Soviet Union were not just different countries in opposite parts of the globe. They seemed like separate planets to me. The world has gotten so much smaller in 2013!

"Hi, Bracha! What can I do for you?"

"I just called to say hi."

"How are your graduate courses going at Hebrew University?"

"Even though I am enrolled in the program for overseas students, most of my classes are conducted in Hebrew or Arabic. As you know, I enrolled in the *ulpan* over the summer, and I got placed in the most advanced class. I strengthened my command of *dikduk* [Hebrew grammar] and gained confidence in my ability to cope with Hebrew lectures. The colloquial Arabic is quite easy. I'm already proficient in classical Arabic. Israeli children's literature is being taught in easy Hebrew. It involves a project at the end of the term. And then there is the course which focuses on the intellectual history of Zionism. I take that course with Israelis, and so far, I understand 90 percent of the lecture.

"I have two English classes as well. I am studying Palestinian history with a Palestinian professor. The course on the land of Israel in biblical sources is fascinating. The class is in English, but the texts are in Hebrew. My teacher is into higher biblical criticism. She embraces the multiple authorship of the Tanach and will probably upset some of my orthodox classmates. Between Palestinian history and the so-called documentary hypothesis, I am getting a very different perspective than I did in my Jewish high school."

"What about Ir Amim?"

"I am working with a couple of lawyers. They are addressing the deplorable sanitation conditions in many of the Arab neighborhoods. We will soon be attending a session at the Knesset."

"That must be exciting. I bet you are looking forward to going to law school."

"Yep."

"I am sure that you are not looking forward to the LSATS!"

"Really, Daddy. I have said many times that any person who can read can easily get an 800 on the verbal section of the SAT."

"Which you did twice."

"Exactly. The same principle applies to the LSATS. I'm not worried."

"If you say so. By the way, where are you right now?"

"As Kristallnacht is only a few days away, I thought that I would visit Yad Vashem. I believe that Baba had an uncle, Berl Valdman, who was murdered during the Shoah. I want to check out the database."

"Where was Berl murdered?"

"In the Ukraine."

"Please let me know what you find out."

"Will do. Afterward, I will pay a visit to our relatives. Perhaps they can fill in the missing information."

"Good luck, Bracha. I'll talk to you soon."

"Love you, Daddy!"

IV

Tuchin, Ukraine
September 23, 1942

The little town of Tuchin was in the Rovno district of the Western Ukraine near the Horyn River. Life was hard for the Jewish population. Between the two world wars, they suffered from the frequent changes of the forces in control of the area (Ukrainians, Soviets, and Poles). Anti-Semitism, both subtle and overt, was very much entrenched in East European society.

The Valdman family lived in Tuchin for generations. Like many of their Jewish neighbors, their extended family was close-knit. They experienced the sweetness of the Sabbath and the great joy of the Jewish festivals. The community educated its children, assisted wedding couples in need, cared for the sick, and buried the dead. While Zionism was strong in this little town and some of its residents found their way to Palestine, Berl Valdman was proud to call Tuchin his home.

After Germany invaded the Soviet Union, refugees from Western Poland migrated to Tuchin, and the Jewish population swelled to three thousand. Jewish life took a drastic turn for the worst when the Nazi army captured Tuchin on July 4, 1941. The signal was given to the Ukrainians, who acted as Nazi surrogates, to carry out pogroms.

That month, twenty Jewish leaders were arrested and shot. Shortly afterward, various forms of persecution including restrictions on movement, the seizure of able-bodied people for slave labor, and the wearing of the yellow badge were introduced. Some members of the intelligentsia were murdered. A ghetto was established in August 1942.

On the Days of Awe, which took place several weeks later, the Jewish community was particularly filled with dread and fear. Berl Valdman, his wife, and his four children spent the entire day of Yom Kippur in the Great Synagogue of Tuchin. As they were pouring out their prayers to God on the holiest day of the Jewish year, they were terrified as to what the *Ribon Ha'olamim* (Master of the Universe) had in store for them. In his somber, melancholy voice, the *chazan* chanted the *Unnetahah Tokef*, one of the central prayers of the High Holy Day liturgy. The words that stuck to Berl were as follows:

> On Rosh Hashanah will be inscribed, and on Yom Kippur will be sealed how many will pass from the earth and how many will be created; who will live and who will die; who will die at his predestined time and who before his time; who by water and who by fire, who by sword, who by beast, who by famine, who by thirst, who by storm, who by plague, who by strangulation, and who by stoning. Who will rest and who will wander, who will live in harmony and who will be harried, who will enjoy tranquility and who will suffer, who will be impoverished and who will be enriched, who will be degraded and who will be exalted.

Two days later, on September 23, judgment came down like an iron fist. An order was given for all Jews to assemble at the ghetto gate. This turn of events could only mean one thing—mass deportation to extermination camps.

The most important phrase of Unnetanah Tokef emphasizes that repentance, prayer, and good deeds annul the severity of the decree. Not in this case. Much more was needed. The head of the *Judenrat* (Jewish Council), Gecel Schwarzman, supported by his two deputies, Meir Himmelfarb and Tuwia Czuwak, decided to revolt. The strategy would be to acquire firearms whenever and wherever possible, to set fires to many houses for defense purposes and for creating a massive diversion, and to escape to the forests.

Berl admired Gecel, Meir, and Tuwia. Although the situation was totally hopeless, they did not want to go like sheep to the slaughter. Jews have survived impossible odds throughout history. Better to fight with their backs against the wall than to resign themselves to death.

However, he thought, *What good was torching his house and running for the forests? Even if we managed to get out of Tuchin alive, there is the risk of succumbing to hunger and exposure. Moreover, the Ukrainians are not our friends. There are several Ukrainian gangs who are only too eager to harass and kill Jews and to complete the work of the Nazis. On the other hand, we can't stay where we are. Either we will be shot on the spot or deported.*

Berl looked toward the sky and asked God for wisdom. He spoke softly to himself the first words of Psalm 121: *Esa einai el heharim, me'ayin yavo ezri; Ezri me'im Hashem Oseh shamayim va'aretz.* (I lift up my eyes to the hills, from where does my help come; from God, the Maker of heaven and earth.)

He contemplated setting fire to his home and burning his entire family inside. While there was the slim possibility of his family linking up with the partisans and living to fight another day, the whole rebellion would inevitably end badly. Even if the Nazis chose to let some of the Tuchin Jews live, what sort of life would it be? Slave labor for able-bodied men and the young pretty women being delivered to German servicemen for their entertainment? Unthinkable!

And yet Berl undoubtedly recoiled from such a thought. He thought of himself as a pious Jew who was a keeper of the commandments. Suicide! A *chilul ha Shem*! A profanation of the divine name!

It's a slap in the face, so to speak, of the Almighty, who granted us life and who commanded us to develop His world.

Soldiers are expendable. They are mere casualties of war. They can be easily replaced. However, as the famous Hebrew writer S. Y. Agnon put it several years later, this is not so with the King of kings, the Holy One, blessed be He. God created humanity in His own image, delights in life, loves peace and pursues peace, and loves His people, Israel. As Jews, we are God's soldiers. Because we are so few, every one of us matters. God doesn't have many to put in our place. When one child of Israel is missing, God forbid, God's entire kingdom is diminished.

Berl Valdman was standing before his God and felt quite alone. The decision that he was about to make opposed the very fiber of his being. However, just as suicide was a desecration of God, so was falling into Nazi hands and allowing German soldiers to become their slave masters, their violators, or their executioners.

He then called his wife and four children to stand with him in the living room. Although there were tears and wailing, he kissed every one of them before lighting the fires that would put an end to life as they knew it.

As the flames began to engulf everything in their path, Berl's final words were "*Shema Yisrael Ha Shem Elokeinu Ha Shem Achad:* Hear O Yisrael, the Lord is our God, the Lord is One."

The fate of Tuchin was sealed between Yom Kippur and Sukkot. Of the three thousand Jews that resided in Tuchin, only twenty survived. While repentance, prayer, and good deeds did not annul the severity of the decree, its residents exercised free choice and stood up to tyranny as best they could.

The remains of those who were murdered lie in nameless graves, either in the town itself or in the surrounding forests. As proclaimed in *Unnetanah Tokef*, many died before their predestined time. Many died by hunger, by thirst, and by exposure. Many died by shooting. Berl Valdman and his family died by fire. May goodness and mercy follow them all their days in the *Olam ha Ba*, the World to Come, and may they dwell in the House of the Lord forever.

The town of Tuchin is no more. No attempt was made to resurrect it. The memories of its glorious days as well as the tragedy of

September 23, 1942, now fall upon the martyrs' descendants. May they tell their stories to their children and their children's children, lest we forget and Tuchin's name be blotted from the face of the earth.

V

Jerusalem
November 6, 2013

Yad Vashem, the premier Holocaust Museum in Israel, is derived from Isaiah 56:5:

> I will give in my house and within my walls a monument and a name better than sons and daughters; I will give them an everlasting name which shall not be cut off.

It was designed to display all the sights, sounds, and artifacts of what took place in Europe from the rise of Adolf Hitler to the defeat of the Axis Powers in 1945. Bracha Levin visited Yad Vashem on three other occasions. We visited it as a family during the summer after her bat mitzvah. She returned there as part of a summer youth tour and shortly before her graduation from the Jewish high school. Each visit provided new and more mature insights.

After visiting the database and researching Jewish life in Tuchin, the tragedy of the Jewish community in 1942, and the tragic fate of Berl Valdman's family, she sat quietly for a few moments. That such things could happen to her great-great-uncle, a major component of her family tree, was too much for her. She had to leave Yad Vashem immediately.

As she departed, she once again came across the plaque that was hanging just above the exit door. Engraved on the plaque was the chilling phrase attributed to the Baal Shem Tov: *Hagolah nimshacha meihashicha, uvzichrona sod ha-geulah.* (Forgetfulness leads to exile while remembrance is the secret of redemption.) Bracha would not forget.

Just two miles north of Yad Vashem was the Jewish neighborhood, Givat Shaul Bet. On a clear day such as today, it could easily be seen with the naked eye. Prior to the birth of Israel, it was the site of the Arab village *Deir Yassin*. Deir Yassin and many other villages were casualties of the war between the Arab population and the emerging Jewish state.

Following the War of Independence, the area was incorporated into the State of Israel. Givat Shaul Bet was built on Deir Yassin's land. In 1951, the Kfar Shaul Mental Health Center was built on the village itself, using some of the village's abandoned buildings. In the 1980s, most of the remaining abandoned parts of the village were bulldozed to make way for new neighborhoods, and most of the Deir Yassin cemetery was bulldozed to make way for a highway.

Upon leaving the building, Bracha stared from a distance at Givat Shaul. She thought to herself, *So many of the exhibitions in Yad Vashem focused on how the Nazis sought to eradicate every vestige of Judaism in Europe. In what was once Deir Yassin, every vestige of its identity was eradicated. Yad Vashem memorialized the six million. There was no monument in Israel to memorialize the life that once existed in Deir Yassin and how its people got driven from their homes. Baal Shem Tov allegedly said that remembrance is the secret of redemption. Did he mean remembrance of only Jewish history and only Jewish tragedies, or did he mean remembrance of world history and all human tragedies? Is not God concerned with all of humanity, or do only Jewish people count?* Bracha would ponder these questions for many years to come. As she was invited to the home of Israeli cousins from her mom's side of the family, she would also share her thoughts with them.

VI

Petah Tikvah, Israel
November 6, 2013

Bracha hopped into a *sherut* and proceeded to the home of Yehudah and Rivkah in Petah Tikvah.

Rivkah was the first cousin of my mother-in-law, who was lovingly known as Baba Masha. Rivkah strikingly resembled her in physical appearance. She greeted us at the entrance.

"Shalom chavivi! Ma Shlomeich? [Hello my beloved! How are you?] Any relative of your baba is welcome in our house. I hope that she is well."

"She's still living independently and getting around town."

"Your grandparents treated us royally when we visited them in Canada a few years ago. Baba Masha is quite a *maven* in the kitchen. If I recall, Zayde Yaakov told the best jokes. This evening, we have a nice dinner prepared for you."

Bracha looked around the house. It consisted of two stories and was quite large by Israeli standards. The children had all grown up and left the nest. Yehudah and Rivkah lived primarily on the first floor.

Yehudah, who was Rivkah's husband, had a lucrative law practice but was semiretired. Before dinner, Yehudah invited Bracha into his home office. She was astounded by the large quantity of books in Hebrew and English. The Judaica collection was quite impressive.

"Wow," said Bracha to Yehudah. You have a *Mikrot Gedolot*, the text of the entire Bible with the major Jewish commentaries. You also own a Talmud, numerous collections of *midrashim*, and books on Jewish history, Jewish thought, and Israeli archeology. Yet you identify yourself as a secular Jew."

Yehudah replied, "*Secular* means something different in Israel than it does in North America. In North America, most secular Jews are estranged from their religion and know very little about Judaism. In Israel, we have Israelis on virtually every street corner who have committed large portions of the Tanach to memory. They may not necessarily take it literally or even believe everything that is written within it. There are also plenty of secular Israelis who can go through a daf [page] of *Gemmorah* as easily as you can read the *Jewish Post* but in the end conclude that it is all *narishkeit* or foolishness. A secular Jew does not have to be an *am haaretz*, an ignoramus on Jewish matters. We are a people of the book."

Rivkah called Yehudah and Bracha to dinner in the large eat-in kitchen. The first courses were Israeli salad and chicken soup.

Rivkah asked, "So how did you spend your day?"

Bracha replied, "I spent most of the day at Yad Vashem, where I researched what took place in Tuchin and the fate of Berl Valdman's family."

Yehudah entered the conversation. "Berl, of course, was one of Rivkah's uncles. The first principle of Jewish survival is memory. The twenty fifth chapter of *Devarim* [Deuteronomy] commands us to remember Amalek and what he did to our ancestors in the wilderness. We must not forget. In the same way, we must remember Berl Valdman. Remember, lest we forget. Once we forget, we as Jews are doomed.

"Bracha, Rivkah tells me that you were named after our dear Berl. Your middle name is Shulamith. Berl was a God-fearing man, and his legacy rests in you. You must help work for a strong Israel so that his memory is for a blessing—the blessing of peace.

"If there is one thing that you should have learned from your research is the importance of keeping Israel safe. We need to protect her from her enemies, both within and outside of our country. In 1942, there was no Jewish state to take in Berl Valdman, and millions of other Jews were murdered."

"There's one thing that I don't understand," said Bracha. "When I left Yad Vashem, I saw what used to be Deir Yassin from a distance. All traces of a formerly vibrant Arab village are erased. Deir Yassin was a central symbol of the *Nakba* (The Catastrophe), but there's no monument to commemorate what took place there."

"There's no need for a monument. The *Irgun* and *Lehi* conducted a military operation there in 1948 to save Jerusalem and, in essence, the fledgling state of Israel."

"The mitzvah to love the stranger is found throughout the Torah. As Jews, shouldn't we care about the other?"

"Not if it is the intention of the stranger to annihilate you. Let me explain. The attack on Deir Yassin took place a few months after the United Nations had proposed that Palestine be divided into an Arab state and a Jewish one. Had the Arabs been smart, they would have embraced partition with both arms. They would be living in a sizeable autonomous state to this very day. Instead, the Arabs foolishly rejected the proposal, and civil war broke out."

Bracha thought that this was a disingenuous argument. The Israelis looked upon the partition, as limited as it was, as a stepping-stone. Settling in the rest of the country was the long game. It would be achieved by other means other than what took place in Flushing Meadows. However, she kept this thought to herself.

Yehudah continued, "In the months leading up to the end of British rule, in a phase of the civil war known as the Battle of the Roads, the Arab League-sponsored Arab Liberation Army, composed of Palestinians and other Arabs, attacked Jewish traffic on major roads in an effort to isolate the Jewish communities from each other. This army managed to seize several strategic vantage points along the highway between Jerusalem and Tel Aviv, Jerusalem's sole supply route and link to the western side of the city where 16 percent of all Jews in Palestine lived. They began firing on convoys traveling to the city. By March 1948, the road was cut off, and Jerusalem was under siege.

"In response, the *Haganah* launched Operation Nahshon to break the siege. The operation was named after the biblical figure Nahshon Ben Aminadav, who was the first to wade into the Red Sea when the Hebrews escaped from slavery in Egypt. On April 6, in an effort to secure strategic positions, the Haganah and its strike force, the *Palmach*, attacked Kastal, a village two kilometers north of Deir Yassin overlooking the Jerusalem-Tel Aviv highway.

"Deir Yassin, lying some two thousand feet above sea level, was an important link in the chain of Arab positions enclosing Jerusalem from the West. Arab forces from Ein Kerem and Bethlehem crossed to the Kastel front, from where they attacked Jewish convoys along the only route to Jerusalem from the coast.

"Both Arabs and certain Jewish officials fearing the Irgun men as political rivals described our military action in Deir Yassin as a massacre. It was condemned by the leadership of the Haganah—the Jewish community's main paramilitary force—by the area's two chief rabbis and famous Jews abroad like Albert Einstein, Jessurun Cardozo, Hannah Arendt, Sidney Hook and others. The Jewish Agency for Israel sent Jordan's King Abdullah a letter of apology, which he rebuffed. He held them responsible for the massacre and warned about terrible consequences if similar incidents occurred elsewhere.

"The hostile propaganda, disseminated throughout the world, deliberately ignored the fact that the civilian population of Deir Yassin was given a warning by us before the battle began. One of our soldiers carrying a loudspeaker was stationed at the entrance to the village and exhorted in Arabic, 'All women, children, and aged must leave their houses and take shelter on the slope of the hill.' By giving this humane warning, our fighters threw away the element of complete surprise and thus increased their own risk in the ensuing battle. A substantial number of the inhabitants obeyed the warning, and they were unhurt.

"The fire of the enemy was murderous, to which the number of our casualties bears eloquent testimony. Our men were compelled to fight for every house. To overcome the enemy, they used large numbers of hand grenades. The civilians who had disregarded our warnings suffered inevitable casualties.

"Without Operation Nahshon and without the military action that took place in Deir Yassin, there would be no Israel."

Bracha interrupted. "What about the accusations that you publicly displayed Arab prisoners in Jerusalem as part of a victory parade?"

"More vicious propaganda! But I don't deny this accusation either. It served two purposes. It was a great morale booster for the besieged Jewish community in Jerusalem. Secondly, it sent a powerful message to the Arab population not to mess with the Jewish people.

"Israeli Jews excel in military operations. In public relations, we stink. The Arabs, I must admit, excel in public relations.

"The propaganda regarding Deir Yassin worked in our favor. It struck fear in the hearts of the local Arab population. It led to the flight of nearly seven hundred thousand Arabs. The legend of Deir Yassin helped us particularly in the saving of Tiberias and the conquest of Haifa.

"The Jewish officials who condemned us were hypocrites. While our political opponents made political capital by their remarks, they certainly were not sorry to see so many Palestinians flee their homes.

While Ben Gurion was publicly conciliatory to the king of Jordan and referred him as a wise ruler, his vision of Israel was no different than the Irgun and Lehi forces. Like many of us, he believed that while the present map of Palestine was drawn by the British mandate, the Jewish people have another map which our youth and adults should strive to fulfill: from the Nile to the Euphrates. He accepted the initial partition of Israel into a Jewish state and an Arab state because he knew all too well that the Arabs would reject it and that the borders of the Jewish state would ultimately be determined by force. He once said, 'The Arabs will have to go, but one needs an opportune moment for making it happen, such as a war.' Because our differences were more about tactics than about philosophy, Ben Gurion's condemnation of Deir Yassin was inappropriate and self-serving.

"My brother-in-law, Avigdor, and I gave blood, sweat, and tears to end British rule and to bring about an independent Jewish state. He was a member of the Haganah. I was part of the Irgun."

Bracha already knew from her family that Yehudah was imprisoned by the British for indelicate activities. She asked, "Why did you spend time in Acre Prison?"

Without directly answering the question, Yehudah replied, "Why not? There is a story in which Ralph Waldo Emerson visited Henry David Thoreau in prison. He asked him, 'What are you doing in there?' He replied, 'What are you doing out there?'"

Bracha retorted, "Henry David Thoreau believed in civil disobedience, but he did not belong to a terrorist organization."

A wry smile appeared across Yehudah's face. "Before I even address the issue of so-called terrorism, let me set the record straight in terms of the Jewish national claim. The traditional argument presented by the Arabs is that the Jewish national entity ceased to exist after the destruction of the Second Temple in 70 CE. They were long gone before there was ever an Arab presence. In the seventh century, the Muslims conquered much of the Middle East and occupied the land. By the fourteenth century, Palestine was incorporated into the Ottoman Empire. Hence the Arab claim to this part of the world. If the Jews have a historical quarrel, it's with the Romans and not with the Arabs."

Yehudah continued, "The *Galut* did not begin with the Roman destruction of Jerusalem. Vibrant Jewish communities in the Middle East, such as Alexandria and Babylon, continued for centuries. Although there was loss of national autonomy, there was still a predominately Jewish presence in Palestine as well.

"In 636 to 640 CE, the Arabs burst into the land and took it over from the Byzantines. The celebrated historian Ben Zion Dinur points out that the Arabs expropriated Jewish homes, Jewish labor, and large amounts of Jewish land. In Tiberias, alone, the Arabs confiscated half the Jews' houses, and most of the Jewish farmers were coerced into the Arab army.[1]

"Under Muslim rule, the Pact of Umar was introduced which governed the behavior of Muslims toward Jews and Christians, the other People of the Book. The respected historian Benny Morris points out that the *d'himmi*, the subject Jewish and Christian communities, were forced to pay a poll tax and a special tax imposed by the Muslim conquerors on nonbelievers whose lands they had confiscated. While Jews and Christians were allowed to cultivate these lands, under Muslim protection, Muslim rulers reserved the right to tear up the agreement and expel the so-called protected communities. Because of the heavy imposition of these special taxes on agricultural land, many Jews were forced to migrate from rural areas to towns.

"There were also restrictions to reinforce the social inferiority of Jews and Christians. The d'himmi were forbidden to strike a Muslim, carry arms, ride horses, build new houses of worship or repair old ones, and they had to wear distinctive clothing. It was a policy of contemptuous tolerance.[2]

"Social and economic discrimination caused substantial Jewish emigration from Palestine. Muslim civil wars in the eighth and ninth centuries drove many non-Muslims out of the country. The Arabs succeeded in doing what the might of Rome had not achieved—the uprooting of the Jewish farmer from his soil. They effectively eliminated the Jewish character from Palestine. While leftist historians currently argue that Jews usurped the land from the Arabs and engaged in ethnic cleansing, it was the Arabs who usurped the land from the Jews."

Up to this point, Yehudah's remarks echoed virtually everything that Bracha learned about Jewish history in her Jewish high school. Indeed, anti-Semitism was a large part of the curriculum. The Arab conquest of Palestine was yet another example. Yehudah simply provided greater details and a more personal slant.

Yehudah continued, "Our job today is to hold on to what rightfully belongs to Israel. Professor Dinur points out that even after the Arab Conquest, we never entirely abandoned the land of Israel and during the entire history of Palestine under foreign rule until the present day there was never a corner of the country where Jews did not live. The fact that we were a tiny minority confined to a specific corner of the promised land for hundreds of years does not diminish our rights. It increases them.[3] Throughout the ages, the Jews have yearned to return to the land, have never ceased to protest the dispossession of political piracy, and to demand the return of its stolen property. The land is Israel's everlasting possession, which only they shall inherit and in which only they shall settle.[4]

"Our prime minister, Benjamin Netanyahu, wrote that the Muslims conquered most of Spain in 711. Over a period of centuries, the Spaniards launched the Reconquista and sought to win back what was taken from them. After the surrender of Granada in January 1492, the entire Iberian Peninsula was controlled by Christian rulers. Spain never ceased to be the Spaniards' homeland. No one seriously suggests that Spaniards who rolled back the Arab tide that had swept over their land committed a historic wrong.[5]

"What the Spaniards achieved after eight centuries, the Jews achieved after twelve. The time frame was different, but the principle is identical."

"There is a flaw in your argument," replied Bracha. "How can you use the Reconquista to justify Israeli policies today? Firstly, through blood and fire, the Spaniards destroyed one of the great intellectual and cultural centers of mankind and threw Europe into the dark ages. Secondly, there was no love for non-Christians, Muslims and Jews alike. Six months after the surrender of Granada, the Jews were expelled from the country. Beginning with the voyages of Columbus, fanaticism against non-Christians was exported to North America.

The Doctrine of Discovery was enforced with great zeal. The natives of the New World were branded as heathens whose purpose was to be enslaved, exploited, and civilized, if possible."

Yehudah argued, "But Zionism was far more humane. During the early years of the *Yishuv,* emphasis was placed on land purchases and peaceful coexistence. While the Spaniards took over a land that was largely cultivated, the first settlers inherited a ruined land which was largely unpopulated. They were a people without a land who were escaping persecution in Eastern Europe and colonizing a land without people. We provided modern technology and created jobs for the indigenous population. By our presence, we were doing the Arabs a tremendous service."

Bracha shook her head in outrage. The events of the War of Independence and the Six-Day War were glossed over. Seven hundred thousand Palestinians became homeless during the War of Independence. When the West Bank and Gaza came under Israel's control in 1967, more Palestinian refugees were added to the list. Yet she politely challenged Yehudah's remarks.

"Taking your argument to its logical conclusion, the War of Independence, which involved taking land by force and driving out people from villages who had lived there for generations, was tit-for-tat retaliation for what the Arabs did to the Jews in the eighth century."

"In a matter of speaking, yes! If Spain could retake its land centuries after it was conquered by Arabs, so should we."

Bracha rolled her eyes at this point. Yehudah was not going to be persuaded. Jewish tradition frowns upon chastising someone if you know in advance that the advice will not be heeded.

"Let's turn to the Balfour Declaration, which promised a Jewish homeland in Palestine. While it is hailed as a watershed moment in Jewish history, it was promulgated out of pure self-interest on the part of the British."

Bracha interjected, "The Balfour Declaration was spoken of in only glowing terms in my Jewish high school. Why are you so cynical?"

"In World War I, Great Britain had its back to the wall. The Allied Armies were bogged down on the Western Front and were in danger of total collapse unless there was more help from Russia and America. Russia was engulfed in a major revolution. The Bolsheviks had no appetite for a war among imperial powers and would likely make a separate peace with Germany. Isolationism governed American politics at that time. Most Americans wanted to live in their bubble and were not anxious to become entrenched in a foreign war.

"The British had a very stereotypical view of international Jewish influence. They believed that Zionist leaders were international button pushers, especially in America. If the government could produce a public document affirming their commitment to a Jewish homeland, this would garner support from both Russian Jews and rich, influential American Jews. Perhaps Russia could be persuaded to stay in the war, and perhaps America would finally enter World War I and put serious boots on the ground.

"Although the British and French were allies in World War I, they had rival colonial claims to Palestine. By endorsing Zionism, Great Britain wanted to legitimize its presence as the protector of Jewish self-determination. Control over Palestine was a strategic imperial interest to keep Egypt and the Suez Canal within its sphere of influence. Access to the Suez Canal was the lifeblood of preserving the British Empire.

"Here's another reason why I challenge the true motivation of the Balfour Declaration. In the early twentieth century, both America and Great Britain were stricken with anti-immigration bias, particularly Jews from Eastern Europe. In 1905, while serving as prime minister, Arthur Balfour presided over the passage of the Aliens Act. The legislature put the first restrictions on immigration into Great Britain, and it was primarily aimed at restricting Jewish immigration. According to historians, Balfour had personally delivered passionate speeches about the imperative to restrict the wave of Jews fleeing the Russian Empire from entering Great Britain.

"The Balfour Declaration was less about providing a home for homeless Jews fleeing pogroms and more about keeping them out of Great Britain. The swarms of East European Jews populating London's East End was a heavy burden on his country. He looked upon them as alien and hostile and as riffraff who could not be absorbed into British society. If they could be dumped into Palestine, the Jewish problem in Great Britain could be solved.

"The McMahon-Hussein correspondence in 1915 to 1916 traded British support of an independent Arab state for Arab assistance in opposing the Ottoman Empire. The Balfour Declaration angered the Arabs because they believed that Palestine was to be part of that independent state. They were threatened by a potential Jewish state in which the Jews would replace the Ottomans as their masters.

"While the Balfour Declaration did not specify the borders, it was our understanding that they would extend from the Mediterranean to somewhere beyond the Jordan River. However, after the Jaffa riots of 1921, the British changed their tune. Sir John Evelyn Shuckburg, the new leader of the Middle East Department at the Colonial Office, and T. E. Lawrence from the Colonial Office felt that Britain's interests would be better served by opposing Zionism and winning the favor of the Arabs. At the time, Winston Churchill was the secretary of state for the colonies and served under the leadership of Prime Minister Lloyd George. Shuckburg and Lawrence persuaded Winston Churchill that Transjordan had been promised to King Feisel and the Hashemites of Mecca during the war. They thereby triggered the installation of Feisel's brother, Abdullah, and his army of Bedouins as rulers of Jordan. Such a move was designed to appease the Arab population. Suddenly, the Jewish homeland got whittled down to a fraction of the size envisioned in the Balfour Declaration. In conjunction with this, the Churchill White Paper of 1922 also recommended putting an end to unrestricted Jewish immigration, which should not exceed Palestine's economic absorptive capacity.

"While most Zionist leaders accepted the White Paper with only mild objections, Ze'ev Jabotinsky wanted no part of this. He insisted that the Zionist leadership attempt to create a Jewish majority in Palestine as soon as possible after World War I. He believed that the future Jewish homeland must include Transjordan, which had sufficient space to incorporate a mass influx of European Jews.

"Given Jabotinsky's vision of the future Jewish state and the increasing rate of Arab violence against Jewish settlers, he founded *Betar* in 1923. It was a Jewish Youth Movement in Eastern Europe designed to foster a new generation of Jews thoroughly indoctrinated in nationalist ideals and trained for military action against all enemies of Judaism. Jabotinsky, who suffered the trauma of pogroms in his native Kishinev, emphasized the importance of military defense. He believed that military training should be as common among Jews as lighting Shabbat candles.

"Jabotinsky was the founder of Revisionist Zionism, differing from Practical Zionism as advocated by David Ben Gurion and Chaim Weitzman. While the practical Zionists sought to settle in Palestine through land purchases, Jabotinsky advocated mass immigration. If the Arabs become the minority, so be it. There were many Arab states in the region to choose from. One branch of the Arab race would have to put up with living in someone else's state.

"Jabotinsky was no fool. He knew that the Arab population would fiercely resist Jewish colonization. In the end, he believed that there were only two possibilities—to either forget about Palestine or to fight a war for it. He believed that the latter was inevitable. Therefore, I would say that *Betar* was the precursor of the Irgun. Jabotinsky was a great man, but not always understood or appreciated by his fellow Zionists.

"Max Nordau was another great Zionist. He negated the Galut and believed that there was no future for Judaism in the Diaspora. In the eyes of their host countries, Jews are a race of accursed beggars. In a speech that he delivered at the First Zionist Congress, he argued that the Jewish body had been destroyed in the cramped quarters of the Jewish ghetto. Jews forgot how to move their limbs freely. In dark houses, their eyes blinked nervously out of fear of persecution, their strident voices turned to mere whispers.[6]

"Max Nordau believed that the solution to this plight was more than just settlement in Palestine. At the Second Zionist Congress in Basel in 1898, he advocated muscle Judaism. He wanted to distance himself from the galut Jew of Europe, from the hunched back *yeshiva* student who was all brain and no brawn. He believed that Jews should be physically fit, become proficient in gymnastics, and compete in sports. He looked upon Bar Kochba and the ancient Maccabees as role models.

"The text of the Shema teaches us that we worship God not only with our minds and souls but also with our might. Jewish learning is wonderful but incomplete without action, without applying our teachings to building a Jewish state. Max Nordau's belief was certainly compatible with what Jabotinsky sought to achieve in Israel."

Yehudah picked up the thread of his history lesson. "Arab riots in the 1920s and 1930s still took place despite the so-called gift of Transjordan. Jewish immigration was blamed for these riots. In response to the riots of 1936 to 1939 and to appease the Arabs further, Prime Minister Neville Chamberlain's government caved in. The duplicity of the British was manifested by the notorious White Paper of 1939. While paying lip service to a Jewish homeland, the White Paper went to great lengths to point out that this did not mean a Jewish State. Thus, Jewish immigration and land purchases from Arabs were virtually choked off. The official position was that under no circumstances was there to be a Jewish majority in Mandate Palestine. Illegal immigrants were turned away from our shores and either sent back to Europe or held in detention camps. A *Haganah* ship even blew itself up in the harbor of Haifa. In the end, the Arabs were never appeased.

"Today, the Jewish world is observing Kristallnacht. From the evening that synagogues and Jewish businesses were destroyed, when Jews were murdered, and when Jews were deported to labor camps, the fate of European Jewry went from bad to worse. What was needed was the world to open its doors. Instead, most countries, including Great Britain and even your country, severely restricted immigrants. To make matters worse, even Mandatory Palestine, the Jewish homeland, was off-limits. When I recall what took place in May 1939, my blood boils.

"Thus, a paramilitary group had to take matters into its own hands. We had to simultaneously provide a deterrent to Arab terrorism and to end the British Mandate as soon as possible. Inspired by the beliefs and actions of that great leader, Ze'ev Jabotinsky, the Irgun was formed. The Irgun's methods were aggressive. There were Jewish leaders who wanted to talk the British out of Palestine. We tried to bomb them out. An eye for an eye. A tooth for a tooth.

"Most Jews around the world call the Irgun a terrorist organization. The real terrorists were the British and the Arabs. To this very day, *Hamas* and many Arab leaders call for the destruction of Israel. Iran's nuclear program is very worrying. The country's mullahs would love to nuke us out of existence. The presence of a democratic state in a reactionary part of the world is an anathema to our enemies.

"The Irgun was, in fact, a counterterrorist organization. Through violence, we defeated those who sought to drive us into the Mediterranean Sea. We were motivated by love of our country and love of our fellow Jews. Israel would be the place where Jews could once again live like human beings. No longer would they have to suffer under the yoke of *goyim*.

"I'm afraid that there is no immediate solution to the current Israeli-Palestinian conflict. It will be an endless conflict until the Palestinians realize the futility of working for the destruction of Israel. Once they come to that conclusion, perhaps negotiation is possible. That is the basis of Jabotinsky's Iron Wall. The dreamy-eyed idealists in Israel and the Diaspora must face reality."

Bracha could not embrace for one minute the notion of endless conflict and bloodshed in the Middle East. She thought to herself, *An eye for an eye. A tooth for a tooth. At this rate, the world will become blind and toothless!* As she and her hosts were finishing the main course of roast chicken, mashed potatoes, and green beans, she spoke out.

"During the birth of the Jewish state, the Six-Day War, and the Yom Kippur War, Israel had the sympathy of most of the world. The Six-Day War even jump-started the Refusenik movement in the former Soviet Union. If the Israeli government continues to violate the civil rights of Palestinians, how can there ever be a just peace in the Middle East?"

"You speak of a just peace. What kind of justice did Berl Valdman and his family receive from the invading Germans? It was the justice that a coyote gives a chicken. President Netanyahu's brother, Yonaton, was killed while trying to rescue Jews from captivity in Entebbe. The ashes of Berl Valdman and the blood of Yonaton Netanyahu cry out to all their descendants in Israel. We have a strong

Jewish state that will never allow any of its citizens to suffer the fate of the six million in Europe. Never again!

"You speak of justice. Throughout the centuries, Jews have had their share of injustice. Let the next injustice work against somebody else for a change. Nothing that the Israeli government does or has done in the West Bank and Gaza compares to what was done to the six million in Europe."

Bracha, who was fuming inside, responded with a touch of defiance. "I suppose that means more outrageous treatment of Palestinians living in the West Bank, more rough treatment at the border crossings, more destruction of homes, more illegal confiscation of privately own land, more harassment of Palestinian families, more illegal deportations, and more torture."

"Let me put it this way. If liberals want to push negotiations, engage in Israeli-Palestinian outreach, and have kumbaya experiences with their local Muslim communities, we have no objections. But consider this. Israel is the only western-style democracy in the Middle East. All the other countries are either theocracies, dictatorships, or complete totalitarian states. We don't have any negotiation partners. It's impossible to reason with authoritarian leaders and with their followers who don't have the foggiest concept of democracy and civil debate. It's impossible to reason with despots whose bottom line is the destruction of Israel. In short, it's impossible to reason with unreasonable people. While the dovish leaders of this world seek to reason with the enemy, our government will continue to build settlements and establish facts on the ground. If in the days of the Messiah there is a final solution to the Middle East crisis, at least we won't be colluding in the dismantling of Israel on the installment plan."

Bracha finished the dessert consisting of coffee and apple strudel. While the visit ended on a sour note, she was invited to come again. As Bracha entered the *sherut* to return to her Jerusalem apartment, she thought, *Yehudah thinks that he will eventually bring me over to his side. He should think again!*

Chapter 2

KRISTALLNACHT

All the Dachaus must remain standing. The Dachaus, the Belsens, the Buchenwalds, the Auschwitzes—all of them. They must remain standing because they are a monument to a moment in time when some men decided to turn the Earth into a graveyard. Into it they shoveled all their reason, their logic, their knowledge, but worst of all, their conscience. And the moment we forget this, the moment we cease to be haunted by its remembrance, then we become the gravediggers. Something to dwell on and to remember wherever men walk God's Earth.

—Rod Serling

I

New York
November 8, 2013

My spacious office at Congregation Rodef Tzedek was on the first floor of our enormous four-story building. On the south side were my two desks, one for the computer and one for my general work. On the north side were the storage closets and a conference table. On both sides were numerous bookcases containing both my

Judaica and general library. The room was bisected by four blue chairs. Two of them were lined up against the wall, just underneath the air-conditioning unit. The other two chairs were facing them. I used the conference table for formal committee meetings and the four comfy chairs for meetings with individual congregants.

I was flicking through the Kristallnacht service when my son reached me on FaceTime. Gregory was named after my mother's first cousin, Georges Garel, who was active in the French Resistance during World War II. This dark-haired, brown-eyed dynamo of medium build resembled my wife's side of the family. When our phones connected, he appeared to be in a very celebratory mood. Greg appeared to be in the middle of a sumptuous meal at a stylish restaurant. Although it was only 1:00 p.m. in New York, it was dinnertime in Berlin. He was sitting with two young men.

"Hi, Daddy! How's it going?"

"Where are you?"

"Inside the famous Berlin Radio Tower."

"You've got guts. Back in 1973, the Radio Tower situated in East Berlin terrified me."

"It's no big deal."

"Berlin was a depressing place when I visited it forty years ago as part of a university field trip. It was a divided city. The Berlin Wall and the Radio Tower were vivid symbols of the Iron Curtain that stretched from Stettin in the Baltic to Trieste in the Adriatic. It was many times worse for Jews in 1938."

As I spoke, my son devoured a piece of schnitzel and washed it down with a glass of local German beer.

I continued, "My synagogue will be observing the seventy-fifth anniversary of Kristallnacht this evening. It will be a heavy-duty service with organ and choir. My *shul* will be in a rather somber mood. Somehow, the mood is quite different on your end."

"It's the end of a hard week of classes, so I'm getting some dinner and chilling this evening."

Greg then proceeded to introduce me to his drinking partners. The heavy-set and good-humored lad sitting to his right was Jake Feldman. The much thinner ruddy-skinned lad was Rusty Bordoff.

"What are your plans for this weekend?"

"As you know, I am lodging with a middle-aged hairdresser who has a sixteen-year-old son, Rudy. Tomorrow afternoon, Rudy and a couple of his German schoolmates are shooting some hoops. They invited me to come along."

"I am sure that there are Kristallnacht observances within the Berlin Jewish community. Are they on your radar this weekend?"

"Not really."

"Is Kristallnacht covered in one of your classes, the Jew in German History?"

"As a matter of fact, my class will be visiting the Sachsenhausen Concentration Camp on Monday, just one day after Kristallnacht. If I remember my history correctly, many Jews were rounded up and deported in Berlin on November 9 to 10."

"That's correct. I hope that it's a good learning experience."

"I have already visited Auschwitz and Birkenau during my high school semester in Israel. I visited Dachau over the summer. I'm not sure that I will learn anything new."

"You certainly know your Jewish history."

"Yep. I know virtually every museum in Berlin which pertains either to the Holocaust or the Cold War. I would make a great tour guide."

"I'll take you up on that someday. You seem to be having a great time so far. I hope that you find some time for your studies."

"I'll think about it." Greg continued, "The Berlin of your youth is not the same Berlin of my youth. Today, Berlin is an exciting seamless city. It's hard to tell where West Berlin ends and where East Berlin begins, and vice versa. There's lots going on here. It's a new world, Daddy!"

The three gentlemen clinked their glasses of beer and drank a toast. "To a new world order on the seventy-fifth anniversary of Kristallnacht!"

Greg concluded, "Daddy, good luck with your service tonight. We'll each observe Kristallnacht in our own way."

On that remark, our conversation ended. Greg knew very well that this act of irreverence would get under my skin. I was the same way with my own folks. I thought to myself, *Heavy is the head that wears the crown of parenthood!*

II

Our Kristallnacht/Kabbalat Shabbat service was scheduled for 7:30 p.m. Although Kristallnacht was observed in most Jewish communities throughout the world, the approach at Congregation Rodef Tzedek was quite unique. While most synagogues must go to great lengths to locate Holocaust survivors to address their members, we still had an ample supply. Indeed, several of our members shared their insights in the public schools and even outside of the New York area. Unlike the current generation of Jews, for which Kristallnacht observance provides an educational function, many of our members know all too well what took place. Kristallnacht for them is a bridge between the twilight of their lives in the Golden Medina and the lives that they once lead in pre-Nazi Europe.

The general trend in reform services was informal interactive worship. Many cantors and a few rabbis strummed the guitar and led the congregational singing of upbeat Shabbat melodies. Lay leaders and even children participated in the English readings. The general mood was happy-clappy.

However, on Kristallnacht, both clergy and lay leaders replicated the worship style that existed in the old country. We recreated what was taken away from so many of our congregants when synagogues were burned and public Jewish worship was terminated. Both the rabbi and cantor wore black robes and kovahs (special high hats.) Indeed, my personal robe was a gift from my first congregation. My kovah was a gift from a Holocaust survivor who felt that I should look like a rabbi while on the pulpit. We used an organ and employed a professional quartet to render the mainly-operatic German melodies.

The architect of our Kristallnacht program was our current synagogue president and music director, Rolf Samuels. He had expertise in the classical music of the Old World and has fought an uphill battle for years to keep it going in the New World. He spends four months out of the year, either teaching at Abraham Geiger College in

Berlin or playing in synagogues in Germany, Poland, and the Czech Republic. As he often said, there is a hunger among the younger generation to revive the lost music of yesteryear.

Yet there was a shade of ambivalence. In one of our conversations, he exclaimed, "When I think of my grandparents being murdered in Auschwitz at the hands of those Nazi bastards, I often wonder why I am even setting foot in Germany and Eastern Europe."

I simply responded, "You are doing God's work."

*****

It was now 7:00 p.m. The doors were opened. I stood in the foyer to greet a few congregants before putting on my robe. The first person to enter was Ruchel Weiser, an elderly woman who was born in Mannheim. Although most of the American-born congregants dressed casually for services, Ruchel firmly believed that a synagogue was a house of God. She always wore dresses or skirts, and her white hair was always immaculate. Indeed, she was a hairdresser during her working days. Her personal grooming was a natural extension of her profession.

"Good Shabbos, Rabbi."

"Shabbat Shalom!"

"We have such a beautiful sanctuary and such a beautiful service. I don't understand why we don't get more people. As a child, I attended services regularly. I would often get beat up either on the way to synagogue or on my way home after services. I can't tell you how many times I was called dirty Jew. *Oy vey iz mir.* Woe is me!

"I came to this synagogue in 1946. It was my first home in America. This synagogue restored what was taken from me since Kristallnacht. When my son, who is about your age, celebrated his bar mitzvah here, it was the highlight of my life. The Nazis killed my family, but they could not kill Judaism."

Just then, Ruchel gazed at the Kristallnacht exhibition. It focused on the lives of six of our Holocaust survivors by using pictures, Jewish artifacts, and brief biographical sketches. Ruchel Weiser was one of the individuals that our talented curator chose to focus upon.

"Very nice exhibit, Rabbi." That was a high compliment coming from her. She demanded high standards. Only a couple of years ago, she complained of a couple of sexually suggestive paintings that escaped my notice. Agreeing with her that a synagogue is different from an art museum, I exercised censorship.

"Are you ready to light your candle this evening?"

"It is a great honor, Rabbi."

"I look forward to seeing you upstairs in the sanctuary."

III

The serene majesty of our place of worship—consisting of two levels with balconies, a high ceiling with a Star of David engraved upon it, and three stained glassed windows on the eastern and western walls—were tailor-made for this occasion. The grandiose design resembled the many places of worship of where so many of our Holocaust survivors prayed in pre-Nazi Germany. Stepping into our sanctuary was like stepping into the Old World.

It was nearly 7:30 p.m. The organist and the quartet took their places in the choir loft behind the pulpit. They were hidden from the view of the congregation as was the case with so many European congregations. The student cantor and I took our respective places on the pulpit.

A few days ago, I invited Dmitri Daniel Glinski to attend our special service. He was the CEO of the Russian-speaking Community Council. I gave him permission to circulate a petition that he was planning to present to the New York City Council on December 13. He wanted to designate the northwest corner of Bennett Avenue and 181st Street as Alexey Murzhenko Plaza.

Normally, I would refuse the signing of petitions after a Shabbat service, but this was a special case. Alexey Murzhenko, who was looked upon as a Righteous Gentile in the Jewish world, became involved in the struggle for human rights and democratic change in the former Soviet Union. He was also one of two Christians in a sixteen-member refusenik dissident group who were activists for the right to emigrate. In 1970, he and other members of this group were incarcerated when they attempted to commandeer a plane with the hope of flying to Sweden and subsequently emigrating to Israel to escape Soviet persecution. They also sought to call attention to the injustices suffered by Soviet Jews and others who were denied freedom to emigrate from the Soviet Union.

Heaven knows how many Righteous Gentiles were responsible for hiding and saving the lives of European Jews. If it weren't for Righteous Gentiles, it is highly likely that some of our older members would not be sitting inside of our synagogue this evening. To refuse Dmitri's request would have been shortsighted and would have smacked of sheer hypocrisy.

My thoughts turned to Alexey Murzhenko's widow, Luba. My partner, Dr. Thomas Barnet, and I visited her in Kiev in April 1981. Although we had eluded the KGB and it wasn't apparent to us that we were being followed, we debated as to whether it was worthwhile to visit her. At that time, she did not speak a word of English, and we did not speak a word of Russian. Nevertheless, we persisted.

Alexey was languishing in prison. Tom took pictures of her with her young daughter, and Luba gave us a picture of Alexey to take back to the West. With minimal use of language, we communicated that Anglo-Jewry still cared deeply about her. For indeed, the language of love is the universal language.

Just as the service was about to begin, Dmitri walked in with a rather portly built middle-aged woman. It was Luba! Dmitri and Luba looked straight at me, exchanged whispers, and then smiled. When we left her one-bedroom apartment in Kiev, I never expected to see her again. Imagine her walking into my synagogue in New York! We have some serious catching up to do.

IV

The service began with a grandiose choral presentation of Lewandowski's *Mah Tovu*, taken from a scriptural verse in Numbers: "How good are your tents O Jacob!" Although this piece of liturgy generally introduces the morning service, we followed German custom and made an exception this evening.

I then followed with the opening prayer written by Abraham Shlomsky.

> In the presence of eyes
> which witnessed the slaughter,
> which saw the oppression
> the heart could not bear,
> and as witness the heart
> that once taught compassion
> until the days came to pass
> that crushed human feeling,
> I have taken an oath: To remember it all,
> to remember—not once to forget!
> Forget not one thing to the last generation
> when degradation shall cease,
> to the last, to its ending,
> when the rod of instruction
> shall come to conclusion.
> An oath: Not in vain passed over the night of terror
> An oath: No morning shall see me at flesh-pots again.
> An oath: Lest from this we learned nothing.

Afterward, we called upon one of our survivors, Gerhard Hertzberg, to turn on the switch of our Holocaust memorial. It was located at the top of the balcony on the western section of the sanctuary. Its light radiated throughout our massive worship space.

Gerhard was a grand gentleman who was in his eighties. He wore a dark suit and a regular hat instead of the traditional Jewish head covering. Given his erect and dignified bearing, one would have never guessed that he was kicked around between four concentration camps and ultimately ended up in Auschwitz. While most inmates at this concentration camp exited via one of the chimneys, he was one of the precious few that made it to the seventy-fifth anniversary of Kristallnacht. While he was ascending the stairs to the Holocaust

Memorial, I silently recited the prayer, "Blessed are You, Adonai our God, Ruler of the Universe, who kept him alive, sustained him, and helped him to reach this day."

Decades ago, Congregation Rodef Tzedek reached out to the general community. As a congregation of members who were among the huddled masses yearning to breathe free, they sponsored other immigrants known as boat people. They adopted Nguyen Be, a former officer in the South Vietnamese Army, and his son, Lam Be. As the owner of a clock and watch business, Gerhard Hertzberg hired Nguyen and taught him how to be a repairman. He eventually started his own business and became a productive member of society. The renowned Jewish sage of the eleventh century, Maimonides, taught that the highest level of promoting economic justice was to give the recipient the tools to make a living. Gerhard followed this teaching to the letter. He truly loved the stranger because he was once a stranger in a hostile land.

*****

The traditional Friday evening service typically begins with the singing or recitation of six psalms, Psalms 95–99 and Psalm 29. As preparation for the welcoming of the Sabbath, they symbolize the six days of creation. On the seventh day, God granted a special gift—a day of rest. Afterward, we welcome the Sabbath bride through the singing of *Lecha Dodi* and then sing Psalm 92, "A Song for the Sabbath Day."

On Kristallnacht, we made an important modification. To my left was a table consisting of six large Yahrzeit candles. We would call up six Holocaust survivors who were present in Germany during Kristallnacht. To make this ceremony multigenerational and to educate the younger generation, each of these survivors was accompanied by either pre-b'nei-mitzvah students or post-b'nei-mitzvah students. The six pairs of individuals coming up would correspond with the six psalms. We were juxtaposing the celebration of creation with the deterioration of German Jewry after Kristallnacht.

The first person to come up was Hilga Eisenberg, accompanied by Noah Kantor.

*****

Offenbach, Germany
November 11, 1938

The horrible events of Kristallnacht represented the culmination of years of Jewish persecution. After 1934, Jewish children were not allowed to go to public schools, so they were taught by Jewish teachers who were also not welcome in public schools. This is how the Jewish school in Offenbach came about. As the perennial optimist, Hilga thought to herself, *I am not deprived. We have our own community.*

Jews were not allowed to go anywhere in the town of Offenbach. There were signs outside of movie theatres and businesses which said, "Jews not wanted." Jews were looked upon as vermin.

When Kristallnacht came to Offenbach, the terror represented a sharp contrast to Hilga Eisenberg's fourteenth birthday. She surveyed the damage and quickly realized that all the apartments were ransacked, and the synagogue was set on fire. Her family's apartment was miraculously spared. Unlike the fathers of other Jewish children, hers was not carted off to a concentration camp. She believed that was attributed to the fact that he did a special favor for the superintendent. Nevertheless, the doorbell could ring anytime, and deportations could occur without any notice. Hilga's family lived in constant fear.

Hilga was getting ready for school. One of her schoolmates met her in front of her home and said, "Don't bother. There's no school to go to."

Hilga decided to see for herself and walked to the school with one of her friends. They peaked through the windows and saw that everything was black and burned.

Jewish businesses were greatly affected. Their stores were empty, and no gentile dared to go in. Hilga's father was pushed out of his position as vice president of a Jewish-owned private bank. The bank was taken over by non-Jews.

It was the beginning of the end of German Jewry. Rabbi Leo Baeck prophesized this reality in 1933:

> For us, the Jews of Germany, an epoch has come to an end… It was our belief that the German and Jewish mind and culture could co-exist and meld on German soil. This was an illusion…the thousand-year history of the Jew in Germany is at an end.

After Kristallnacht, Hilga's family realized that they had to get out of Germany as soon as possible.

*****

New York
November 8, 2013

Noah read the first line from Psalm 95, "Come let us sing joyously to Adonoy. Raise a shout for our rock and deliverer."

Hilga lit the first candle and recited, "I am from Offenbach. I came to America in 1939 and joined Congregation Rodef Tzedek in 1973. This candle is lit in memory of the six million."

The second Holocaust survivor to come up was Heinz Fleishman, accompanied by Alex Fishman.

*****

Jena, Germany
November 9–10, 1938

Young Heinz Fleishman heard sounds of windows and glass breaking as well as yelling and screaming coming from outside. His parents came into his room and told him and his brother not to worry, that the police would be there shortly to stop what was going on. The police were there, but they did nothing to stop the destruction. The department store and other Jewish businesses in town were owned by Jews, and after Kristallnacht, the windows were broken, and the store had been vandalized. During that night, Heinz's parents informed him and his brother that they would have to leave them behind for a little while, but not to worry. Heinz's father's secretary was due to come in the next morning, and she would check on them. His parents left them alone in the house. They were taken to police headquarters.

The next day, the secretary came for a little while, but that did not comfort the boys. Heinz went to school and was soon called into the principal's office. The principal was part of the same veteran's organization as Heinz's father. When he was brought into the office, the principal told him in a very kind way that he was no longer allowed in school. He said, "Go home. Your parents will explain everything to you."

Heinz lowered his head in utter despondence and did what he was told.

Later that afternoon, Heinz's mother came back. She told him that his father, grandfather, uncles, and basically every German Jew in town would be held in prison for a few days and then sent to Buchenwald, a concentration camp located about fifteen miles outside of Jena. After the men were taken to Buchenwald, Heinz, his brother, and his mother moved into his grandmother's house, which was a villa right outside the town. This same house would go on to be a *Judenhaus* (a Jewish house) in which many Jews would move in and out during their escape.

Heinz's father spent about four weeks in Buchenwald. He was released a little bit earlier than everyone else. Apparently, he scored a few points because he was a German officer in World War I. He was a radically changed man upon returning from Buchenwald—twenty-five pounds lighter, no hair, and totally depressed. Heinz's grandfather was less fortunate. He was beaten so severely that he died shortly after his release from Buchenwald.

The Fleishmans received their wake-up call and began planning to escape Germany.

*****

New York
November 8, 2013

Alex read the first line from Psalm 96: "Sing to Adonai a new song. Sing to Adonai all the earth."

Heinz lit the second candle and recited, "I am from Jena, Germany. I came to America in August 1941. I, along with 450 refugees, was on the last ship to arrive in the United States. I joined Congregation Rodef Tzedek in 1971. This candle is lit in memory of my grandfather who died shortly after Kristallnacht due to the beatings in Buchenwald."

The third Holocaust survivor to come up was Leah Fleishman, accompanied by Rose Cornblatt.

*****

Berlin, Germany
November 9, 2013

Leah's father was working, and her mother was out. She was home alone with her grandmother, who lived with the family. Leah was thirteen at the time. On that inauspicious day, the doorbell rang, and her grandmother opened the door. Two SS officers had come to arrest Leah's father.

"Just a minute," the grandmother told the officers.

She then knocked on the door of Leah's bedroom and said, "Leah, please say hello to the officers."

Leah, who was scared silly, curtseyed in front of the men.

The grandmother pleaded with them, "Don't arrest him. He's a wonderful man, and this is his only child."

The SS officers left their card and said that when her father returned home, he should call the telephone number for instructions.

When her father came home, he was informed of what happened, and he decided to go into hiding with a non-Jewish family, who were friends of her grandmother. He did not come home for a couple of weeks. Before he would come home, he would call to make sure that it was safe. They never heard from the SS officers again.

It became abundantly clear that it was time to get out of Germany.

New York
November 8, 2013

Rose read the first line from Psalm 97: "Adonai is sovereign. Let the earth exult, the many islands rejoice."

Leah lit the third candle and recited, "I am from Berlin, Germany. I came to America in 1940 via London. I met my husband, Heinz, at a Vermont ski resort in 1943. Along with my husband, I also joined this synagogue in 1971. This candle is lit in memory of my grandmother, who had to stay behind."

The fourth Holocaust survivor to come up was Ruchel Weiser, accompanied by Shira Snyder.

*****

Mannheim, Germany
November 10, 1938

Kristallnacht descended upon Mannheim a day later than most other cities and towns in Germany. It was 6:00 a.m. as Ruchel, who was only seven years old, gazed upon all the burning buildings. Her beloved liberal shul, the Haupt synagogue, was destroyed. So was the family store. The beautiful color picture of her older brother, Hugo, was ripped off one of the walls and put out into the street. Underneath the picture was written the words *Dirty Jew*.

Ruchel's family, like many of their neighbors, considered Germany to be their home. Despite the burning of the synagogues and the burning of the most important possessions they have as a people, their Torahs, many German Jews were so stunned that they refused to believe that life for them in Germany would become unbearable. Many believed that all this would blow over, and life would return to normal. On the contrary, Kristallnacht was only the opening chapter.

*****

JEFFREY GALE

A Convent in Vichy-Controlled France
1942

Ruchel was standing in front of the convent with one of the OSE leaders, Georges Garel, and a French social worker, Claudine Basset. OSE was the acronym for *Oeuvre de Secours aux Enfants* (Children's Aid Society). OSE was a French Jewish organization that saved hundreds of refugee children from the Holocaust.

She reflected on the sequence of events that took place after Kristallnacht. Three weeks after her brother's bar mitzvah at an orthodox synagogue in Mannheim, Ruchel's family was rounded up and sent to Camp Gurs. The camp, about fifty miles from the Spanish border, was situated in the foothills of the Pyrenees Mountains northwest of Oloron-Sainte-Marie. The barracks were infested with rats, mice, lice, and other unwanted insects. About twenty people were housed in each building. Food was far from plentiful.

A representative from the OSE removed Ruchel from Camp Gurs. She was taken to Chabannes and was later placed with a non-Jewish family. When the family appeared on the radar of the local police, the OSE determined that her new residence would be the convent. Going forward, she would go by the name of Renee Latty.

*****

Georges Garel was a rather handsome man and wore a small mustache. With great earnestness, he explained to Ruchel what she needed to do to stay alive. Having been educated as an engineer in Germany, he was able to speak to her in her native language.

"You know that you are Jewish, but you have to put that aside for a while. You must follow the nuns in all things. You must go to mass. You must go into the confession booth. Even though the cross symbolizes pools of Jewish blood that have been shed by Christians over the ages, you must make the sign of the cross when required to do so. Do you understand, my dear Ruchel?"

Ruchel sadly nodded.

"Above all, Ruchel, you must be a brave girl."

After giving all these directions, Georges Garel and Claudine Basset walked her into the convent. There she remained until France was liberated by the Allied Army. Eventually, she was reunited with her brother, Hugo, and the two of them sailed to America in 1946.

Ruchel narrowly escaped the concentration camp. She and her brother never saw their mother again. She was eventually murdered in Auschwitz.

New York
November 8, 2013

Shira read the first line from Psalm 98: "Sing unto Adonai, a new song, for God has worked wonders.

Ruchel lit the fourth candle and recited, "I am from Mannheim, Germany. I came to America and began attending services at Congregation Rodef Tzedek in 1946. This candle is lit in memory of my mother."

The fifth Holocaust survivor to come up was Alfred Seidman, accompanied by Nate Kushner.

*****

Breslau, Germany
November 10, 1938

On the morning of November 10, Alfred went to school as usual. As he walked to school, he saw main shop windows smashed in and the word *Jude* smeared on the shards of glass still left in the windows or on the doors. Cash registers were strewn in the streets, and nobody was attending the stores. Much of the merchandise had been looted from the display cases.

As he entered the street where his school was located, he was met by his teacher, Mr. Marx.

"Alfred, go home quickly. Turn around. Go home," he ordered him.

Alfred turned around and started walking home. Something terrible must have happened. He turned the corner and quickly looked back. As he turned around, he saw what was happening. The dome of the New Synagogue in Breslau was on fire. The big dome was just imploding. Terrified of what he saw, he ran home as fast as he could. Alfred's body shook as he told his parents, "Daddy, Daddy, our synagogue is on fire!"

Alfred's parents lived on one of the main streets in Breslau and had a window facing the street. Occasionally, they would peek out the window and see what was happening outside their apartment. People were being dragged, beaten, kicked, and pushed onto trucks.

Paramilitary youth groups were marching and singing "Horst Wessel Lied," the anthem of the Nazi Party. It was a frightening scene to watch. Kristallnacht came to Breslau with a vengeance. The events of the day made it clear that the Seidmans had to get out of the country before it was too late.

NEW YORK
NOVEMBER 8, 2013

Nate read the first line from Psalm 99: "Exalt Adonai our God and bow towards God's holy hill, for Adonai our God is holy."

Alfred lit the fifth candle and recited, "I am from Breslau, Germany. My family came to the United States in 1959. I have been an active member of Congregation Rodef Tzedek for many years. I light the fifth candle in memory of my parents."

The sixth Holocaust survivor, Fritz Bernstein, came up to light the sixth candle and was accompanied by Davida Dubinsky.

I was glad that Davida was participating. She was a Russian-American girl. Considering my work with Soviet Jewry thirty years ago, it seemed *bashert* (destined) that I would be the one to train her for her bat mitzvah. While the Nazis sought to kill Jews, the Soviet Union sought to kill Judaism. Her parents immigrated to America in 1990. Life was certainly no fun for them prior to that time.

*****

LÜDENSCHEID, GERMANY
NOVEMBER 10, 1938

The insanity of Kristallnacht also descended upon the home of Horst Bernstein, the father of our sixth Holocaust survivor. There was the ominous knock on the door.

When Horst opened it, he found four or five policemen standing at the entrance.

"Are you Horst Bernstein, the Jew?"

"*Ja*," he replied.

The policemen loaded their pistols, pointed them at him, and told him, "You are under arrest!" His wife, Freda, screamed.

There was little that Horst could do. In a final act of defiance, he grabbed his half-dozen military medals and put them on, hoping that the police would feel shame and recognize that they were arresting not some faceless Jew. After all, he was a decorated war veteran. Four years ago, to the day, he received one of the medals in the name of the führer and chancellor of the Reich. He deserved much better treatment than this.

None of that mattered. With the Cross of Honor draped across his chest, he emptied his pockets as police took him into custody to become a prisoner of Hitler's Reich.

*****

SACHSENHAUSEN CAMP
1938

The daily routine was brutal. Wake-up time was 4:30 a.m. Roll call took place at 6:15 a.m. The work detail began at 8:00 a.m. Horst's work detail included shoveling sand, carrying rocks, and toting forty-pound sacks of sand. Lunch, consisting of a single piece of dry bread, took place at 11:30 a.m. Labor would continue until 4:00 p.m. when evening roll call would take place. If the prisoners were lucky, they were dismissed by 6:00 p.m. They would stand by the barracks for the evening meal. By that time, they were so hungry that they lunged over their bowls of food like starving animals.

While Sachsenhausen was primarily designated as a labor camp rather than an extermination camp, deaths still took place at a fast and furious pace. The usual causes were starvation, exposure to inclement weather conditions, untreated medical conditions, and downright torture.

The SS meted out punishments for any infractions as if back in the Middle Ages. Horst witnessed the hands of many "offenders" being tied behind their backs, hoisted up, tied to a pole, and left hanging for five to ten hours. Others were tied and strapped to a rack then clubbed with a wooden stick on their naked buttocks between fifteen and twenty-five times. Horst thought to himself, *The same could happen to me.* He feared that he would die in Sachsenhausen without ever seeing his family again.

*****

Reprieve came twenty-two days later. A beloved uncle sent a large sum of money to a business associate, who in turn greased the right palms so that the Bernstein family could obtain landing permits and visas so that they could immigrate to Cuba. Paying off corrupt Cuban officials was a small price for being able to provide a written guarantee that they truly intended to leave Germany.

When the reality of his imminent release from Sachsenhausen sunk in, Horst cried profusely and collapsed to the ground. He couldn't understand what was happening. Finally, the flood of emotion slowed down, and he regained his composure. Someone picked him up and sat him down.

He was given a haircut and a shave. Then he gave away every single belonging that he had with him, regardless of whether it was originally his. It was as if he wanted no connection to anything that had been part of this place. At the same time, he could not believe his sudden good fortune. He gazed into the eyes of the poor souls he was leaving behind and understood the blessing that was being bestowed upon him this day.

At the time of discharge, the camp commandant explained the policy of the Third Reich toward its Jews.

"Your release is not due to good behavior," he said. "You are being released on condition that your family leaves Germany as quickly as possible. Germany doesn't want Jewish shit like you!"

To Horst Bernstein, a decorated war veteran who loved his country, this was the ultimate humiliation.

Escorted by a sentry to the camp, Horst and twenty other prisoners watched the barrier being raised and rejoiced for the first time in their golden freedom. The Bernsteins would soon be on their way to Cuba and eventually to America.

New York
November 8, 2013

Davida read the first line from Psalm 29: "May Adonai grant strength towards God's people, may Adonai bestow peace upon God's people."

Fritz lit the sixth candle and recited, "I am from Lüdenscheid, Germany. My family came to the United States in 1940. I light the sixth candle in memory of my parents, who lost everything in Germany and who rebuilt their lives from broken glass."

*****

As the six Yahrzeit candles shone brightly from the *Bima*, the choir sang "Ashrei Hagafrur," a rousing song written by one of the Holocaust martyrs, Hannah Senesh.

> *Ashrei hagafrur shenisraf v'hitzit l'havot*
> *Ashrei halehavah shebaarah b'sitrei l'vavot.*
> *Ashrei hal'vavot sheyad'u lachadol b'chavod.*
> *Ashrei hagafrur shenisraf v'hitzit l'havot.*

> Blessed is the match consumed in kindling flame.
> Blessed is the flame that burns in the secret fastness of the heart.

> Blessed is the heart with the strength to stop its beating for honor's sake.
> Blessed is the match consumed in kindling flame.

The remainder of the service, for the most part, was straightforward. The only difference was the primary use of lofty German music. We concluded Kabbalat Shabbat with *Lecha Dodi* and Psalms 92–93. The *Chatzi Kaddish* provided a transition to the standard evening prayers. After the cantor chanted *Oseh Shalom*, a prayer which asks God to make peace not only in the heavens but also on earth, he then proceeded to chant a prayer for personal and congregational healing. Then came time for the sermon.

*****

Speaking about Kristallnacht or the Shoah in front of Holocaust survivors is a daunting task. How can I as, an American who was born after World War II, presume to speak about the atrocities that took place? Yet as a senior rabbi who attended a seminary founded by Holocaust survivors, who was largely taught by Holocaust survivors, who attended interfaith conferences in Germany, and who had worked with these individuals for over three decades, I had both the credentials and the duty to speak from the pulpit.

If my years of working with Holocaust survivors had taught me anything, it was that they were not a monolithic group. They interpreted their experiences in different ways. Some wore their ordeals on their sleeves and even spoke at public gatherings. Some kept to themselves and pretended that nothing happened in the 1930s and 1940s. Some clung to the Jewish community for dear life and circled the wagons at every instance of anti-Semitism. Some believed in interfaith cooperation in building a better world. Some have lauded me for my views on civil rights and Israel. Others have chastised me for the very same views. I concluded that the best policy was to comment on the issues of the day through the lens of Torah and to just be myself. No Jewish leader ever had a 100 percent approval rating. That included Moses!

My strategy was to progress from the least controversial comments to remarks that will raise eyebrows and ruffle feathers. I began by pointing out that the American reformers of the late nineteenth century believed that American Jewry was in splendid shape and heading toward the Messianic Age. They believed that scientific progress would ensure a better quality of life and that moral progress would take place in lock step. America was to be the new Babylon, and there was no need for a return to our Jewish homeland or for a Jewish state.

I also pointed out that advances in modern science certainly did not bring about the golden age in the Third Reich. Indeed, technology enabled the Nazis to carry out their barbaric crimes in a more efficient manner. Discoveries in medicine were designed to reduce human suffering. Yet in Auschwitz, sadistic medical experiments were performed by Dr. Josef Mengele on Jewish subjects. The purpose of scientific inventions was to make human existence more enjoyable and to raise the general standard of living. Yet in Nazi Germany, the discovery Zyklon B gas and the establishment of death chambers were intended to exterminate large quantities of Jews in the shortest space of time.

I then quoted a story from Professor Emil Fackenheim, a well-known Holocaust theologian who addressed a large group of Jewish leaders during my student years in London, England. He related an incident in which an SS officer ordered a group of children to be burned alive on a funeral pyre. A Russian official asked the SS officer how he could justify such a barbarous act. The reply was quite simple: "I'm not sure whether it was to economize on the gas or because there wasn't enough room in the pits." Such a callous statement reminds us that the Nazis did not regard killing as a moral issue. For them, murder was a technical detail. By using all technology which was at their disposal, the Nazis attempted a final solution of the Jewish problem which could achieve maximum results at a low cost.

As painful as that story was, there appeared to be general assent within the congregation and a general nodding of heads. My second point was that while it was appropriate to observe Kristallnacht in a solemn, dignified manner, we could not be a faith forged by foes.

I remarked that there was often a bump in synagogue attendance whenever there was a crisis or an anti-Semitic incident. I mentioned that in my previous congregation, on the first Friday night service after 9/11, attendance jumped to over four hundred. Congregants were afraid and needed to be reassured. While we need religion and while we need to reconnect with God and our community in times of crisis, anti-Semitism can't define our religious identity.

I continued with this argument by posing a series of rhetorical questions to the good people of Congregation Rodef Tzedek. Does Jewish survival depend upon living in a constant state of emergency? Will we still listen to God after the tumultuous events of the world have quieted down? Will we still turn to God when there are no longer anti-Semitic attacks or states of emergency? Will we show up for Shabbat every week or only one when we are fearful? Will we still need God when life is treating us well? Do we keep God as a domestic pet to comfort us when we are needy? Do we tell God to butt out when words of the Torah tell us what we don't want to hear?

Again, there was general assent, but it was more reserved. There were undoubtedly some individuals who defined their religious identity in terms of circling the wagons rather than in terms of responding to God's call or in terms of celebrating the Sabbath and festivals with joy. I was clearly challenging this mentality.

Finally, I pointed out that remembering what took place in Nazi Germany or responding to anti-Semitism in the present should not lead to tribalism. When it comes to dealing with the ills of this world, we are in this together. I then inserted a piece of news which had been recently voted upon by the Congregation Rodef Tzedek board of trustees. As of January 2014, we would be renting out our sanctuary to an eclectic multiracial church on Sunday mornings and a Hispanic congregation on Sunday evenings. I heard a few sighs and gasps within the congregation. I then concluded the sermon with a gripping comment:

> Our health as individual faith communities are connected to the overall health of our neighborhood. What takes place east of Broadway

impacts upon those who live west of Broadway and vice versa. When Yeshivah students are harassed by anti-Semites, the whole community suffers. When Latinx and African Americans are the victims of discrimination, the whole community suffers. When Muslims are singled out because of the fanaticism of a handful of self-radicalized terrorists, the whole community suffers. When African American men are shot for no good reason or when police officers are targeted as reprisals for the senseless killing of African Americans, the whole community suffers. When undocumented immigrants become scapegoats for the ills of society and become unfairly targeted for deportation, the whole community suffers.

Jewish law requires us to worship in a sanctuary with windows. We look through them, and we respond to the pain which exists outside the building. Indeed, an assault on immigrants or a particular faith community is ultimately an assault upon us. In the famous words of Pastor Martin Niemoller:

> First, they came for the socialists, and I did not speak out—because I was not a socialist.
> Then they came for the trade unionists, and I did not speak out—because I was not a trade unionist.
> Then they came for the Jews, and I did not speak out—because I was not a Jew.
> Then they came for me—and there was no one left to speak for me.

The response was far more mixed. The majority smiled, vigorously nodded, and enthusiastically shouted amen after the sermon was finished. A minority of individuals responded with a cold, hostile silence which spoke volumes. The subliminal message that was sent to me was "How dare you, as a rabbi, speak of interfaith and multicultural cooperation at a service which focuses on Jewish suffering?"

*****

After a brief organ interlude, I invited the congregation to rise as we proceeded with the Martyrology Kaddish, which I borrowed from the Jules Harlow *Machzor*. It was to be chanted by both the cantor and the choir. The Aramaic and Hebrew words make no reference to death. It is the Jewish custom to face death bravely by singing lavish praises to God. Despite the great tragedy of the Shoah, we still need God to be part of our lives. I inserted after each line of the Kaddish the various concentration camps and venues where Jews were slaughtered. The text was as follows:

>*Yit-gadal* Exalted
>Kishinev
>*ve-yit kadash* and hallowed
>Warsaw.
>*shemei-rabah* be God's great name.
>Auschwitz.
>*b'alma divra khir'utei* in the world which God created according to plan
>Dachau
>*ve-yamlich mal-khutei* May God's majesty be revealed
>Buchenwald.
>*be-hayei-khon uve'yomei-khon* in the days our lifetime
>Baba Yar
>*uve-hayei di-khol beit yisrael* and in the life of all Israel
>Baghdad.
>*b-agala u-vizman kariv* speedily, imminently.
>Hebron.

v'imru amen. To which we say Amen.
Ye-hei shmei raba meva-rakh l'alam ul'mei 'almaya.

Blessed be God's great name to all eternity.
Yit-barakh ve-yish-tabah blessed, praised
Ravensbruck
ve-yit-pa'ar ve yitromam honoured, exalted
Mayence
ve-yitnasei ve-yit-hadar extolled, glorified
Terezin
ve-yit'aleh ve-yit halal adored and lauded
Treblinka
shmei di-kudshabbrikh hu be the name of the Holy Blessed One,
Bergen Belsen
l'eila l'eila beyond, beyond
Vilna
mikol bir-khata ve-shirata all earthly words and songs of blessing,
Usha
tush-be-hata ve-nehe-mata praise and comfort.
Massada
da-amiron b'alma v'imru amen. To which we say Amen.
Jerusalem
Ye-hei slama min shmaya ve-hayim aleinu v'al kol yisrael v'imru amen.

May there be abundant peace from heaven, and life, for us an all Israel. To which we say Amen.
Oseh shalom bimromav, hu ya'aseh shalom aleinu v'al kol yisrael v'imru amen.

May the One who creates harmony on high, bring peace to us and to all Israel. To which we say Amen.

*****

Because the Martyrology Kaddish was one of the most emotional components of the service, I invited the congregation to sit and pause for a moment of silent remembrance. We continued with the *Aleinu,* which proclaimed the hope of a better world under the rule of one God, and the Mourner's Kaddish, which focused primarily on recent deaths and yahrzeits. Rolf Samuels, our president, gave some brief reflections and then proceeded with the announcements. The closing hymn was the Lewandowski interpretation of *Adon Olam.* I then invited the congregation for the closing benediction:

Adonai oz l'amo yetain, Adonai yivareich et amo shalom.
May God give strength to the people. May God bless the people with peace.

Barukh ata b'vo-echa uvarukh ata b'tzeitecha.
Blessed are we when we enter and blessed are we when we go out.

V

Immediately after the Kristallnacht commemoration, I made a beeline for Dmitri and Luba. Luba and I embraced each other tightly for minutes. It was a reunion that I never expected. She certainly made an impression on me thirty-two years ago, but I never expected that the feeling would be mutual.

I asked Dmitri what he and Luba were smiling about.

Dmitri said, "I asked Luba if she recognized you."

"And what did she say?"

"You put on some weight since 1981."

Just at that moment, the cantor tapped me on the shoulder and reminded me that there was a fair crowd in the exhibition gallery and that people were waiting for the blessing over the wine and the blessing over the *challah.*

"Right away. Dmitri and Luba, please make an appointment with me, and let's really get caught up. Good luck with the Alexey petition. I wish that I had met him in person before he died."

With everyone assembled, I explained my Soviet Jewry work in England and my connection with Luba Murzhenko. Out of respect for the righteous gentiles that supported and even hid Jews during World War II, I urged my congregants to support the petition of designating the northwest corner of Bennett and 181st St. as Alexey Murzhenko Plaza.

After the cantor chanted the appropriate blessings, the reception continued. A short elderly white-haired woman, who frowned throughout much of the service and especially at my remark about renting to two churches, was ready to tear a strip off me. Rina, who had been a widow for several years, always struck me as being an angry person.

"What is the meaning of renting our holy sanctuary to Christians?"

I kept my cool and replied, "The primary reason is to promote good will in the community. As you know, this community, which was once known as Frankfort on the Hudson, is much smaller today. We need additional revenue to keep this massive building running."

Rina quickly responded, "I would rather see this synagogue close than to take money from Gentiles. If my husband were alive, he would also be upset. Non-Jews hate us, and we hate them right back. That's the reality." She gnashed her teeth as she spoke.

"The fact is, Rina, is that the board of trustees supports our new tenants. We are considering others as well. If we can establish enough connections, we might even have the critical mass to organize an interfaith Thanksgiving celebration in our very own sanctuary."

"Oh my god!" she exclaimed as she disappeared into the crowd. It was obvious to Rina that she wasn't getting anywhere with me.

As the petition was being circulated and garnering much support, I was approached by a young man who appeared to be in his mid or late thirties.

"Let me introduce myself. I'm David Thompson. I was invited to the service by your president. I currently sit on the Board of Grace

Afternoon School and, wearing the attorney hat, I attend to the school's legal issues.

"I was impressed by the beauty and the power of the service. Congratulations on opening your doors to the outside community. You strike me as a maverick. Few clergy seem to have such a global perspective of the community."

I replied, "It's the only way to function in a society where most people are insular and tribal, where clergy people define themselves as parish priests rather than as community leaders, and where cooperation gives way to polarization."

Donald Thompson continued, "I would like to give Congregation Rodef Tzedek an opportunity to put your idealistic views into practice."

"I'm listening."

"Would you consider providing space for our afternoon school?"

"Wow! I see tremendous potential. Obviously, this is a decision for the board of trustees. However, let's get the ball rolling. We could ask several board members to visit the school and to examine its programs."

"How about you?"

"I would love to. Where is the school?"

"On Wadsworth Avenue, south of 181st St. and east of Broadway. It's a relatively short walk from your synagogue."

"Ah, 181st St. and especially Broadway are not only physical boundaries within this community but also psychological ones as well."

"True enough. When can you come?"

"As you probably know, I am not in New York every day. However, I'll check my calendar and give you an answer soon. I promise!"

"That's all I ask."

"Shabbat Shalom!"

As the reception was winding down, I was approached once again by Ruchel Weiser. "So now we have churches in our building. *Oy vey iz mir*! Will there be crosses?"

"Not to my knowledge."

"Will the people be praying to Jesus?"

"Of course. That's what we signed up for. I am sure that there will be communion ceremonies as well."

"Oh well. I also prayed to Jesus every day when I was living in the convent. I had no choice. The convent saved my life."

"Out of respect for the convents that saved Jewish children in Vichy France, we open our doors to non-Jewish religious groups in our synagogue."

"By the way, Rabbi, I want to compliment you. Beautiful, beautiful service!"

Paramus, New Jersey
November 2018

Five years later, shortly after the eightieth anniversary of Kristallnacht, I stood at the burial plot of Ruchel Weiser. She had died of natural causes. As family and friends were shovelling earth upon the coffin, a profound thought popped into my head. My mother's first cousin, Georges Garel, and I turned out to be good partners. He rescued little Ruchel from an early grave or more likely from the crematorium. I am reciting prayers at the final resting place as the aged version of Ruchel lies in sweet repose. She passed into the next world surrounded by her older brother, her son, her daughter-in-law, and her grandchildren. As I eventually left the cemetery, the daughter-in-law touched my shoulder and said tenderly, "Beautiful service!"

VI

Sachsenhausen Concentration Camp
1938

Pastor Martin Niemoeller was sitting in his cell as he was contemplating the bizarre sequence of events that brought him to this God forsaken place. After all, he was once a staunch supporter of the Nazi Party. With the benefit of twenty-twenty hindsight, it was a knee-jerk reaction to the declining role of religion in Germany in the 1930s.

Under the Weimer Republic, the Communist labor unions fought against the church savagely. They adopted Karl Marx's line that "religion was the opiate of the people." The masses were influenced by fiery speeches against religion. This occurred at the time when the sense for morality and respect for authority were at a low ebb. Marriage under religious auspices became more and more infrequent. People preferred to have the rites performed by civil authorities.

Attendance at church declined. Fewer and fewer children were being baptized. The new constitution had abolished compulsory attendance at religious courses in the school. Children over fourteen could decide for themselves whether they wished to learn anything about religion or not. For children under fourteen, the decision rested with the parents.

The government ceased all support of the church, which then had to resort to taxation of its followers. The lack of funds made it impossible for us to fulfil our charitable tasks, and the struggle became one for bare existence. Statistics showed that if these conditions continued, the church as an organization would be destroyed within thirty years.

Because of the growing atheistic movement in Germany and because of the growing hostility toward the church, which was fostered by Communists and Social Democrats, he pinned his hopes on Adolf Hitler. Indeed, he had an audience with him before he became chancellor in 1932. He promised on his word of honor to protect the church, to ensure its financial support, and not to issue any anti-church decrees. He also assured him that while there will be restrictions on the Jews, there will be no ghettos and no pogroms in Germany. What a boldface lie! As it turned out, he was betrayed.

After the Nazis seized power in 1933, it became apparent to Martin Niemoeller that Hitler had no intention of keeping any of his promises. While attacks on Jews and Communists, as well as others who were not perceived as true-blue Aryans, were stepped up, he was primarily interested in the fate of the church. He was greatly distressed that the Christian state of Germany was being replaced by the nationalist paganism of the Nazi Party. He was granted a meeting with the führer on January 5, 1934, to express his displeasure.

Hitler emphatically stated, "It will be necessary to adjust the Christian dogma which we National Socialists represent. You are mistaken in believing that this would be harmful to the church. The National Socialist ideology is more than a mere political program. It is a *Weltenshaung* [worldview], comprising everything of importance for mankind, including religion. An adjustment of the Christian dogma to the demands of our times will not weaken the position of the church but strengthen it and will secure its unconditional backing by the great power of the National Socialist State."

Pastor Niemoeller adamantly responded, "Christian doctrine is not dependent upon any time or any occasion. It is God's Word, and we believe that political doctrines should be founded on Christianity and not Christianity on political ideology."

A futile war of words continued in which Pastor Niemoeller knew that he could not win. Hitler became increasingly hysterical and pounded his fists. Pastor Niemoeller remained calm but persistent. Finally, he said, "Then I have come in vain to you."

As he turned to leave the room, Hitler screamed, "Pastor Niemoeller, you will either come to terms or you will die. Everyone will die who gets in my way." Just as the Third Reich turned on so-called non-Aryans, so it turned on Niemoeller.

Pastor Niemoeller was arrested on July 1, 1937. On March 2, 1938, he was tried by a Special Court for activities against the state. He received a 2,000 Reichmarks fine and seven months of imprisonment. But as he had been detained pretrial for longer than the seven-month jail term, he was released by the court after sentencing. However, he was immediately rearrested by Himmler's Gestapo, presumably because Rudolf Hess found the sentence too lenient and decided to take "merciless action" against him.

He was given the opportunity to avoid further punishment by promising not to speak out against the National Socialist Party and against the führer from the pulpit. He was immediately rushed in a private car to the Sachsenhausen Concentration Camp.

When he walked on the grounds in his prison uniform, a Jewish prisoner approached him. He beckoned, "Pastor Niemoeller, do you realize what you have done? This place is a hellhole."

He replied, "I am ready to see it through the bitter end. Perhaps I am lost. I may never be released. But I will keep my conscience clear to the last. God will give me the strength."

Just like his fellow inmate Horst Bernstein, Pastor Niemoeller recalled executions at Sachsenhausen. He once saw a Jew with tears in his eyes. He had collapsed the day before and had hidden himself in the camp to avoid being taken to the quarry. There he would have collapsed again and been brutally beaten once more. The guards finally found him and shot him in cold blood.

Niemoeller trembled. Tears rolled down his cheeks, and he said, loud enough for the Nazis to hear him, "Lord, forgive them, for they don't know what they do." One of the guards who had heard this remark walked up to him and gave him a dirty look.

"Into the barracks with you," he cried, pushing him. "Get going!"

The same guard slapped Niemoeller a few days later, taunting him, "Where is your dirty God now? Why doesn't He help you get out of this concentration camp?" A moment later, he shouted, "Salute Heil Hitler!" Niemoeller stood silent. The guard slapped him again. "Salute Heil Hitler!" he roared.

Pastor Niemoeller remained silent, but just then, another prisoner, a Jew, stepped out of line, and the guard rushed away to beat the man to the ground. All the prisoners realized that the Jew had done that deliberately to lure the brutal guard away from Niemoeller.

*****

At Sachsenhausen Concentration Camp, Pastor Martin Niemoeller finally realized how shortsighted he had been when he initially embraced National Socialism. He did not see the big picture. He was focused primarily on the fate of the Protestant churches but somehow rationalized the persecution of others. *Why care about the Socialists, the Communists, and the Trade Unionists?* he thought. After all, weren't they responsible for the atheism and loose morals in German society? Why care about the Jews? Did he not say in one of his sermons that the Jews were punished for centuries because they brought the Christ of God to the cross? Why risk incurring the wrath of the Third Reich?

Finally, the Nazis turned against him. There was nobody left to speak on his behalf. He realized far too late that the fate of humanity is interconnected. When fighting oppression, all religious and ethnic groups are in it together. He thought to himself, *I am paying for that mistake now, and not me alone but thousands of other persons like me.*

After the Allied victory in World War II, Pastor Martin Niemoeller became a free man. Like Horst Bernstein, he lived to tell of his ordeal and of the lessons learned.

VII

November 11, 2013
Sachsenhausen Concentration Camp

Gregory Levin boarded the train at the Berlin station with his professor, Fräulein Elsie Shultz, and his twenty classmates. He felt very much at home in Germany. He knew the streets and subways of Berlin as intimately as he knew the streets and subways of New York.

His thirst for Jewish history began when he spent a high school semester in Israel. The integration of classroom studies with field trips in Israel and Eastern Europe fired his imagination. He wanted to know more and more. Over a period of a few years, he had obtained vast knowledge. All the background information on the Shoah and its context within modern world history was locked in his head. What stood out in Gregory's mind was the memorial of the burning books in Bebelplatz. The memorial, which was located near Humboldt University, commemorates the notorious evening of May 10, 1933. Twenty thousand books were burned before a large audience. The memorial is a five-by-five-by-five-meter underground room which was set into Bebelplatz. On the walls of the completely whitewashed room, there were empty shelves for twenty thousand volumes. The empty room was not accessible. A glass plate in the pavement of the square provided a view for visitors.

In addition to the glass plate, two identically inscribed bronze plates embedded in the floor informed passersby about the monument. They carried the following texts, which began with a quotation from Heinrich Heine's tragedy *Almansor*: "That was a prelude only, there where you burn books, you end up burning people, too." How prophetic those words were!

The train ride was approximately thirty-five minutes. Greg's class dismounted the train and proceeded through the squeaky-clean streets of Oranienberg. Walking in the footsteps of Horst Bernstein and Pastor Martin Niemoeller, they passed by rows of immaculately kept "suburban-type homes." Many of them housed the staff of the Sachsenhausen Camp. Greg wondered how ordinary residents of the town could harmoniously live just outside the local hellhole of torture and death. He thought of the biblical narrative in Genesis when Joseph's brothers tossed him into a pit and later sold him as a slave. While Joseph was screaming and trying to claw his way out, his eleven brothers were leisurely eating and drinking.

After briefly walking through the pine forest, they arrived at the main gate. On the front entrance gates to Sachsenhausen was the infamous slogan *Arbeit Macht Frei* (work makes you free). Fräulein Schultz provided a cynical explanation: "The harder a person worked, the quicker he would die and be free of torture and starvation."

Sachsenhausen was intended to set a standard for other concentration camps, both in its design and the treatment of prisoners. The camp perimeter was approximately an equilateral triangle with a semicircular roll call area centered on the main entrance area in the boundary running northeast to southwest. Barrack huts could be found beyond the roll call area, radiating from the gate.

Fräulein Schultz pointed out that Herschel Grynszpan's assassination of German diplomat Ernst vom Rath was not the cause of Kristallnacht. It was merely an excuse for the Nazis to do what they had been planning for a long time. The deportations to Sachsenhausen and other places were carried out to provide labor for several specific projects.

She said, "Sachsenhausen was the site of Operation Bernhard, one of the largest currency counterfeiting operations ever recorded. The Germans forced inmate artisans to produce forged American and British currency as part of a plan to undermine the British and American economies. Who better to carry out this wicked scheme than the Jews!

"Heinkel, the aircraft manufacturer, was a major user of Sachsenhausen labor, using between six thousand and eight thousand prisoners on the Heinkel He 177 bomber. Many prisoners worked in a brick factory. Albert Speer, the Minister of Armaments and War Production in Nazi Germany, had a grandiose vision of rebuilding Berlin and transforming it into a dream city."

Greg took note of where each of these projects took place within the Sachsenhausen Camp. His class was then taken to the death strip. While Sachsenhausen wasn't a death camp per se, it featured guard towers, high walls with barbed wire, and a lethal electric fence. Any prisoner entering the zone was shot on sight. Public hangings were also commonplace.

The class then proceeded to the parts of the camp where torture was carried out. Some prisoners were required to march fifteen to twenty-five miles a day over a variety of surfaces to test military footwear. As witnessed by Horst Bernstein seventy-five years ago, some were suspended from posts by their wrists tied behind their backs.

Then came, perhaps, the most gruesome part of the tour. Greg's class visited a small room where prisoners were told that they were being measured and weighed. Without any inkling as to what was about to take place, with music playing in the background, they were shot through a sliding door located directly behind their necks. Fräulein Schultz pointed out everything.

While those shootings were done behind the scenes and caused little commotion, they were an inefficient way of committing mass murder. A small-scale gas chamber and a small-scale crematorium was created to step up the volume of executions. They provided a model for death camps, such as Auschwitz and Birkenau, to follow later. Greg's class saw both the gas chamber and the crematorium. Such a sight, however, was not new to Greg.

During this part of the tour, a German-born classmate, Johanna Thal, burst into tears. She was a sturdily built young woman with a very pleasant face and long brown hair reaching below her shoulders. Although Greg and Johanna had less than perfect command of each other's language, Greg tried to offer words of solace as best as he could. With a somewhat broken German tongue, he articulated what he was feeling in his American heart.

"I was born on the other side of the Atlantic, and everything here is so gut-wrenching, how much the more must it be for you who was born in this country and lost an ancestor."

Johanna replied, "My great-grandfather, my grandmother's father, was sent to Sachsenhausen just after Kristallnacht. He was not one of the lucky ones. He never came back. Perhaps he went on one of those long marches, collapsed out of exhaustion, and was shot like a dog! Or perhaps he was suspended on a post with his wrists tied behind his back. Or perhaps he was shot when he was supposedly measured and weighed. Or perhaps he ended up in one of the crematoria. No one in our family knows how he died."

Sensing Gregory's display of empathy, Johanna sobbed on his shoulders. Gregory gently embraced her. Fräulein Schultz gazed upon them with sympathetic eyes and patiently waited for Johanna to collect herself before the outing resumed. Out of Sachsenhausen, a friendship emerged.

The tour of Sachsenhausen ended with the tour of the barracks. Greg stood outside the bleak cell of Pastor Martin Niemoeller for several minutes. He knew his famous poem backward and forward. He allowed Nazism to turn on his enemies, the atheist Communists, the trade unionists, and even the Jews who he had accused of being Christ-killers. Finally, the Nazi Revolution turned on him.

Fräulein Schultz now stood beside him.

"You are awfully quiet, Gregory. That's not like you. You usually have a lot of comments to say in class."

He replied, "This is primarily a business school. Why do you have a course entitled the Jew in German History?"

Fräulein Schultz replied, "For the German people, teaching the Holocaust is a very modest form of repentance. We obviously cannot bring the six million murdered Jews back to life, but we can tell the full unvarnished truth about what took place between 1933 and 1945. With the population of Holocaust survivors and eyewitnesses diminishing and with Holocaust denial being so prevalent in academic circles, our school has a sacred obligation."

For the first time, Gregory became truly conscious of the two men that he was named after. Neither were Jewish intellectuals, but both were Jewish doers. The middle name, Henry, came from his great-grandfather, Chaim. He was once the president of a conservative synagogue. His congregation raised thousands of dollars to send to Jewish refugees after the war. His grandfather, or father's father, who was stationed in Europe and almost sent to invade the mainland of Japan, was the conduit who provided food for the hungry, shelter for the homeless, and medicine for the infirmed.

Gregory was proud of the fact that he was named after a major player in the French Resistance. Back in Lithuania, Georges Garel's original name was Grigory. I personally made sure that he knew about how he hid Jewish children in Vichy France, how he sometimes smuggled them out of the country and prevented many of them from ending up in places such as Sachsenhausen. His full Hebrew name was *Gibor Chayim*, "warrior of life."

Gregory left Pastor Niemoeller's cell. As the group made its way back to the Oranienberg Train Station, he gazed at the *Arbeit Mach Frei* sign for the last time. He made a pledge to himself:

> The happy go lucky image is but a mask I wear.
> It hides the sense of ancestry that my soul bears.
> The mask will drop and I will cast this loose behavior away,
> Questioning religious truth, but standing with my people I pray.
> Like a diamond lying on a barren ground,
> My reformation glittering over my faults will surely resound.
> I'll make my mark and apply my skill.
> Redeeming myself when men think least I will.

Chapter 3

THE WORD WOULD BE GOODBYE

As we stood there reliving the past and as we paused at the edge of the future, we bid our childhood farewell forever.

—Shalom Aleichem

I

New York
November 18, 2013

Since I became the spiritual leader of Congregation Rodef Tzedek in 2009, I got to know Davida Dubinsky very well. She seemed to have one foot in America and one foot in the land of her ancestors. Although she was born in New York and spoke English with an American accent, her father was from Khielnitsky in the Ukraine and her mother was from Moscow. Russian was the primary language spoken in their home, and she was much immersed in Russian culture. Many of her friends in school were Russian.

Over the past four years, Davida bloomed into a beautiful lady. She was about five feet six inches tall. She wore her long soft brown hair in various styles—ponytail, pigtails, ballet bun, or loose and flowing on her shoulders. Her deep penetrating brown eyes clearly portrayed an amazing level of sensitivity and emotional intelligence that belied her youth.

Davida, of course, was the first female in her family to celebrate a bat mitzvah in the traditional sense. It was going to be a big event and involved major planning. Davida and her mother, Larissa, joined me at the conference table to get the ball rolling.

"Rabbi," Larissa said. "We are looking for a late spring date that will be convenient for our out-of-town guests. Of course, the Torah portion must also be taken into consideration. As you know, some portions lend themselves better to these ceremonies than others."

As Larissa was speaking, all I could think of was Simone Da Costa's bat mitzvah, which took take place thirty years ago on June 2, 1984. The Torah portion then was *Parshat Naso*. Perhaps Davida could read the same Torah portion on May 31, 2014.

I prefaced my words to Davida and Larissa by saying, "Of course, the final decision is yours, but why don't you choose May 31? Almost thirty years ago to the date, I twinned an English girl, Simone Da Costa, with a Russian girl, Sanna Tsivkin. If you choose this date, the bat mitzvah will be particularly special. As a Russian American, Davida, you will be able to celebrate a milestone that was unavailable to Sanna thirty years ago. For that matter, bat mitzvah was not an option for your mom as well."

Davida came to a decision instantly. "It would be an honor to be connected to that bat mitzvah. I choose May 31."

Larissa nodded.

"Let's have our first lesson next Monday," I chimed in.

"Sounds good," Larissa said. "Rabbi, Davida and I feel close to you. Were you close to Simone and her family?"

"Yes," I replied with a tone of nostalgia in my voice.

"Were you sad when you left England?"

"That's a long story all by itself."

II

London
October 13, 1984

On May 18, I officially gave my notice to the Settlement Synagogue that I accepted a new position in mid-Michigan. I would be serving a small pulpit and would become the prison chaplain for Jewish inmates being incarcerated at the nearby federal penitentiary. I would assume my new duties on November 15. It was an odd time to go to a new synagogue, but I promised in my contract to give six months' notice. Ironically, my insistence on honoring my commitments did not turn the new congregation off but endeared me to them all that much more. They were willing to find a retired rabbi to cover September, October, and half of November.

My resignation was one of the most bittersweet moments of my rabbinate. On the one hand, I had lots of friends in Great Britain, both within and outside the Settlement Synagogue. I adapted well to the temperament of this country. Not only did I acquire *Yiddishkeit* but also *Britishkeit* as well. On the other hand, my American family trumped everything.

I lived in Great Britain for over nine years. As hospitable as my congregation was and as comfortable as I felt in my adopted country, it was time to go home. My new congregation was only an hour's drive from where my brother's family lived. As one of the perks, I would be living in a three-bedroom parsonage and would be able to make a special room for my nieces whenever they visited me.

At my personal request, the officers of the Settlement Synagogue kept the news quiet until after Simone's bat mitzvah. I did not want anything to spoil the day for both Simone's family and the congregation.

*****

It was the Saturday that fell during Sukkot, and I was sitting quietly in my compact Ilford flat. Several weeks ago, I replaced the carpet in the living room to make the flat more attractive for perspective buyers. My strategy worked! Another young man would take it over when I vacated it in mid-November.

Next to the bay windows which looked out into the street was a small alcove which could fit a round table and four chairs. The bathtub and sink were just off the living room. This spacious living space ran directly into the kitchenette without any kind of partition. At the end of the kitchenette was a glass door which led to a small corridor. On the right was the toilet. On the left was my bedroom.

At 4:00 p.m., Simone, Allison, and Rachel arrived. While the young ladies were quite different from each other, I bonded with all three of them. During the last two years, at one time or another, I spent time in each of their homes and got to know their families. Simone continued to be the thoughtful one. Rachel, who was a few years older than the other two, continued to wear dresses, tights, and high-heeled shoes at all my classes.

Allison was a live wire. She laughed at all my jokes even when they were not particularly funny. Once in an act of desperation, I said sternly, "Apply yourself to your lesson, sunshine!"

To which she replied with a page from my own joke book, "I'm not sunshine. I am Daughter-shine!"

"Okay, Daughter-shine."

More raucous laughter. "Ha ha ha! Daughter-shine!"

*****

The b'not mitzvah of Simone, Rachel, and Allison took place within a few weeks of each other. Therefore, I decided with the strong support of their families to hold a few post-b'not-mitzvah sessions in my Ilford flat before my return to America. We used the text *Churban*, a Holocaust textbook written by Rabbi Tony Bayfield, one of my teachers at Leo Baeck College. It was specifically geared toward teenagers. However, we often used the textbook as a springboard to discuss other issues which were relevant to young people in those days.

As there were four of us, we fitted comfortably around the table. As these were British teenagers, tea and cakes were served while class was taking place. For the first part of the session, I kept to the lesson plan. Afterward, I took out a doll dressed in Ukrainian costume.

I said to Simone, "I am sure that you remember this doll that I used at your bat mitzvah. It was given to me by a Hebrew teacher and prisoner of conscience from Kiev. Back in the old country, the doll was used to warm the teapot. I keep it for only display purposes."

Simone nodded.

"At the bat mitzvah," I said. 'The name of this doll is Alanna. She symbolizes the refusenik child who could not receive a Jewish education and had to hide her Jewish identity while she was still living in the Soviet Union.'"

The heads of my students were lowered. "That's so sad," Allison remarked.

"It is. Simone, I am sure that you remember the empty chair at the front of the synagogue with the tallit draped over and the siddur on the seat."

Simone nodded again

"The empty chair with the tallit was a reminder that Sanna could not celebrate a bat mitzvah herself, nor could she be present in London to celebrate with you."

"All three of you have the opportunity to continue learning after bat mitzvah, to become lay readers, and to really get involved in synagogue life. As Jews, learning is a lifelong task. I expect to continue studying until I draw my last breath. When I am gone in a few weeks, please promise that you will continue where we left off."

"We promise," my three students said in unison.

The class ended, and my long-awaited reunion with Katarina would take place tomorrow.

III

October 14, 1984

Katarina and I corresponded regularly for the past several months. There were even occasional phone calls. Ever since that wonderful evening in Paris when we dined at a café on the Champs

Élysée and took in a Russian movie with French subtitles, I thought about her constantly. I longed for the day when she would come to England. That day was today.

Yet I was also worried. How would she react to my move? Given our commitments and financial means, arranging trips from England to France or France to England was challenging enough. How would the greater distance between us affect our budding relationship?

She had arrived in London a few days ago and was staying with English friends. They would drive her to the Settlement Synagogue at noon. That was the time when religious school classes ended.

Simone Da Costa had volunteered to help with the *cheder*. I was counting on her to apply her Jewish day school education and help the children in the younger grades to learn their Hebrew alphabet. School was over as scheduled. I put on my soft British hat and coat and left the premises with Simone. Just as we walked out the front door of the Stepney Jewish Settlement building, a car drove up. Katarina got out of the car with her two friends, obviously a husband and wife. She was casually dressed in brown slacks and wore a light brown jacket. Her long hair flowed effortlessly down her back. Katarina was as beautiful as ever! She had a violin case tucked away under her arm.

"Isaac!" she exclaimed with enthusiasm. "How are you?" I promptly kissed her on both cheeks according to European custom. I was greatly tempted to break with convention and to simply give her a strong hug, but I chose to restrain myself.

"I missed you so, Katarina. How I waited for this day!"

Simone had that knowing grin on her face. What's the matter with her, anyway? Isn't a single rabbi allowed to have a social life?

As Katarina and I reunited, she momentarily forgot her host and hostess. She turned around and thanked them profusely for putting her up in their home, for furnishing her meals, and for their general warm hospitality.

The woman said, "It was a sheer delight to have you. Have a wonderful afternoon!"

"Thank you, thank you," Katarina replied. The couple drove away.

"So, Katarina, how would you like a tour of the synagogue before we begin our adventure?"

"That would be wonderful!"

"Simone, could you give us a few minutes before I take you home?"

"Take your time, Rabbi." She was still grinning.

I showed her the small indoor sukkah. It technically met the requirements of a kosher sukkah as the roof over it could be manually opened. It would be closed outside of working hours or during inclement weather. I then showed her the main hall.

"This is where Simone Da Costa's bat mitzvah took place. This is the empty chair that was reserved for the bat mitzvah girl that was still in Leningrad, Sanna Tsivkin. This is the stage where the organist played and the women's choir sang. All the action took place in this very room."

"I am impressed."

I then showed Katarina the two multipurpose rooms that were on the opposite side of the second floor. One of them contained a piano. I sat down and played the first measures of "Ballade for Adeline" by heart.

"It's a beautiful piece. I didn't know that you played the piano."

"When I visited Paris last April, I heard this song while riding the bus from Calais to Paris. To me, it's a song of anticipation. It's a song of longing."

"Longing for who?"

I took her hand. "I think you already know."

"Oh!"

Her head was slightly bent down. My remark obviously took her off guard.

Katarina and I walked down the stairs and caught up with Simone. We then boarded my car and made our way to Simone's house. Katarina sat on the passenger side while Simone got in the back seat. Simone's facial expression remained until the very moment she got dropped off. She said to us with that ironic smile of hers, "Have a nice outing!"

After making a brief stop, my orange Vauxhall Chevette, which I named Gertrude, was ready for its last major voyage. At Katarina's request, we proceeded to Cambridge. Once we got on the M11, it was a straightforward one-hour run.

During the drive to Cambridge, I asked Katarina why she was bringing a violin case with her.

"Just as you surprised me at the piano, I am going to surprise you with the violin. I am going to play something special for you, Isaac!"

When we arrived in Cambridge, Katarina stored her violin in the trunk of the car. We proceeded to leisurely stroll the massive grounds. We would make frequent stops and take pictures of each other, either standing by an academic building or a fountain or sitting on one of the benches. Occasionally, we would ask a passerby to take a picture of the two of us together.

Although we hadn't seen each other since last April, there was no awkwardness whatsoever. Katarina took my arm at the very beginning of our stroll. We soon graduated to walking hand in hand and then walking with our arms around each other. We finally stopped for an early dinner at a local pub. Katarina ordered a salad. I ordered fish and chips.

"You've become quite an Englishman," she said.

"After living in this place for nine years, I adapt to my surroundings. How is it possible that two children of the Cold War, who grew up on opposite sides of the world, who were taught to despise each other's way of life, find each other?"

"I am not surprised. We have similar interests. We both love literature and music. Our special sensibilities and our ability to love the beautiful triumphs over our upbringing. Friendship transcends nationality and political systems."

Unable to contain my feelings any longer, I turned my head downward.

"You look serious. Is something on your mind?"

"I accepted a job in the United States. My pulpit is in a small town in Mid-America."

Katarina's countenance fell. "I don't know what to say," she responded. "Everything was going so well today. Even though we live on opposite sides of the English Channel, I was hoping that we would find a way to see each other more often."

"I'm devastated," I replied with a quiver in my voice.

"Why would you leave London to live in a small town in the American Midwest? It's a very boring area."

"My brother's family lives nearby. The other day, I got a sweet letter from my older niece. She wrote to me about her school, her friends, and her petty quarrels with her sister. She's glad that I am coming home for good and will be able to see her more often. My family needs me."

"I understand."

When we left the pub, our animated conversation turned to silence. We stopped by my car, and Katarina picked up her violin. The sun was setting, and we proceeded to one of the benches.

"And now, Isaac, I want to give you your surprise."

Katarina took out the violin and proceeded to play the Romance from Shostakovich's *The Gadfly Suite*. She played the five-minute heartrending piece to perfection as her long hair flapped lightly in the breeze. We then sat on the bench and paused for a few moments of silence.

I finally spoke. "You played so beautifully, Katarina. Did you take lessons in Leningrad?"

"Music is important in our family. My mother could make the balalaika strum like two guitars. I took some violin lessons for a couple of years. Although I can read music, I can play by ear as well. It seems to run in the family."

"Then it's a gift."

Suddenly, the emotion and passion that had been building up inside of us for months was released. In the elegant melancholy of twilight, we embraced and kissed passionately for what seemed an eternity. I caressed her beautiful brown hair, which stretched to the middle of her back while she was caressing my back with her delicate fingers. The flame that was kindled in Paris suddenly became a bonfire in Cambridge.

We paused for a short break as I grasped her hand.

"Oh, darling, I love you. Why didn't we meet sooner? I wish that I could take you back to America."

"It cannot be. My life is here for right now. I have to finish my coursework in Paris."

"If there is one person that could keep me in Europe, it would be you. We belong together."

"Oh, Isaac, I am touched, but now you really belong with your family."

"Living on the opposite side of the Atlantic will be tough. I leave not only you but all the friends that I made in this part of the world for the past nine years. I'm in for some reverse culture shock!"

"It's not our time, Isaac. We may be farther away, but we can still keep in touch."

"We can still write letters. We can make overseas calls and hold hands across the Atlantic. You will always have a special place in my heart, Katarina."

"I have faith that our paths will cross again, even though it may take a while."

"I suppose that we have to get going soon if I am going to drive you to Victoria Station. Don't you have a train to catch?"

"I'm taking a midnight train. Let's stay in Cambridge a bit longer and nestle together on the bench."

I opened my mouth to speak, but Katarina put a finger on my lips to silence me. "Not another word, Isaac. You'll spoil it. Just hold me."

As we had no way of knowing what the future held in store for us, Katarina and I cuddled on the bench under the comforting blanket of a star-filled sky.

We corresponded after my return to the United States, but over the months, our letters and rare transatlantic phone calls became fewer and far between and finally disappeared. Many years later, our paths would unexpectedly cross again. To this day, my memory of Katarina is as sad and as sweet as the cry of a night bird drifting across the lush English fields of spring.

IV

November 9, 1984

My last Friday night service at the Settlement Synagogue signified an end and a beginning. It marked the last episode of the

European chapter of my story. It also marked the beginning of a totally new life in North America. On the surface, I was officiating at a typical service. However, this night was different from all other nights, so to speak. The women's choir was fuller and would sing from the stage instead of adjacent to the Holy Ark. The social hour after the service would be far more ornate as there were tables of sumptuous food in the two back social halls. No matter the occasion, there was never a shortage of food at the Settlement Synagogue. Instead of the average attendance of perhaps forty to sixty congregants, there were two hundred people sitting in our makeshift sanctuary.

As the extended choir and I prepared to enter the large room together for the very last time, Leisel Harrison came up to me and pointed to her watch. She said, somewhat tongue in cheek, "Rab, we're running three minutes late. Disgusting!" Coming from Leisel, it was music to my ears.

Conspicuously, my mentor and friend, Sigmund Feinberg, was not present. He died of a massive heart attack in Majorca just a few weeks ago. How I loved the man and how he was loved by the congregation! In addition to Lillian Goldwasser, he was the person I turned to for counsel and advice. I turned to him to discuss my dilemma of remaining in London or accepting the new pulpit. He advised me to look after my own interests. The Settlement Synagogue was rich in lay leadership and would survive. He was like a father to me.

I missed Sigmund at this service. I will sorely miss him at all future services. I will always remember his *heimishe* style and how he would announce in his thick German accent, "Psalm 92, *Mizmor Shir Yom ha Shabbos.*" Officiating at his burial in the Cheshunt Cemetery was a privilege and allowed me to have closure before my departure.

Appropriately, the honorary president of the congregation, Sam Kaiser, led the first half of the service. I continued with the second half. It included an English scriptural reading from the week's Torah portion, *Parshat Vayera*. Lillian Goldwasser read Genesis, chapter 21. It described the birth of Isaac, who represented a new link in the chain of Jewish tradition. In many ways, my life as Isaac Levin was about to be reborn.

I then continued with my sermon. The Settlement Synagogue did not formally observe Kristallnacht at that time. However, I chose to weave it into my remarks as today was the forty-sixth anniversary of the November pogrom. As the late Sigmund Felnberg, Leisel Harrison, and others in the congregation were Holocaust survivors, it seemed to be totally appropriate.

In the first half of the sermon, I remarked that the Settlement Synagogue has been around for two world wars. After the First World War, the congregation took in East European immigrants. After Kristallnacht spelled the beginning of the end of Germany Jewry in 1938 and especially after World War II, the congregation took in Holocaust survivors. I then referred to the wonderful work of Sir Basil and Lady Rose Henriques, better known as the Gaffer and the Missus. I pointed out what was obvious to everyone in the sanctuary, how they founded the Oxford and St. Georges Settlement which provided a range of social services from the cradle to the grave. I pointed out how they took the children of immigrants and attempted to integrate them into British society. I pointed out how they founded the Settlement Synagogue as they could not conceive of social services without the spiritual influence of religion. I pointed out how the missus built the women's choir and set some the Jewish prayers to the music of Bach, Beethoven, and Mozart. I pointed out how the Settlement Synagogue stared at the tragedy of war in the face and established new beginnings.

In the second half of my sermon, I referred to some of the pleasant moments that we celebrated together. To add a bit of levity, I mentioned my ill-fated attempt to sing the *Avinu Malkeinu* solo during Rosh Hashanah. That got a few laughs from the choir and some of the lay leaders. I also mentioned celebrating the joint twenty-fifth anniversaries of Kate Tenenbaum and Anita Robbins, Lillian's sisters, and their husbands. Indeed, Kate and Anita each took one of my arms, marched me on the dance floor, and got me to dance! I was considered family after working only a couple of months at the Settlement Synagogue. I recalled the moments in which we invited schoolchildren to some of our Friday night services, filled the multipurpose room, and drove the organizers of the Oneg crazy. I recalled the interfaith weekends that had been part of Settlement Synagogue programming before I arrived and our participation in a special interfaith service in which our organist, Jacob Walsh, skillfully played the pipe organ.

I then turned my attention to the special benefit concert for the Jewish Blind Society. It featured the American singer Maureen Scanlon, as well as our local talent. When Kate and Anita sang such songs as "Bei Mir Bistu Shein," "Sunrise, Sunset," "This Is My Song," and "I Enjoy Being a Girl," a smile came to my face. When I mentioned this, a smile also came to the faces of most of the congregation as Lillian, Kate, and Anita were among the pillars of the congregation.

Finally, I referred to Simone's bat mitzvah, her twinning with Sanna Tsivkin, and the use of Tchaikovsky's music. At that remark, Simone turned her head downward. Tears streamed down her face. Rachel sobbed her heart out.

I concluded my sermon by emphasizing that just as biblical history made a new beginning with the birth of Isaac, the Settlement Synagogue has made new beginnings throughout its history. I continued this legacy by offering innovations of my own and inviting the leaders to also think outside the box. My last statement was "Soon the Settlement Synagogue will have a new rabbi, and you will also make a new beginning. May your highest dreams be your only boundaries."

My sermon was followed by remarks and a presentation from Sam Keiser and Lillian Goldwasser. What particularly moved me were my two gifts—the British reform siddur, *Forms of Prayer*, with a heartfelt inscription from the congregation, as well as a snazzy framed *Mizrach*. Inside the Jewish home, the Mizrach points eastward toward Jerusalem. Today, the 1980s version of *Forms of Prayer* is an integral part of my Judaica library, and the Mizrach decorates the stairway of my Long Island home.

Before the concluding hymn, *Yigdal*, I put my foot in my mouth. I invited the entire congregation to attend the elaborate *oneg* and that I would be happy to say goodbye to everyone. I got a boisterous laugh from the congregation. It unintentionally broke the tension in the room. Of course, what I really wanted to say was that it was sad to say goodbye, but I would be happy to greet everyone for the last time.

At the social hour, I shook a lot of hands, received a multitude of good wishes, and became a "professional model" by being photographed in several group pictures. I was promised copies of them after I settled in Michigan.

On my way out the door, Sam Kaiser touched me on the shoulder and said with great earnestness, "Don't forget to find your way home, son."

"I never will," I replied.

V

November 14–15, 1984

In the days that followed, members of my congregation came to my flat and collected my car. She had her last major run when Katarina and I drove to Cambridge. As the new rabbi had a car of his own, the plan of the lay leadership was to sell it.

I shipped my books and other items to Michigan about two weeks ago. I packed up the remainder of my belongings and returned my keys to the real estate agent. On Wednesday afternoon, Allison's parents picked me up at the flat and took me to the home of my longtime friends in Wembley, Ivor and Naomi. They met me when I was a young insecure student and guided me over the past nine years. They were among my surrogate parents. Whenever I had a large Shabbat meal at their home, Naomi would always say, "Eat it all. The food is not for decoration."

Naomi even went so far as to type my rabbinic thesis at a very reduced rate. Therefore, I was not surprised when they attended my ordination ceremony at the Liberal Jewish Synagogue. They felt that they played a large part in my achievement.

A lot of water has gone under the bridge since we first met. We spent the rest of the day reminiscing over the wonderful moments that we spent with each other during the past nine years.

The next day, Allison and her parents picked me up and took me to Heathrow Airport. As I got out of the car, Allison began to bawl. She was such a happy girl that her outburst took me aback. I thought to myself, *O Daughter-Shine, how could you do this to me just as I am about to leave?* Her tears reminded me of my tears when I left my family nine years ago. I shook the hands of Allison's parents. I gave her a big hug, but it didn't seem to have much impact on her. She still bawled.

*****

I climbed the stairs to the entrance of the British Airways plane. Before I entered the portal that would transport me back to the New World, I turned around and gazed at the British landscape for the last time. As Shakespeare might have expressed it, "This blessed plot, this earth, this realm, this England."

If there is one word to describe what life is all about, the word would be *goodbye*. Life always appears to have its entrances and exits. As I paused at the edge of my future, I bid my young adulthood farewell forever.

In the years that followed, I married and raised a family of my own. Today, my wife and I live in suburban New York. As far as the Settlement Synagogue is concerned, it merged with Southwest Essex Reform Synagogue in one of the London suburbs. The new entity is now called Southwest Essex and Settlement Reform Synagogue, popularly known as SWESRS. The East End location was vacated. The building which housed the Settlement Synagogue remains, but the multipurpose room that once served as a synagogue was transformed into a suite of laboratories.

When one of my teachers and mentors, the late Rabbi Lionel Blue, installed me at the Settlement Synagogue, he translated a Yiddish phrase, "East Stepney, East Stepney where love comes from heaven. Every Sadie is a lady, and every Sam is a gent." I will never forget the ladies and gentlemen that made up the Settlement Synagogue. In memory, I stand before that venerable building on Beaumont Grove where the sweet voices of the women's choir must echo still.

Chapter 4

Leaving Mother Russia

> We are leaving Mother Russia,
> We have waited far too long.
> We are leaving Mother Russia,
> When they come for us, we'll be gone.
>
> —Safam

I

Long Island, New York
November 19, 2013

Tova came home at last from her European adventure. When I met her at Kennedy Airport, she was maneuvering two heavy suitcases and some carry-on luggage as well. I promptly took them from her, dragged them to the outdoor parking lot, loaded up my car, and drove home. After she unpacked the luggage, we sat down to unwind before having supper.

"Great to have you home, sweetie! So how was St. Petersburg?" I asked.

"I didn't see much of it. I was running around nonstop at the conference."

"It's the most European of all Russian cities. I was there three times. As a university student, I went to the circus and saw a production of the ballet *Giselle*."

"There's also a lot of dingy high-rise apartments."

"That's true. Perhaps you walked down the same streets I walked and used some of the same subways that I used."

"Very few free moments, I'm sorry to say. Most of my time was spent at the hotel."

"How did your lecture on neutropenia go?"

"Very well. There were about sixty physicians representing many countries in the conference room. I knew most of the North American oncologists, including two from my native Canada. A few came up to me afterward. I got mostly positive feedback."

"Excellent!"

"I couldn't wait for the next leg of the journey—Paris. What a beautiful city!"

"It was one of my favorites as well."

"Great stores. I did some power shopping. I got a few blouses and skirts and two pairs of shoes."

"You really cleaned up!"

"I got a couple of things for you. I know you like hats, so I got you a gray French beret."

I tried it on for size. "I love it."

"I had coffee with Michel, one of Georges' sons. They wanted you to have this book."

I took a quick look. It was entitled *Le sauvetage des enfants par l'OSE* (The Rescue of the Children by the OSE). It was a detailed description of Georges Garel's activities, especially his efforts to prevent French children from ending up in German concentration camps.

"That's a valuable book. Thank you. I wish I could have gone on this trip with you."

"They'll be other opportunities. We've had our share of exotic trips."

"Especially our honeymoon in the Far East."

"I remember going to a restaurant on the water and our famous cruise of the Hong Kong harbor. You put on that crazy sailor hat. As we were cuddling, you sang 'True Love.'"

"You joined in."

"Who did you think that we were, Bing Crosby and Grace Kelly?"

"We were newlyweds on a honeymoon. In the eyes of the groom, every bride looks like Grace Kelly. In the eyes of the bride, every groom looks like Bing Crosby."

"You have a vivid imagination."

"You must admit that it was a magical moment in our lives. You and I had a guardian angel on high with nothing to do."

"But to give to you and to give to me, love forever true!"

After the bantering, it was time for supper, which I served in the dining room, complete with a nice tablecloth and candles. I then sang one of Tova's favorite pop songs, "Through the Years," composed by Kenny Rogers

"Oh, Isaac," she said. "You have always had a flare for the romantic."

"Or perhaps for the corny," I replied.

After giving her a big hug and kiss, I served up my signature dish, spaghetti and meatballs and cut-up hotdogs in a delicious Italian sauce.

Afterward, Tova was exhausted from her travels, and we quickly retired to bed.

Tomorrow would be a working day for both of us.

II

New York
November 25, 2013

Having set Davida Dubinsky's bat mitzvah date for May 31, the tutorials in my office began in earnest. Davida indicated that her Hebrew reading was shaky, so I decided to give her a refresher course in the Hebrew alphabet. We went through the beginning of the blue Hebrew primer. Within an hour, we covered the first twenty pages. I had every confidence that Davida would be a great success.

As we were winding down, Davida asked, "When you visited the Tsivkins in Leningrad, did you try to teach the Hebrew alphabet to Sanna?"

I replied, "Not successfully."

When I attempted to give Sanna a mini Hebrew lesson, it turned out to be about the same time in the afternoon that I used to give my lessons to Rachel, Allison, and Simone. I introduced the Hebrew vowels *patach*, *qames*, *and seghol* as well as the Hebrew consonants *beit*, *veit*, *and aleph*. I taught her how to put consonants and vowels together and how to read from right to left. Sanna figured out how to put the consonants together, but the concept of reading two syllable words from right to left really spoofed her. After a few minutes, she lost her concentration and became more interested in playing with the Rubik's cube.

Trying to prevent a small revolution from taking place in the apartment, Irina firmly said, "Enough."

I decided to quit while I was ahead. Nevertheless, I went through the twenty-two letters of the Hebrew alphabet with Vladimir, and he put down the sound equivalents in the Cyrillic alphabet. He vowed to work with Sanna on Hebrew reading on a more appropriate occasion.

Davida persisted in her questioning. "Do you know what became of the Tsivkins? Did they eventually leave the former Soviet Union? Are you still in touch them?"

My answer is yes to all your questions. While my departure from London was a bittersweet tale, their departure from Leningrad was a long involved saga that eventually had a happy ending."

III

Long Island, New York
June 2002

When I returned to North America in November 1984, Soviet Jewry was slowly moved to the back burner of my priorities. Small-town USA was worlds apart from London, and I had to adapt accordingly. After I joined the Kiwanis Club and the interfaith clergy council, I found that lofty social action goals gave way to local causes. Furthermore, I became a prison chaplain, a position for which I had absolutely no training, and I had to deal with a whole new set of issues. When working with Jewish inmates, human rights issues reentered my life through the backdoor, but that's a totally different story.

Over the next two decades, I changed pulpits and countries two more times. I moved from the US to Canada and then back to the US. I eventually became the rabbi of a six-hundred-family congregation in suburban New York. I attempted with great difficulty to balance the demands of a huge workload, even with full secretarial and professional staff, with the challenges of looking after my young family.

My rabbinate changed drastically after September 11, 2001. The Twin Towers in New York were obliterated by terrorism, and one of my congregants was among the victims. I visited the sorrowing family many times, conducted a memorial service without a body, and officiated at a shiva. Eventually, when parts of the body were found, I officiated at the burial.

On top of this were community memorial services, both within and outside of my synagogue. Countless sermons, especially those on Rosh Hashanah and Yom Kippur, were devoted to 9/11. I held a special school assembly and, over two Sundays, visited every class of our religious school, which consisted of over four hundred students.

My recurring theme was not to let this tragedy become a convenient excuse for blanket hatred towards Muslims. Indeed, I represented the synagogue at the opening of a nearby mosque. While terrorism was perpetrated by a handful of fanatics, the biblical commandment to love the stranger still applies.

Now that synagogue life was returning to normal, I could breathe a sigh of relief. It was under those conditions in which Russian Jewry made a major comeback in my rabbinate. The attention, however, shifted from refuseniks to Russian anti-Semitism in the post-Soviet era. Loving the stranger appeared to be the antithesis to what was taking place on the other side of the world.

A letter coming from an East Meadow address appeared in my mailbox. It was from Lynn Singer. She was a local activist who steered both the Long Island Committee for Soviet Jewry and the Union of Councils for Soviet Jewry during the heyday of the Soviet Jewry movement. She wrote a heartfelt letter updating me on the current conditions, especially the rise of anti-Semitism and its toll on Jews electing to remain in the former Soviet Union. Within the letter, there was a request for a donation, which I was happy to give.

However, I wanted to do more than that. I wanted to know what happened to some of the people that I visited in the early 1980s. I wanted to reconnect, so I picked up the phone in my study and contacted Lynn Singer.

"Lynn Singer. This is Rabbi Levin. My pulpit is not too far from where you live. I got your letter, and I want to do more than just give money. I was active in Soviet Jewry while working in the UK for several years."

Lynn was delighted to hear from me and was very pleasant on the phone. "Just give me the names, Rabbi Levin. Chances are that I have the information in my computer files."

I rattled off the names, and sure enough, Lynn provided the information. Some had emigrated to Israel, of course, but many are living in other parts of the world, especially the United States.

"How about the Tsivkin family?" I asked.

"Oh, I know them well. They live in Connecticut."

"Connecticut!" I exclaimed. "Less than two hours away by car. Practically in my own backyard!"

Lynn gave me the necessary information. "By all means, see them," she said. "I look forward to hearing from you, soon."

"You will," I replied.

IV

Connecticut
August 2002

The next step was to phone the Tsivkin family. Irina picked up the phone. I hadn't heard her voice since that memorable moment in my Settlement Synagogue study.

"Hello," she said in her booming voice.

"This is Isaac Levin. A blast from the past!"

"Were you Simone Da Costa's rabbi back in 1984?"

"Yes."

"Were you the rabbi who visited us in Leningrad?"

"Yes."

"I remember you very well."

"As it turns out, I don't live that far away from you. Is it possible for me to visit Vladimir and you on a Sunday morning?"

"Of course, Isaac. It would be a pleasure. Come for early lunch. I'm glad that you still remember us!"

I could not wait for my rendezvous with yesterday!

*****

Our reunion was set for the first Sunday in August. I would visit the Tsivkins en route to the Berkshires. Afterward, I would join the faculty of Eisner Camp, a well-established reform Jewish camp in Great Barrington, Massachusetts. I needed a break from the tension of the entire year. I needed to return to nature and be involved in the nurturing of Jewish youth. I needed to believe in humanity again.

I arrived at the house, a comfortable two-story home, a far cry from the cramped apartment on 2/99 Moskovskoe Shosse in Leningrad! From few resources in 1990, Vladimir and Irina made a pleasant life for themselves in the Golden Medina.

With my heart pounding, I knocked on the door. Irina answered.

There was instant face recognition. Irina and I embraced for a couple of minutes. She then showed me to the living room, where Vladimir got up from his chair to greet me. His dark hair had turned completely white. My hair was headed in that direction. All three of us had aged during the last eighteen years, but miraculously time and distance did not make us strangers.

The first order of business was to present Vladimir and Irina with souvenirs. I presented them with a copy of our group picture, Irina, Vladimir, Sanna, and myself sitting on the sofa in their apartment.

"How lovely it was to be young them," Irina remarked.

"I was a carefree bachelor in those days," I replied.

Then I presented a picture of Simone as she appeared in 1984 as well as a copy of the sermon that I delivered at the bat mitzvah in London. It was one of my few saved sermons that was typed on a manual typewriter. How times have changed!

We then retreated to the kitchen, where we had a light lunch of cold borscht and a nutritious salad. No wine this go-round as I still had a couple of hours to drive after this visit. Coffee and cakes were served for dessert.

As we returned to the living room, we began with small talk. Vladimir and Irina emphasized that their work in the United States had little to do with their training back in the former Soviet Union. Vladimir got involved with software, which was virtually nonexistent in the 1980s. Irina had two patents in the field of cosmetics. They went on to speak of Sanna's studies in Princeton and her doctorate in psychology. Sanna married a nice Jewish boy and was making sure that their granddaughter, Esther, got the Jewish education that she couldn't receive herself. Of course, as Sanna was an accomplished pianist, she made sure that Esther would also get a sound music education.

I spoke briefly about Tova's work and what my children were up to. However, I said very few words. I wanted to hear the Tsivkin's story. They were happy to oblige me.

V

Leningrad
1988–1990

In 1988, the Soviet premier, Mikhail Gorbachev, introduced the concept of *glasnost*—political openness and greater freedom. Glasnost eliminated traces of Stalinist repression, like the banning of books and the omnipresent secret police. Political prisoners were released. Newspapers could print criticisms of the government. For the first time, parties other than the Communist Party could participate in elections.

Greater religious freedom was also extended to Soviet Jews, including the right to emigrate from the Soviet Union. The trickle of Jews that were being allowed to leave when I visited the Tsivkins became a veritable flood. Glasnost, of course, led to the growth of democracy in Eastern Europe, in countries which were once Soviet puppet states. It also led to nationalist sentiment within the Soviet Union's own borders, to the decline of communism throughout the world, and to the ultimate collapse of the Soviet Empire as we understood it.

It was a bitter irony that one of the prominent beneficiaries of the new political openness was a virulently anti-Semitic and nationalist organization known as *Pamyat* (Russian for memory). Its mixture of anti-Semitism and anti-Westernism and its contempt for democracy had considerable traction. Its rhetoric was deeply rooted in Russian thought and history. Pamyat espoused the statement made by the nineteenth-century theorist Konstantin Leontev: "The Russian nation was not created for freedom." Pamyat also reinforced officially sponsored Zionist propaganda by blaming Zionism for any number of past and present Western social ills and for even helping Hitler to carry out the Holocaust.

The crumbling Soviet Empire had become a more open society, but it also became more open to anti-Semitism. Even after Gorbachev came to power, the Tsivkin family realized that for a long time, anti-Semitism was still smart politics in Russia. Befriending anti-Semites won more political influence than befriending Jews. That reality will never change.

For eleven years, the Tsivkins were refusniks. Even though their applications to leave the Soviet Union were routinely turned down every six months on the spurious grounds that Vladimir had access to state secrets, Vladimir and Irina at least had their jobs. They could at least send their daughter to an English school and give her piano lessons. However, in 1989, life for the Tsivkins took a turn for the worse.

On March 14, 1989, they were granted permission to emigrate. After quitting their jobs, selling almost all their belongings, and returning their official documents, they were notified after eight days that their permission had been a mistake and had been rescinded. Vladimir and Irina were now unemployed, destitute, and trapped in a country where they no longer wished to be. Unemployment was technically a crime in the Soviet Union. Offenders could be arrested for parasitism.

In June, just a few months later, there was a glimmer of hope. Vladimir was permitted to attend the international conference on human rights in Paris. Perhaps they would be able to leave the Soviet Union after all. Once again, Vladimir and Irina were denied. They were then told that not only was their permission to emigrate a mistake, so was the permission for Vladimir to travel to Paris.

In January, the Tsivkins had a family meeting.

"Irina," Vladimir said earnestly. "The French authorities are willing to get tourist visas for both you and Sanna. You must get out of this God forsaken country. Sanna is seventeen, and she can't spend the rest of her life hiding her Jewish identity. She needs to be around other young Jews. She deserves better. You deserve better. We just have to hope and pray that I will be allowed to join you soon."

Sanna did not want to leave her father behind without knowing when or if she would see him again. Considering Vladimir's thyroid condition, Irina felt guilty about walking out on him as well.

"You and Sanna have an opportunity to be free at last. You can do more for me in the United States than you can here. You can speak with Soviet Jewry activists and public officials who can put more pressure on the Soviet government to let me go. The more publicity we generate from the outside, the better it will be for us."

In January 1990, Irina and Sanna left for Paris and eventually made their way to the United States. They settled in Connecticut, where they were sponsored.

The Tsivkins were high-profile refuseniks. They were well-known by Soviet Jewry activists in both the United States and the United Kingdom. They were well-known by politicians in the houses of Congress and in the hallways of Parliament. Vladimir personally met Prime Minister Margaret Thatcher at the British Embassy in Moscow as well as Senator Frank Lautenberg and Professor Alan Dershowitz at the American Embassy.

I was humbled by these revelations. Both the Settlement Synagogue, the synagogue which adopted the Tsivkins, and I were but cogs in a very large machine which was specifically designed to get them out of Russia. But important cogs we were, because the information that we gleaned and shared with future visitors advanced their cause further and further. The grim reality was that the better known a refusenik was to the western world, the better his or her chances of being allowed to emigrate. I was proud to be part of this entire campaign.

Irina spent months touring the United States and speaking to local Soviet Jewry chapters. She also spoke with Senator Frank Lautenberg of New Jersey in Washington, DC. Senator Lautenberg was considered a hero for Soviet Jews. The first Lautenberg Amendment passed in 1990 facilitated the emigration of Soviet Jews by relaxing stringent standards for refugee status, granting immigrant status to those who could show religious persecution in their native lands. The amendment led to the emigration of tens of thousands of Soviet Jews and was extended to religious minorities in Iran, Vietnam, Burma, and other countries.

Good news came at last. On July 26, 1990, the US Senate with the strong backing of Senator Lautenberg approved Resolution 313 petitioning Vladimir's release. In addition to recapping the hardships of the Tsivkin family since 1978, it pointed out that the Soviet Union was a signatory to the Final Act of the Conference on Security and Cooperation in Europe and the United Nations Universal Declaration of Human Rights. The Soviet government was obligated to allow all citizens to leave the country if they so desired, to facilitate the reunification of families, and respect human rights and fundamental freedoms. It scolded the Soviet government for violating these commitments by refusing Vladimir Tsivkin permission to emigrate. It further argued that the Soviet Union's actions violate the spirit of statements made by President Gorbachev before the United Nations and in other forums that the problem of entry and exit from the Soviet Union will be dealt with in a humane spirit.

In August 1990, Vladimir Tsivkin got permission to leave the Soviet Union so he could visit Senator Lautenberg. Senator Lautenberg arranged his plane ticket. It would be a direct Pan American flight from Moscow to New York. Vladimir was on his way to freedom!

*****

After Vladimir's plane landed, he had to go through passport control, collect his luggage, and then proceed through customs. It was difficult and confusing to navigate through this maze in a country so different from his own. Despite his imperfect and sometimes broken English, he finally got to the finish line. Through the double doors, he would begin an entirely new life.

Irina and Sanna were the first to greet him. They had a group hug that seemed to last forever. Accompanying them were a group of Soviet activists. Their spokesperson was Lynn Singer.

"Welcome to your new country, Vladimir," she said.

Between his thyroid condition, the emotional anguish of the past several months, and plain old-fashioned jet lag, he was totally exhausted. He still managed a few words.

"Coming to America is like coming out of the darkness of totalitarianism into the light of freedom. So bright a light! It's hard to see at first. It's hard to understand. It's so bright a light that it makes the eyes water."

Lynn and her team put Vladimir, Irina, and Sanna into a limousine and escorted them to their new home in Connecticut.

*****

A few days later, the Tsivkins stood at the foot of the Statue of Liberty. Vladimir and Irina kissed the ground as my grandmother once did on Ellis Island. Lady Liberty was lifting her lamp toward the Golden Door. They were now among the huddled mass yearning to breathe free. Gone were the days of hiding their Jewish identity and living as second-class citizens. Gone were the days of harassment by the KGB and the Soviet bureaucracy. Gone were the telephone calls and knocks on the door in the middle of the night.

The American dream beckoned Vladimir, Irina, and Sanna. As they awaited the ferry that would take them back to Manhattan, they gazed at the New York skyline. With a mixture of sadness and relief, they left Mother Russia and would embrace America the Beautiful as their new country.

> Thine alabaster cities gleam,
> Undimmed by human tears!
> America! America!
> God shed his grace on thee,

And crown thy good with brotherhood
From sea to shining sea.

VI

Connecticut
December 2013

After my first few sessions with Davida Dubinsky, I began to think about Simone and Sanna more frequently. Ever since our first meeting, I made a greater effort to touch base with the Tsivkins. My rejuvenated relationship with them was every much as miraculous as my unexpected meeting with Luba Murzhenko.

As far as the Da Costas were concerned, we occasionally stayed in touch since I left England. We initially communicated via snail mail and occasional overseas calls. More recently, this form of communication had given way to emails, Facebook, and Skype. Jerry Da Costa was a whiz with Skype and was frequently online during the wee hours of the night, Greenwich Mean Time.

I suggested to both the Da Costas and the Tsivkins that we finally reunite Simone and Sanna via Skype. Both families were excited. And so I made another trip to Connecticut.

As I drove my car, I remembered the international telephone conversation which took place between Simone and Sanna thirty years ago as if it had taken place yesterday.

VII

London
June 2, 1984

We had placed the initial call to Leningrad but were told by Irina that Sanna was not available, but she would be home soon. The Russian operator, who was transferring the call from London to Leningrad, was undoubtedly listening in to our conversation. She promised to call our synagogue phone number soon.

A few minutes later, the telephone in my office rang. Simone answered it. It was the same Russian operator.

"I have Leningrad," she said.

"Hello."

"Is this Sanna?"

"I am Sanna."

"I want to congratulate you on becoming a bat mitzvah with me on Saturday."

"Thank you very much."

"Do you like Tchaikovsky?"

"Very much. He's my favorite composer. I played a Tchaikovsky piece for your rabbi."

"In your honor, our organist played Tchaikovsky music during the service. After the closing prayer, Jacob played the opening measures of Serenade for Strings."

"Simone, excuse my poor English."

"You're doing fine, Sanna."

"I also want to congratulate you on your bat mitzvah. I am sure that you had a wonderful celebration with family and friends."

"I did. Thank you for your kind words. Perhaps we can meet some day."

"I would like that. For now, it's time to say goodbye."

"Goodbye, Sanna."

I added through the speaker phone, "God bless your entire family."

Jerry and Suzanne were beaming throughout the conversation. The grandparents, Johnny and Bessie, were *kvelling* as well.

Then came the venerable words of Sam Kaiser: "The mother tongue of Simone and Sanna are so different, and yet they communicated. How marvelous!"

I replied, "The language of love is the universal language."

I remember to this very day the dramatic events that brought together two girls from their respective sides of the Iron Curtain. I remember the intercontinental telephone call in my office that allowed Simone and Sanna to hold loving hands across a war-torn continent. I will remember it all, lest my ears and my heart forget the bittersweet ballad of East and West.

VIII

Connecticut
December 2013

During this trip, after Irina opened the front door, we directly walked up the stairs to the computer room. Not only was I greeted by Vladimir but also by Sanna and Esther. Sanna and I briefly exchanged hugs. She remembered me as well, or at least she remembered the Hebrew lesson and the Rubik cube! Esther, who was now nine years old, and I simply shook hands. With that long dark hair, she was the spitting image of her mother.

Vladimir proceeded to make the Skype connection. Jerry Da Costa's image appeared on the screen.

"Hello," he said.

Vladimir and Irina appeared in front of the screen. "We are Sanna's parents," Vladimir responded.

"We meet at long last."

I chimed in, "Today the shoe is on the other foot. In 1984, I was standing with Suzanne, Simone, and you in my study, and we were placing an overseas call to the Soviet Union. This afternoon, I am standing with Vladimir, Irina, and Sanna to make an overseas connection with the three of you."

"How remarkable," Suzanne added.

Vladimir continued, "Many changes have taken place since your Simone spoke to our Sanna." He then provided a synopsis of the events that took place from the time the two girls held hands across the Iron Curtain to the present.

Jerry remarked that the Settlement Synagogue is no longer in Stepney Green but merged lock, stock, and barrel, with a larger congregation in the suburbs. He then spoke with puffed-up pride about his grandson and granddaughter as only a proud grandfather could do. Having known Jerry and Suzanne from the time they were in their thirties, it was difficult for me to image them in that role.

Vladimir said, "Let's put the two young ladies in front of our respective computers." Simone and Sanna took their respective places.

Subconsciously, I still think of Simone as a child, but the truth of the matter is that she had reached middle age. It was evident in her appearance and mature voice, but she still had the basic Simone face. "Alas, Sanna, I not only hear your voice, but I see your face as well. It was an honor to be your bat mitzvah twin."

"It is good to see you in the flesh as well," Sanna responded.

"So are you still playing the piano? Do you still like Tchaikovsky?" That was the exact same question that Simone asked her almost thirty years ago.

"I remember playing the piece 'April' for Rabbi Levin in our apartment. I still like Tchaikovsky. I don't play piano as much anymore, but I make sure that Esther gets music lessons."

The rest of the conversation became more stilted and superficial. Simone and Sanna discussed the activities of their kids but really didn't touch upon their personal feelings about this reunion. Simone appeared more enthusiastic than Sanna. For Sanna, Simone was a painful reminder of all that was horrible about Communist rule under the iron fist of Yuri Andropov. It was a period of her life that she would prefer not to dwell upon. At least her daughter is growing up in a free country with many more opportunities.

The conversation soon winded down as both Simone and Sanna were running out of things to say. I appeared in front of the screen and showed all three Da Costas the double picture of Simone and Rachel as teenagers. She presented that picture as a going-away present. Suzanne acknowledged the picture with a smile. It captured the good old days when I was a close friend of the family.

As we signed off, I promised that they would hear from me very soon.

I continued my conversation with Vladimir, Irina, Sanna, and Esther for a little while longer over some coffee and dainties. Then I made my way home. During the two-hour drive to Long Island, I yearned for the day when Simone and Sanna might meet face-to-face. Maybe in America. Maybe in England. Perhaps someday they will become close friends.

In the months which lay ahead, the bat mitzvah of Davida Dubinsky and the prospect of an emotional reunion were eclipsed by social issues in the community. My rendezvous with yesterday ended abruptly as I turned my attention to the challenges of the present.

Part Two

CHALLENGES OF THE PRESENT

Be in the Present; Learn from the Past;
and Help Create the Future.

—Spencer Johnson

Chapter 5
TWO SOLITUDES

> Two nations; between whom there is no intercourse and no sympathy; who are as ignorant of each other's habits, thoughts, and feelings, as if they were dwellers in different zones, or inhabitants of different planets; who are formed by a different breeding, are fed by a different food, are ordered by different manners, and are not governed by the same laws.
>
> —Benjamin Disraeli

I

New York
Early Part of 2014

Bat mitzvah lessons took place on most Monday afternoons. They lasted forty-five to sixty minutes. We sat on the comfy blue chairs that bisected my office.

Although Davida had serious doubts as to whether she could master the material, she soon made rapid progress. With the help of the primer, she polished off the entire Hebrew alphabet in only a few weeks. We proceeded directly with the Torah blessings and Torah portion as this was the most difficult part of the process. Once this was mastered, the rest of the training would be downhill.

In learning to read Torah, we used a *tikkun*. A tikkun contained all fifty-four portions within the five books of Moses, from the beginning of Genesis to the end of Deuteronomy. The Torah verses appeared in two columns. On the right-hand column was the vocalized version containing Hebrew vowels and trope marks. On the left-hand column was the version as it appears in the Torah scroll—special writing, no vowels, and no trope marks. My methodology was to introduce a verse by first teaching the vocalized side and to immediately switch to the non-vocalized Torah side. Of course, I also recorded the Torah portion for practice at home.

Davida responded very well to this approach. In accordance with our custom at Congregation Rodef Tzedek, she would eventually chant twelve *pesukim* or verses. She already learned the first three. The rest would fall into place a few weeks later. At that point, I would then introduce Davida to the actual Torah scroll.

"You are doing splendidly," I said to Davida. "I am completely confident that you will learn all the material way ahead of time. I am proud of you!"

Davida smiled politely and quietly responded, "Thank you."

"How is your speech coming along?"

"I think that a Russian invasion of Crimea is imminent. Their excuse is liberating the local Russian-speaking population. I might wish to say something about it in my speech. As you know, my mother is Russian, and my father is Ukrainian."

"Ukraine was always a thorn in Russia's side," I responded.

"Ukraine is too pro-West for their liking. The last thing they want is for the country to join NATO."

"Russia has historically mistrusted the West. When I travelled to the Soviet Union thirty years ago, I told my fellow travelers that from the dawn of time, the Mediterranean Sea flowed from west to east and facilitated the flow of new ideas throughout Europe. However, the Volga flows from north to south, and for centuries, Russia was cut off from new ideas—the Renaissance, the Reformation, the growth of democratic institutions, and industrialization. The Soviet Union's distrust and fear of the West did not begin with the Cold War."

"How deep-rooted?" Davida asked.

"Charles XII invaded Russia in 1708. Napoleon invaded Russia in 1812. Hitler invaded the former Soviet Union in 1940. All three countries were ultimately defeated, but not before they wreaked tremendous death and destruction. For much of World War II until the Allied invasion of Normandy in 1944, the Soviet Union took on the Nazi war machine by itself. Millions of Russians perished during World War II. This has caused bitter feelings toward the West until this very day. When East and West Germany came together and the Berlin Wall fell, there was tremendous anxiety. As you know, President Putin was enraged about the collapse of Communism in Eastern Europe and the dissolution of the Soviet Empire."

"Wow!"

"It is ironic that Tchaikovsky's 1812 Overture celebrated the defeat of Napoleon's forces in Borodino and that today, Putin and his thugs wish to do to Ukraine what France once did to Russia."

"Lots of food for thought when writing my speech."

I brought a large scrapbook of my Soviet Union adventures to the synagogue that day and placed it on the conference table near my personal library. I turned to the section, which contained all the refusenik families that I encountered.

"Let's change the subject for a few minutes. Look at the Tsivkins sitting on a sofa in their tiny Leningrad apartment."

In the picture, Vladimir was sitting on the far right. His wife, Irina, was sitting in the middle, and Sanna was sitting on the left. Sanna looked like a typical twelve-year-old with short black hair and a somewhat mischievous face.

I then took out photographs of Allison, Rachel, and Simone, which were displayed on one of the windowsills. "This rather petite girl in the white dress is Allison, another one of my English bat mitzvah students. She was quite a character in her day. This rather mature girl is Rachel. She was a few years older than the other students and celebrated a late bat mitzvah. Today, she is about the same age as your mom. And here is Simone." Simone had long hair hanging down her back and a sweet face that I adored for the last thirty years.

"I am pleased to tell you that Simone is planning to come to New York to attend your bat mitzvah! She might even offer a few words on the *Bima*."

Davida exclaimed, "When I return to my home, I am going to ask my mom to dig up some pictures from her life in Moscow in the 1980s."

"I will never forget the twinning of Sanna and Simone to the end of time. Davida, you are an important part of that story."

II

Jerusalem
August 2013

The *ulpan*, which Bracha attended, was being conducted on the Mt. Scopus campus of Hebrew University. There were beautiful buildings with modern air-conditioned classrooms. The campus was far more built up than when I attended classes there more than thirty years ago.

The teacher of the most advanced Hebrew class, Ronit Zuckerman, made valiant attempts to liven up the class. Reviewing the conjugation of irregular Hebrew verbs in seven *binyanim* and three different tenses and discussing the finer points of Hebrew grammar did not exactly cause great excitement. For the past several weeks, Ronit interjected academics from the social science and humanities departments to give mini presentations in Hebrew and to stimulate discussion on sensitive issues. Students will tolerate a certain degree of drudgery if they see their newly acquired language skills put to good use. At that level, the class was highly motivated. They all wanted to get to the stage of attending highbrow lectures with Israeli students.

While there were some North American students like Bracha, the majority in the class were children of immigrants from the former Soviet Union, young people who were only a few years older than Davida Dubinsky. Many Russian immigrants imported Russian-style nationalism to their new home and viewed Judaism through these lenses. While the parents of many of the students were victims of Russian-style nationalism and the anti-Semitic canards of *Pamyat*, they often projected their victimhood unto the Arabs.

One girl, Svetlana Furman, became friends with Bracha. The Furmans had extended family in Hebron. One weekend, Bracha spent Shabbat with them and learned more about life in the old country. Their hospitality was impeccable.

Ronit knew her clientele. The topic for today's class discussion would be "Should all Israeli children be required to learn Arabic from elementary school to high school?" Not only would it stimulate fiery discussion, but it would also give the students an opportunity to practice their spoken Hebrew in a meaningful way. She announced the topic a few days in advance so that the students could prepare their arguments. Bracha brought a special book to class.

From the moment class began, the sparks were flying. The American students offered the standard arguments in favor of making the study of Arabic required for all Israeli children.

Liz Cohen argued, "The Arabic language is the language of Islam, which Jews need to speak to build bridges of understanding with Muslims. It is also the language of the Palestinians and the surrounding Middle East countries, whom Israel should strive to make peace with."

Sandy Hertz added, "Integrating Arab teachers into Jewish schools and training them to address sensitive topics will prevent children from adopting negative stereotypes. Furthermore, it's good for Israeli children to be exposed to Arab teachers."

Then the detractors chimed in. First came Ilene Malamud. "Teaching Arabic to all Israeli children sounds nice in theory but is unrealistic in practice. In fact, it is a waste of time and resources. Israeli students will learn Arabic and quickly forget it since they would not employ the language in their daily lives. A government decision to make the teaching of Arabic mandatory will require Israel's educational institutions to train no fewer than five thousand specialized teachers at the highest level, but it is not possible at present because there is a limited supply."

Tonya Abramovitz argued, "Why learn the language if Arabs use hateful and aggressive language? Until their rhetoric changes, how can we have cultural and humanitarian exchange with Arabs in general and Palestinians in particular? How can we have reasonable communication with unreasonable people?"

Mara Kazekevitch was even more extreme. "We have nothing in common with Arabs. Arab culture promotes violence. Our culture promotes Torah. If I was a parent, I wouldn't want my children to be influenced by the warped ideologies of Arab teachers in Israeli schools."

Liz Cohen reentered the fray. "Let's forget about Arabs for a moment. The waves of immigration of Iraqi, Yemenite, Egyptian, Moroccan, and other Arab Jews have meant that a plurality of Israelis had Arabic speaking ancestors. The speaking of Arabic is not confined to Arabs. Many of our Sephardic brothers and sisters speak it as well!

"It is also important to note the literary overlap between Arab and Jewish writers in the past. Arab-Jewish writers such as Sami Michael, Shimon Ballas, and Isaac Bar Moshe wrote their works in Arabic. Arab authors like Anton Shamas, Naim Araidi, Siham Daud, Faruq Mawasi, and Salman Masalha have also written works in Hebrew."

Bracha was the last speaker of this debate. "I would like to read an Arabic passage for the class's consideration."

"*B'vakasha* [please]," added the teacher.

Bracha took the book and came to the page with the paperclip marking the passage to be read.

The general object of the law is twofold: the well-being of the soul and the well-being of the body.

The well-being of the body is established by a proper management of the relations in which we live one to another. This we can attain in two ways: first by removing all violence from our midst. That is to say, that we do not do every one as he pleases, desires, and is able to do, but every one of us does that which contributes toward the common welfare. Secondly, the law teaches every one of us such good morals as must produce a good social state.

The well-being of the body is also attained by creating the healthiest condition of his material relations, and this is only possible when man has all his wants supplied, as they arise. If he has his food and other things needful for his body, e.g., shelter, bath, and the like. But one man alone cannot procure all this. It is impossible for a single man to obtain this comfort. It is only possible in society, since man, as is well-known, is by nature social.

The welfare of the body is treated in the law most carefully and most minutely. While the welfare of the soul is the superior kind of perfection, it can only be attained when the first perfection of the body has been acquired. For a person that is suffering from great hunger, thirst, heat, or cold cannot grasp an idea even if communicated by others, much less can he arrive at it by his own reasoning. Only when the perfection of the body is achieved can there be the possibility for the perfection of the soul."[1]

Bracha then proceeded to translate all this to Modern Hebrew. Ronit Zuckerman had a twinkle in her eye as she was fluent in Arabic. She commented that Bracha's translation was more or less accurate.

Bracha summarized the passage. "In other words, before you can live a life of Torah, you need a stable and just society in which there is law and order and in which everyone's material needs, food and shelter, are met. Judaism is about social action. Judaism is about *tikkun olam*—repairing our world."

Sandy Hertz commented, "What beautiful words! What beautiful thoughts!"

Other American students threw in some comments in English.

"Cool!"

"Awesome!"

"This passage rocks!"

The teacher interjected, "Rak b'ivrit, b'vakasha!" (Only in Hebrew, please!)

Bracha concluded, "This passage is from *Moreh Nevukhim, The Guide for the Perplexed*, written in classical Arabic with Hebrew characters on Medieval Jewish philosophy. It was written by Moses Maimonides in 1190, who was both a learned rabbi and physician who interacted extensively with Muslims. It was later translated into Hebrew by his contemporary, Samuel ibn Tibbon, in 1204. In Egypt, Maimonides was appointed court physician to al-Qadi al-Fadil, the chief secretary to Sultan Saladin, then to Saladin himself, after whose death he remained a physician to the Ayyubid dynasty. He also compiled the *Mishneh Torah*, one of the most important Codes of Jewish Law."

At that point, all debate ended in that class.

III

New York City
Early Part of 2014

Davida and I sat around the conference table in my study. For this lesson, I decided that we should take a break from the weekly grind of Torah reading and turn to the Torah portion itself. The main feature of *Parshat Naso* were the laws pertaining to the Nazirite.

"So, Davida," I asked. "What do you think about the Nazirite who leads a more limited lifestyle to become closer to God? What do you think about abstaining from wine, not visiting a beauty salon, or coming near a dead body for a designated period? Would you be prepared to drink only grape juice after our Shabbat services, let your hair go down to your waste, or avoid funerals, even for loved ones?"

"That would be horrible," she replied. "I could handle the grape juice, but I could not cope looking like Rapunzel or not attending the funeral of someone who I cared about."

"The rabbis were divided on this. After a Nazirite completed his vow, sacrifices were performed on his behalf. Some rabbis argued that it was a good thing to be extra pious. Sacrifices were performed because the Nazirite was giving up extra piety and returning to normal life. Rabbi Eleazar argued, 'If a person who denies the enjoyment of wine is considered holy, how much the more holy would he be if he denies himself other pleasures of life?'

"Other rabbis believed that the Nazirite was a sinner. Sacrifices were performed because he was denying what God has permitted and was separating himself from the community. Maimonides, a Medieval Jewish philosopher, believed that it was sinful to avoid wine, to avoid nice clothes or nice dwellings, and to shun marriage.

He abhorred the Nazirite. He believed that we must participate in the community before we can get closer to God.

"There is a Hasidic story in which one of the disciples wanted to get into the good books of a famous rabbi by boasting how much he denied the pleasures of life. His meals consisted of dry bread with salt.

"The famous rabbi chastised him for his ascetic lifestyle and forced him to give it up immediately.

"Another disciple asked the rabbi why he found fault with this very pious man. 'What difference does it make if he eats the minimum?'

"The rabbi replied, 'If this man eats only dry bread with salt but could afford to eat much better food, he will soon expect the poor to eat stones. He would have no social consciousness.'

"Let's go upstairs and look at the stained-glass windows."

"All right," Davida replied.

We walked the two flights of stairs and entered the sanctuary.

As I pointed to the windows, I said, "All the windows of our sanctuary have either biblical or Talmudic quotes. Our tradition invites us to view what lies beyond these walls through Jewish eyes and to take stock of it, both in its beauty and its ugliness.

"The synagogue was never meant to be a fortress to shut Jews away from the outside world. The fine ethical principles coming from our prayers and our Torah and Haftarah portions compel us to go out and repair our world. Jewish teaching at its best is applied ethics.

"Davida, hatred of the other is pervasive in our society. In northern Manhattan, you are fortunate to live in a diverse community. In combatting hatred of the other, we as Jews must work with many different people who are not like us. Extra piety is not about being a Nazirite or giving up pleasures. It's about getting involved, sacrificing time, and being a participant rather than a spectator. Are you ready for that?"

Davida nodded.

"Great. I'm sure that I can count on you long after the bat mitzvah is over."

IV

Jerusalem
Middle of January 2014

Miri Rosenberg, the Israeli Children's Literature professor, was a dynamo of energy. A plumpish middle-aged woman, she had a personal mission to share the insights of this special genre of literature to her predominantly American students. Although her class was conducted in easy Hebrew, the profundity of the reading assignments belied her modified presentation to young people whose mother tongue was not Hebrew.

Today, she was assigning the term projects. Just as her father, many years ago, put together a high school project in which he researched the treatment of African Americans in traditional high school textbooks, Bracha wanted to research the treatment of Arabs in Israeli textbooks and children's literature.

Miri was enthusiastic about this project. She told Bracha, "Don't feel that you must produce a final product that will please me. You will find some disconcerting realities in your research. Go where the facts lead you!"

For the projects, the students were to work in pairs. Before the pairing officially took place, Bracha made two observations. The first one was that more than half the class consisted of young ladies who attended the University of Michigan and were spending their junior year at the Hebrew University Overseas School. Most of them seemed to know each other very well. There was a sense of cliquishness that Bracha didn't find in her other classes.

The second observation was that a Palestinian student was sitting by herself at the end of the third row. She had darkish skin and was rather tall and slim. She wore a long dark dress, and her black hair was covered by the traditional hijab. Her modest clothing and retiring nature were certainly in character with Muslim tradition. During roll call, she responded to the name Anwar.

Bracha remembered a story told by her father when he was a junior in high school. He was the vice president of the debate team. At the various competitions, the debaters participated in pairs. During one of the early sessions, the eight members of the team were choosing partners. There was an African American member on the team, the only African American debater in the entire Greater St. Louis league! Her dad went up to him immediately and asked, "Jeremy, will you be my partner?" Not only did they become partners, but they also developed a friendship which lasted for over thirty years until Jeremy's death.

Bracha immediately went up to Anwar before any other pairs were formed and said, "I would love to be your partner on this project!"

Anwar smiled. "I would love to work with you as well."

Bracha continued, "I am interested in doing research on the treatment of Arabs in Israeli textbooks and Israeli children's literature. We may not like everything that we find. Does that interest you as well?"

Anwar responded, "You seem very interested in producing serious work. I would love to work on that topic with you. It's close to my heart as well."

"Miri will support our conclusions whatever they are."

"Let's get coffee afterward."

"I'd like that."

And so the first meeting took place at a Starbuck's coffee shop.

Bracha gave her general bio. Her mother was a physician, a cancer specialist. Her father was the rabbi of a New York congregation. Her brother was in university, currently studying in Berlin.

Anwar lived in East Jerusalem with her parents. Although she was only in her early twenties, she had two younger sisters who were already married. She chose a different path as she wanted to obtain her master of education before any consideration of starting a family.

Anwar posed a question. "Bracha, do you think your father would object to you working with a Palestinian Muslim?"

Bracha responded, "Are you kidding? He would probably light Roman candles. He attended the official opening of a mosque in our neighborhood soon after 9/11. As president of the local interfaith clergy council, he invited Muslim leaders to attend the meetings and to participate in the annual interfaith Thanksgiving celebration. Despite all the antipathy toward Muslims after the destruction of the Twin Towers, including members of his congregation, he brought high school students to the local mosque for an educational outing. I attended the special class. That marked the beginning of my social activism and indirectly led to interest in human rights in Israel."

Anwar relaxed considerably. "I had no idea," she responded.

"In 1984, my dad dined in a Parisian café with a Russian woman. She had met with her uncle and aunt and cousins in Leningrad only a short time ago. He delivered presents from them and sent her their good wishes.

"My dad's Russian was virtually nonexistent. Her English was limited at the time. They achieved a common ground by speaking French!"

Anwar interjected, "Our world would be a much better place if everyone found common ground."

"We can do better than this. We know each other's language. We can use both Hebrew and Arabic at will."

As Bracha and Anwar sorted through many books and gathered the necessary information, many meetings took place, often at pastry shops or restaurants. Most of the time, they spoke Hebrew. On other occasions, they would speak Arabic. Other variations included Bracha speaking Hebrew and Anwar answering in Arabic or the role reversal of Bracha speaking Arabic and Anwar answering in Hebrew. Through their collective research, through their meetings, and through their breaking bread together, was the emergence of a lasting friendship.

V

New York City
January 15, 2014

It was a frosty Wednesday afternoon when I found myself in between synagogue functions. Earlier, I attended a sisterhood luncheon in which most of the participants were elderly women, mostly in their eighties and beyond. Many were the last remnants of our

Holocaust survivors. Having worked with Holocaust survivors for my entire career, especially in England, I felt a special connection even though I did not speak a word of German. I would bring a sandwich from home and enjoy a nice strudel and coffee provided by the synagogue.

As I knew in advance that I would not have religious school responsibilities that day and that I would have to return to the synagogue for a board of trustees meeting at 7:30 p.m., I chose that day to take David Thompson's offer to visit the Grace Afternoon School and explore the possibility of a future rental. On the way back, I would stop at the Hudson View Restaurant for a quick dinner.

My trip was a fifteen-to-twenty-minute walk from Congregation Rodef Tzedek. Although the neighborhood changed drastically over the decades, there was still a formidable Jewish presence. On Saturday mornings, I would invariably see Orthodox Jews walking on Fort Washington Avenue toward the synagogues of their choice. The men would be attired in dark suits and *kippot* (head coverings), and the women would be wearing long dresses, always the finest clothing to honor the Shabbat. As I would walk a few blocks to my own synagogue, I would sometimes overhear them discussing the Holy Books which represented the word of God.

As I crossed 181st St., I found myself entering another world. The farther south I walked, the more Latinx (mostly from the Dominican Republic) I would encounter. I went down 176th St. and came to Broadway. There, I found many restaurants and stores with Spanish signs. Across from the United Palace Theater, the major entertainment center of the neighborhood, was a market where a passerby, such as me, could buy fruits and vegetables as well as clothing and household objects.

I crossed Broadway and continued my walk eastward. East and West Broadway seemed to be a major dividing line in northern Manhattan. It was assumed that west of Broadway, which is where my synagogue and most of my membership were located, was the more affluent area. East of Broadway, where the plurality of the Dominican population was located, was considered by the local population to be the poor relation to those who lived on the other side.

During the 1980s, when I travelled to the former Soviet Union, I felt that I was visiting an entirely different world. East was east, and west was west, and never the twain shall meet. Of course, Russia and my country of birth were on opposite sides of the globe. Here, two worlds were less than one mile apart! As someone who was not born in New York, I experienced two solitudes. I wondered how many Orthodox Jews left their enclaves and had meaningful relationships with Latinx. I wandered how many Latinx in this area have met a Jew let alone strike up a friendship. The thought made me sad.

I crossed the street and found the church where Grace Afternoon School was located. Entrance, however, was not through the main level of the church. I went down a separate flight of stairs. There was a musty, dank smell which followed me all the way down the staircase. I entered the heavy door to the school.

The school belied the external appearance of the entryway. It was a beehive of activity. The one hundred plus children had just come from the local playground. They were marching into the various classrooms with joyful hearts and eager minds. The school catered to mainly elementary and middle school youth and the classrooms were carefully organized by age. Many children wore school uniforms. Others wore plain street clothes.

In the foyer, which was the nerve center of the school, I saw the two office mangers sitting behind a large desk. In the foyer, I was met by David Thompson.

David vigorously shook my hand and said, "Rabbi Levin, I would like to introduce you to the two joint directors of Grace School, Anton and Maria Muharsky. Maria mainly functions as the parent coordinator."

Both, one of Polish background and the other of Latina background, greeted me enthusiastically.

"Come," said David. "Let's enter the main room and sit around the long table."

"Please excuse me, Rabbi," asked Maria. "I must meet with some of the parents. I hope that we meet again soon."

A large framed picture of Jesus Christ with a multiracial group of children was firmly attached to the main wall. Also on the picture was an apt quotation form Matthew 19:14: "Let the little children come to me, and do not hinder them, for the kingdom of heaven belongs to such as these."

Noticing that my head was glued to the picture, Anton chimed in, "You gathered that we are a faith-based organization. That picture succinctly summarizes the philosophy of our school. All our children, regardless of their background, are created in God's image and are deserving of our help. The kingdom of heaven does belong to them. It was so in the time of Jesus. It is also so in 2014."

Anton added, "Are you comfortable that we are faith based? The faith happens to be Christianity. Most of the children come from some form of Christian home."

I responded, "I am perfectly comfortable with a faith-based school. About one hundred years ago in London, Sir Basil Henriques founded the Settlement Synagogue several years after he found Jewish youth clubs. He believed that religion was an inseparable part of youth education and, in fact, social services in general. Religion for him was the lifeblood of all the social action that he ever undertook. As far as Christianity is concerned, we already rent out our facilities to two churches."

A broad smile appeared on Anton's face. "Then we are on the same page!"

"Absolutely."

"Let me give you some background about our school. Grace Afternoon School has a long history of working with the Latinx community of New York City, established through its origins in Washington Heights, a predominantly Latinx and Dominican community in Manhattan's most northern section. In 1998, we launched the After School Program in response to the community's under-resourced schools and the significant language barriers of its residents. Employing a literary focus coupled with positive reinforcement and community building, the After School Program remains the cornerstone of our service model with students continuing to make strong academic and socioemotional gains."

I interjected, "What I am feeling is how little has changed since I went to public schools. In 1954, in the landmark case *Brown v. the*

Board of Education of Topeka, the Supreme Court ruled that separate was inherently unequal. Yet on the sixtieth anniversary of *Brown v. Board of Education*, little has changed in my hometown, St. Louis. Through white flight, red-lining, blockbusting, and gentrification, also known as urban renewal, separate White and Black neighborhoods were perpetuated. Because the upper middle-class White neighborhoods got the lion's share of tax money for schools while the Black neighborhoods in the outer-rim suburbs and inner city were starved for tax dollars, predominantly Black schools could not maintain their buildings, attract quality teachers, and enrich their curriculums."

Anton continued, "The same applies here. New York is the most segregated state for Black students and the second most segregated for Latinx students, trailing only California. In 2018, in New York, 90 percent of Black students attended predominantly non-White schools, while Latinx student enrollment in predominantly non-White schools has remained at 84 percent. Three-quarters of the students enrolled in gifted and talented programs are White or Asian. Meanwhile, 70 percent of all New York students are Black or Hispanic, and a majority attend schools where less than 10 percent of their classmates are White.

"If I may, I would like to shift my focus to this neighborhood. The average income is about $3,000 a month. The average rent for a two-bedroom apartment is $2,500 a month, and $500 a month is left for food and clothing and extras. That's poverty in my book. Therefore, one-third of all Washington Heights families with children live below the poverty line. Close to 20 percent are unemployed. Also, 46 percent of Grace students live in a single parent household, and 30 percent of Grace students live in linguistically isolated households. Neither parent nor grandparents can read and write in the English language.

"Latinos and Latinas collectively are the poorest educated of NYC's major race and ethnic groups and are behind other ethnic groups in other important outcomes. By 2009, only 15 percent of Latinx adults had graduated college, and 39 percent had not graduated high school. Furthermore, Latinos and Latinas have the lowest median incomes, the highest poverty rates, 27 percent for all ages, 37 percent for children, among the highest unemployment and out-of-the workforce rates, and the lowest health insurance coverage."

"These are very grim statistics," I replied. "There must be a tremendous need for schools such as yours. Tell me all the services that you provide."

"In addition to the After School Program for elementary school and middle school children, we also have a separate high school program which meets at a different time. That large room off the main room is the man cave for our teenagers. It's a safe space and great for teenagers to hang out.

"We also have a Saturday mentoring program designed for career mentoring and field trips. It is one of the jewels in our crown, and we receive lots of grant money for it. There's a full summer achievement program which reinforces what is learned during the regular school year. While there are also excursions and recreational activities, it's designed to prevent children from falling behind on their grade levels during July and August.

"There's also health and nutrition services, a teenage pregnancy prevention program, school placement, and family engagement."

"Please take me through a typical day."

"Sure. The children arrive anytime between two and four. They are brought by parents, grandparents, and other caregivers. They are escorted by a faculty member to the local park. At four, we assemble in the main room for about ten minutes. That's the time for general announcements. In addition, I give some spiritual inspiration. From 4:10 p.m. to 5:30 p.m., the children disperse to the various classrooms for homework help or perhaps to work with the computers. The last child is out of the building by six.

"During the afternoon, we serve a snack. We often serve rice in various combinations, such as rice beans or rice and chicken. Other times, we serve eggs, pancakes, or hot dogs. Snack time is one of the most important parts of the afternoon. Unfortunately, for too many of the children, it's the main meal or perhaps the only meal for the day."

I sighed at that remark as I stated, "Im ayn kemach ayn Torah. If there is no meal, there is no Torah. It's impossible to teach hungry children how to read and write." With that remark, I completed my copious notes on my laptop.

As a rejoinder to that remark, Anton added, "Feeding the body is important, but our chief mission is to feed the soul."

"I've got one more broad question. What are your broad goals for this school year?"

Anton responded, "We are working toward the following outcomes: maintain an average daily attendance of 90 percent, achieve a year-to-year retention rate of at least 80 percent, 80 percent of participants will maintain a grade point average of 2.0 or higher, 50 percent will maintain a grade point average of 3.0 or higher, 80 percent will complete one hundred hours of independent reading, 80 percent will meet program curricula outcomes, 100 percent will be promoted to the next grade, 100 percent will graduate high school, and 100 percent will be enrolled in a postsecondary educational institution.

"Any more questions, amigo?" asked David Thompson.

"I am sure that I will have many more later. Although there are special issues associated with a Jewish institution, such as High Holy Days and Shabbat, I believe that we can make this work. I see only a win-win situation by renting our facilities to you. From your side, we can offer improved facilities. With the two pastors of the two churches to which we are renting space, we can offer spiritual mentoring. There is the possibility of offering intergenerational programing by pairing your children with our elderly Holocaust survivors. We could invite some of your children to break bread with us at our monthly Shabbat dinners. We can also get your teenagers together with our teenagers. Perhaps they can work together at the Hebrew Union College soup kitchen. The sky is the limit.

"From our side, we can use the additional revenue to beef up our infrastructure, our office, and custodial staff. If we can get the place hopping seven days a week with organizations such as yours, we'll attract more members. A busy place which is bursting at the seams is certainly more attractive than an empty building with little activity going on."

"I like how you think," replied David Thompson.

"I will give a very positive report to our licensing committee. Probably, our synagogue president, Rolf, and our religious school principal, Sanford, will want to look at your program as well. I hope that our paths cross many times. I am excited."

"We're excited too," David replied.

At that point, we got up from the table. We shook hands, and I returned to Congregation Rodef Tzedek for my evening meeting.

*****

Long Island, New York
January 21, 2014

On Long Island, as a service to local congregations whose clergy was overwhelmed by the size of their large bar and bat mitzvah programs, I occasionally tutored students. On Tuesday afternoons, I met with the Rubin twins, Jake and John, at their home. Their Hebrew background was nonexistent, but I drummed the Hebrew alphabet into their heads and got them to begin their respective Torah portions.

As I was about to finish with the second son, the father, Matt Rubin, walked in. As most of my interactions were with the mother, Matt attempted to engage me in some small talk.

"You've been teaching my boys for several weeks, and I still don't know where you work."

I replied, "I commute to northern Manhattan a few days a week."

"That's a *shlep*!"

"I work in Washington Heights."

"Is that where all the *shvartzes* live?"

I cringed. *Shvartze* is the derogatory Yiddish expression for a Black person. In my mind, it's not that far away from *nigger*. I said so once from the pulpit and surprisingly got pushback from a congregant. He defended his God-given right to objectify African Americans!

Controlling my anger, I responded, "More African Americans live farther south in Harlem. Many Dominicans live in Washington Heights."

Matt replied, "Shvartzes, spicks. They're all the same."

This time, I lost it. "If you want me to continue teaching your sons, please do not use this terminology in my presence."

"All right! All right! Don't be so touchy!"

I collected my payment for the lesson and returned home. We never spoke again about the racial composition of northern Manhattan.

VI

Jerusalem
Middle of January, 2014

Bracha had butterflies in her stomach as she entered the lecture hall. She was attending the first class of the Intellectual History of Zionism. There were more students in this class than in the others. What was more significant was that it was a regular Hebrew University course. Most of her classmates were Israelis.

The lecture and required readings were entirely in Hebrew. While the essay questions on the final exam would also be in Hebrew, the school offered one concession. Bracha would be permitted to write her responses in English so that she could express herself fully. While she could easily write in Hebrew, she did not protest the levelling of the playing field, so to speak.

Bracha sat in the front row. Seated next to her was a tall, slender, and rather handsome Israeli. He was dark-skinned, and Bracha surmised that while he might be a sabra (native-born Israeli), his family origins were likely outside of Europe.

The professor, Eliezer Spiegel, got right down to business. For the opening lecture, he stated the obvious: Israel is both a Jewish State and a democracy. The entire history of Zionism revolves around the tension between ethnic nationalism and democracy. His thesis was that democracy cannot exist without nationalism and nationalism cannot exist without democracy.

In terms of the first statement, Professor Spiegel pointed out that patriotic feelings are not in themselves incompatible with a democratic outlook, insofar as they mean a preferential solidarity with one's own nation, the attachment to national cultural heritage and language, and the desire to make one's nation better off and more civilized. Nationalism fosters feelings of common heritage, common history, and civic responsibility. Nationalism emphasizes that we are all in this together and provides the sense of internal cohesion that is necessary for a people to be able to govern itself.

In terms of the second statement, Professor Spiegel also argued that in an ideal society, nationalism has checks put upon it by the belief that people remain distinct individuals embedded in important family, religious, and community networks. We need to respect differences while acknowledging shared nationalist values that unite people around common moral and political ideals. Democracies reject *organicism*, the notion that the state is an organic being that is larger than the sum of its citizens. The country may be bound by majority rule, but individual minorities have civil rights.

Professor Spiegel then made the distinction between closed nationalism and open nationalism. Nationalism is a coin with two sides. The closed side is exclusive; the open side is inclusive. The closed side limits freedom to some; the open side expands it to all. The closed side practices discrimination. The open side abhors second-class citizens. The closed side denies Israel can do no wrong; the open side acknowledges Israel's flaws and endeavors toward improvement. The closed side must be turned down to prevent worship of the state, a form of idolatry which had its antecedents in biblical history. The open side must be turned up to support human rights and human flourishing.

*****

After the lecture, the dark-skinned student turned toward Bracha and said, "Shalom, Shmi Shmuel Sassoon. Hello, I am Shmuel Sassoon."

"I am Bracha Levin. I am from New York."

Immediately detecting the American accent, he asked, "Did you understand the lecture?"

"About 90 percent of it. Professor Spiegel's jokes usually go above my head."

"If you are around here long enough, you'll pick up the Israeli idioms. Anyway, you speak good Hebrew for an American."

Bracha smiled. "Many years ago, my father was looking at artwork at the Montmartre in Paris. A Parisian thought that he was German. He replied, 'Je suis American.' [I am American.] He replied, 'Vous parlez bien…pour un American.' (You speak well… for an American.) My dad smiled and thanked him for probably the highest compliment that he could receive in France."

"I am a sabra, but my family is from Yemen. My parents, my two younger sisters, and I live in a Yemenite *moshav* not far from Jerusalem. While my major is mathematics, I am taking this course as an elective. I am interested in hearing Professor Spiegel's spin on the intellectual history of Zionism."

Bracha and Shmuel decided to leave the lecture hall and continue their conversation in a school cafeteria.

"So, Shmuel, do you think the Israeli government practices open nationalism or closed nationalism?" Bracha's question was rhetorical. Having visited *Susya*, having participated in the Breaking the Silence tour, having witnessed daily Arab Israeli interactions on the street, and currently working as an intern with Ir Amim, her mind had been made up a long time ago.

"Based on the historical treatment of my people and other immigrants from Arab lands, I would say mostly closed nationalism."

"That's an understatement," Bracha replied.

"In 1949, the journalist Arye Gelblum branded immigrants from Arab and Muslim countries as primitive, ignorant, lazy, and subordinate to savage instincts such as drunkenness and prostitution. Most of us have serious eye, skin, and sexual diseases. With all our deficiencies, we are still one grade above the Arabs and the Negroes.[2] How comforting! Arye Gelblum obviously wanted no part of us in the *kibbutzim*.

"What is particularly sad was that his sentiments were echoed by major Israeli leaders. David Ben Gurion insisted that Israelis should not be corrupted by Arab culture. Abba Eban stated that Mizrachim should be infused with the Occidental Spirit. We should not allow them to drag us into an unnatural Orientalism.[3] Golda Meir believed that Mizrachim belonged to the Middle Ages and had serious doubts as to whether they could be assimilated into Israeli society.

"Black Jews was often a canard used by European anti-Semites. How ironic it is that American Jews often refer to Black people as shvartzes, especially Black housekeepers. Here, the terms *shvartze Mizrach*, Blacks from the east, and even worse, *shvartze chayes*, Black animals, are often applied to us."

Bracha responded, "It's equally ironic that anti-Semites branded Jews as an alien Eastern people and that the early Zionists claimed that Western culture was decadent and led to assimilation. And now, here, they wish to impose European culture upon their Middle East homeland!"

Shmuel continued, "Just as public schools were separate and unequal in America, so they were for my people as well. Ashkenazi pupils were being oriented toward white-collar occupations while Sephardi pupils were being oriented toward low-status blue-collar jobs. The schools in Ashkenazi neighborhoods had better facilities, better teachers, and higher status. Most Oriental children, including Yemenites, studied in schools designated by the Ministry of Education as schools for the *te'unei tipuach*, those in need of nurture or culturally deprived. These schools assumed the cultural inferiority of Mizrachi children. What the Israeli government was saying, 'Don't expect much from Oriental children and their parents.'

"The policy of separate and unequal educational facilities coupled with the ideal of the White Europeanized Sabra in Israel has caused many Mizrachim to hate themselves. They became ashamed of their skin color, their speech, and their culture. Children became ashamed of their parents.

"Such a policy created a vicious circle. Weak education leads to bleak job opportunities. Bleak job opportunities lead to poverty and substandard living conditions. Substandard living conditions lead to poor health, poor self-esteem, and less motivation and access to education. And so the cycle continues. It is a rigged system designed to perpetuate the economic superiority of the Ashkenazim.

"Of course, the percentage of Ashkenazim who have received higher education is higher than that of Mizrachim. When my grandparents came to this country in the 1950s, the gap was huge. Today, in 2014, the gap has narrowed, and more Mizrachim are attending university. I hope to get my PhD in mathematics. Despite everything that I have said, I am one of the lucky ones."

"On this rather somber note, I need to move on to the next class," said Bracha. "I look forward to attending more lectures with you. Perhaps you can help me with the 10 percent of the lecture that I don't understand, including the inside jokes."

"Will do. We should have coffee more often. We can reflect on what we have learned and exchange notes."

"I'd like that."

Another lasting friendship was born.

VII

New York City
January to February 2014

When offering our facilities to the wider community took effect several months ago, there was great excitement. Operating a large aging building with a small membership was challenging. The additional revenue would help offset the high cost of utilities and maintenance. However, the reality of larger numbers of people walking through our doors soon set in.

Mendel Kornblum, the housing chair, attended more services and volunteered more of his personal time than just about any other member of Congregation Rodef Tzedek. The synagogue was his second home, and he was totally devoted to the upkeep of our facilities. He was as zealous about them as the fictitious character, Scotty, was about the good working order of the *Starship Enterprise*! If the building was left in anything less than pristine condition, if food was left in the sanctuary, if there was a broken chair, or if the occasional cigarette butt was lying on the social hall floor, he got rather testy.

Thus, the initial enthusiasm of the licensing committee toward tenants was slowly replaced by more sober realism and even ambivalence. This was hardly the time to propose a new organization which would turn everything topsy-turvy and make the entire congregation think outside the box. Such was my challenge when I wanted to paint a glowing picture of Grace Afternoon School.

The licensing committee meeting was scheduled for 7:30 p.m. The first ninety minutes were spent going over the picayune details regarding the other two rentals. Many of Mendel's concerns were mauled over *ad nauseum*. Additional time was spent on any modifications that we would like to see in their contracts. Much of the nattering that took place did not require the attention of a whole committee. With all the attention to minutiae, the big picture of outside tenants and their impact on the wider community was totally lost.

Finally, attention was magnanimously given to Grace Afternoon School. Most of the members were already emotionally exhausted. The prospect of a major tenant bringing in substantial revenue was tempting enough for the beginning of negotiations between our lawyer and longtime member, Monroe Morgenstern, and the Grace lawyer, David Thompson.

Sanford Kantor, the principal of the religious school, along with another teacher who belonged to Rodef Tzedek, recently visited the Grace Afternoon School. He reported that both were greatly impressed by how the school was managed, by the rarity of discipline issues, and by the tremendous value of the school to the Latinx community. Sanford concluded his report by saying, "We can make this work. Let us be strong and of good courage."

I then had the floor. I wanted to communicate my own enthusiasm and make the big pitch. I first attempted to appeal to the enlightened self-interest of the congregation. I began with finances.

"By offering our facilities to Grace Afternoon School, we would obtain enough revenue to convert our senior custodian from part-time to full-time with health benefits. He is a great handyman. He is also Latino, bilingual, and personable. He would be the perfect man to work in this new environment.

"Our increased revenue would enable us to beef up the office staff and to keep the building open day and night, seven days a week. Grace has deep connections with various social services in the area which could become future rentals. Because we would be open most of the week, we would potentially become a beehive of activity. Busy places are more likely to attract potential members, particularly younger families, than white elephants.

"In terms of potential programs, the sky is the limit. Can you imagine an intergenerational program in which the children meet some of our elderly Holocaust survivors on Wednesday afternoons? Many of our old-timers whose children and grandchildren live outside the city are starved for contact with youngsters. The children from single-parent homes might profit from a surrogate grandmother.

"Can you imagine the Grace High School students and the Rodef Tzedek High School students coming together on Monday evenings to discuss the social issues of the day or working together at the Hebrew Union College soup kitchen downtown?

"Can you imagine an adult education evening in which the clergy or representatives of the four occupants of the building offer an array of courses that appeal to members of all four organizations? *A Taste of Judaism* or *Introduction to Judaism* would likely appeal to non-Jews as well as Jews. Perhaps some of us would like to hear a non-Jewish slant on the Bible. Perhaps a specialist from the Grace Afternoon School could teach a class on child-rearing. This might appeal to our families who have toddlers or young children at home.

"Can you imagine our four organizations rolling up their sleeves and participating in social action projects? Can you imagine our four organizations offering an interfaith Thanksgiving celebration next November?

"The potential is breathtaking. We could become the synagogue under the bubble, a model for the rest of New York City. We could become a safe space in a turbulent community. Everybody would be a winner in our building—our tenants and our congregation."

Despite my pitch, little emotion was generated by the others seated around the table.

Monroe Morgenstern was a prim and proper gentleman. He came to the meeting almost directly from work and was wearing a dark three-piece pinstripe suit. His roots were deep in the synagogue. His father, a Holocaust survivor, was a past president. Not responding directly to my pitch, he said, "The congregation does have a precedent for social action. Years back, we did help one of the boat people from Vietnam and found him gainful employment."

After a pause, Mendel Kornblum shook his head, took a deep breath, and responded, "You know, Rabbi. I admire your innovative thinking. Despite skepticism from some families and from me, you introduced Jewish camping to our youth, and our children derived great benefit. But, if I must say so, you have gone over the top this time. This idea of yours sounds very nice, but I am concerned how the Grace Afternoon School will affect our own programming. How will it affect the religious school?"

Sanford Kantor immediately inserted, "Our school is small. We can find alternative space, perhaps even in our exhibition area."

"It could make it difficult to grow the school."

"Not an immediate problem."

Mendel shook his head again. "What about our family service dinners? We can't have Grace kids hanging around when family service begins at 6:30 p.m."

I responded, "I was assured that it wouldn't be a problem. It gives us an opportunity to invite the entire school to one of these services, to interact with our children, and to see how we operate. Thirty minutes prior to the service, I could give a rundown on the symbols of the sanctuary. Or perhaps we can invite a couple of Grace families to our dinner and practice true Jewish hospitality."

Another shake of the head came from Mendel. "What about our annual rummage sale? It's a major event in the life of our congregation. How would we accommodate that?"

"We could persuade Grace families to help and publicize the sale. We would be able to attract an even larger clientele. In addition to raising money for the synagogue, we would also be expanding our service to the needier elements of our wider community."

"What about the wear and tear on the building? We could get to the point where the increased costs of utilities and repair would significantly offset revenue gains."

"While it's not my place to quote figures, we would obviously require a damage deposit and set an appropriate rent that would reflect all of your concerns."

"In terms of hours, rooms, and office space, Grace seems to want a lot for a relatively low price. I am worried that we could be overrun and overwhelmed by the school with no way out. Financially, we could end up worse and not better."

Monroe Morgenstern found his opening. "Renting to the two churches is relatively easy. They come here on Sunday, when none of us are around, and do not interfere with our programs. This group is much more intrusive. Now as the son of Holocaust survivors, I'm all in favor of reaching out. However, if this doesn't work out, are we going to throw out one hundred Latinx children? It would be morally unconscionable."

I responded, "True enough. However, a contract is only as good as the trust between the two parties. There's plenty of mistrust in race relations to go around. We trust the two churches. Maybe we should have a bit of trust in this organization as well."

Monroe smiled. "A bit naïve on your part, Rabbi Levin, if I must say so. Our first commitment is to our membership and to protecting our synagogue. You obviously do not think like a lawyer. You think like a rabbi."

"I would hope so. I speak like a social reformer who is optimistic about human nature."

Mendel sighed and shook his head once again.

Out of nowhere, Dena Schwartz, the president of Sisterhood, joined the conversation. "Rabbi, while I applaud your reaching out to other religious groups, I am totally opposed to bringing in the Grace Afternoon School. I come to this synagogue to seek inspiration and inner peace. If we have one hundred kids hanging around while Shabbat morning services are taking place, how will it be possible to worship in peace?"

I got exasperated at this point. "We have an elephant in the room. This discussion is very much about how we view ourselves as a congregation. Are we a tribe, or are we players in the outside world? Are we an isolated enclave, hiding behind Fortress Rodef Tzedek, or are we a community center open to the wider community?"

"The tribe, as you call it, must obviously come first," said Mendel emphatically. "Don't get me wrong, Rabbi. I'm delighted that our shul has had a greater presence in the neighborhood than ever before. Some of the members of the Uptown Church live in my building and are among my best friends. I even shoot pool with one of my neighbors on the second floor. However, I wouldn't want our rooms to be used to the point that our personal space becomes constricted. The last thing that any of us would want is less ability to run programs that our members have cherished for many years."

Just then, we heard from the chair of the committee and the vice president of the congregation, Jane Lieberman. She was a blondish middle-aged woman who had kept the synagogue on an even keel for many years. Her messages from the pulpit were often warm and fuzzy as she avoided controversy at all costs.

"Rabbi, I second Dena's praise of your interfaith work. As all you know, I have lots of connections with politicians and organizations in this neighborhood. However, the proposal appears so overwhelming," she said. "My head is spinning. It's hard to wrap my arms around everything that you are recommending. While the concept of a community center sounds nice in theory, we could be biting off more than we can chew.

"As the daughter of Holocaust survivors, I can say that not all our old-timers would be happy. Many of them are emotionally scarred. Non-Jews destroyed many of their families in Europe. They come here to seek shelter from the outside world. While the neighborhood has changed drastically over the years, they want to recreate some semblance of the Jewish life that they once knew before the Nazis took over Germany.

"Perhaps we should attain balance between Jewish and non-Jewish tenants. There is a modern orthodox group that is unhappy with its current location. Perhaps we should steer the group here."

I responded, "This is a massive four-story building that consists of thousands of square feet. We can handle many organizations. We can accommodate this group by finding a space or by changing the times of our own services so that we can accommodate two different congregations. If they want some educational programs for children, we could merge the two religious schools and even hire qualified staff from the other congregation. I already spoke about communal adult education. This group would be welcome to join."

Mendel had a definite edge in posing his last question. "Rabbi, you seem to have an answer to everything."

"All of these challenges are solvable if there is creativity and flexibility on everybody's part. What we cannot allow to happen, however, is for us to talk ourselves out of the low-hanging fruit. As Rabbi Chaim Nachman of Bratslav once said, 'The world is a narrow bridge, and the important thing is not to be afraid.'"

Discussing minute details was more in Jane Lieberman's comfort zone. Delving into larger philosophical issues and entertaining the possibility of redefining the synagogue's identity was too daunting. It didn't seem to interest the other committee members either.

She said, "It's ten. The hour is late. I want to go home. Let's table this discussion for the next meeting. Do we have a motion to adjourn?"

Dena replied, "So moved."

"Meeting adjourned."

Sanford Kantor and I rolled our eyes and shook our heads. On the one hand, Sanford believed in proper due diligence when entertaining the possibility of new tenants. On the other hand, from his student protest days in the sixties, he was also a radical and a shit disturber. We began to appreciate how Joshua and Caleb felt when they gave a glowing report of Canaan to Moses, only to be rebuffed by the pessimism of the other ten leaders who also spied out the land.

Sanford shrugged his shoulders and said, "Congregations are conservative by nature. People fear change, even if they will likely benefit from it. They want to hold on to the past at all costs."

*****

For the next few weeks, the mixed feelings toward tenants in general and the prospective tenancy of Grace Afternoon School carried over into the negotiations and subsequent meetings. The second and third rounds of discussion followed the pattern of the first round. Most of the time was devoted to tiny agenda items regarding the other two rentals. When we got to Grace Afternoon School, there would be a report on the latest negotiations, followed by the same arguments and concerns being trotted out repeatedly. Talking *tachlis*, the bottom line, the big picture, was deliberately avoided. Invariably, the discussion would be abruptly ended by Jane Lieberman uttering the familiar phrase, "The hour is late. I want to go home. Let's table this discussion for the next meeting."

The suspension of the negotiations became inevitable. I held a conference call with Anton Muharsky and David Thompson and told him them how disappointed I was.

David responded, "It was equally difficult on our end. Many families were concerned about sending their children to a school that was farther away from their neighborhood. Most of them live several blocks south of 181st and east of Broadway. Your building is north of 181st St. Most of your congregants live west of Broadway. Crossing Broadway is a big deal in this part of the world.

"Secondly, it is true that operating in a basement without windows and which is a potential firetrap is challenging. While our relationship with our current landlord is complicated, we know the situation well and make the necessary adjustments. Your building and your community are an unknown quantity. People in our community fear the unknown."

"The same in my community," I responded.

"Thirdly, our board of trustees, rightly or wrongly, got the impression that deep down inside, your licensing committee doesn't really want the likes of us around them."

"That sentiment applies to some individuals, but certainly not to the licensing committee as a whole, nor most of the congregation. I do think that you hit upon something that is very important. Despite all the discussions, the negotiations weren't really about money and facilities. Underneath it all, it was about comfort level. Our congregation knows little about you, and your community knows almost nothing about us. We are two solitudes dwelling on opposite sides of Broadway.

"We've been going about this all wrong. I'm not ready to give up on the negotiations, but something else must happen first. We must do our homework. We must make much greater efforts to know each other. We must cross Broadway."

"How do you propose to do that?" asked David Thompson.

"For my part, I wish to become one of your reading buddies on Friday afternoons. I will lose the suit, put on blue jeans, a sweater, and sneakers, and become part of your community for one to two hours."

"That would be wonderful," responded Anton. "The majority of our students are boys. We need male role models."

"I'll work with both genders. I'll start next week."

"I'll make that happen."

"Secondly, I will arrange for your children to mingle with our children on a Monday or Wednesday afternoon. I will take your high school students and give them a tour of the sanctuary. We will serve pizza to all age groups. Breaking bread breaks down barriers. I will subsidize the pizza from my discretionary fund. I don't need the approval of the licensing committee to invite guests, especially if I foot the bill!"

"What a wonderful idea! I like your vision, amigo," said David.

I concluded the conference call by saying, "The important thing, gentlemen, is not to be afraid and not to give up on each other."

*****

For my Friday afternoon volunteer work, I was performing a double mitzvah. By walking to and from my destination, I got in my daily quota of exercise and performed the mitzvah of taking care of my body. By serving as a reading buddy, I was nurturing young minds and establishing a meaningful connection between Congregation Rodef Tzedek and Grace Afternoon School. If we could only get this school into our building, we would be able to provide many volunteers, young and old, to donate their time.

As a reading buddy, I was reprising my volunteer work in university. I was a tutor of elementary school children in Hamilton, Ohio. In our student center, we had an orientation center conducted by Mrs. Evelyn Dister, who coordinated the entire program.

One young lady posed the question, "Are the children White or Black?"

Mrs. Dister's answer was right on the money. "In the Harrison School, which we visit on Tuesday, the children are a mixture. In the church in downtown Hamilton, which we visit on Wednesday, the children are predominately Black. In the Van Buren School, which we visit on Thursday, the children are predominately White. But what difference does that make? They are all children."

When I entered the walls of Grace Afternoon School with an almost exclusively Latinx student body, that would be my motto: "In the end, they are all children." I might add, "They are all children of God, created in the image of God." If I remember that, I'll be okay.

I was soon met by the real button pusher of this institution, Maria Muharsky. She had an encyclopedic knowledge of every family that was served by this school. She was regarded by their children as their "earth mother."

"Welcome, Rabbi," she cheerfully greeted me. "Let me put you in the capable hands of Kimberley."

Kimberley was a tall lanky lady who took me in hand and escorted me to the main room. "We're delighted to have you here, but I want to point out a few points of our policy.

"Unlike the public schools, we don't forbid teachers and students from hugging. In fact, many of our children require a hug now and again. However, you cannot lift any child above your waste. And as you can appreciate, you cannot be in a room alone with a child with the door closed."

"I'll probably use this long table in the big room to work with the children."

"In addition, you'll be given a form and will record what you read with each of your students. Often, you will read to them. However, if a child reads to you, you should briefly describe their progress. We want to be always accountable to their parents.

"One suggestion. The relationships that you build with the children are even more important than anything that you might teach them. The most important skill is to be an active listener. Listen carefully to everything that they might say to you about themselves, their families, their friends, and their likes and dislikes. Try to discern what they really need from you and from Grace Afternoon School. Hold still, be quiet, and really listen to the people you say you want to help. Although the emotional pain cries out and it's tempting to intervene, don't try to fix troubled children. None of their lives can be quickly fixed.

"We have had problems with a few volunteers from the suburbs who offer ready-made solutions to various children's problems. They are the so-called do-gooders. Addressing the staff in condescending voices, they offer unsolicited advice as to how we should run this school. At bottom, they have hidden agendas."

"I know what you mean. I was once a prison chaplain a long time ago. There was a social worker who would also make patronizing comments and tell me how to do my job. As it turned out, her true motive was to visit the inmates to obtain male companionship that she was not receiving in her marriage. She had no sense of boundaries. I finally had to bar her from the prison."

"That's dreadful," Kimberley remarked. "I think that we are on the same page. Volunteers who offer solutions but can't handle the simple act of listening are not really our allies. They're simply armchair White liberals with White savior complexes."

"I have a second cousin who is a teacher in this area and who certainly doesn't fit that mold. In fact, I was named after her grandfather."

"What's her name?"

"Barbara Feinberg."

"I had her as a teacher in fifth grade. She's a dynamo. Very caring. You'll have to give her my love."

"Will do. If you see me fall in the trap of trying to fix things, please call me out. Along with Anton and Maria, you are my boss."

"I look forward to a great partnership. Let's bring on the children."

*****

Over the next several weeks, there were several children to tend to. The children had almost complete freedom to choose their books. Depending upon the situation, I could either read to them or have them read to me.

The first child up to bat was Mia. She had short black hair and was usually dressed in school uniform. On the surface, she was a very quiet girl. The first book that I read to her was Dr. Seuss's *Green Eggs and Ham.* It was a classic that had a certain rhythm to it. Mia's shtick was to turn the pages faster and faster so that the rhythm in which I would read would go faster and faster as well. She found this to be amusing and softly chuckled from beginning to end. In subsequent weeks, she would try this tactic with other books as well.

Then came Samantha. She had long brown hair that extended over her shoulders. Unlike Mia, she wore civilian clothes, usually trousers, sweaters, and sneakers. She felt comfortable with me almost from day 1. On subsequent weeks, she would immediately greet me by saying, "Hi, Isaac." Maria once corrected her and said, "You should call him Rabbi Levin. He's your teacher."

Samantha replied, "He's my friend as well."

I chipped in, "I like you too, Samantha. I hope that our friendship never dies. Maria, I'm okay with first names. It places less of a barrier."

Samantha's personality was the exact opposite of Mia's. She was a veritable chatterbox. Based on the numerous questions that she asked me about my home, my family, my hobbies, and my vacations, I thought that she was my official biographer. I learned that she had two sisters, loved to read, and liked to spend time at the beach.

Samantha came across as an old soul. As a third grader, she appeared to have a sense of discernment which was well beyond her years. Every time I would exchange small talk with her, I felt that I was speaking with an adult.

At any rate, she would read two books to me every week and read them rather well. Samantha certainly read at grade level, if not beyond. I wondered if she really needed extra help from me.

I once shared my observations with Maria. She surprised me when she said that it wasn't always this way and that Samantha had made enormous progress in the past two years. She wanted us to continue reading together to maintain our positive relationship.

Then came Joel. He was a plump fellow with short black hair. He had an older sister in the program. He was interested in only one book—the Bible. Without saying a word, he would present me with a Bible, point to a story, and expect me to read it. Most stories came from the Old Testament. Occasionally, I would read a narrative from the New Testament.

Over time, I asked Joel to use his words. Instead of pointing to a story, I asked him to give me the title of the story that he wished me to read. Afterward, he would read a few paragraphs himself. Joel was a fair reader, but very shy and self-conscious.

Following Joel was a nervous dark-skinned little guy called Christian. Observing that Joel and I had quite a good time reading Bible stories, he asked me to read them as well.

Unlike Joel, there was nothing shy about Christian.

"Please read me the Bible, the whole Bible, and nothing but the Bible."

Christian obviously watched too many courtrooms portrayed on television. I asked, "Why do you like the Bible so much?"

"I love God!"

"A good reason. Let's begin."

I shared my conversation with Maria.

"So Christian said he loved God," she replied. "What a troubled little soul! Based on what I know about his family life, I sometimes wonder in my darkest moments if God loves him in return."

I had no response to that statement. Weeks later, Christian was no longer part of the afternoon school. During the time I had with him, I met him on his own terms. Not every child can be saved.

My biggest handful was Anna Leah. She wasn't satisfied with having just one or two books read to her. She ransacked the bookshelf in her classroom. She was also a live wire. She couldn't sit still. She constantly interrupted our reading sessions to use the bathroom or to get a drink but would expect me to keep her place even if I had to wait more than ten minutes.

Once, Anna Leah climbed on top of the big table and did a tap dance. Before coaxing her back onto the floor, I clapped my hands and sang, "Anna Leah, Anna Leah, tiny little thing Anna Leah dance, Anna Leah, sing. What's the difference if you're very small. When your heart is full of love, you're nine feet tall!"

Noticing this escapade, her older darker-skinned brother came up to me and asked, "Is my little sister driving you mad?"

I replied, "She's a bit high-spirited."

"I'll speak to her and ask our grandmother to speak to her as well."

The most heart-wrenching part of my encounter with Anna Leah was if she was left to her own devices, she would take up the whole afternoon with me. Of course, that could not be as there were others who required my time.

On one occasion, I asked her to return to her classroom after we had worked for twenty minutes. She replied, "No! No! No! I want to stay with you." In fact, she would grab on to me for dear life. Maria came by and noticed what was happening. Maria emphasized that sharing time with me was just as important as sharing toys and gently led her back to her classroom. Sadly, our relationship was never quite the same again.

*****

A few weeks after I began my work at the Grace Afternoon School, the "subway series" resumed in my synagogue. Although Grace was walking distance from Rodef Tzedek, the two locations were separated by one stop on the A line. As it was a rather cold Monday afternoon in February, the subway was the preferred mode of transportation.

We were to play hosts to two distinct groups: about twenty children between grades three to seven, accompanied by Anton Muharsky, and five high school students accompanied by Kimberley. The younger children arrived at 4:30 p.m. and entered through the Ft. Washington entrance.

This is the first time these young people saw me in a blazer and tie, my usual synagogue attire for weekdays. Then Samantha said, "I remember you," and put her arms around me. This act was repeated by Mia and Joel. Afterward, I led them to the penthouse, where our youngsters were eagerly waiting for them.

This inaugural meeting was meant to be a low stress event with emphasis on social interaction. Sanford and Anton prearranged the seating so that all the tables had roughly equal representatives from the two schools. As both Rodef Tzedek and Grace were faith-based schools, nobody had any trouble with Eleanor, one of our students, reciting the blessing over bread, the *Motzi*, in Hebrew and English. Sanford, with the help of two high school aides, distributed the cheese and vegetarian pizzas, the salad, and the apple juice. When it comes to bringing children together from different backgrounds, pizza is the great unifier!

Although the youngsters were temporarily taken out of their comfort zones through the rigging of the tables, their interpersonal interactions became seamless within ten minutes. Young people were chirping way about their interests, their hobbies, their likes, and dislikes as if they had been together for months. In the end, they were all children. At one table, Lazlo provided impromptu instruction in constructing paper airplanes; both Latinx and Jewish children were getting into it. The interest spread to the other tables as well. Fortunately, Sanford and Anton intervened before too many paper airplanes were given a test run.

Then came the second part of the program. Sanford taught the group a song of thanksgiving. The Rodef Tzedek group already knew the first two lines consisting of Hebrew and English:

> Ve-al zeh, ani modeh/modah
> And for this, I am thankful.

We explained to our guests that if you were a boy, you would use *modeh*. If you were a girl, you would use *modah*.

We then introduced a new wrinkle, the Spanish translation, to the Rodef Tzedek group.

> Y po resto, doy gracias

In essence, the Latinx children learned a line of Hebrew, and the Jewish children learned a line of Spanish. Both groups came together with the English lyrics. Within a few minutes, both groups were joyously singing all three lines. In addition, representatives from each group shared things that they were thankful for. Children from both groups mentioned family, friends, good health, being able to pursue their passions, and making new friends this afternoon. It was interculture sharing at its finest!

I remarked, "I am planning an interfaith Thanksgiving celebration in this synagogue in late November. *Ve-al zeh* would be a perfect contribution to the program!"

Throughout the time, my mind went back in time when I used to watch *Art Linkletter's House Party* as a young child, particularly the section "Children Say the Darndest Things." I know of no television celebrity that could relate to children as well as Art Linkletter.

Sanford Kantor was the New York version of Art Linkletter. While being firm, he put our guests at ease and made them feel comfortable. He had all the children eating out of his hands! I sat at his feet in admiration.

I staggered the timing of the two groups so that I could participate in all the proceedings that afternoon. As soon as this event was winding down, I went downstairs and greeted Kimberley and the teenagers. They arrived like clockwork at 5:15 p.m. We proceeded to the sanctuary.

*****

The names of the teenagers were Isabella, Mariana, Sofia, Tomas, and Mateo. They were wowed by the size of the building and by the large seating capacity of the sanctuary. I pointed out that it was built for a much larger congregation back in the day. The synagogue was well over one hundred years old. The membership elected to move to our current location in the 1970s. The building was purchased from a church and was slowly converted to a synagogue.

I then introduced some Hebrew terminology. First, the *ner tamid*. It called to mind God's abiding presence and His providential care of the Jewish people. The *ner tamid* also represented the light that burned continuously in the western section of the ancient Temple of Jerusalem. I also pointed out the *Bima*, the elevated platform from which services were conducted, and the *Aron ha Kodesh*, the Holy Ark where the Torah scrolls were contained.

Most of the teenagers were silent. I didn't know whether it was sheer awe, discomfort, boredom, or some combination of the three. Nervous laughter came from Mariana and Isabella. All of this was so foreign. So as not to lose this group, I proceeded to the main event.

I took out a Torah scroll which was already set to the Ten Commandments. I invited the five teenagers and Kimberley to ascend the *Bima* and examine the writing. I explained that the text of the scroll contained the Five Books of Moses in their entirety. It was handwritten with a special pen and special ink. The writing had to be word perfect. The Hebrew text was written from right to left.

None of my six guests had seen anything like this. Isabella, who was a tallish young lady, exclaimed in amazement, "Praise the Lord!"

"Praise the Lord, indeed," I replied. "Before a passage could be read, it was customary to recite a blessing and praise the Lord who gave us the Torah."

I then read each of the Ten Commandments, one by one, and translated them into English. At that point, the students were in more familiar territory. Seeing these commandments in their original language was a revelation to them.

Afterward, I rolled the scroll to the nineteenth chapter of Leviticus and read verses 33 to 34 in Hebrew and translated it to English.

> When a stranger sojourns with you in your land, you shall not do him wrong. You shall treat the stranger who sojourns with you as the native among you, and you shall love him as yourself, for you were strangers in Egypt: I am the LORD your God.

"I bet all of you can relate to these verses."

Tomas and Mateo vigorously nodded.

"Bigots and demagogues may say otherwise, but don't believe anything they say. These words come directly from the Torah. They are repeated thirty-five additional times. They are the words of God."

With that, I rolled the Torah scroll together, dressed it up, and returned it to the Holy Ark.

All of us left the sanctuary, went down into the social hall, and had slices of cheese pizza together.

"I am delighted that all of you came to share the afternoon with me. How would you like it if I lose the jacket and tie, put on some real street clothes, come down to your place, sit with you in your man cave, and have a real bull session? You can say anything that comes to your mind and ask any question that you would like. I tell students of all ages that there is no such thing as a stupid question. Is that something that might appeal to you?"

"We'd like that. Let's do it soon," replied Isabella.

*****

After a few weeks, I requested and received permission to lead the opening assembly at Grace Afternoon School. Every time I walked inside the building, I thought of the sharp contrast between the Supreme Court decision of *Brown v. Board of Education in Topeka*, articulated sixty years ago, and the grim realities of 2014. As a newcomer to this school, I did not want to address this sore point head-on. I would create a twist of my own and provide a more positive message.

I brought four dolls with me: the Ukrainian tea cozy that I was given to me as a gift in Kiev, a classical Raggedy Ann doll, a twelve-inch biracial doll who was both African American and Latina, and a Bahama doll, purchased in Nassau, which was carrying a basket of fruit on top of her head. I laid them out together on a medium-sized table. The dolls caused a sensation, especially among the girls, as they gathered around the table.

Kevin, who occasionally read to me, asked, "Isaac, did you play with dolls as a child?"

I replied, "Not exactly. They certainly aroused my curiosity, but in my day, it wasn't cool for boys to play with dolls, so I directed my interests elsewhere. Today, I collect ethnic dolls, dolls from different countries. They remind me of the huge beautiful variety of human beings. Have any of you visited Disneyland?"

Very few children raised their hands.

"My favorite ride was It's a Small World. I would get into a boat and ride through a cave with hundreds of dolls coming from all corners of the world. In the background, you would hear a children's choir sing 'It's a Small World.' If the rest of my family would have allowed me, I would have stayed on that ride all day!"

Anna Leah pointed to the biracial doll and exclaimed, "That doll looks like me!" If she had her way, she would have snatched the doll, taken it home, adopted it, perhaps given it a warm bath, and added it to her dollhouse. Kimberley intervened in time.

I asked the group, "Which of the dolls do you like?"

For a few moments, animated discussion took place among the children. Samantha, the old soul, volunteered to speak. Pointing to the biracial doll and the Bahama doll, she said, "These dolls look more like us, but the Ukrainian doll is the most beautiful."

I replied, "Is this the consensus of this group?"

Most of the children raised their hands, but Anna Leah still preferred the biracial doll.

"All four of these dolls have a special story."

"The Ukrainian doll, which has beautiful blond braided hair and a beautiful costume dress, was actually very sad. Back in the 1980s, Jewish children could not go to a Jewish school to learn Hebrew, Jewish history, and Jewish customs. Alanna, the name of the Russian doll, was one of those children.

"What if Grace Afternoon School made a rule stating that the speaking of Spanish was forbidden in the building? How many of you would think it's a good idea?"

Only one child raised his hand, mainly to be contrary, I suspect.

"How many of you think it's a bad idea?"

Everybody else raised their hands.

"That's the way it was for Jewish children in the 1980s in the former Soviet Union.

"Let's turn to Raggedy Ann. There is sadness in her life as well. She was created by Johnny Gruelle. When she came on the market in 1915, his daughter, Marcella, died of an infected vaccination. The anti-vaccination movement at that time adopted Raggedy Ann as a symbol. Raggedy Ann has stringy red hair. All of you thought that Alanna was more beautiful. Yet she has given pleasure to children for almost one hundred years.

"Let's look at the Bahama doll. On the one hand, she carries a burden upon her head and has a hard life. On the other hand, she lives in a warm climate and has a loving family.

"Now we come to the doll that Anna Leah loves so much. Perhaps she represents all of you. She might have a tough life in her home, but she has a special family in Grace Afternoon School."

Kimberley and some of the other instructors smiled at this remark.

"We often think of family as father, mother, and children, and perhaps some pets. But I think of family differently. It is about people bound together by loving relationships. This school could also be thought of as your extended family. Belonging to a family has less to do with being born than with being loved. DNA does not make a family. Love does. What lesson did all of you learn today?"

Joel surprisingly spoke up. "You can't judge a book by its cover."

"Something like that. The cover of the Bible is not always glamorous, but the content teaches us very important lessons. The dolls are the same. I think of them as miniature people. They all look different. But within each of them, there is a mixture of happiness and sadness. Like these dolls, all human beings are worthy of respect and dignity."

A lot of buzzing took place after I finished my session. I collected my four dolls, put them in my small blue suitcase, and proceeded to begin my reading sessions with my pupils.

"Great message," remarked Anton.

"Thank you."

"I'm looking forward to participating in the symposium that you organized. The topic—The Other: A History of Hate in America—is incredibly timely. What an ambitious agenda! I am bracing myself for an intensive twenty-four hours! After Sunday church, I'll hop in my car and be in Cold Spring Harbor for the opening dinner."

"I look forward to really getting to know you better."

*****

The exchanges that took place between Congregation Rodef Tzedek and Grace Afternoon School, of course, did not fix the shattering impact of de facto segregation in New York City. With all the hurts and fears and wants that these children faced in their daily lives, they were softened by an accepting community, by a caring staff within the humble walls of a church basement, and by their new friends who dwelled on the other side of Broadway. Truly, it was a beginning.

VIII

Jerusalem
May 2022

Bracha and Anwar made a very good team. In researching the treatment of the Arab in Israeli children's literature, they combed through well over a dozen textbooks and works of historical fiction. Together, they came up with a gold mine of valuable information. After numerous meetings in pastry shops and restaurants, they came up with a well-documented project.

Anwar felt uneasy after they turned in their work. She said to Bracha, "Hebrew University is one of the crown jewels of the Zionist project. We're making statements that not too many people in Israel want to hear. What if our teacher is displeased with our conclusions and recommendations! Will she give us a poor mark and conclude that this is the work that you can expect from a Palestinian student?"

"I wouldn't worry so much," replied Bracha. "Hebrew University has come a long way since Arthur Ruppin purchased the land for it in 1925. While Ruppin at that time embraced the Zionist narrative, favored working the land over academics, and even developed Zionist racial theories, Hebrew University today is an academic institution which encourages freedom of thought and doesn't demand its professors to adhere to a party line. Didn't our teacher, Miri Rosenberg, tell us to not worry about pleasing her and to go where the research leads us? She strikes me as a fair-minded teacher."

*****

Here is a synopsis of their project.

Textbooks in most countries reflect their societies' ideology and ethos, their values, goals, and myths. Although most students perceive textbooks as objective, truthful, and factual, they do not impart neutral knowledge but rather provide a view of their society through a biased lens. Deciding what should go in a textbook is a political process. Educators are aware that for students, textbooks are often their first and sometimes their only early exposure to books and to reading.

Ben-Zion Dinur was the minister of education in the 1950s. Believing that the Arabs, even more than the Babylonians, the Persians, the Romans, and the Byzantines, were the *real usurpers* of Jewish land and continue to threaten the Jewish state, he advocated a strong Zionist orientation in public education. He wrote in 1953:

> The position of our country must form the underlying premise of the civil education system. The State of Israel was born after a long and difficult struggle. It was established in the middle of a civil war. The struggle continues… Officially we are living in that vague shadowy situation which is neither war nor peace. We resemble a city under siege… We are surrounded by enemies whom we fought during the War of Independence and who yet to reconcile themselves to our existence.[3]

Children's literature, like textbooks, are agents of socialization and communicating society's values. Literature can play a role in how children perceive other groups and influence their prejudices. Because children have limited face-to-face experience with people who come from different religious and ethnic backgrounds than their own, they tend to accept what they read as the gospel truth. As a result, it's very easy to shape Israeli children's image of Arabs and to foster negative and even destructive stereotypes.

During the pre-state period, both textbooks and children's works of fiction emphasized that the Jewish homeland was conquered by different peoples including Arabs, was neglected through the centuries, and waited to be redeemed by Jews. One book backed the historical theory of Ben Zion Dinur by writing that the Arabs did indeed conquer the land 1,300 years ago, did settle in it, and did see it as their own country, but they did not do anything to protect it from destruction and ruin.

The textbooks perceived Arab society ethnocentrically, as was the customary European view, with a feeling of Jewish superiority. The adjectives of backward and ignorant were constantly applied. Textbooks through the present day ignored the fact that there were Arabs who were middle class, professional, and intellectuals. This is especially puzzling as there are plenty of Arabs, citizens of the State of Israel, who occupy a noticeable place in Israeli society, for example in hospitals as doctors or auxiliary personnel, or in schools in the role of teachers. Also, in the occupied territories, there is a considerable segment of intelligentsia, which does not appear in the books.

As acts of Arab violence increased in the 1920s, and especially in the late 1930s, textbooks began to present the Arab as the enemy. They were perceived as ungrateful, since the Jews came to contribute to the development of the country, and the Arab leaders nevertheless incited their people against the Jewish settlement. The violence that Jews suffered in the pogroms of Eastern Europe was projected unto the Arab people. Thus, many history books described Arabs as a "mob which threatens, assaults, destroys, eradicates, burns and shoots, incited by haters of Israel."

From the establishment of the State of Israel until the early 1970s, textbooks were influenced by the Holocaust trauma and used extreme words to describe the Arab role in the Jewish-Arab conflict. Most of the books failed to mention the existence of the Palestinian nation, its aspirations, or the driving force of Palestinian nationalism. The events of 1936 to 1939 were presented as disturbances and riots by "Arab gangs" who had ties to Nazi and Fascist movements. As one textbook wrote, among the Arabs, "inflammatory Italian and German political propaganda, fell on the fertile ground of religious and national fanaticism." The presence of Nazis, references to Hitler, and threats of completing Hitler's work can be found in some Israeli stories for children.

In Israeli textbooks, the 1948 war was presented as a struggle between the few (Israel) and the many (the Arabs), starting with attacks by local Arab gangs and followed by invasion by seven Arab states. The reason for the refugee problem was that the Arabs fled following their leaders' propaganda, despite Israeli attempts to persuade them to stay. The Arabs were deluded into thinking that they would soon return victorious to the country, expel the Jews, and seize their assets as spoils of war. The 1960 classic film *Exodus* embraced that narrative. After the UN voted in favor of partition, Barak ben Canaan addressed a large crowd from the balcony and exclaimed, "To the Arabs, we implore you to remain in your homes. We will work together as equals in building the free state of Israel."

During the 1970s, the Ministry of Education initiated a major shake-up of the curricula, which led to changes in the content of textbooks. The role of classical Zionist ideology was diminished, and more emphasis was placed on critical thinking. In the 1970s, descriptions delegitimizing Arabs almost disappeared in history school textbooks. These books permitted the acknowledgment of the existence of Palestinian nationalism, used less pejorative terminology in the description of violent Arab resistance to Jewish immigration and settlement, and began to present a more balanced picture of the origins of the Palestinian refugee problem.

By the 1990s, Arabs in some textbooks were presented "not only as mere spectators or as aggressors but also as victims of the conflict." For the first time, there appeared to be a genuine attempt to formulate a narrative that not only glorified Zionist history but also touches on certain shadows in it. Controversial questions such as the Palestinian refugee problem, Israel's presence in Lebanon, and the desirability of establishing a Palestinian state were taken seriously. They described in a balanced way the violent acts of Palestinians against Jews in periods of conflict and offered an objective description of the wars. In general, they provided a new perspective to the Arab-Jewish conflict, presenting a more complex and multidimensional picture of the Arabs, in general, and the Palestinians, in particular. However, it should be noted that such books are still scarce. Often their publication is accompanied with political outcry and political debate in the media.

We arrived at the following conclusion. While the rhetoric in children's literature has been toned down over the decades, negative stereotypes and delegitimizing labels persist. They have been passed down from grandparents to parents to children. Inevitably, it will take further generations to change societal beliefs about Arabs. It goes without saying that a parallel undertaking by the Arab states and Palestinians in particular, whose textbooks are similar in nature to those of the Israeli books, would help such a process. We fear that the upswing in conflict might lead to the reversal of the gains made in the 1990s.

The trauma caused by the pogroms in Eastern Europe and by the Shoah continues to be perpetuated throughout the generations. The brutal and self-serving agendas of both Israeli and Palestinian extremists receive their oxygen from the perpetuation of objectifying and vilifying the other. Israeli-Palestinian dialogue and resolution of the Israeli-Palestinian conflict will make little or no progress until more persistent attempts are made to reform Jewish civic education and Palestinian civic education on both sides of the Separation Wall. The Shoah must be taken seriously by Palestinians. The Nakba must be taken seriously by Israelis. Attaching negative labels must give way to empathy. Otherwise, we will continue to remain two solitudes.

Bracha and Anwar received a mark of 97 for their term project, a mark rarely awarded at the Hebrew University.

Chapter 6

A Tale of Two Nations

We hold these truths to be self-evident, that all men are created equal, that they are endowed by their Creator with certain unalienable Rights, that among these are Life, Liberty, and the pursuit of Happiness.

—American Declaration of Independence

When the architects of our great republic wrote the magnificent words of the Constitution and the Declaration of Independence, they were signing a promissory note to which every American was to fall heir. This note was a promise that all men, yes, black men as well as white men, would be guaranteed to the inalienable rights of life, liberty, and the pursuit of happiness. It is obvious today that America has defaulted on this promissory note insofar as her citizens of color are concerned. Instead of honoring this sacred obligation, America has given its colored people a bad check, a check that has come back marked "insufficient funds."

—Martin Luther King

The state of Israel will be open for Jewish immigration and for the Ingathering of the Exiles; it will foster the development of the country for the benefit of all its inhabitants; it will be based on freedom, justice and peace as envisaged by the prophets of Israel; it will ensure complete equality of social and political rights to all its inhabitants irrespective of religion, race or sex; it will guarantee freedom of religion, conscience, language, education and culture; it will safeguard the Holy Places of all religions; and it will be faithful to the principles of the Charter of the United Nations.

—Israel Declaration of Independence

Except for those who were born blind, they realized long ago that it is utterly impossible to obtain the voluntary consent of the Palestine Arabs for converting "Palestine" from an Arab country into a country with a Jewish majority.

—Vladimir Jabotinsky

I

Jerusalem
Middle of January 2014

In the Palestinian history class, Professor Abdul Habib knew his audience well when he delivered his opening lecture. He was determined to tear a strip off those smug upper middle-class American Jewish students, many of whom came from traditional Jewish backgrounds. He began his remarks by branding both America and Israel as malevolent colonialists determined to continue their domination of much of the non-Western world, including indigenous people on the North American continent and Palestinians on the Asian continent.

Bracha believed that one of three things was going on with Professor Habib. Either he woke up on the wrong side of the bed, or he was interested in pure shock value, or he had a gigantic chip on his shoulder. Perhaps it was all three.

"Could you explain yourself further?" she asked.

"It's common knowledge that the US has enabled Israel to sustain the occupation of Palestine. Israel is the largest recipient of foreign aid since World War II. Billions of dollars are given each year, much of which is used to bolster its military might.

"Israel, for its part, has had its footprints on many US interventions in Africa, South Asia, and South America. This excludes numerous locales throughout the Arab world. Wherever the United States sticks its nose where it is not welcomed, Israel is a ready tool for direct or indirect assistance."

Such remarks tore Bracha up. She was taught to love both America and Israel in her Jewish school. Every day, she would recite the Pledge of Allegiance with her fellow classmates and sing "Ha Tikvah," Israel's national anthem. She marched for Israel in New York City, participated in a youth tour to Israel, and even studied in Israel as a college undergrad and worked as an intern for a human rights organization.

Bracha knew both America and Israel were far from perfect and have come nowhere near the lofty principles expressed in their respective Declarations of Independence. However, she felt that the Palestinian professor had gone off the deep end.

"What you are saying is outrageous!" she exclaimed.

"The truth hurts," replied Professor Habib. "In this class, I will open your eyes as to what is really taking place throughout the world, particularly in Israel.

"So-called American exceptionalism and so-called Israeli exceptionalism are joined at the hip. American and Israeli settlers shared a common origin myth. Both groups envisioned themselves as travelling in the footsteps of their biblical ancestors. Both groups envisioned themselves as gloriously predestined for greatness. The Puritans were influenced by the ideas of John Calvin, while Zionists who claimed to be secular, still quoted from the Old Testament.

"The early American colonists looked upon themselves as God's New Israel. Settlers followed the example of Joshua crossing the River

Jordan into Canaan, where God commanded them to exterminate the indigenous populations and establish for themselves an exemplary nation which is currently underused and underappreciated by the natives.

"The early Zionists were influenced by American models of colonization and ethnic cleansing of the various Indian tribes. Vladimir Jabotinsky, who was considered a visionary Zionist leader by the Israeli right-wing politicians, compared the conquest of America to the proposed conquest of Palestine. He argued that the Indians fought against the White settlers because they viewed their lands as their home and were not willing to accept new masters. The same would apply to Arabs. In fact, the same would apply to any indigenous population, whether savage or civilized. Jabotinsky was willing to negotiate with the Arab population only after the Zionists became the majority and effectively controlled the country. He embraced negotiations only after the victor set the terms.

"So you see, America and Israel have a vested interest in each other's colonial successes.

"America has the Statue of Liberty. The phrase 'Give me your tired, your poor, your huddled masses yearning to breathe free' is great poetry but total garbage. Africans were brought to its shores in chains almost four hundred years ago, and many African Americans still can't breathe. That's before we even address the ethnic cleansing of many Indian tribes, Islamophobia, or crackdowns on immigration.

"Israel has the Knesset, a multiparty system, and claims to be a democracy. Yet the major parties pander to the smaller nationalist and religious parties to stay in power. Thus, Palestinians and Israeli Arabs continue to be treated as second-class citizens, and the Occupation continues. Jerusalem is supposedly a city which is holy to all three religions. Yet one religion dominates."

Bracha wondered how a so-called academic like Professor Habib could be allowed to teach at Hebrew University. Yet as she was researching the treatment of Arabs in Israeli children's literature, her teacher advised her to be guided by hard facts rather than by political considerations.

"Academic freedom must apply to all even if it provokes controversy and violent disagreement," she concluded. She was determined to learn from Professor Habib, no matter how biased his beliefs. Whatever doesn't kill her makes her stronger.

II

Cold Spring Harbor, New York
February 9, 2014

At 6:00 p.m., the twelve participants in the symposium were seated at the dinner table at the Harbor Mist Restaurant. Two tables were put together to accommodate everyone. Before orders were taken, everybody introduced themselves. As the two representatives of Congregation Rodef Tzedek, Sanford Kantor and I were the first two participants to introduce ourselves. Sanford was truly in his glory as he wore his trademark Hawaiian shirt. Next came the Japanese and Latino clergy who served the two churches utilizing our facilities, Pastor Renjiro Suzuki and Pastor Antonio Vasquez. Pastor Renjiro Suzuki was the spiritual leader of the Uptown Church while Pastor Vasquez was the spiritual leader of the Church of the Heights. Next came the two ministers serving the Washington Heights Community Church down the street, the seasoned senior minister Doreen Williams and the fiery assistant minister, Brenda Corbett. Both were very much into human rights issues. Afterward was the Mormon minister, Bishop Steven Young; the Lutheran minister, Pastor Lars Munson; the interdenominational minister from the United Palace, Pastor Helen O'Shea; a Native American leader from the Cherokee tribe, Austenaco (meaning "Chief") Kanoska; the Cuban-born social activist minister from the Northern Manhattan Episcopal Church, Father Lorenzo Burgos; and my new buddy, Anton Muharsky from the Grace Afternoon School. In addition, we were joined by two resource people, Dr. John Kirby, an associate professor from New York University, and Anna Fuentes, a knowledgeable human rights attorney who specialized in immigration law.

At one time or another, I ate breakfast, lunch, or dinner with most of these colleagues at the Hudson View Restaurant on 181st St. While the ambiance was rather ordinary and I would not recommend it as a place to take a date, the diner served an unbelievable French toast which I enjoyed on rare occasions.

I looked upon Hudson View Restaurant as the holy town hall, the place to break bread and to establish lasting relationships with colleagues. Hence, when planning this conference, I sought to break barriers from the start with a communal meal. For dinner and tomorrow's breakfast and lunch, one colleague would recite a prayer before the meal, and one would recite a prayer after the meal.

After the participants gave their mini bios and after the orders were taken, I got things underway by giving a short introduction.

"Many of us wanted to have a retreat outside of New York City for a long time, so I thought this venue would be the perfect opportunity. The Cold Spring Harbor Laboratory, as you can see, is situated on a major campus consisting of fifty-two laboratories, six hundred researchers, and a staff of over 1,200. Cutting-edge research has taken place in such areas as cell biology, cancer, neuroscience, plant biology, and population genetics. The Cold Spring Harbor Laboratory prides itself on diversity and inclusion. Great minds are attracted to this facility from all over the country and from all over the world.

"I bet you're wondering why we are here. This was an entirely different place about a century ago. In 1904, Professor Charles B. Davenport became director of Cold Spring Harbor Laboratory and also founded the Eugenics Record Office in 1910. For over a quarter of a century, the location became an international center of eugenics research. Dr. Davenport was a dour, humorless man who came from a staunch Puritan background. His not so hidden agenda was to create an Anglo-Saxon master race in America. He engaged in heavy-duty research to create findings that would back his beliefs. The findings had catastrophic consequences, particularly with compulsory sterilizations and with the mistreatment of immigrants. Dr. Davenport was no lover of foreign-born people unless they came from Nordic countries and certainly no lover of non-White people who were already American citizens."

Father Lorenzo Burgos, who never minced words, chimed in, "So it's safe to say that if he was living in 2014, at least half of us around this table would be on Professor Davenport's shit list!"

"A good way of putting it. As a Jew, I probably would be near the top," I responded. "During this symposium, we are briefly reviewing the treatment of the other throughout American history and how it provides the backdrop of the immigration crisis of today. As we all know, the challenges of ICE and the existence of sanctuary religious institutions and sanctuary cities did not spring up overnight. They are the byproducts of hatred of the other, which has become deep-rooted in American culture."

Pastor Renjiro Suzuki added, "We are eating in a very nice restaurant and staying in a rather fancy bed-and-breakfast place, the Harbor Rose. The area itself is less diverse than what we are accustomed. We appear to be very detached from the ethnic reality that all of us face in New York City."

"Right you are," I replied. "It seems to me that it's much easier to make pronouncements about so-called inferior ethnic groups if you don't have to work or live among them. By contrast, our diverse group will be studying, praying, and living together for twenty-four hours. Hopefully, we will get to know each other better and forge a more permanent bond in the future."

"Amen to that," said Anna Fuentes.

Pastor Brenda Corbett chimed in, "As I have said to you many times before, Rabbi Levin, you are a radical!"

The food came. It was time to feed our bodies as well as our souls.

*****

After we completed our desserts, I told an anecdote. "A Border Control guard stationed in San Diego is assigned to watch the border between California and Mexico. He thought of his profession in Christian terms and believed it to be his calling. He was guarding the border to serve a divine purpose.

"A clergy person, who could have been anyone of us, asked him, 'How do you reconcile that with your biblical principles of giving hospitality to a stranger?'

"He responded, 'I don't see the conflict that some others see. I go back to the original sin, to the Garden of Eden. There were consequences. Adam and Eve got deported out of the Garden of Eden, and God created a border around it. The Bible teaches us that there are always consequences for our actions. We perform our job very compassionately every day, but we didn't create borders. They've been around since the beginning of time. We didn't create the concept of deportation. It comes directly from the Holy Bible.'

"The border guard further quoted Romans 13: 'Let everyone be subject to the governing authorities, for there is no authority except that which God has established. The authorities that exist have been established by God. Consequently, whoever rebels against authority is rebelling against what God has instituted, and those who do so will bring judgment upon themselves.'"

Austenaco Kanoska, our Cherokee participant, was visibly offended. "So the border guard was saying that God was the first deporter in chief and that he was doing God's work by chasing out trespassers on American soil. How presumptuous! I don't have to tell any of you how many crimes against humanity have taken place because people presumed to be carrying out God's will."

Austenaco continued, "The true original sin was taking more from Mother Earth than what we need. In this case of Adam and Eve, it was from the tree of knowledge. Nobody owns Mother Earth, not even the original inhabitants. From the Cherokee point of view, when one takes from Mother Earth, one also gives back. The American settler project in which the land was violated and exploited in the name of greed and western expansion all stemmed from the original sin of Adam and Eve. Equating Adam and Eve with illegal immigrants is preposterous."

"I don't disagree," I replied. "However, I would go one step further. The first time that the Hebrew word for sin, *chata*, appeared in the Bible was when Cain slew Abel because God had a better regard for his sacrifice and seemed to favor him. Chata is only used in the realm of interpersonal relationships. In essence, Cain committed his crime because he believed that the other, namely Abel, had something that he wanted. He also had the *chutzpah* [nerve] to deny all responsibility for his actions and to pose a rhetorical question to God, 'Am I my brother's keeper?' I would argue that the entire history of hate in America and elsewhere emerged from the fact that many human beings negatively brand the other and turn him into a scapegoat to justify usurping a disproportionate share of the world's resources and taking what they believe is rightfully theirs. Like Cain, they believed that they were more worthy of God gifts than the other. I maintain that everything that we will discuss for the next twenty-four hours will fit this pattern."

After dinner, we left the restaurant and reconvened in the conference room. The next session was scheduled to take place at 8:30 p.m.

III

Jerusalem
Mid-January 2014

Professor Nechama Yehezkel's class in the Rothberg International School was entitled "the Land of Israel in Biblical Sources." It appealed to American and European students who came from either conservative or modern orthodox backgrounds. Most of the students either attended four-day-a-week afternoon schools and day schools and were generally more Judaically educated than the average Diasporan Jew. They were expected to handle texts in Hebrew.

Professor Yehezkel was a scholarly woman and was a formidable presence. She generally wore a plain white blouse, a blue or black skirt, and in the winter, high black boots.

Her syllabus was well organized and comprehensive. The first topic that was covered was *B'reishit* 10 (Genesis), "The Table of the Nations."

She said, "On the surface, chapter 10 appears to be a telephone directory. What earthly purpose was achieved by presenting an exhaustive genealogy which began with the three sons of Noah?"

She explained, "Because the nations of the world ultimately descended from the three sons of Noah, all of humanity is intrinsically equal. Maimonides stated in *Guide for the Perplexed* III:50 that because of the centuries-long time lapse between Adam and Moses, the Torah wanted to explain how the diverse nations formed after the Flood and how they branched off from a common root, namely Adam, the first man. There was no racial commentary whatsoever. The peoples were consciously and deliberately related to each other as brothers. No one, not even Israel, was elevated above anyone else, and no disparaging remark was made about any people, not even the enemies of Israel."

Although Professor Yehezkel labeled herself as a secular Jew, she came from an Orthodox background and dabbled into Jewish liturgy.

She said, "Judaism respects and embraces diversity. The prayer that is recited upon seeing people of unusual appearance is *Baruch Ata Ha Shem, Elokeinu Melech ha-olam, mishaneh briyot*—Blessed are You, Lord our God, ruler of the universe, who varies the form of creation."

She concluded the class by saying that the Table of the Nations appears immediately after the ninth chapter of *B'reishit*, verses 20 to 27, which describes Noah's drunkenness after the Flood, Ham's failure to cover Noah's nakedness, and Noah's cursing of Ham's son, Canaan.

"Regarding the curse of Canaan, I will explain how it was connected to the Abrahamic narrative and how it was used as a biblical pretense to displace the Canaanites and the other nations that were already in the land. On the other side of the Atlantic, the text was used as the chief text to justify America's peculiar institution, slavery, as well as institutionalized segregation."

IV

Cold Spring Harbor, New York
February 9, 2014

During the first part of the evening session, I was the presenter. I commented that prior to the introduction of the concept of evolution in the nineteenth century and later, the eugenics movement racial ranking occurred in two modes known as monogenism and polygenism. Monogenism upheld the religious notion that all people emerged from the single creation of Adam and Eve, while polygenism abandoned scripture, considering it allegorical, and held that human races were separate biological species from the dawn of human history. As I direct our attention to the biblical origin of racism, I am focusing on monogenism.[1]

I explained to my colleagues that in Jewish exegesis, that there is a difference between *p'shat* (the plain level meaning) and homiletics, which provides the symbolic and allegoric meaning of a biblical text. "The p'shat of the Table of Nations is simply an explanation of how the nations of the world ultimately came from Noah's sons, Japhet, Shem, and Ham. The equality of humanity was implicit. There was no attempt to rank humanity. In fact, there were no value judgments whatsoever. However, regarding the curse of Ham, homiletics set in.

"Some rabbis were disturbed by Noah's curse of Cain. Here is a wild homily from the Talmud, Sanhedrin 108b:

> "The Sages taught: Three engaged in intercourse while in the ark, and all of them were punished for doing so. They are: The dog, and the raven, and Ham, son of Noah. The dog was punished in that it is bound; the raven was punished in that it spits, and Ham was afflicted in that his skin turned black.

"This Midrash was the basis of explaining Canaan's dark skin. It goes without saying that it was taken to a different level centuries later to justify the inferiority of those with darker skin color."

*****

Dr. John Kirby, the specialist on American history, took over at this point. He argued that monogenism took hold in the antebellum South. Indeed, most Southern clergymen explained the degeneration of Black people as the direct result of Ham's curse.[2]

"I would like to introduce you to Pastor Benjamin Palmer, a Southern Presbyterian minister who was active during much of the nineteenth century. He advocated heavily for the secession of Louisiana from the United States to join the Confederacy, with his infamous Thanksgiving sermon serving as a major catalyst for the Confederate movement.

"His interpretation of Shem, Japhet, and Ham had no basis in scripture whatsoever. In 1858, as a guest speaker in La Grange Synodical College in Tennessee, he argued that Japhet and his race were the top dogs who were designated to be the organs of human civilization. The Japhet Whites, stationed in Europe, were destined to develop the higher powers of the soul in politics, jurisprudence, science, and art. The race of Shem, stationed in Asia, dispersed over a more monotonous continent, embarked in those pursuits of industry fitted to the lower capabilities of our nature in cultivating the intellectual powers. The descendants of Ham, on the contrary, in whom the sensual and corporeal appetite predominate, were driven like an infected race beyond the deserts of Sahara, where, under a glowing sky, nature harmonizes with their brutal and savage disposition."[3]

I added, "This mode of thinking was not confined to Southern Protestants. Rabbi Morris Raphall, who was born in Scandinavia, served a congregation in Birmingham, and who ended up in Congregation B'nai Jeshurun in New York, was undoubtedly familiar with the text that I quoted from the Talmud. In 1861, Rabbi Raphall delivered a controversial sermon at his synagogue which was entitled *Bible View of Slavery*. He reiterated what be believed to be the Jewish justification of America's peculiar institution.

"'May God enlarge Japheth, and may he dwell in the tents of Shem. And to this day, it remains a fact which cannot be denied, that the descendants of Japhet [Europeans and their offspring] have been enlarged so that they possess dominion in every part of the earth. While at the same time, they share in that knowledge of religious truth which the descendants of Shem were the first to promulgate. Noah did not bestow any blessing on his son Ham but uttered a bitter curse against his descendants. And to this day, it remains a fact which cannot be gainsaid that in his own native home, and generally throughout the world, the unfortunate Negro is indeed the meanest of slaves.'"

Pastor Doreen then asked, "Rabbi Raphall must have been in a quandary. How could he possibly defend slavery when Egyptian oppression was the origin story of the Jewish people? From my experience of interfaith seders, doesn't the *Haggadah* say that every Jew should regard himself or herself as if he or she had personally come out of Egypt? Wasn't the experience of slavery in ancient times the chief motivation for Jewish participation in the civil rights movement and other human rights causes?"

I responded, "Rabbi David Einhorn, his contemporary, took Rabbi Raphall to task on these issues. In Baltimore, he preached against slavery even though many of his congregants held slaves and was forced to flee the state of Maryland.

"Rabbi Raphall felt that as a rabbi, he was obligated to teach the word of God as he understood it despite his personal feelings. He rationalized his view by claiming that indentured servitude was sanctioned by the Torah and was much more humane than heathen slavery as practiced in the South. Indentured servitude existed only to allow certain people to pay off their debts. Servants were granted their freedom after seven years. All servants were freed in the Jubilee year. Servants were regarded as human beings, not property. Nevertheless, he still used the biblical curse of Canaan as the root justification for the enslavement of Black people.

"Deep down inside, Rabbi Raphall found slavery to be distasteful. However, he felt it was more important to preserve the union rather than end slavery. Speaking from his pulpit in New York, if he could get the north to accept that slavery was not antithetical to biblical principles, maybe the Civil War could be averted."

Dr. John Kirby continued, "In the aftermath of the 1954 Supreme Court decision, *Brown v. Board of Education of Topeka*, Reverend Guy T. Gillespie, a Southern Presbyterian who was president of Belhaven College in Jackson, Mississippi, for thirty-three years, tied the narratives in Genesis 9 to 11 together. When Noah cursed Canaan after the Flood, Black people were designated for eternal inferiority. As it was God's divine plan to segregate the races, the sons of Noah became the progenitors of three distinct peoples. He agreed with Pastor Palmer in arguing that the progeny of Japhet migrated toward Europe, the progeny of Shem migrated toward Asia, and the progeny of Ham migrated toward Africa.[4]

"Gillespie cited the Tower of Babel narrative to oppose integrated schools. Or for that matter, integrated facilities in general. The confusion of tongues at Babel and the consequent scattering of peoples was an act of special divine providence to frustrate the mistaken efforts of godless men to assure the permanent integration of the earth. Gillespie feared that forced integration of public schools would either lead to interracial marriage or to a constant state of tension and friction which would lead to a breakdown of discipline and administration and would eventually imperil the social order and welfare of the White race."[5]

Pastor Brenda Corbett was visibly fuming. She was a truly spiritual person who loved God and who loved the Bible but resented this perversion of scripture. She attended segregated schools in her youth and busted her butt to earn both a bachelor's degree and a master's degree and eventually became an ordained minister. Indeed, I attended and participated in her ordination ceremony. It was a proud day for both the church and for her.

Pastor Corbett spoke up. "While I and many others look to the Bible for inspiration, we have a clear example of how religious leaders used homiletics to serve their political agendas. These interpretations of the curse of Canaan and the Tower of Babel have done tremendous damage to African Americans. I really resent this!"

Upon listening to this, I thought of my eleventh-grade classmate, Candy. While most of her African American friends sat sullenly in American studies classes, Candy spoke up. She would constantly say, "I'm tired of listening to all this smack. Why do we only hear about Black people when we're discussing slavery or Jim Crow? Have we been invisible for almost two hundred years?"

I remember myself saying to the history teacher, "Why do we only study the contributions of only a handful of Blacks like Frederick Douglas, Booker T. Washington, W. E. B. Du Bois, and Martin Luther King? Why don't we study the contribution of Blacks as they occur throughout American history?"

"I agree with you," Candy replied.

While Candy and I never became friends in high school, we achieved a quiet level of understanding between us from that time onward.

My thoughts returned to our session. I replied to Brenda, "For the next day, we are going to hear things that will turn our stomachs. Dr. Kirby's presentation is important because we see the ideological origins of White supremacy that are with us today. Quoting the Bible to promote a political agenda, I agree, is dangerous. Often, people follow these dangerous ideas because they genuinely believe that they are the words of God. We will see their implications later."

Our symposium adjourned for the evening. We made our way to the Harbor Rose Hotel. Tomorrow would be another day.

V

Jerusalem
Middle of January 2014

Professor Yehezkel continued where she left off during the last lesson. "Alongside the concept of the racial equality of all descendants of Shem, Japhet, and Ham, the entire known world population at that time, there was the concept of *am segulah,* a treasured people. A lot of people have difficulties wrapping their arms around it. If the Bible did not acknowledge a superior race, how can there be an am segulah?

"In biblical thought, this term was about establishing an exemplary society which served as a model for the surrounding nations. The origin story for chosen people began with Avram in *Bereishit* chapter 12. He was commanded to leave his native country, Mesopotamia, with his family and to immigrate to the promised land. In return, his name will be great throughout the ancient world and his newly formed community will become a light unto the nations. This does not imply any innate Jewish superiority but additional responsibilities toward God and fellow human beings. Later in the Torah, our ancestors were commanded to become a kingdom of priests and a holy nation with obligations and duties which flowed from our willingness to accept this status.

Mara Cohen, one of Bracha's classmates, added, "Whenever Jews are called up to the Torah reading, they are required to say *asher bachar banu mikol ha-amim*—who has chosen us from all peoples. Only Jewish people read from a Torah scroll during services. We have a special mission to share and promote Torah throughout the word."

"Precisely," responded Professor Yehezkel. "Being a light unto the nations meant serving as a moral example. When the Torah prohibited our ancestors from assimilating into Canaanite society, the purpose was not to preserve racial apartheid but rather to prevent them from adopting the depraved mores of the marketplace. For instance, *Vayikra* chapter 18 [Leviticus] states the following commandment: 'You must not do as they do in Egypt, where you used to live, and you must not do as they do in the land of Canaan, where I am bringing you. Do not follow their practices.' The passage then continues with the various incest laws.

"There are two ways at looking at this text—the religious point of view and the historical point of view. The religious point of view emphasizes that coming to the land is the first cause of Israel. This is the view generally espoused by the highly nationalistic Orthodox community.

"The historical point of view emphasizes that the migration of Avram occurred for political and economic reasons. I personally espouse the historical point of view. As I embrace the Documentary Hypothesis, which suggests multiple authorship of the Tanach, an acronym for Torah, Prophets, and Writings, I would like to share with you that Avram's mission, as well as many other passages, were probably written in the fifth to sixth centuries BCE, after the Babylonian Exile and during the restoration of Jewish life in Judah under the newly formed Persian Empire. I would like to suggest that God's promise to Avram was a back projection of Israelis after they settled in the land to justify and describe their history."

Shaul Mendelbaum, who always wore a black *kippah* and *tzizit* [fringes] which were visible outside his clothing, was hot under the collar. From his second-row seat, he protested, "Are you trying to tell us that the Torah is not the word of God!"

The professor answered, "The Torah was certainly divinely inspired, but its transmission was likely human. Many of the passages did not necessarily describe events in the present but reflected realities which took place centuries later."

Shaul shook his head in disgust.

"Now let's examine an excerpt from Jubilees, an extra-canonical work, which was written much later than the *B'reishit* version of Avram's mission, probably in the second century BCE. This excerpt filled in additional details that did not appear in the Tanach.

"For a moment, let's go back to the Noach narrative. After the ordeal of the Flood, Noach got drunk and became completely naked. While Shem and Japhet carefully covered him, it was Ham that reported the nakedness in the first place. When Noach woke up, he pointed the accusing finger at Ham and said, 'Cursed be Canaan! The lowest of slave will he be to his brothers.'

"The biblical problem was that Canaan was guiltless. If there was a guilty party, it was Ham. Therefore, Jubilees 9 came up with an explanation. Noach divided up the world between his sons, and Shem's portion included the center of the earth, Canaan, Mt. Zion, and the Garden of Eden. Noah then had his sons swear by oath to curse everyone who wanted to occupy the share which did not emerge by his lot. Subsequently, when Canaan, the son of Ham, was on his way to Africa to possess his appointed lot, he 'saw that the land of Lebanon as far as the stream of Egypt was very beautiful!' and chose to usurp Shem's portion, incurring his father's wrath and curse. Ham, his father, and Cush and Mizraim, his brothers said to him, 'You have settled in a land which is not yours. Do not do so, for if you do so, you and your sons will fall in the land and be cursed with rebellion… Dwell not in the dwelling of Shem, for to Shem and to his sons did it come by their lot. You are cursed and you will be cursed more than all of Noach's children…' But he did not listen to them. And for this reason, the land is named Canaan.

"According to scholarly opinion, this narrative solved a lot of problems. It explained that Noach cursed Canaan rather than Ham because of Canaan's land grab. It explained why the land promised to Avram was called the land of Canaan. It also provided justification for the conquest of Canaan and why the Israelites were commanded in the Torah to make no treaties with the Canaanites when they enter the land, to exterminate them, and to engage in ethnic cleansing. Moreover, Avram should not be looked upon as a sojourner from another country or as a usurper. His arrival in Canaan was a restoration of his true inheritance.[6]

"The Torah said little about Avram's background aside from the fact that he came from Ur and immigrated from Haran. Jubilee 12, however, explicitly stated that he left Ur, settled in Haran for fourteen years, and immigrated to Canaan to reject idolatry and to flee persecution for his religious beliefs.

"Thus, the *Bereishit* 12 narrative was not simply a nice story. It was a polemical narrative. If you add the supplementary material from Jubilees, it justified the conquest of Canaan. Because Canaan was cursed centuries ago, this provided justification for conquest. The descendants of Avraham were not colonists. They were simply taking what rightfully belonged to them.

"Zionists, whether secular or orthodox, or somewhere in between, often quoted the Tanach to justify their project. Avram's mission and Moses's mission, coming directly from God, trumped the rights of the current inhabitants of the land. Just as Avram fled a dangerous idolatrous society in Mesopotamia and the Israelites escaped slavery to enter the promised land, so Jews in the Diaspora fled assimilation, pogroms, and Nazism to enter the promised land. Just as Avraham's and Moses's communities came home, despite the presence of nations already living in the land, so Zionists perceive that those who made *Aliyah* were coming home as well despite the presence of an Arab community. The needs of Jewish refugees trumped the needs of people who have lived in this country for generations.

"The implications of the Avram narratives, both in the Tanach and in Jubilees, were enormous! The next natural step was to follow the commandment in *Devarim* 7, Deuteronomy, which was to annihilate the seven nations—Canaanites, Girgashites, Amorites, Hittites, Perizzites, Hivites, and Jebusites. Many Zionists regarded Arabs as modern-day Canaanites. Many modern-day Israelis do the same.

"The Jewish texts were the precursor to the Doctrine of Discovery. This doctrine gave papal permission to drive out or enslave the heathens on the other side of the Atlantic. In the American colonies, the Indian tribes were seen in the same light as the seven ancient nations that had to be removed by the Israelites.

"At the next class, I will offer another radical concept that may make some of you feel very uncomfortable. *L'hitraot!* Until next time!"

There were no comments from the class. Many of the students were stunned when they left the classroom.

VI

Cold Spring Harbor
February 10, 2014

After a hardy breakfast in the Harbor Rose dining room, the group reassembled in the conference room at 8:00 a.m.

Father Burgos had special expertise in psychology and alcoholism. Many of the homeless people who had found refuge in the basement of his church also had substance abuse issues. He began our session by transitioning from what was presented last evening. Commenting on Noah's infamous curse, he said, "What it really amounted to was the punitive action of an abusive father diverting attention from his shameful drunkenness by attacking his son. When an alcoholic is exposed, watch where the attention goes from the drunk to the witness. Noah disowns and condemns Ham in the strongest possible way, feeling justified in doing so. Also typical of an abusive attitude. God only knows, I have also found this behavior in so many families."

A few colleagues around the table nodded.

Professor Kirby inserted, "The curse of Ham and his descendants had major consequences. The belief that the descendants of Canaan were condemned by Noah to be slaves in perpetuity was used to justify enslaving people from Africa, introducing Jim Crow laws after Reconstruction, and practicing various forms of discrimination to this very day. It was also used to justify the maltreatment of indigenous peoples during colonization."

Bishop Steven Young chipped in, "Until 1978, the Church of Jesus Christ of Latter-day Saints did not allow Blacks in positions of leadership because they believed they were cursed. I and my parishioners totally reject this position."

*****

At this point, Dr. Kirby moved the topic in a different direction. In the days of Christopher Columbus, polygenism existed alongside monogenism. The *great chain of being*, which emphasized the hierarchical structure of all matter and life, came to dominate European thought. The chain begins with God and descends through angels, humans, animals, and plants and minerals. This worldview was formulated by Plato and Aristotle, and medieval Christianity believed that God decreed this chain.

The great chain of being was the ideological underpinning of both the Spanish Inquisition and the Doctrine of Discovery. If the world was determined by a hierarchical structure, it was a natural step for Europeans to create a hierarchy of human beings as well. They placed White European Christians at the top of the ladder and assigned the lower rungs to non-Christians. Such an ideology provided justification for religious persecution in Spain and Portugal. It also provided justification for the seizing of land on the American continent that was not inhabited by Christians and for enslaving local populations.[7]

*****

I continued the discussion. "The humiliation of Jews and Arabs, which included forced conversions, violence, the burning of books, and expulsions in Spain and Portugal was the dress rehearsal for the Doctrine of Discovery.

"In March 1992, during the Central Conference of American Rabbis' mission to Spain, five hundred years after the Edict of Expulsion, I remember gathering in a palace with my colleagues. The palace was graciously provided by the municipality of Granada at the foot of the Alhambra in a majestic courtyard adorned with handsome pillars and budding springtime foliage. The darkened clouds and intermittent raindrops no doubt expressed our somber and mournful mood. The liturgy of our ceremony, elegantly composed by the late and venerable Rabbi Simeon Maslin, a member of our delegation, captured our innermost feelings."

I quoted from the text which I had saved for over twenty years:

> In this place of beauty and of unspeakable tragedy, in this place where psalmists and sages sang praises to the God of Israel through golden centuries, in this place, settled as Granat al-Yahud by Jews in antiquity; in this place where a king and queen, poisoned by religious fanaticism and greed, inflicted untold suffering on our people; in this place where Samuel Ha-Nagid, Solomon ibn Gabirol, Moses ibn Ezra, Judah Ha-Levi, and so many others sang of wine and gardens and love, of battles and death and of God, we raise our voices and join them in song… To this place, emptied of Jews five hundred years ago, this place where we were warned not to return, "either as residents, travelers, or in any other matter whatever," on pain of death, we have returned today to raise our voices in prayer and to sing praises to the God who rules over temporal kings and queens.

I inserted my commentary: "We had indeed returned, with heads held high, but with an enormous sense of loss, a sense of isolation, a sense of how erasing both the physical presence and the memory of Jews who had once constituted 20 percent of the city's population. Today, in 1992, we Jews were alone in this place.

"It was futile to identify any meaningful remains of pre-1492 Jewish life in Spain—no synagogues, no schools, not even cemeteries. Most of the synagogues that remained were preserved as churches. On Friday evening, we did pray in a Madrid synagogue made up primarily of North African Jews who had come home in recent decades.

Ironically, we entered the building via an x-ray machine, and all bags were carefully checked. Five hundred years later, we still feared violence perpetrated against Jews. So little has changed.

"We had come to mourn for the victims, to celebrate their dignified and creative lives, and to remember the more pleasant times when Christians, Muslims, and Jews had lived together in relative harmony. And despite the threatening clouds and the chilling wind, it never rained. When we recited our kaddish, one could even detect a few rays of sunlight."

There was silence for a few moments. Then Pastor Helen O'Shea, the true embodiment of empathy, said quietly, "Your mission to Spain, especially to Alhambra, must have been draining."

I nodded.

*****

Professor Kirby continued, "The fanatic assault on non-Muslims that Rabbi Levin spoke about was exported to the New World. The atrocities that would potentially be committed would all be justified by the Doctrine of Discovery. Let me give you a behind the scenes account of Columbus's first voyage to the New World."

*****

ROME
MAY 3, 1493

Pope Alexander VI was the leader of the Catholic Church. Portugal and Spain were competitors in terms of discovering the New World. Portugal had a head start. On June 18, 1452, Pope Nicholas V issued a papal bull, *Dum Diversas*, granting permission to King Alfonso V of Portugal to:

> Invade, search out, capture, vanquish, and subdue all Muslims and pagans whatsoever, and other enemies of Christ wheresoever placed, and

the kingdoms, dukedoms, principalities, dominions, possessions, and all movable and immovable goods whatsoever held and possessed by them and to reduce their persons to perpetual slavery.

Christopher Columbus was chomping at the bit to travel to the New World. He first approached King John II of Portugal to finance his voyage, but he was turned down as the king's scholars determined that it would be much longer than Columbus estimated. He made the trip anyway, and it caused a rift in diplomatic relations between Spain and Portugal.

Columbus sent a glowing report of the New World to King Ferdinand and Queen Isabella while in Lisbon. They had colonial designs of their own and did not wish for Spain to play second fiddle to Portugal. On April 11, 1493, the Spanish ambassador urged Pope Alexander VI to urge a decree which was favorable to Spain. Papal bulls were important in those days as the two Catholic countries respected the Pope's authority, and his decrees prevented colonial rivalry from degenerating into warfare.

Pope Alexander VI felt that he was under pressure. He was a Spaniard and the former administrator of Valencia. Furthermore, as the ruler of the Papal States, he was embroiled in a territorial dispute with Ferdinand's first cousin, Ferdinand I, king of Naples. Hence, he was eager to please King Ferdinand and have him in his corner. Therefore, on May 4, 1493, the year after Columbus began his expedition, Pope Alexander VI issued the papal bull *Inter Caetera*. It was addressed to King Ferdinand and Queen Isabella of Spain. Like the papal bull of Pope Nicholas V, it also offered spiritual validation for European conquest. It stated:

> In our times especially the Catholic faith and the Catholic religion be exalted and everywhere increase and spread, that the health of souls be cared for and that barbarous nations be overthrown and brought to the faith itself.

*****

JEFFREY GALE

Cold Spring Harbor
February 10, 2014

Professor Kirby concluded, "The Doctrine of Discovery, first directed toward Portugal then directed toward Spain, affirmed the imperial ambitions of these two European powers. It gave theological permission for the European body and mind to view themselves as superior to the non-European bodies and minds. The European conquerors became the new insiders on the North American continent. The original inhabitants of the discovered land became outsiders, not welcome in their own home.

"How did the Doctrine of Discovery impact upon Christopher Columbus? When he came to what we know now as Haiti and the Dominican Republic, he was shocked to discover that this was not a land without a native population. Instead of finding primitives, he encountered a complex society. The Taino and Arawaks who had inhabited the islands were experts in agriculture and lived in harmony with the land. However, Columbus saw them as subhuman godless creatures who were to be used as fodder to enrich himself and his Spanish benefactors. He exploited the Taino, using them to find gold in newly constructed mines, and as commodities in themselves, becoming one of Europe's first slave traders. Between 1492 to 1509, the Taino population plummeted from eight million to one hundred thousand. By 1542, there were only two hundred left. Ethnic cleansing was relentlessly carried out.

"*Inter caetera* is on the books to this very day. Groups such as the Shawnee, Lenape, Taino, and Kanaka Maoli organized protests and raised petitions seeking to repeal this obnoxious papal bull and to remind Catholic leaders of the record of conquest, disease, and slavery in the Americas, sometimes justified in the name of Christianity, which they said has a devastating effect on their cultures today.

"*Johnson v. M'Intosh*, which was decided on February 28, 1823, was a landmark decision of the US Supreme Court that held that private citizens could not purchase lands from Native Americans. In giving the opinion of the court, Chief Justice John Marshall traced the outlines of the Doctrine of Discovery. He concluded that when the United States declared independence from the Crown, the United States government inherited the pre-emption over Native American lands. The legal result is that the only Native American conveyances of land which can create valid title are sales of land to the federal government. In essence, the Doctrine of Discovery was legitimized in American law."

*****

"We now turn our discussion to John Winthrop, an English Puritan lawyer and one of the leading figures in founding the Massachusetts Bay Colony. He was a Puritan through and through. He embraced the Calvinist concept of double election. Some people, such as the Puritans, were predestined by God to receive grace. Others, such as non-Puritans, especially Native Americans, or people who did not agree with him, were destined for hell.

"Like most people of their day, the Puritans subscribed to the hierarchical view of the world organized in the great chain of being. When they arrived on our shores, they fervently believed that they were God's New Israel. They were walking down the same path as their ancestors from the Old Testament. In 1630, Winthrop delivered his famous speech, 'A Model of Christian Charity.' He stated, 'We must consider that we shall be as a City upon a Hill, the eyes of all people will be upon us.' It was the statement of exceptionalism par excellence. It drew from Jesus's exhortation to be a city on a hill in Matthew 5:14 and referred to the land covenant that the God of Abraham established with the people of Israel. Winthrop asserted that the colonists were on the shores of their own promised lands, about to take possession of them. While there was no direct reference to the Doctrine of Discovery, Winthrop's message to his community certainly reflected its spirit. The Puritans were clearly the chosen people. Winthrop implicitly affirmed the European body to be superior to the Native body."

Pastor Brenda remarked, "Winthrop made that speech only eleven years after the first Black people were brought to these shores in chains."

Austenaco Kanoska, our Native American attendee with Cherokee background, observed, "The curse of Canaan reared its ugly head again. If you juxtapose Winthrop's claim of special status for Puritans, his intent to follow in the footsteps of our biblical ancestors, and the commandment to dispossess the Canaanites and the other occupants of ancient Israel, you have religious justification for genocide and ethnic cleansing.

"May I point out that in 1636 to 1637, just a few years after Winthrop made his statement of Puritan exceptionalism and implicitly reaffirmed the Doctrine of Discovery, an alliance of the colonists from the Massachusetts Bay, Plymouth, and Saybrook colonies and their allies from the Narragansett and Mohegan tribes fought against the Pequot tribe. The primary cause of the Pequot War was the struggle to control trade. English efforts were to break the Dutch-Pequot control of the fur and wampum trade, while the Pequot attempted to maintain their political and economic dominance in the region. The Puritans had a major hand in decimating the Pequot for financial gain. John Winthrop sat on the council which decided to send an expedition under John Endecott to raid Indian villages on Block Island in the war's first major action. Winthrop persuaded the Narragansetts to side with the colonists against the Pequots, who were their traditional enemies. The strategy of divide and conquer was applied. The war ended with the destruction of the Pequots as a tribe, whose survivors were scattered into other tribes or shipped to the West Indies as slaves.

"As far as John Winthrop was concerned, the slave trade was around before he arrived in Massachusetts. After the Pequot War, he kept one male and two female Pequots as slaves for himself.

"Brenda, John Winthrop was very much aware of the slave trade when he proclaimed the city on a hill. Exceptionalism applied to his community, but not to non-Whites.

"There was a bitter irony regarding the Puritans. While they fled England in the seventeenth century to escape the persecution perpetrated by King James I and King Charles I, they in turn oppressed people in the New World who were not like them. The intolerance that Puritans experienced in the Old World was projected unto the other in the New World."

VII

Jerusalem
Middle of January 2014

Professor Yehezkel began the class with this overarching question: "When we speak of the promised land, what specifically is God promising to the children of Israel? There are many passages in the *Chumash*, the Five Books of Moses—Genesis, Exodus, Leviticus, Numbers, and Deuteronomy—that refer to the promised land. Let me just list a few.

"*B'Midbar* 34, Numbers, gave a very specific description of borders of the promised land. The tribe of Reuben, the tribe of Gad, and the half tribe of Manasseh, which are east of the Jordan River, were not included as part of the promised land. *D'varim* 3, Deuteronomy, by contrast, included these lands as part of the promise. In Yechezkel 47, Ezekiel, the prophet provided his vision of the future borders of the land. While the borders were like the borders described in *B'Midbar* 34, all twelve tribes are allotted portions west of the Jordan River.

"The land promised to Avraham in *B'reishit* chapter 15 was totally different altogether. It was the biggest border description in the entire Bible! It was never achieved in Ancient Israeli history, not even by King David! The borders in this passage represented an idealization of Israel as an empire between the powers of Egypt and Mesopotamia. They were more aligned with Yesheyahu's [Isaiah's] vision in Yesheyahu 19:24–25. In this passage, Yesheyahu longed for the day when Israel will be the third, along with Egypt and Assyria, a blessing on the earth. 'The Lord Almighty will bless Egypt his people, Assyria his handiwork, and Israel his inheritance.'"

"So I ask, why the discrepancies? Was God inconsistent? Was God being wishy-washy, as you would say in America? Or did these discrepancies reflect different visions of the promised land?"

Shaul Mendelbaum was indignant. He said, "God can't possibly be inconsistent. Throughout the Bible, God expanded or contracted

His promises, based on how conscientiously the children of Israel fulfilled the commandments."

Professor Yehezkel smiled. She has heard that argument before—many times!

Bracha spoke up. "I favor the second interpretation. It's too much of a stretch to try to reconcile contradictory passages."

Shaul and others in the classroom gave her a dirty look.

Professor Yehezkel jumped in. "According to the Documentary Hypothesis, which I embrace, there are four major sources, J [Yahwist], E [Elohist], P [Priestly], and D [Deuteronomist]. For instance, many scholars attribute P to Numbers 34. The Priestly source rejected all lands east of the Jordan as defiled lands because of the immorality of their inhabitants. They should not be part of the promised land. In fact, there are passages in the Talmud which also rejected lands east of the Jordan because the rabbis wanted to discourage immigration to Babylonia after the destruction of the Second Temple and curb the brain drain of scholars leaving Palestine for more comfortable living conditions. The passage in Deuteronomy, however, did consider lands east of the Jordan as part of the promise and therefore the scholars assign D."

"This is outrageous," replied Shaul. "First, you say that the promise to Avram was written long after his time as a polemic to justify the conquest of the land. Today, you point out contradictions in some of the texts which give the borders of God's promise."

"Modern Jewish leaders have different visions of the land of Israel. Many Israeli leaders want a two-state solution to the current Israel-Palestinian conflict and are willing to trade land for peace. Some, in the interests of peace, might wish to return to the pre-1967 borders. Others would like to establish settlements in the West Bank, create facts on the ground, and grab as much territory as possible. Others would be happy if Israel annexed the entire West Bank and Gaza. Still others would love to expand Israel's borders farther, as far north as Lebanon and as far east as Syria. Many Zionists favor nationalism over religion and try to distance themselves from the slouching Yeshivah student in the Diaspora. Others, such as Tzvi Yehudah Kook, the founder of Gu*sh Emunim,* a very right-wing nationalist group, believed that religion was indistinguishable from nationalism. According to Tzvi Yehudah Kook, we live in Israel because God tells us so. Judaism is incompatible with Western democracy, and God's word is not subject to majority rule. He further argued that because the land of Israel belongs not only to Israelis but to millions of Jews throughout the world, the halacha forbids any man to make territorial concessions and create a truncated state. To do so would not only be a disgrace and a sorrowful shame, but also a violation of the Torah.

"If modern leaders have different ideologies pertaining to the borders of the Jewish state, why shouldn't there be different ideologies within the Tanach?"

Shaul almost barked at Professor Yehezkel, "If we accept multiple authorship of the Bible, what is the purpose of keeping any of the mitzvot? If they are human in origin, what incentive is there to take them seriously?"

Mark Cohen, an Orthodox student from Glasgow, Scotland, said in a whining voice, "If we continue to speak about the Torah in this way, none of us will have any share in the World to Come."

Shaul replied, "Exactly!"

By this time, Bracha was really getting agitated. Facing Mark, she exclaimed, "Your remark is pure bullshit!"

The professor interjected, "Bracha, b'vakasha! Derech Eretz [courtesy]."

The arguments backing both sides of the argument went back and forth for at least five or ten minutes. Students were really getting passionate about expressing their clashing points of view.

Professor Yehezkel was the master of *utzing* (needling) and provoking discussion. As the class was about to end soon, she interjected herself into the discussion. She said, "This sounds like the Knesset. Mah zeh?" (What is this?)

A student, David Zuckerman, responded, "B'nai chorin." (Free men.)

Bracha chimed in, "Two Jews, three opinions!"

"*Bediuk*—exactly! The hallmark of democracy is civil discussion and free debate. It was true among the Talmudic sages, so it is true today. We can disagree without being disagreeable. I believe that the late Winston Churchill once said, 'To jaw-jaw is better than to war-war.' While there continues to be active listening, hearing all sides of a *machloket* [argument], and passionate discussion, democracy will ultimately thrive in Israel.

"And my final point. Using biblical texts to justify the Zionist project is tricky business. Just as the authors of the Bible were governed by differing ideologies, so modern leaders often selectively find quotes to support their respective agendas as well. On the other side of the Atlantic, the use of the Bible to justify the conquest of land and American exceptionalism has led to the annihilation of many indigenous tribes."

As the class was about ready to leave, Professor Yehezkel thought of the Talmudic debate when the sages were debating about the *kashrut* of an oven. Rabbi Eliezer could not win his colleagues over to his opinion even though God moved a carob tree, made a stream flow backward, made the walls of the study move inward, and even spoke from heaven, "Why don't you accept the ruling of Rabbi Eliezer?" God finally laughed and said, "My children have defeated me! My children have defeated me!"

Professor Yehezkel laughed to herself and said, "My students have defeated me! My students have defeated me!"

VIII

Cold Harbor Spring
February 10, 2014

After the morning coffee break, Austenaco Kanoska continued the discussion.

"Middle East studies, in recent years, has attracted great interest among Native Americans. Many of us feel a special kinship with Palestinians. Just as they have been victims of colonial duplicity, so have we. For indigenous people, this country has been a graveyard of broken treaties, broken promises, and broken dreams. Dr. Kirby spoke of the ethnic cleansing which took place in Columbus's time and of the massacre of the Pequot in 1637. That was only the beginning.

"In 1814, Major General Andrew Jackson led an expedition against the Creek Indians climaxing in the Battle of Horseshoe Bend, where Jackson's forces soundly defeated the Creeks and destroyed their military power. He then forced upon the Indians a treaty whereby they surrendered to the United States over twenty million acres of their traditional land—about one half of present-day Alabama and one-fifth of Georgia. Over the next decade, Jackson led the way in the Indian removal campaign, helping to negotiate nine of the eleven major treaties to remove Indians. These treaties whittled away at Cherokee land during the first two decades of the 1800s.

"It became clear to the Native American tribes that they could not defeat the Americans in war. An important strategy that the Cherokees used to hold on to their land was assimilation. In 1825, they adopted a written alphabet of their language which was created and taught widely within a generation. In 1827, they created a constitution based on the United States, which formed judicial, legislative, and executive branches. The Cherokees believed that they were doing everything right by the standards of the White government leaders they wanted to appease. They practiced and advocated for Christianized education and religion, English fluency, land holding, plantation owning, and slave owning. If they could convince the US government that they weren't savages, perhaps they would be respected as a legitimate sovereign people.

"An important lesson can be learned. Assimilation into the society of the racial majority never wins their respect. In this instance, assimilation was also ineffective. Georgia residents resented the Cherokees owning six thousand square miles of tribal lands within the state and governing themselves. In 1828, Georgia passed a law pronouncing all laws of the Cherokee Nation to be null and void after June 1, 1830. The Cherokee government was forbidden to meet for legislative purposes.

"When gold was discovered on Cherokee land in northern Georgia in 1829, efforts to dislodge the Cherokee from their lands were intensified. President Andrew Jackson became an interested party. Back in 1815, after the Battle of Horseshoe Bend, Jackson had promised the Cherokee that their people would forever stay on their rightful ancestral land. The Indian Removal Act, which he signed in 1830, essentially stripped the words of their value and dissolved all remaining hope for the Cherokee. Native Americans were betrayed once again! The president was now able to legally remove the Cherokee people by force.

"President Jackson agreed that all Native Americans must be removed and transplanted somewhere west of the Mississippi. As incentives, the law allowed the Indians financial and material assistance to travel to their new locations and to start new lives and guaranteed that the Indians would live on their new property under the protection of the United States government forever. With the Indian Removal Act in place, Jackson and his followers were free to persuade, bribe, and threaten tribes into signing removal treaties and leaving the southeast.

"The Cherokee nation fought back. In 1831, the state of Georgia indicted Samuel Worcester, a White missionary for living in Cherokee territory without a license. Worcester was convicted and sentenced to four years of hard labor. The case, *Worcester v. Georgia*, was appealed and reached the Supreme Court.

"The chief justice, John Marshall, clearly sent a mixed message in the ruling. On the one hand, he argued that the Cherokees were an independent nation, that Georgia's Indian laws were unconstitutional, and that Georgia did not have the right to make laws on Cherokee land. On the other hand, he also argued that the Cherokees were not a foreign state in the sense in which the term was used in the Constitution. Rather, they and other Indian tribes were 'domestic dependent nations who were in a state of pupilage.' Marshall then explained, 'Their relation to the United States resembles that of a ward to his guardian. They look to our government for protection, rely upon its kindness and power, appeal to it for relief to their wants, and address the President as their Great Father.'[8]

"The contradictory statement that the Cherokee people were both an independent nation and a protectorate of the American government played right into President Jackson's hands. He was given license to not take the chief justice seriously. President Jackson allegedly said, 'John Marshall made his decision. Let him enforce it.'

"The state of Georgia, emboldened by President Andrew Jackson's disdain for the Supreme Court's sovereignty ruling, moved in on the Cherokee. In 1832, the Cherokees' land was surveyed and split into 160-acre lots. Draws were sold at $18 each for a chance to win a lot. Over eighty-five thousand people bought chances for eighteen thousand lots. As winners were announced, Cherokee families were forced from their homes.

"All of this culminated in the treaty of New Echota on December 29, 1835. It obliged the Cherokees to surrender all their lands in the east and remove to the country set aside for them in the west by previous treaties. The United States agreed to pay $5 million to appraise and compensate for the value of all improvements left behind, to set aside money for schools, orphans, and a national fund, and to pay the cost of removal to and subsistence in the west during the first year. The Cherokee Nation received assurances that the United States would respect the right to self-government in the west, that the nation could never be included into any state or territory without its consent, and that the United States would protect its borders and defend the Cherokees from hostile neighbors.[9]

"The Cherokees were deeply divided. The chief, John Ross, and most of the Cherokee Nation were bitterly opposed to this agreement. They did everything that they could to prevent the treaty of New Echota from coming into fruition. However, other powerful leaders, Major Ridge, his son John Ridge, and his nephews Elias Boudinot and Stand Watie usurped John Ross's role to negotiate treaties and dealt with the US government on their own. They believed that the Cherokees' backs were against the wall. If they persisted in their opposition to removal, there would be much loss of life, and they would lose their lands anyway. It was an illegal negotiation from start to finish as these men were not authorized to sign away Cherokee lands that had been held for generations. They had violated Cherokee law.

"In 1836, the Treaty of New Echota was approved by the senate and signed into law by President Jackson. It would go into effect two years later. In 1838, Major General Winfield Scott was put in command of seven thousand soldiers whose job was to remove the Cherokee Indians and send them on their way.

"When we think of treaties, they are conducted between equal partners. There is negotiation in good faith, compromise, and give and take. Not with the Treaty of New Echota. It was the mother of all disastrous treaties. It was governed by harassment and coercion. President Jackson's administration dictated all the terms. The Cherokees were doing all the giving while the US government officials were doing all the taking. The US was happy to participate in an illegal negotiation because the negotiators were totally willing to play ball with them.

"When Pope Alexander VI issued the papal bull, *Inter Caetera*, almost 350 years earlier, he set the precedent for the Treaty of New Echota. Just as he gave permission to conquer the lands of the indigenous population as long as they weren't Christians, so this treaty gave permission to relocate my ancestors. Just as Pope Alexander VI authorized ethnic cleansing, so the Treaty of New Echota virtually cleansed Georgia and neighboring states of indigenous peoples.

"The Treaty of New Echota was a watershed moment in the history of the Cherokees. We were the victims of greedy gold-digging settlers. We were literally crucified on a cross of gold."

IX

Jerusalem
Middle of February 2014

For the next few weeks, Professor Habib continued his tirades. The topic of today's lecture, according to the syllabus, was the Balfour Declaration. Ironically, thought Bracha, this was a topic in which Yehudah and Professor Habib, representing opposite ends of the political spectrum, agreed. The Balfour Declaration was a fraud! For my Israeli cousin, the fraud was perpetrated against the Yishuv, the early settlers. For Professor Habib, it was perpetrated against the Arabs!

"During World War I, the British felt that their backs were against the wall. On the Western Front, the war was at a stalemate with countless loss of life. The British equally feared that if the Germans achieved mastery of the Middle East with all its natural resources, their empire would be in jeopardy. They needed a game changer and looked to both the Jews and the Arabs to achieve that purpose.

"Back in 1915, the British needed the help of the Arabs in defeating the Ottoman Empire. In a set of letters called the McMahon-Hussein Correspondence, they promised the Arabs that if they rebelled against the Ottoman Empire, which had sided with Germany in the war, that they would get their own independent state. Sharif Hussein, who negotiated from the Arab side, was led to think that Palestine would be part of this independent Arab state, but as it turned out, that arrangement was never on the table.

"At the very same time the British made this promise, there was a clandestine agreement in the works with Britain and France to carve up the Ottoman Empire among themselves. This was known as the Sykes-Picot Agreement. Suffice it to say, the territory promised to the Arabs was not taken seriously. Indeed, the Sykes-Picot Agreement was without doubt a watershed event in the creation of the modern Middle East."

Professor Habib then displayed two maps. The first map was the area that the Arabs perceived they were getting as a result the McMahon-Hussein Correspondence. The second map displayed a more truncated area for Arab autonomy.

He continued, "The creation of states like Iraq, Syria, Lebanon, and Jordan, all under British or French influence, were a product of Sykes-Picot. The creation of artificial countries was consistent with the British policy of promoting a state of disintegration in the region and to establish puppet political entities under European control.[10] The policy of divide and conquer was recommended to British Prime Minister Sir Henry Campbell-Bannerman in 1907, well before Sykes-Picot.

"The Arabs fought and died for the British, thinking that they would gain their independence as a reward for their sacrifice. Yet what ended up happening instead was that the British and French marched into their territory and claimed the remains of empire for themselves.

"Many of the people living within these borders felt that the division was arbitrary, and indeed this has been a catalyst for bloody ethnic conflicts that continue up until today. Sykes-Picot sowed the seeds of hostilities between the Western and Arab world. I bet you Jewish students didn't learn about this in your Jewish schools back home!

"Imagine if the French had promised America that they would help them fight the British in the Revolutionary War, only to march into America themselves and take over in the aftermath of the war.

"In the eyes of the British and the Zionists, the Palestinians were put on the same level as the American Indians. American Indians were ignorant savages that could easily be deceived by empty promises, which was what the McMahon-Hussein agreement was all about. The British architects didn't expect much from Palestinians either. Just as high-sounding treaties and double-dealing was used to force Indian tribes off their lands, so the same principles were applied to my people."

Many of Professor Habib's remarks were eye openers for the students.

Jane Miller exclaimed, "In Sunday school, I learned about Herzl and the Balfour Declaration, but never about this."

Professor Habib continued, "As for the Balfour Declaration, it laid bare our belief in the collusion of Zionist colonialism and British colonialism. Not only were Arab lands carved up to the victors, but the British intended to set up a buffer state which would be populated by a strong foreign human presence hostile to its neighbors and friendly to European countries and their neighbors.[11]

"In cooperation with Chaim Weizmann and his Zionist team, Britain granted a land it did not possess to a group who did not own it at the expense of those who possessed and had the right to it. The Balfour Declaration stipulated that nothing shall be done which may prejudice the civil and religious rights of existing non-Jewish communities in Palestine.'

"Who did the British think that the Palestinians were? Chopped liver? In truth, my people were regarded as a non-Jewish community, not as Palestinians. What about political rights? What about economic rights? The Balfour Declaration treated us an inconsequential minority when in fact, 90 percent of the population was Arab!

"While there were always Arab suspicions about Zionist intentions, the distrust reached a new level after the Balfour Declaration. Before the Balfour Declaration, the sharif of Mecca called upon the Arabs to welcome the Jews as brethren and cooperate with them for the common welfare. What many people in the West don't understand today is that before World War I, relations between the Arabic and Jewish population in the Middle East were relatively tolerant. Much of the Israeli-Palestinian conflict today is a direct result of the territorial divisions made in the aftermath of World War I and World War II.

"The underlying assumption by both the British and the Zionists was that Palestine was a land without a people. The so-called promised land was empty, desolate, and barren. There was no infrastructure whatsoever.

"Professor Ilan Pappe was a leftist Israeli historian who moved to England in 2006 because of his underlying stance that Israel has engaged in the ethnic cleansing of the Palestinian population. As a fellow academic, he argued that Palestine began to develop long before massive immigration from Central and Eastern Europe. He also emphasized that my people were opened to change and modernization and that we were not isolated from the civilized world. The Palestinian people were readily exposed to interactions with other cultures as part of the wider Ottoman Empire. There were extensive trade connections with Europe. Agriculture and commerce served a population of half a million people on the eve of the Zionist arrival.[12]

"The British and the Zionists enjoyed a symbiotic relationship. Britain will help them build a country of their own while the Zionists, with their international influence, would prevent Russia from engaging in a separate peace with the Germans and help bring America into the war. Make no mistake about it. Zionism was an extension of European colonialism."

With those strong words, the class ended.

X

Cold Spring Harbor
February 10, 2022

"I would now like to share with all of you a personal story," said Austenaco after he outlined the events leading to the Treaty of New Echota.

*****

"When Halona and her parents finally arrived at their destination, she was totally exhausted. She completed a long journey of over one thousand miles that lasted many weeks. She tried to pull her blanket over her, but sleep didn't come. Instead, memories of the past year whirled round and round inside her head.

"Halona remembered her teacher reading a letter from a White man who called himself the superintendent of Cherokee Removal. The letter stated that the treaty signed two years ago will soon be enforced in Tennessee, Georgia, and Alabama, as well as here in North Carolina. Removal to the West will begin on May 23, 1838.

"The teacher said, 'There will be no more school for you here. Maybe in the West.' Halona, who was ten years old that year, had tears in her eyes. Why must she stop going to school because of a letter from the White man?

"Halona remembered the door of her house flying open and soldiers entering uninvited. One of them stomped toward her and pulled on her arm. Her precious doll fell on the floor. Another soldier with a gun kicked the doll under the bed. Her mother pulled blankets from the bed and put as much as possible in them, including bread, bacon, spoons, pans, dishes, a knife, and three cups. Halona held Grandmother's hand until she was pulled away from her. She would never see Grandmother again.

"Halona remembered other helpless Cherokees arrested and dragged from their homes and driven at the bayonet point into the stockades. She saw some of them loaded like cattle or sheep into the 645 wagons that would take them to the West.

"Halona remembered, during the early part of the journey, riding on one of the wagons arriving at a large pen with high sides. One of the soldiers shouted, 'Out of the wagons. Everyone in the stockade!' Halona mumbled, 'This is the stockade? It's a pen of logs that would normally hold animals. Instead, its holding people, my people!'

"The pens were very uncomfortable. Babies were crying. The heat and sweat were unbearable. Flies were buzzing about. Men and women had no privacy to relieve themselves unless they hung some cloth in their tents. As it was impossible to bathe, there were a lot of bad smells around the pen. People were coughing. Many contracted measles. There were stomach sicknesses as well. Many people could not get to a bucket in time. Some of the illnesses were undoubtedly contracted from the White men.

"Halona remembered the journey taking place over rivers, valleys, and mountains. Wagons often got stuck in the streams or had to be pushed up rocky hills. Animals were beaten when they could not pull the load. Old people would have to trudge up the rough roads. Winter nights were bitterly cold, accompanied by heavy snow. Old people, babies, and children died every day. There was no time to bury the dead properly, for each morning they started walking early.

"Halona was glad that she and her parents survived the journey from North Carolina to Oklahoma. *Halona*, in English, means 'good fortune.' Unlike the four thousand men, women, and children, one quarter of the Cherokee population, who perished and who were buried in nameless graves along the length of the journey, she had the good fortune to survive.

"Measuring the disaster in terms of the number of casualties, however, is a mistake. Even if there were no casualties at all, the dispossession and deportation of thousands of people from their homeland under a fraudulent treaty would still be a tragedy. The dark cloud that appeared as my people left the East may well be regarded as the omen of that tragedy. It was truly a Trail of Tears.

"Halona would soon make a new beginning. But there was a lingering sadness that would never go away. Cherokees regarded the land as Mother Earth, which gave birth to them and which sustained them. Mother Earth had to be cared for. Land was not merely an entity to dig gold and exploit.

"Halona would always have precious memories of her early life in the East. I am proud to say that she has a prominent place on my family tree!"

Pastor Helen O'Shea from the United Palace put a comforting arm around Austenaco's shoulder. On that dismal note, we broke for lunch.

XI

Jerusalem
End of February 2014

Professor Habib's angry lectures did not abate. The next item on the agenda was the War of Independence in the aftermath of the recognition of the new Jewish state. As predicted, he chose to focus on Jewish atrocities and Deir Yassin in particular. Most of Bracha's Israeli family strongly maintained that the Arabs, both within and outside of Israel, were determined to drive the Jews into the sea. They emphasized that Israel's very existence hung on a thread unless decisive action took place. Yehudah looked upon Deir Yassin as another unfortunate military operation and dismissed the very concept of massacre as propaganda. Professor Habib, on the other hand, saw the events quite differently.

Professor Habib began his discourse by questioning the attack on Deir Yassin in the first place. "Months before the attack, the elders of Deir Yassin agreed not to allow the village to become a base for attacks against the neighboring Jewish areas of West Jerusalem. The agreement was supervised by the Haganah. In turn, Deir Yassin would not be attacked. The village was not situated on the main road. It was located on the other side of the hill and was over a kilometer away.

"By the late 1940s, however, the village had developed a good working relationship with the nearby Jewish settlement, Givat Shaul. Deir Yassin made its own decisions in the 1948 conflict. Having chosen mutual nonaggression with their Jewish neighbors, the village elders stuck to the deal. Even Lehi officials, who worked closely with the Irgun, admitted that the village had remained steadfast in honoring their end of the bargain.

"The attack, therefore, had little to do with actual security. Security was a pretense for capturing booty for nearby military bases and beleaguered Jerusalem. Security was also a pretense for settling old scores and for striking fear in the hearts of the Arab population. The ensuing violence was far out of proportion to the so-called strategic value of Deir Yassin.

"Deir Yassin is the ultimate result of Vladimir Jabotinsky's Iron Wall. He sought to establish a strong Jewish state, put the Jews into a commanding position, motivate the Arabs to overthrow their extremist leaders, and dictate peace terms to a relatively weak, more moderate Arab community. Jabotinsky embraced violence as a necessity."

Then Professor Habib's tone became much more somber as he read a brief account of the atrocities. It came from a girl who was ten years old at the time.

They started with one man. They shot the son-in-law, and when one of his daughters screamed, they shot her too. Then they called my brother Abdul and shot him in our presence, and when my mother screamed and bent over my brother, they shot my mother as well. She was also carrying my little sister, who was still being breastfed.

The children began crying and screaming. They were told that if they didn't stop, they would shoot us all. The children did not stop crying. So the attackers lined us up, shot us, and left.

"Across the Atlantic, about 175 years ago, the Indian Removal Act, signed by President Andrew Jackson, precipitated the removal of sixteen thousand Indians from North Carolina, Georgia, Tennessee, and Alabama and brought about the Trail of Tears. Almost eighty-six years ago, the Iron Wall, formulated by Vladimir Jabotinsky and which provided the ideological basis of Deir Yassin, precipitated the removal of nearly seven hundred thousand Arab residents of Palestine and created our own Trail of Tears."

Wiping his eyes with a handkerchief, Professor Habib said, "The woman who gave that grisly account was my mother. I am named after my murdered uncle, Abdul."

There was stone silence in the classroom. For the first time, Bracha was able to walk in the shoes of her bitter Palestinian history professor.

XII

Cold Spring Harbor
February 10, 2014

For lunch, Sanford Kantor ordered cheese and vegetable pizzas as well as salad from Hunki's Kosher Pizza. I made a special request for anchovies.

Sanford replied, "You must be kidding, bro! In this group, you are a minority of one!"

I took that as a no.

As we concluded our meal, we got ready for the next big topic of this symposium. Professor Kirby resumed his presentation.

He suggested that the Doctrine of Discovery, which originated in Europe, which was transplanted to North America and used to justify the removal of Native American tribes from their ancestral lands, metamorphized into the concept of manifest destiny.

"John O'Sullivan was an American columnist, editor, and diplomat who used the term *manifest destiny* in 1845. He sincerely believed that God sought to establish the supremacy of the Anglo-American race in North America. God chose America to spread democratic principles and to bring the whole continent into the American Union.

"According to John O'Sullivan, democracy was the highest stage of society,[13] and the White race was the pinnacle of humanity. Life, liberty, and the pursuit of happiness applied to White people only. The African and Native Americans, because they cannot be assimilated into American society, would disappear completely from the mainland of America. Such thinking rationalized both the ethnic cleansing of Native Americans and slavery.[14]

"Manifest destiny was used to justify the annexation of Texas in 1845 and the Mexican American War in 1846 to 1848. In the Treaty of Guadalupe Hidalgo, the United States gained undisputed control of Texas as well as the states of California, Nevada, Utah, most of New Mexico, Arizona, Colorado, and parts of Oklahoma, Kansas, and Wyoming. Before the war, the area of Mexico consisted of 1,700,00 square miles. After the war, the area shrunk to eight hundred thousand square miles. Mexico effectively lost 55 percent of her land.

"Manifest destiny was used to justify the Spanish-American War in 1898. In the Treaty of Paris, Spain ceded ownership of Puerto Rico, Guam, and the Philippine islands. Spain also granted temporary control of Cuba. American military operations extended to both the Caribbean theaters and the Pacific theaters.

"Manifest destiny was articulated by Senator Albert Beveridge as he justified America's recent military action. To use Rudyard Kipling's words, he believed that America should 'take up the White man's burden.' At a Republican rally taking place in Chicago in 1900, he said, 'We are this at last, a great national unit ready to carry out that universal law of civilization which requires of every people who have reached our high estate to become colonizers of new lands, administrators of orderly government over savage and senile peoples.'[15]

"Manifest destiny was the governing principle of the Roosevelt Corollary of 1904. While the Monroe Doctrine of 1823 was designed to keep European powers out of the western hemisphere, President Theodore Roosevelt proclaimed the right of the United States to exercise international police power such as sending American troops into other countries of the western hemisphere. As a result, the US Marines were sent into Santo Domingo in 1904, Nicaragua in 1911, and Haiti in 1915, ostensibly to keep the Europeans out."

Anna Fuentes, the specialist in immigration law, took over at this point. She pointed out, "Manifest destiny was also the governing principle behind what has taken place in Guatemala. In the mid-twentieth century, United Fruit Company, based in New Orleans, owned 42 percent of the land in Guatemala, all the country's banana production, all the country's telephone and telegraph network, and all its railroads. The company took advantage of Guatemala's weak and corrupt government. Guatemala was literally a banana republic!

"Leftist Jacobo Arbenz rose to power in 1944 and spoiled things by passing a New Agrarian Reform Law. It was designed to break the United Fruit Company's stranglehold on the nation's best land. His government allocated forty-two acres to each individual farmer from the unused land on banana plantations. Within two years of the law's implementation, one hundred thousand indigenous families had received land and credit to begin cultivation.

"This was obviously bad for business. The United Fruit Company campaigned for US government intervention. First, it persuaded Secretary of State John Foster Dulles, United Fruit's former attorney, and his brother CIA Director Allen Dulles, and a former member of United Fruit's board of directors that Guatemala's democratically elected president posed a communist threat. As it was now the 1950s, the middle of the Cold War, President Dwight D. Eisenhower was eager to respond. While containment of communism was, indeed, a central component of American foreign policy at that time, it was also a pretext for economic self-interest.

"In 1954, Eisenhower ordered the CIA's covert overthrow of Arbenz. The CIA raised a private army to invade the country and force Arbenz to resign. The name of the operation was PBFortune. The land reforms were rolled back. Essentially, the United States government illegally overthrew the democratically elected president of a country to benefit one of its politically well-connected corporations.

"A series of coups and countercoups followed a revolving door of American-backed dictators going in and out of the presidential palace—with every American president implicated. More than two hundred thousand Guatemalans died over the next four decades in civil strife. As a result, Guatemala, to this very day, has been characterized by political instability.

"Guatemala in 2014 is a hyperviolent society. Given its turbulent history, its legacy of corruption and genocide, and the clout of the drug cartels, it is not surprising that many have migrated to our country without legal authorization to enter the United States. Only one in four of the 1.5 million Guatemalan Latinos has American citizenship, meaning that three in four live in the shadows. There is exploitation by American workers and the constant fear of arrest or deportation. Deportation back to Guatemala, for many, is a death sentence.

"Illegal immigrants are often perceived in a negative light. Most people think twice before leaving their country of birth to enter a foreign land with a different language. This is true of Guatemalans. Many Guatemalan refugees are here because American military troops were there. Though many of them are accused of breaking our laws, the US government broke international law with impunity and helped create the current situation."

Father Lorenzo Burgos spoke up. "At our church, we currently have a family receiving sanctuary—a woman from Guatemala and her three American born children. Only a short time ago, they were living in a nice modest home in Long Island, and they were sleeping in comfortable beds. Then Amelia received a summons to US Immigration Customs Enforcement and was told to bring her passport. That could mean only one thing—deportation! Now Amelia, her two daughters, and her son are now cramped into two tiny rooms off the church sanctuary and sleep on bunk beds.

"Sanctuary takes many forms. We can offer facilities to refugees just as we offer our basement to the homeless. Our congregants provide material support and some companionship. However, the faith community which is ably represented by those assembled in this room can help as well. Not every church or synagogue can open its doors to undocumented immigrants, but they can provide other levels of sanctuary such as providing meals and other implements that are needed in daily life. As clergy, all of you can really help by visiting and comforting Amelia."

Pastor Doreen was the eager beaver. "We'll get our membership mobilized right away," she said. "We have lots of Spanish speakers."

"Count our congregation in as well," said Pastor Antonio.

"Give us a week," said Pastor Lars Munson. "We'll have a visiting roster."

Father Lorenzo Burgos chimed in, "You don't have to be a Spanish speaker. We can provide interpreters. Extending a caring hand is the language of love. It transcends linguistic barriers."

Then I joined the bandwagon. "I will organize a vigil on a Saturday evening. While it will have a Jewish flavor, I will invite participation from one or more of the churches as well."

The response was enthusiastic.

Anna Fuentes continued, "Toward the end of the symposium, I will address the issue of illegal immigration in greater depth, especially as it applies to Amelia and her family. Professor Kirby, I believe that in the next session, you are covering the eugenics movement and its disastrous impact upon American immigration policies."

"I am, indeed."

"It's 2:00 p.m. Let's resume in fifteen minutes."

XIII

Cold Spring Harbor
February 10, 2014

"To understand the American eugenics movement and its impact upon immigration," said Professor John Kirby, "it's important to understand the Progressive movement in the late nineteenth and early twentieth centuries. That period, also known as the Gilded Age, was characterized by the rapid transition from an agricultural economy to an industrial economy. Indeed, economic output quadrupled between the 1870s and the 1890s.

"While the US economy ultimately surpassed that of major European countries, it led to gross disparities of wealth. Large corporations, headed by wealthy elites, existed alongside disgruntled rural homesteaders and the urban poor. The mass migration from rural areas to the cities lead to crowded tenements with substandard housing, poor sanitation, and recurring unemployment.[16] By 1897, only 1 percent of the American population possessed about half the wealth of the entire country!

"The Progressives blamed the gross inequality of wealth and the plight of the impoverished on classic Anglo-American individualism with its natural rights foundation. In the classically liberal model, a well-ordered society was governed by self-interested market behavior. The unbridled free market would guarantee solid social and economic progress. Government's function should be limited to ensuring a healthy environment for mutually beneficial trading. The Progressives branded this ideology as *laissez-faire*.[17]

"As enemies of rugged American individualism, the Progressives embraced holism. They were heavily influenced by German academics. They advocated a historical school of thought which emphasized that a nation was an organism, something greater than the sum of the individuals it comprised. Individuals were deemed organs or cells within the greater organic state. They are made subordinated to the whole.

"President Woodrow Wilson embraced the organic state as the ideal model for the United States government. He believed in a strong central government in which all power rested with the executive branch and was bitterly opposed to the system of checks and balances that were built into the Constitution and which are central to how our government functions today. In fact, Wilson argued that an organism, such as a nation-state, cannot survive internal conflict.[18]

"You may ask, 'What does the concept of the organic state have to do with eugenics and immigration policy?' The liberal conception of American nationality is inclusive. It admits all who agree to abide by our country's basic principles. An organic state, by contrast, is exclusive. American nationality is not governed by social contract but by biology. A healthy organism is constituted by healthy cells. Uninvited parasites and microbes are potential threats to its survival. By analogy, a healthy nation consists of physically, intellectually, and morally healthy individuals. In an unhealthy nation, there is a preponderance of individuals who have physical or mental disabilities and individuals who are prone to crime.

"Relating this theory to the early twentieth century, racial minorities already living in the country and immigrants coming from non-Anglo-Saxon countries were viewed as undesirable parasites or microbes which threaten the health and very survival of America. Thus, the overarching goal of the eugenics movement was to ensure the survival of White Anglo-Saxon stock and to weed out the undesirables."

Professor Kirby continued, "The eugenics movement was naked racism which was given the respectability of pseudoscience."

Pastor Brenda Corbett hastily added, "The biological inferiority of Black people and Native American people has been part of this country's DNA long before the Declaration of Independence. Centuries ago, the Bible, the great chain of being, the Doctrine of Discovery, and Calvinism with its emphasis on election and predestination were put in the service of racism. The rationale was that if God proclaimed that there is a hierarchy of races, then it must be so. In the early twentieth century, God's word was backed up with bogus statistics."

"Right on the money," Professor Kirby replied. "Before this complex in Cold Spring Harbor became completely operational, Dr. Charles Davenport argued that eugenics was largely based on the scientific work of Gregor Mendel, who was considered the father of genetics. Davenport argued that man was an organism, an animal, and the laws of improvement of corn and racehorses hold true for him also.

"Such ideas attracted the newly formed American Breeders Association. One New York state breeder clearly stated that what we can do for racehorses, bulls, and pigs, we can also do for man. 'The results of suppressing the poorest and breeding from the best would be the same for them as for cattle and sheep.'"[19]

Pastor Renjiro Suzuki chimed in, "I have an undergraduate science background. It seems to me that a true scientist doesn't start with a far-gone conclusion. While he or she might begin with a hypothesis, he or she engages in exhaustive experimentation and follows the data. Quite frequently, hypotheses are modified or discarded altogether. A responsible scientist doesn't fudge data to promote his or her agenda."

Professor Kirby responded, "That's exactly what Dr. Davenport and his followers did. His book, *Heredity in Relations to Eugenics*, was published in 1903, several years before his laboratory in Cold Spring Harbor was set up. His agenda was made very clear. He argued that it is a reproach to our people, proud in other respects of our control of nature, should have to support about half a million insane, feeble-minded, epileptic, blind and deaf, eighty thousand prisoners and one hundred thousand paupers at a cost of over $100 million per year.[20] He was equally upfront about immigration control and utilizing American resources to weed out potentially undesirable immigrants, particularly from southeast Europe.

"As Dr. Davenport believed Judaism to be a race rather than a religion, he referred to Jews as Hebrews. He embraced stereotypes about Jewish greed by claiming that while Hebrews rarely commit offenses of personal violence, they commit gainful offenses such as thieving and receiving stolen goods. He disparaged the morality of many Jewish immigrants by linking them with prostitution. Worst of all, Dr. Davenport embraced anti-Semitic trope by accusing Hebrews coming from Russia and the extreme southeast of Europe as intense individualists, the exact opposite of early English and Scandinavian immigrants who were God-fearing and community minded."[21]

I interjected, "Rabbi Max Reichler embraced eugenics as a defense mechanism against intermarriage between Jews and non-Jews. He quoted from Dr. Davenport's book which mentioned undesirable immigrants who originally came from Calabria, known as home of the brigands.[22] Just as the biblical Abraham refused to have his son, Isaac, married off to one of the Canaanite women, so it was equally unacceptable for Jews to marry anyone coming from Calabria or, for that matter, any non-Jew, even if conversion does take place. It was ironic that Rabbi Reichler quoted from Dr. Davenport's book and made similar remarks about non-Jews as Dr. Davenport made about Jews! It's almost as if he embraced and internalized anti-Semitic rhetoric."

Dr. Kirby continued, "In order to persuade the trustees of the Carnegie Institution to underwrite the new eugenics laboratory at Cold Spring Harbor, Dr. Davenport played the race card. He wrote:

> "We have in this country the grave problem of the negro, a race whose mental development is, on the average, far below the average Caucasian. Is there a prospect that we may through the education of the individual produce an improved race so that we may hope at last that the negro mind shall be as teachable, as elastic, as original, and as fruitful as the Caucasian? Or must future generations, indefinitely, start from the same low plane and yield the same meager results? We do not know; we have no data. Prevailing opinion says we must face the latter alternative. If this were so, it would be best to export the black race at once.[23]

"In essence, both the Cold Spring Harbor Laboratory and the Eugenics Record Office sought to provide the raw data which would buttress Dr. Davenport's views concerning the treatment of racial undesirables, such as the disabled non-Whites and immigrants from Eastern and Southern Europe. There were lots of statistics put forward, but in the end, it was pseudoscience.

"Much of Davenport's study of human inheritance was predicated on one gigantic scientific error—his belief that characteristics as complex and as unmeasurable as memory, loyalty, and shiftlessness were determined by a single unit character. In other words, that the origin of each was, genetically speaking, no more complicated than the color of the flowers of one of Gregor Mendel's pea plants.[24]

"Dr. Davenport was very much influenced by the work of Sir Francis Galton in Great Britain. Galton was the originator of the early twentieth-century eugenics movement but did not go anywhere near the extremes of his counterpart on the other side of the Atlantic. In fact, the original Galtonian eugenicists were horrified by the sham science. British scientist David Heron excoriated the work that took place in Cold Spring Harbor. His accusations: 'Careless presentation of data, inaccurate methods of analysis, irresponsible expression of conclusions, and rapid change of opinion.'[25]

"Heron emphasized 'that the material has been collected in a most unsatisfactory manner, that the data had been tabled in a most slipshod fashion, and that the Mendelian conclusions drawn have no justification whatever.' He also complained that the data has been deliberately skewed. Rather than letting it speak for itself, Davenport and his assistants deliberately searched for families that had the greatest number of defectives to prove his theories and generally overlooked similar families with fewer amounts of defectives. In other words, Heron called American eugenics rubbish."[26]

One of the educators among us, Anton Muharsky, added, "Both the IQ and college entrance exams, the SAT and ACT, are remnants of the eugenics agenda. While they allegedly measure intelligence and aptitude for college, they have historically been used to exclude racial minorities. The verbal and numerical skills that were tested and the manner which questions were worded often put non-Caucasian children who lived near the poverty line at a disadvantage.

"This also applies to standardized testing in New York. Many of the children at the Grace Afternoon School have a rough time. The authors of these tests often have preconceived ideas as to who will do well and who will not do well. The aim is less about diagnostics and more about sorting. When the results come out, the neo-eugenics experts come out and say, 'We knew that this would happen all along.'"

I added, "I am no fan of standardized tests. Contrary to eugenics thought, environmental and health factors rather than heredity effect most scores."

"Hear! Hear!" Anton replied.

Dr. Kirby continued, "The social consequences of the Cold Spring Harbor Laboratory and the Eugenic Record Office were enormous. President Theodore Roosevelt was an early convert to social Darwinism, which led him to embrace the racist pseudoscience of eugenics. He looked upon Columbus's discovery of the New World as a red-letter date in American history. As president of the United States, he perceived his mission as Americanizing Columbus. He envisioned a country dominated by the superior White race, which in America consisted of Anglo-Saxons, Scots, Irish, French Huguenots, Scandinavians, and German and Dutch Protestants. The prosperity of the Caucasian represented the survival of the fittest.

"Not so for other ethnic groups in America. In Theodore Roosevelt's view, all the darker peoples were inferior, particularly Native Americans, who were destined to disappear completely. Such individuals were not among the fittest. The work of ethnic cleansing, began by the Doctrine of Discovery, would eventually be completed."

Austenaco Kanoska interjected, "Indian residential schools were one method used to make Native Americans disappear. Their goal was to expose Native American children to Christianity and to assimilate them into mainstream culture. This assimilation came at a steep price to Native people across North America, a price we are still paying today in terms of the erosion of indigenous languages, cultures, lifeways, and the very loss of life among some students.

"Children were separated from their parents. Many of them were prohibited from speaking their native languages. They were only allowed to communicate in English. Many of them endured routine injury and abuse. Some perished and were interred in unmarked graves. The legacy of Indian boarding schools remains. It manifests itself in indigenous communities through intergenerational trauma, cycles of violence and abuse, disappearance, premature deaths, and other undocumented bodily and mental impacts."

I responded, "One of the major reasons for this symposium is to impress upon all of us that the legacy of the Doctrine of Discovery, reinforced by the removal of Native peoples from their lands in the nineteenth century, and given the ideological stamp of approval by the eugenics movement, is with us to this very day. Thank you, Austenaco, for reinforcing this point for us."

Dr. Kirby continued, "While President Roosevelt recognized that America was a country of immigrants, he saw America as a melting pot and not as a mosaic of different cultures and ethnic groups. On Columbus Day 1915, he gave a speech to the Knights of

Columbus. He stated that while American citizens are by blood and culture kin to each of the nations of Europe, they are also separate from each of them. Americans are a new and distinct nationality.

"Columbus Day in 2014 is an anathema for most Native Americans and other ethnic minorities. In Roosevelt's day, Columbus Day was not only a moment to reflect upon European roots. This national holiday was also the occasion to reinforce Americanism. Hence, Roosevelt made it clear that there was no room for hyphenated Americanism."[27]

*****

"Another repercussion of the eugenics research taking place in Cold Spring Harbor was compulsory sterilization. President Theodore Roosevelt advocated sexual sterilization of criminalized individuals and those with cognitive differences from the norm, alleging that otherwise, the United States would be committing race suicide. In 1907, Indiana passed the first eugenics-based compulsory sterilization law in the world. Thirty states would soon follow their lead. In the 1927 case *Buck v. Bell*, the Supreme Court, led by Roosevelt-appointed justice Oliver Wendell Holmes, upheld compulsory sexual sterilization laws which gave the states the power to regulate the breeding of its citizens. Between 1907 and 1963, over sixty-four thousand individuals were forcibly sterilized under eugenic legislation in the United States. Shockingly, sterilizations in the United States took place many years before they were performed in Nazi Germany and long before Josef Mengele's sadistic medical experiments on German Jews.

"A few years after the Supreme Court decision on *Buck v. Bell*, the Nazi regime that took power in Germany in 1933 adopted US race law and eugenics as a fundamental platform for their governance. Hitler intently studied American eugenics laws. He tried to legitimize his anti-Semitism by medicalizing it and wrapping it in the more palatable façade of science. Hitler was able to recruit more followers among reasonable Germans by claiming that science was on his side."[28]

"While Hitler's race hatred sprung from his own mind, the intellectual outlines of the eugenics Hitler adopted in 1924 were made in America. He simply adapted long-established race science to his anti-Jewish agenda. Hitler's version of eugenics shaped both the institutions and the machinery of the Third Reich's genocide.[29]

"In fact, America funded Germany's eugenic institutions. By 1926, Rockefeller had donated some $410,000—almost $4 million in twenty-first-century money—to hundreds of German researchers. In May 1926, Rockefeller awarded $250,000 to the German Psychiatric Institute of the Kaiser Wilhelm Institute, later to become the Kaiser Wilhelm Institute for Psychiatry. Among the leading psychiatrists at the German Psychiatric Institute was Ernst Rüdin, who became director and eventually an architect of Hitler's systematic medical repression.[30]

"Madison Grant, a geneticist, was a close friend of Dr. Charles Davenport. He sought to translate Davenport's ideas and genetic experiments into concrete political action. As a firm advocate of the genetics movement, he embraced polygenism rather than monogenism. His views of racial hierarchy were based on so-called science rather than on religion. In his openly racist book, *The Passing of the Great Race*, published in 1916, he rejected the Table of Nations in Genesis 10 that we had discussed earlier during this symposium. According to Grant, Genesis 10 did not prove the racial equality of all of humanity. He stated quite specifically that in the modern and scientific study of race, 'we have long discarded the Adamic theory that man is descended from a single pair, created a few thousand years ago in a mythical Garden of Eden somewhere in Asia, to spread over the earth in successive waves.'[31] Like others before him, he divided humanity into White Europeans, Negroid, and Mongoloid. Whites can be subdivided into Nordic, Mediterranean, and Alpine [Central and East European]. The superior, elite people were the Nordics.

"Grant concluded that unless concrete steps were taken to counteract the numbers of racial minorities and immigrants, America will be committing race suicide. President Theodore Roosevelt was extremely impressed with *The Passing of the Great Race*. Hitler even wrote a fan letter to Madison Grant calling his race-based eugenics book his bible.

"In addition to sterilization of undesirables, Germany also embraced American continental imperialism and ethnic cleansing. Removal of Native Americans from their ancestral lands under the guise of the Doctrine of Discovery and wars with Mexico and Spain under the guise of manifest destiny was the American counterpart to the German program of *Lebensraum*, living space. Lebensraum led to death camps for Jews, communists, gypsies, and the disabled.

*****

"Potential immigrants to America also were casualties of the eugenics movement," continued Professor Kirby. "In the late nineteenth and early twentieth centuries, immigration patterns shifted away from northern and western Europe and toward southern and eastern Europe. By 1910, more than two million Italians and over one million Yiddish-speaking people became American residents.[32]

"Support for immigration restriction has had a long history in our country. It was directed against German immigrants in the mid-nineteenth century by the xenophobic Know Nothing Party. The Asian Exclusion Act, directed against Chinese and Japanese, took place a few decades later. During World War I, Germans became public enemy no. 1. After the 1917 Bolshevik Revolution in Russia, foreign communists and anarchists—typically Italians, Russians, and Jews—supplanted the German Hun as perceived threats to the peace and security of the United States. What became known as the Red Scare of 1919 to 1920 involved a period of national hysteria. Political pressure was brought upon Congress to greatly restrict potentially dangerous elements from entering American society.[33]

"Madison Grant, the author of *The Passing of the Great Race*, served as the key advisor to Representative Albert Johnson, a Republican from the state of Washington. Albert Johnson, a vehement racist and anti-Semite, chaired the House Committee on Immigration and Naturalization and was determined that Congress should pass draconian immigration restrictions. He needed the intellectual input from an academically credible expert to achieve his objective. Madison Grant recommended the eugenicist Harry H. Laughlin. Laughlin was a former high school teacher and principal from the rural Midwest and had very little graduate education. Yet he was appointed by Dr. Charles Davenport in 1910 to become the superintendent of the Eugenics Record Office. He emphasized the importance of basing immigration policy on racial rather than on economic considerations.

"In the spring of 1920, Laughlin was presented to Johnson's committee as a representative of the Eugenics Research Association, which was founded by Charles Davenport in 1913 and in which Madison Grant became its president five years later. For much of his two days before the committee, Laughlin used copious visual aids and charts to unspool a series of assertions concerning the physical, mental, and moral qualities of immigrants. He declared that charity extended to the eugenically inferior was biologically unfortunate because it bolstered up individuals who, under a lower civilization, would have perished. Laughlin explained that the character of a nation is determined primarily by its racial qualities. Because immigrant women are on the average more fertile than the native-born, their genetic material would eventually dominate the American population. His charts purported to demonstrate that the foreign-born population of state institutions was disproportionately higher than their presence in the population at large. He recommended adding general shiftlessness to the list of conditions such as trachoma and tuberculosis that guaranteed the automatic rejection of immigrants.[34]

"Although Laughlin's presentation was based on shoddy science, Representative Albert Johnson was most impressed and decided to appoint Laughlin the committee's official expert eugenics agent. For the next decade, Laughlin would be the most visible advocate of eugenics in the entire nation. He would repeatedly testify at length before Johnson's committee, elaborating on studies he had conducted on its behalf.[35]

"To make a very long story short, the final product was the Immigration Act of 1924. As the architects of this law were Congressman US Representative Albert Johnson and Senator David

Reed, it was also called the Johnson-Reed Act. It unquestionably legitimized exclusion and restriction based on race as an acceptable policy of the United States. The new law froze the ethnic composition of the United States population and tried to reset it back to what it was prior to 1890. Countries like Great Britain, Germany, Ireland, Sweden, and others in northwestern Europe received nearly 87 percent of the visas, while countries like Poland, Italy, Czechoslovakia, and Russia received just over 11 percent. The Immigration Act constructed a White American race that included all people of European descent in a common whiteness. At the same time, it hardened the line between Whites, non-Whites, and those who were not White enough.[36]

"The Immigration of Act of 1924 was praised by Nazi Germany. The Nazis admired not only America's system of Jim Crow segregation but also its immigration and naturalization laws and the creation of de jure and de facto second-class citizenship for African Americans, Mexican Americans, Asian Americans, and the subjects of American colonies like Filipinos. In his unpublished sequel to *Mein Kampf*, drafted in 1928, Hitler applauded the 1924 Immigration Act as an effort to exclude the 'foreign body of strangers to the blood of the ruling race.'[37] The United States recommitment to being a Nordic-German state was to be commended. America became, in Hitler's view, a racial model for Europe.[38] Indeed, the Immigration Act was the precursor of the notorious Nuremburg Laws which were enacted in September 1935. As Nazi racism, which took its lead from American racism, was put into practice, German Jews were stripped of their political rights.

"Nazi racism and American xenophobia converged over the tragic voyage of the *St. Louis*, a German ocean liner carrying 937 passengers, most of them Jewish refugees, to Cuba in May 1939. Although most had proper landing certificates entitling them to enter Cuba, the ship was turned away in Havana. The Cuban president, acting on the country's own xenophobia, and covertly assisted by Nazi agents who fanned the flames of anti-Semitism in the general population, refused to let all but twenty-six of the refugees disembark. The *St. Louis* tried to seek refuge in the United States instead.

They sailed so close to Miami that the passengers could see the city lights twinkling, but with the US Coast Guard tailing the ship to prevent anyone from swimming ashore, the US officials refused to let them dock. The *St. Louis* was forced to return to Europe. Some passengers were sent to Great Britain, where all but one survived the war. The rest went to Belgium, the Netherlands, and France—all countries that would eventually be invaded by the Nazis. By the end of the war, 254 of the *St. Louis* passengers had been murdered in the Holocaust.[39]

*****

Our immigrant resource person, Anna Fuentes, took over the remainder of this session.

"The Immigration Act of 1924 was replaced by the 1965 Immigration and Nationality Act. This revolutionary piece of legislation abolished the discriminatory national origins quota. In terms of the issuance of immigrant visas, it explicitly prohibited discrimination based on race, sex, nationality, place of birth, or place of residence. There would be an annual per country cap at twenty thousand, an annual cap of one hundred seventy thousand from the eastern hemisphere, and an annual cap of one hundred twenty thousand from the western hemisphere. Spouses, minor children, and parents of American citizens were exempt from these numerical ceilings.

"But xenophobia did not end with the 1965 Immigration Act. The end to racial discrimination only masked the perseverance of xenophobia and the inauguration of its more subtle version, color-blind xenophobia. Claiming to be color-blind, those who wish to restrict immigration refer to so-called objective factors such as economics, national security, and legal status. They avoid referring to race, religion, or national origin. Nevertheless, racial anxieties and bias remain in the background. The new target of the bias was directed to potential immigrants who lived south of the border.[40]

"Indeed, a special hardship was created for immigrants from Latin America, particularly Mexico. Between 1942 and 1964, US recruitment of Mexican laborers under the *bracero* program brought

4.6 million workers. This excluded immigrants who were admitted through normal channels. When the program was allowed to lapse by Congress, it cut off an important source of legal immigration. What had been a massive amount of legal immigration, two hundred thousand braceros and thirty-five thousand regular admissions for permanent residency was reduced to the annual twenty thousand quota.[41]

"Hence, there has been an increase in undocumented immigration over the decades. American employers continued to rely on labor from Mexico, but with no legal way to enter the country to fill these jobs, Mexicans turned to entering without inspection. In many cases, migrants were returning to the same jobs and to the same employers they had before the new law went into effect. But now they were illegal. At the same time, undocumented immigrants already in the United States began to remain in the country rather than risk multiple cross-border trips across an increasingly militarized border. Both trends resulted in record members of undocumented immigrants coming to and staying in the United States.[42]

"In response to the crescendo of undocumented immigrants was a new regime of immigration enforcement focused on arrests, detention, and deportation. Such a policy crossed party lines. No American president wanted to be perceived as being soft on enforcing immigration laws.

"Beginning with Clinton, the US government also increased the list of offenses that triggered deportation for all immigrants, regardless of legal status. This meant that immigrants could be detained and deported for even minor crimes and everyday legal infractions, such as drunk driving, failing to appear in court, filing a false tax return, passing bad checks, shoplifting, minor drug possession, and traffic violations.[43]

"Hence, there was the merging of criminal and immigration law. Immigrants, both undocumented and lawfully present, became subjected to a double standard that allowed the American government to inflict a far greater punishment, deportation, than the crime merited and treated noncitizens far more harshly than citizens. By the first decade of the twenty-first century, immigration-related offenses constituted the largest share of prosecuted federal crimes in the United States. Over 60 percent of all deportations from the United States were triggered by criminal convictions, most of which were minor offenses like traffic violations, nonviolent drug crimes, and immigration violations.[44]

"The terrorist attacks of September 11, 2001, in which Americans were attacked on their own soil, rocked our country to the core. Xenophobia rose to new levels, especially against Muslims. Fear of the other became rampant. In essence, our country went apeshit.

"In response, the US government's ability to keep track of, arrest, detain, and deport immigrants grew exponentially. During the Bush administration, Congress established the Department of Homeland Security [DHS], the Immigration and Customs Enforcement, better known as ICE, US Citizenship and Immigration Services, and the US Customs and Border Protection. To this very day, we see how ICE—through targeted raids, detention without due process of law, and deportation—strikes terror in the hearts of undocumented immigrants.

"Deportations increased dramatically during the Obama administration. In 2012, the DHS removed a record high of 419,00 people—ten times the number of people deported in 1991 and higher than the number of people deported during the entire decade of the 1980s. President Obama was famously labeled deporter in chief by critics.[45]

"To President Obama's credit, he announced a series of executive actions that granted temporary reprieve to millions of 'dreamers,' immigrants who entered the United States without documentation when they were children, from deportation. The Deferred Action for Childhood Arrivals [DACA] eventually allowed approximately eight hundred thousand immigrants to temporarily stay in the United States and work."[46]

At this point, Anna Fuentes distributed two handouts. The first one was a copy of the Fugitive Slave Act of 1850. She called special attention to Section 7, which prohibited harboring runaways and the penalties for doing so. The second handout was a copy of Title 8, USC 1324 (A) Offenses, which was promulgated in 1994. She called our attention to the first few paragraphs. It was a series of prohibitions concerning the smuggling, the domestic transportation, and the harboring of undocumented aliens as well as prohibitions against encouraging or enabling them to enter the country illegally. As was the case with the Fugitive Slave Act, there were penalties for noncompliance.

Anna urged us to lay the two handouts on the table side by side. If we read them carefully, their language was similar. The Fugitive Slave Act, in plain language, stated that any person even in the free states of the North, who willingly or knowingly attempted to rescue a fugitive slave or prevent his owner or his representatives from arresting him, was subject to a fine not exceeding $1,000 and imprisonment not exceeding six months. Title 8, USC 1324 (A) Offenses, in plain language, stated that any person who knowingly or in reckless disregard of the fact, who transports or harbors an undocumented alien, was subject to a fine and imprisonment of no more than five years!

This statute got our attention. As we learned earlier today, Amelia and her three children were already being harbored in Father Lorenzo Burgess's church. We were all devising strategies for giving this family living in sanctuary physical and spiritual comfort. Some of my colleagues, including myself, were also considering the possibility of converting our own places of worship into sanctuary congregations. Considering the aggressiveness of ICE and the xenophobic climate of our country, we knew that we would be operating on shaky ground. Nevertheless, New York was a "sanctuary city."

As always, Pastor Brenda Corbett was outspoken. "We call ourselves a nation of laws. Just as slavery was a flagrant violation of the Declaration of Independence, so American intervention in Latin America, however covert, was a violation of international law. Just as slaves ran to the North and to Canada to save their lives, so refugees like Amelia cross our border to save their lives. In the antebellum period, Black slaves were property and were counted as three-fifth of a human being in terms of determining the number of congressmen that a state was allotted. In 2014, a refugee from Latin America has no more value in the eyes of the American government than a common slave!"

All of us around the table nodded.

"At my church, we are clearly breaking the law," said Father Burgos. "I have received several threatening telephone calls from ICE. The bottom line has been 'Turn over Amelia or else!'"

Doreen responded, "At present, ICE is reluctant to conduct raids in sensitive areas such as churches or synagogues."

Father Burgos continued, "There are no guarantees that my church will not be raided by ICE someday, but I am not afraid. Over the years, I have been arrested sixty-five times for civil disobedience. We have a moral obligation to break the law. Remember, back in Nazi Germany, everything that Hitler did was legal."

I interjected. "In all fairness, a major problem is our broken immigration system. If we have a purely open border, we invite chaos. However, proper regulation as to who enters our country must be balanced by compassion and sensitivity as to why immigrants choose our country in the first place."

Anna responded, "I agree, Rabbi Levin. However, the legitimate need to control our borders has often become the fig leaf to hide naked racial bias. As for you, Pastor Brenda, you hit the nail on the head! Behind the rhetoric of being a nation of laws and behind the rhetoric of national security is the desire to preserve White Anglo-Saxon domination. Xenophobia is always the elephant in the room.

"Samuel P. Huntington, a political scientist from Harvard University, wrote the book *Who Are We?* It expressed the ideological underpinnings of current immigration policies and of Title 8, USC 1324 [A] Offenses. He unabashedly described the glorious White Anglo-Protestant legacy of our country. In this book, he wrote that the combination of high levels of Mexican and Hispanic immigrants combined with their allegedly low rates of assimilation into American society could eventually change America into a country of two languages, two cultures, and two peoples. We would have people who are living in our country, but you are not part of it. Huntington then made the cryptic remark: 'There is no Americano dream. There is the American dream created by an Anglo-Protestant society. Mexican

Americans will share in that dream and in that society only if they dream in English.'"[47]

Anton Muharsky interjected, "Such a statement also provided the ideological backdrop of de facto segregation in so many school systems. Many Latinx children are excluded from the so-called American dream. I see it every afternoon, Monday through Friday."

Anna Fuentes concluded her presentation: "Professor Huntington also complained about the Hispanic takeover of Miami and of the southwestern part of the United States. In this book, he called for America to force immigrants to adopt English and the US to turn to Protestant religions to save itself against the threats of Latino and Islamic immigrants."

I responded, "History has a peculiar way of repeating itself over the centuries. Thus, it was written in the first chapter of Exodus, 'And Pharaoh said unto his people, Behold, the people of the children of Israel are more and mightier than we: Come on, let us deal wisely with them; lest they multiply.'"

The afternoon session concluded at 4:15 p.m. We paused for a coffee break. I suggested that we resume in fifteen to twenty minutes. We would then have a wrap-up session and finish no later than 5:30 p.m.

XIV

Jerusalem
February 10, 2014

In the Intellectual History of Zionism class, Professor Spiegel focused on the ideological underpinnings of Zionism.

"With regard to Zionist thought, there is the perennial argument: Is Zionism primarily biblical in its origins, or is it the product of European philosophy? I would contend that the yearning for the land which God promised to the patriarchs—Abraham, Isaac, and Jacob—began in biblical times, was reinterpreted through the rabbinic period, was captured in the poetry of Judah Ha Levi in the eleventh century and by others, and has permeated the minds and souls of Jews throughout the centuries. The Bible provides the basic building blocks of Zionist thought. Even the secular Zionists of the early twentieth century who have shunned Jewish observance knew sections of the Bible by heart and employed its teachings to support their messages.

"However, the frame of reference for modern Zionism as we understand it was Central and Eastern European nationalism. The celebrated Israeli political scientist Zeev Sternhell stated that east of the Rhine River, the criteria for belonging to a nation were cultural, linguistic, ethnic, and religious. German, Polish, Romanian, Slovakian, Serbian, and Ukrainian identities were based on biological or racial differences.[48]

"Hence, Zionism in the late nineteenth and early twentieth centuries was essentially a Jewish version of nationalist socialism. Nationalist socialism was based on the idea of the nation as a cultural, historical, and biological unit. The individual was regarded as an organic part of the whole, and the whole took precedence over the individual. The blood ties and cultural ties linking members of the nation, their partnership in the total national effort, took precedence over the position of the individual in the production system.[49]

"American Progressivism and Zionism were contemporary ideologies of the early twentieth century. Both espoused the organic state as espoused in Central European thought. Both were reactions against political liberalism which sanctified the individual.

"Professor Sternhell cited A. D. Gordon as an exemplar of early Zionist thought. As the spiritual force behind practical Zionism and Labor Zionism, he categorically rejected the liberal expression of society as a collection of individuals. He called this a society that is an artificial conglomeration, devoid of the spirit of life.[50] The nation represents the spirit of the individual.[51] The individual *I* always draws from the wellspring of the nation.[52]

"Thus, for A. D. Gordon, political liberalism was a fraud. Negation of the *galut* or diaspora was central to his thinking. The ethos of individualism coupled with the absence of Jewish peoplehood represented the spiraling staircase to assimilation and to the complete disappearance of the Jewish people in the Diaspora. He believed that if we, as Jews, do not have a complete and absolute national life embracing our entire existence and if the national idea is not considered to be the loftiest of ideals, it would be better that there shall be a total end to things.[53]

"A few words about Arthur Ruppin. I will have a lot to say about him during this lecture. Although he was not a household name like Theodore Herzl, A. D. Gordon, Vladimir Jabotinsky, or David Ben Gurion, he was an important Zionist thinker. He was a Zionist proponent of pseudoscientific race theory and one of the founders of the city of Tel Aviv. Appointed director of Berlin's Bureau for Jewish statistics in 1904, he moved to Palestine in 1907, and from 1908, he was the director of the Palestine Office of the Zionist Organization in Jaffa, organizing Zionist immigration to Palestine. In 1926, Ruppin joined the faculty of the Hebrew University of Jerusalem and founded the Department for the Sociology of the Jews.

"Arthur Ruppin became the father of Jewish settlement during the Second Aliyah to Palestine, 1904 to 1914. He was eventually regarded as the father of Jewish sociology. Like Gordon, he was a proponent of both organic nationalism and practical Zionism. Like Gordon, he believed that either Jewry exists as a nation or it dies out altogether through assimilation. Ruppin expressed even stronger views than Gordon regarding the role of the individual within the Jewish nation:

> "Human individuals as such are worthless, that only as part of a nation can they be said to be worth something, and that the nation is the means to the higher breeding or cultivation of humanity. Work for one's nation is the metaphysical purpose of human beings and must replace the false dream of individual immortality.[54]

"Just as the concept of the organic state in American Progressivism was a reaction against rugged individualism which led to huge disparities of wealth and numerous social problems, so Zionism was a reaction to the so-called political emancipation of Jews in Europe. Theodor Herzl argued that despite political emancipation and greater acceptance in European society, anti-Semitism persisted. Herzl concluded that if the Dreyfus Trial could evoke such virulent anti-Semitism in France, the bastion of liberal democracy, there was no hope for Jews anywhere in the Diaspora. Herzl pointed out that despite all attempts by Jews to merge with the national community with the caveat that they preserve the faith of their fathers, they will always be regarded as aliens. They shall never be left in peace.

*****

"As was the case in America at the turn of the century, the Zionist project also embraced the notion that organic nationalism and eugenics went hand in hand. The early Zionists, to a large extent, embraced and internalized the biologizing of the Jewish people by European anti-Semites. They adopted stereotypical anti-Semitic images such as homelessness, weakness, and cowardice in discourses about European Jewry. Thus, early Zionist ideologies, long before the establishment of the State of Israel, posited the need for the construction of a 'new Jewish person who will resemble physically and psychically, his tall and strong European neighbors.' He would be the opposite of the Jewish male of Eastern Europe.

"As the early Zionists sought to rise above the anti-Semitic stereotypes that were used against them in Europe, they projected European-style racism unto the non-European native population, the Arabs, and to non-European Jewish immigrants coming mainly from Asia and Africa. They regarded themselves as racially superior to both the current inhabitants of Palestine, the Arabs, and to the Jews immigrating from Arab lands. The Occident was superior to the Orient. The new Jews coming from the West were far more advanced than those who hailed from the East.

"In the words of Vladimir Jabotinsky, the architect of the Revisionist movement:

> "We Jews have nothing in common with what is called the 'Orient,' thank God. To the

extent that our uneducated masses have ancient spiritual traditions and laws that call the Orient, they must be weaned away from them, and this is in fact what we are doing in every decent school, what life itself is doing with great success. We are going to Palestine, first for our national convenience, second to sweep out thoroughly all traces of the 'Oriental soul.' As for the Palestinians, Arabs in Palestine, what they do is their business; but if we can do them a favor, it is to help them liberate themselves from the Orient.[55]

"Arthur Ruppin spoke even more disparagingly of Arabs. He internalized the negative Jewish stereotypes of preoccupation with mercantile interests and projected it upon the Arab population. He argued that the Arab has a strong materialistic conception of life and that in the daily life of the Arab peasants, making money plays the principal role.[56]

"There was a consensus among Zionist thinkers that the Arabs were a backward people and had no concept of caring for the land of Palestine. Palestine was awaiting a more cultured people, said Chaim Weizman, who would take much better care of it. The Arabs would profit from the wisdom and technology of the new European inhabitants.

"This sense of racial superiority, the belief that the Jewish people are the rightful owners of the land which was taken from them by the Arabs in the eighth century, and the duplicity of the British during the Mandate Period form the crux of the Israeli-Palestinian conflict. Many Israelis believe that there is no such thing as a Palestinian people. They are simply part of the larger Arab population in the Middle East. Many Israelis argue that there are many Arab-speaking countries in which they would fit in better, especially Jordan.

"In the past, there were Israeli leaders who wished to annex Gaza and the West Bank and transfer the inhabitants to neighboring Arab countries. Eliahu ben Chorin, a disciple of Jabotinsky, said in the 1940s that a population transfer would benefit both Palestinians and Israeli Jews. Palestinian farmers will get better soil and more promising life conditions, and the city Arab will better be able to realize his ambitions in a purely Arab state unit.[57] The Israelis would simultaneously transfer Iraqi, Yemeni, and Syrian Jews to Palestine. A win-win situation.

"At present, outright annexation is no longer on the table. Instead, we have the policy of creeping annexation which translates to increased settlements and restricting Palestinian inhabitants to ever-shrinking enclaves. Along with making it more difficult for farmers to make a living, creating havoc on border crossings, deporting so-called troublemakers, destroying the homes of suspected terrorists, and other civil rights violations, the unofficial strategy is to make Israel less livable, to encourage emigration, to reduce the Arab population, and to maintain a Jewish majority.

"Eugenics even figures in the Law of Return. Automatic Israeli citizenship applies to Jews, not to descendants of Arab families who fled their homes during the 1948 War of Independence. In the past, the Orthodox rabbinate has sought to offer immigration only to those Jews whose religious status is certified by a competent Orthodox rabbi or to those individuals who converted under strict orthodox auspices. In other words, only so-called pure Jews are acceptable. At present, matters of Jewish status, marriage, and divorce are relegated to the orthodox rabbinate. This, of course, caused a great outcry in America as most of the Jewish population is non-Orthodox.

*****

"Returning to Arthur Ruppin, he not only believed that Jews were racially superior to Arabs. He also believed European Jews to be superior to Jews immigrating from Africa and Asia.

"Concerning Ethiopian Jews, he wrote, 'Negroes, who came to Judaism by force of the sword in the sixth century BC have no blood connection to the Jews. Therefore, their number in Palestine should not be increased.'[58]

"Furthermore, Ruppin argued that the original Semitic race was considered akin to the inferior Bedouin type who were known for their commercial instinct. He thus segregated the Ashkenazic Jews from the main Semitic stock and associated them with Indo-Germanic races. This enabled Ruppin to accept European theories concerning the inferiority of the Semitic race. It was not the Jews who were avaricious. It was the Semites.

"The good Jews were the Ashkenazim who were responsible for the good qualities of Jewish culture. The bad Jews were the Semites with their oriental germ plasma. According to Ruppin, the Oriental and Sephardic Jews were in a state of biological degeneration. They have assimilated the way of life and the mores of the local Arabs. Therefore, they should not represent the Jewish race in the modern period. He pointed out that it was a well-known fact that Ashkenazi Jews were better than Sephardi Jews in their abilities and inclinations to the sciences and that Ashkenazi school children were superior to Sephardi school children.[59] Therefore, Zionism must focus on the regeneration of the new Ashkenazi Jew.

"Just like the pseudoscience known as eugenics, which was peddled on the other side of the Atlantic, notably at Cold Spring Harbor, New York, so Arthur Ruppin peddled it in Israel. Instead of cold, hard measurable data, Ruppin based his observations on casual observation, nonrationalized or unmeasured intuition. Influenced by racist thinkers, including the British-German philosopher Houston Chamberlain, he defined his racial theories as instinctual objectivity.[60]

"Ruppin's unscientific explanation of the inferiority of Sephardim, of course, was a thin veil for outright bigotry. In subsequent decades, Ruppin's ideas took on a life of their own. In a 1949 article published in *Haaretz*, during the mass immigration from Arab and Muslim countries, the journalist Arye Gelblum made Arthur Ruppin's beliefs about the racial inferiority of the Sephardim even more explicit:

> This is immigration of a race we have not yet known in the country… We are dealing with people whose primitivism is at a peak, whose level of knowledge is one of virtually absolute ignorance, and worse, who have little talent for

understanding anything intellectual. Generally, they are only slightly better than the general level of the Arabs, Negroes, and Berbers in the same regions. In any case, they are at even a lower level than what we know regarding the former Arabs of Eretz Yisrael... These Jews also lack roots in Judaism, as they are totally subordinated to the play of savage and primitive instincts... As with the Africans you will find card games for money, drunkenness, and prostitution. Most of them have serious eye, skin, and sexual diseases, without mentioning robberies and thefts. Chronic laziness and hatred for work, there is nothing safe about this asocial element.[61]

"Like the pseudoscience in America, Ruppin's ideas had enormous consequences. Historically, Jews coming to Arab lands were treated as second-class citizens. Ethnic discrimination against Sephardim began with their initial settling. Upon arrival in Israel, the various Sephardi communities, despite their will to stay together, were dispersed across the country. Families were separated, old communities disintegrated, and traditional leaders were shorn of their positions. Oriental Jews were largely settled in remote villages which had recently been emptied of Palestinians.[62]

"In cases where Sephardim were moved into preexisting housing—and in Israel preexisting housing means Palestinian housing—the Sephardim often ended up living in precarious conditions because the Orientalist attitudes of the Israeli authorities found it normal to crowd many Sephardi families into the same house, on the assumption that they were accustomed to such conditions. These poor Sephardi neighborhoods were then systematically discriminated against in terms of infrastructure needs, educational and cultural advantages, and political self-representation.[63]

"As a cheap, mobile, and manipulable labor force, Sephardim were indispensable to the economic development of the state of Israel. Many Sephardim were ill-paid construction workers. In terms of agricultural settlements, they received poorer and fewer lands than the various Ashkenazi settlements such as the *kibbutzim* and much less adequate means of production, resulting in lower production, lower income, and gradually the economic collapse of many Sephardi settlements.[64] In terms of industrialization, a large section of the Sephardim came to form an industrial proletariat. The wages were the equivalent of similar workers in Third World countries.[65]

"While the Sephardim were relegated to the lowest rung of Israeli society with relatively few means to improve their lot, Ashkenazim nicely climbed the social ladder. There was ample mobility in management, marketing, banking, and technical jobs. European immigrants were deliberately privileged. Educated Sephardim became unskilled workers while less educated Ashkenazim came to occupy high administrative positions. For Ashkenazim, immigration to Israel raised their stature and standard of living. For Sephardim, immigration to Israel had the opposite effect.[66]

"In the United States, President Theodore Roosevelt emphasized that there was no room for hyphenated Americans. In Israel, there was no room for hyphenated Israelis, namely Arab Israelis. Deliberate attempts were made to remove the Arabness from Jews who came from Muslim lands. As Sephardim arrived in Israel, violent measures were taken to strip them of their heritage. Yemenites were shorn of their sidelocks, and religious artifacts were stolen by Zionist emissaries with false promises of return. Sephardim, under the control of Ashkenazi religious authorities, had to send their children to Ashkenazi Orthodox schools, where they learned the 'correct' forms of practicing Judaism, including Yiddish-accented praying, liturgical-gestural norms, and centuries-old Polish styles of dress which emphasized dark colors."[67]

Shmuel Sassoon stood up and posed a question to Professor Spiegel. "Professor Spiegel, could you comment on the Yemenite Children Affair?"

"Of course." Professor Spiegel was not one to avoid difficult or even embarrassing questions. "Traumatized by the reality of life in Israel, some Sephardim, most of them Yemenites, fell prey to a ring of unscrupulous doctors, nurses, and social workers who provided hundreds of Yemenite babies for adoption by childless Ashkenazi couples, some of them living outside of Israel, while telling the natural parents that the children had died. The conspiracy was extensive enough to include the systematic issuance of fraudulent death certificates for the adopted children and to ensure that over several decades, Sephardi demands for investigation were silenced. Information was hidden and manipulated by government bureaus."[68]

"As a result of that scandal, I never met one of my great-aunts" was Shmuel's somber response.

"I am very sorry to hear that. It was a complete national disgrace!"

Bracha stood up. "In both America and Canada, there were boarding schools especially designed for Native Americans. Just as Ashkenazi schools were designed to remove all traces of Arabness from Sephardim, so these schools sought to remove all traces of Indian culture from Native Americans. While some Indian children were probably kidnapped as well, it was done quite openly. Many Indian families were pressured to send their children to boarding schools as the government did not deem Indian parents and Indian tribes competent enough to raise and educate their own children. That was undoubtedly the message that was also sent to Sephardi families."

"Excellent observation, Bracha. While the purpose of Zionism was to provide a homeland in which all Jews, regardless of their country of origin, could live in dignity, its execution, tainted by racial and ethnic bias, was frequently a disaster."

*****

Although Professor Spiegel stuck to eugenics, he changed subjects.

"Just as the American eugenics movement fueled the German eugenics movement and American eugenicists had contacts with Nazi eugenicists, so some Zionist leaders had connections with Nazi officials and Nazi thinkers. Once again, I return to Arthur Ruppin.

"In August, 1933, Arthur Ruppin met with Hans Gunther, a major Nazi ideologue, in Jena, Prussia. Ruppin spoke positively about the event and felt that there was a meeting of the minds. Both men viewed nationhood through racial lenses. Just as Gunther viewed Aryans as the purest, most beautiful, and the most creative people, at the top of the racial pyramid,[69] so Ruppin viewed the Ashkenazim at the top of the racial pyramid in Palestine. Both Gunther and Ruppin shared the belief that Jews could not be assimilated within German society. Ruppin went further to say that the Jewish people could only reach their highest potential by building a country of their own. Thus, Gunther welcomed Zionism as a positive development, praising it for recognizing the genuine racial consciousness [*Volkstum*] of the Jewish people.[70] For his part, Ruppin recognized that there were irreconcilable differences between German and Jewish national agendas that could not be removed by arguments and reason.[71]

"Ruppin's historical meeting with Gunther and his friendly meetings with Nazi officials as well as with Jewish and Zionist leaders were the preliminary discussions for the *Haavara Agreement*. Under the agreement, Jews emigrating from Germany could use their assets to purchase German-manufactured goods for export, thus salvaging their personal assets during emigration. The agreement provided a substantial export market for German factories in British-ruled Palestine. Between November 1933 and December 31, 1937, 77,800,000 Reichmarks, or $22,500,000, values in 1938 currency, worth of goods were exported to Jewish businesses in Palestine under the program. By the time the program ended with the start of World War II, the total had risen to 105,000,000 marks, about $35,000,000 in 1939 values.

"Emigrants with capital of £1,000,(about $5,000 in 1930s currency value, could move to Palestine in spite of severe British restrictions on Jewish immigration under an immigrant investor program. Under the Transfer Agreement, about 39 percent of an emigrant's funds were given to Jewish communal economic development projects, leaving individuals with about 43 percent of the funds.

"The *Haavara Agreement* benefitted both the Third Reich and the fledgling Jewish community in Palestine. For Hitler's regime, it was a solution to the Jewish problem as it removed 15 percent of the Jewish population. In addition, it stimulated the German economy and broke the worldwide anti-Nazi boycott of German goods. From the Jewish standpoint, the agreement enabled fifty-five thousand German Jews to leave their country of birth and retain a substantial portion of their assets, much more than what would have been possible under other circumstances.

"Nevertheless, much of the Jewish world believed that it was an anathema to do business with such a vibrantly anti-Semitic regime. Opposition came from the mainstream US leadership of the World Zionist Congress, in particular from Abba Hillel Silver and from American Jewish Congress president, Rabbi Stephen Wise. Wise and other leaders of the Anti-Nazi boycott of 1933 argued against the agreement, narrowly failing to persuade the Nineteenth Zionist Congress in August 1935 to vote against it. The right-wing Revisionist Zionists and their leader, Vladimir Jabotinsky, were even more vocal in their opposition. The Revisionist newspaper in Palestine, *Hazit HaAm*, published a sharp denunciation of those involved in the agreement as betrayers, and shortly afterward, one of the negotiators, Haim Arlosoroff, was assassinated.

"The Haavara Agreement was not simply an agreement based on pragmatic and economic self-interest. It was propelled by eugenic principles. It was clearly the outcome of a congruent *weltanschauung*. The mutual perception of Ruppin and Gunther, which served their mutual self-interests, was that Jews must be excluded from German culture and eventually expelled from Germany. In August 1933, Zionists and Nazis alike did not realize the ultimate outcome of this *weltanschauung*, the Final Solution.

*****

After the lecture, Shmuel and Bracha met outside the auditorium.

"That was a dreary lecture," exclaimed Bracha. "Much of the misery that is occurring in this country stems from Israel's adaptation of organic nationalism and eugenic principles imported from both America and Central Europe."

"I couldn't agree more," responded Shmuel. "While the lecture dished out all of the negative stereotypes about Sephardim, how would you like to see Yemenites in a much more positive light?"

"What do you mean?"

"I would like to invite you to my moshav for the first day of Pesach. It will be quite different from anything you have ever experienced."

"I would love that."

"You will eat well. We will provide a nice bedroom for you in our house. Yemenite hospitality is legendary."

"We have a date!"

*****

XV

Cold Spring Harbor, New York
February 10, 2014

After twenty minutes of feasting on coffee cakes from Zucker's bakery and sipping chocolate fudge coffee that I percolated in my Cuisinart coffee machine, we reconvened.

Throughout the morning and afternoon sessions when we focused on the Doctrine of Discovery, the Trail of Tears, manifest destiny, eugenics, and immigration, Pastor Doreen Williams was quietly fuming. Although less vocal than her associate pastor, Brenda Corbett, she finally poured out her feelings.

"I feel depressed," she said. "Although the presentations were informative and sometimes eye-opening, I come away from this symposium with a very bad taste in my mouth. I get it. I realize that the problems that our country is facing with racism, anti-Semitism, de facto segregation, and undocumented immigrants didn't come about overnight. Nevertheless, the final message that institutionalized white supremacy and hatred of the other is so deep-rooted in American history makes me feel helpless. Although I love the way that this group has gelled, how can we make a difference when we leave this comfortable setting and return to hard reality in northern Manhattan?"

Pastor Lorenzo Burgos added, "The Puritans have a lot to answer for. Their Calvinist beliefs in predestination and election set the tone for a hierarchical society in which the superior elite, wealthy White men with property, rule over everybody else and trample upon the rights of the so-called undesirables—Native Americans, African slaves and their descendants, and immigrants. We can draw a straight line from the Puritans to the American pioneers of the Wild West, to the Southern plantation owners, to the eugenicists, and to the White supremacists of our own times. Correct me if I am wrong, Dr. Kirby. Based on your lectures, I recall that Dr. Charles Davenport came from an Anglo-Saxon Puritan background. His buddy, Madison Grant, wrote *The Passing of the Great Race* and had his fingerprints all over the Johnson-Reed Act of 1924."

"Correct on all accounts," answered Professor Kirby.

Father Lorenzo Burgos continued, "In my church, we live with the legacy of the Johnson-Reed Act. It may have been repealed by Congress in 1965, but it has not ended xenophobia any more than *Brown v. Board of Education of Topeka* has ended segregation. In our church, we protest the legacy of the Johnson-Reed Act by providing sanctuary to Amelia and her three children.

"Doreen, I understand your frustration. From the day that Christopher Columbus set foot in the western hemisphere until now, our country has grown mightily in terms of technology but has hardly advanced in its political institutions and its empathy towards the other."

Desperate to end the symposium on a more positive note, I responded to both Pastor Doreen Williams and Father Lorenzo Burgos. "I have a more optimistic view of our current situation. Yes, hatred of the other has gone back to the biblical moment when Cain slew his brother. He perceived that he was God's favorite and further denied that he was his brother's keeper. Yes, the hierarchical view of society and the division between higher and lower forms of humanity has gone back long before the Thirteen Colonies became a new nation. But just as the power of hate has been strong throughout the generations, so is the power of love and the power of curiosity."

"Could you elaborate?" asked Bishop Steven Young.

"I organized this symposium because I have broken bread with many of you seated around the table, feel comfortable with all of you, and care for you. Your work in your respective communities inspires me every day."

"Aw!" exclaimed Pastor Helen O'Shea.

"Curiosity is one of the most basic of human emotions. Instead of keeping apart from the other, I am curious. I am interested in how different ethnic groups do things, how they approach the world, how they solve problems, and even how they eat."

Pastor Vasquez inserted, "Rabbi Levin, if food makes you curious, I will take you out to a nice Latino restaurant, and you can satisfy your curiosity with Latino cuisine."

There was a general laugh among the participants. The mood of the group was now moving in a positive direction.

I continued, "I was hoping that this symposium would be a springboard for us to do real projects together, projects that make a difference in our community."

Father Lorenzo Burgos chimed in, "As you can gather, I am no Puritan."

More laughter from the group.

"In addition to rejecting the hierarchy of society into haves and have-nots, I also reject the Puritan notion that human action has no bearing on salvation. I do not believe in justification by faith alone. Rather, I believe in the efficacy of social progress. I believe in justification through good works. In the words of the second chapter of James, 'What good is it, my brothers and sisters, if someone claims to have faith but has no deeds? Can such faith save them? Suppose a brother or a sister is without clothes and daily food. If one of you says to them, Go, in peace, keep warm and well fed, but does nothing about their physical needs, what good is it?'"[72]

Pastor Helen O'Shea commented, "I accept what you are saying, but I am sure that around this table, there are a variety of views as to what extent clergy people should get involved in politics. My congregation does not really want the clergy to make waves. They want a preacher who is pleasantly boring. Every Sunday, they would prefer to listen to clean thoughts in clean underwear. My membership generally frowns upon addressing hot button issues from the pulpit."

Father Lorenzo Burgos argued, "The problem is that we do not live in a clean world. To some extent, everything that we preach from the pulpit has to do with politics. When we take a stand on a controversial issue, we are obviously making a political statement. However, if there is a burning issue in the community and we choose to ignore it, we are also making a political statement. The question is not whether or not we are making political statements but what type of politics we are advocating—engagement with our community or passivity.

"In our case, if we tackle immigration and sanctuary in our respective places of worship, we will obviously provoke the wrath of those congregants that either believe that it's not our concern or that we shouldn't be challenging immigration laws. However, now that we all know what's taking place in my church and we choose to ignore it, we make the political statement that the pain of the destitute doesn't concern us and that religion has nothing to say about loving the stranger."

I responded, "Right on, Father Lorenzo. As I had mentioned earlier in our symposium, Rabbi David Einhorn spoke out against slavery to many congregants who owned slaves. His pronouncements had consequences for him and his family. However, he felt that if he had kept quiet, he would be sanctioning 'America's peculiar institution.'

"Only a few months ago, my congregation observed the seventy-fifth anniversary of Kristallnacht and mourned the death of the six million. Although Nazism was defeated and Adolf Hitler committed suicide in the bunker, Nazism is very much alive today. Hitler's phantom roams the earth in search of trouble. He can be found in any place where there's hate, where there's prejudice, where there's bigotry. He's alive because humanity has kept him alive."

Our group nodded vigorously.

"My friends, based on the vibes that I have been getting, the last thing that we want to do is to leave this meeting, go our separate ways, and not see each other again until the next blue moon. We must build on this moment and meet more regularly."

"We have our work cut out for us," said Pastor Lars Munson.

"Indeed, we do. I also believe in social progress and justification through good deeds. We have a family in sanctuary that we must attend to. I'll keep you informed as to the exact date of the vigil.

"As for you, Anton, let's get those children from Grace Afternoon School into our building. If we can do that, there will be plenty to keep all of us busy for a very long time. Many projects can spring out of it as well.

"We may be a small group, but we are cohesive. We can do great things together. We might not be able to change the world overnight, but we can still make a huge difference in northern Manhattan. We can be an example to the rest of New York City. Let's begin with small projects. They may eventually lead to big results."

"Amen to that," said Sanford Kantor.

The symposium adjourned at 5:30 p.m. We ended the proceedings with a round of handshakes and hugs. From a collection of individual clergy people, we emerged from the symposium as a formidable group.

XVI

New York/Jerusalem
February 12, 2014

After an intense twenty-four-hour symposium at Cold Spring Harbor, I was delighted to return to my community. I promised Father Lorenzo Burgos that I would stop by on Friday afternoon, before erev Shabbat services, to meet with Amelia and her family. Until I had become the spiritual leader of Rodef Tzedek in 2009, I had very little contact with Hispanic people. Although New York was a sanctuary city and I had heard of sanctuary congregations, my life was relatively sheltered in the suburbs of Long Island. I was nervous about my upcoming meeting. Neither my seminary nor my many years in the rabbinate prepared me for such an encounter.

I was in between rabbinic functions. I mingled with the sisterhood in the morning and was awaiting the religious school in the afternoon. I usually led the assembly and visited the various classes as a resource person. It was 2:00 p.m. when my daughter contacted me on Facetime. It was nighttime in Jerusalem.

"Hi, Bracha! What can I do for you?"

"I just called to say hi."

"I suspect that something is on your mind."

"For several weeks, I listened to contradictory visions of Zionism."

"How so?"

"Well, our cousin, Yehudah, argued that the Jews were betrayed by the Balfour Declaration, while the Palestinian professor argued that it was the Arabs who were betrayed. Yehudah argued that the Irgun attacked Deir Yassin in 1948 because the Arabs were blocking the highway to Jerusalem and preventing the city from receiving vital supplies. My professor argued that the Deir Yassin offensive was a massacre in which members of his own family were killed. Some of my classmates are biblical fundamentalists and are sympathetic to *Gush Emunim*. They believe that the land of Canaan was promised by God to the children of Israel, and the borders are specified in the Torah. On the other hand, one of my professors adheres to the multiple authorship of the Tanach and pointed out that the borders of the promised land vary among biblical passages. She argued that just as Zionists have different visions of the boundaries of the Jewish state, so did the authors of the Tanach. The professor of intellectual Zionist history acknowledges that the yearning to return to the promised land has existed since biblical days but seems to believe that Zionism is more about biology and eugenics than about scripture. Many Zionist thinkers, especially Arthur Ruppin, spoke of Judaism as a race more than as a religion. While many of them were indifferent or even hostile to formal Jewish practice, they still quoted the Bible to support their beliefs. And there was the children's literature class. For my project, I collaborated with my Palestinian friend,

Anwar, and we determined that Israeli textbooks portrayed Arabs in a very negative light and perpetuated stereotypes that have been passed down through the generations. Yet as an Israeli, our teacher told us to go where the evidence leads us and even praised our conclusions. Everything seems so contradictory."

"What does all of this tell you about Israel?"

"That it is a schizophrenic country?"

"I think the word that I would use is diverse. Just as it is wrong to stereotype Arabs or any other ethnic group for that matter, it is equally wrong to attach one label to Israel. Israelis are as diverse in their opinions as anybody else."

"Which version of Israel am I supposed to believe?"

"Perhaps there is some truth in all the narratives that you have heard. Israel has provided a Jewish homeland for homeless Jews, particularly targets of anti-Semitism throughout Europe, those who were victims of Russian pogroms, and survivors of the Shoah. On the other hand, the birth of the Jewish State was also known as the Nakba from the Palestinian point of view as many Arabs either fled or were driven from their homes.

"During the world wars, Great Britain's primary agenda was to preserve its interests in the Middle East. The interest of both the Jews and the Arab inhabitants came in second place. They viewed themselves as racially superior to both groups. In performing a balancing act to maintain stability in the Middle East, both groups perceived that they were receiving the short end of the stick. In fact, both groups felt that they were royally screwed!

"Atrocities have taken place on both sides. On the one side, we have stabbings and suicide bombs. On the other side, we have disproportionate use of force, wanton destruction of Arab homes, and clear-cut violation of both civil rights and international law.

"On the one hand, there is no shortage of religious fundamentalism in Israel. On the other hand, there are Israeli academics, like your children's literature teacher and your Bible professor who are engaged in serious scholarship. Unlike the eugenicists and pseudo-scientists of the early twentieth century, they draw their conclusions from careful research. They do not manipulate data and historical facts to buttress their foregone conclusions."

"So I guess I have to live with ambiguity in Israel," replied Bracha.

"Life itself is ambiguous. During your undergraduate semester in Israel, didn't you study some Talmud in *chavruta* [study partnership]?"

"Yes. What are you getting at?"

"The premise of chavruta is that two heads are better than one. No one person has a monopoly on truth. In interpreting sacred text, we need discussion and debate with the other. Study partners bring their different backgrounds and different strengths to the table. In essence, you studied Israeli children's textbooks with Anwar in chavruta. The two of you brought different perspectives to the table.

"When two people study together, there is a greater likelihood of getting to the bottom of a passage of Bible or Talmud. In fact, the Talmud teaches that a dispute for the sake of heaven has a lasting result. What is an example of a dispute for the sake of heaven? Hillel and Shammai. The two sages often disagreed with each other, but they argued out of mutual respect.

"The Talmud is a record of debate and discussion. Our sages were not fundamentalists. Although they accepted the Torah as the word of God and believed in observance of the mitzvot, they weren't Orthodox in the sense that we would understand it today. *Orthodox* is a Greek word meaning 'right thinking.' In the Talmudic world, there was pluralism in terms of interpreting Jewish laws. Minority opinions were respected and recorded. There was also pluralism in terms of Jewish thought. Rabbis had different ideas on such issues as capital punishment, the Messiah, whether or not we should have a fixed date for celebrating the giving of the Torah, or whether or not Torah study should take precedence over earning a living or community action. Considering that disagreements were often substantive and that the Talmud was formulated during contentious times, the discussions were amazingly civil and respectful, far ahead of the historical curve.

"The same principle applied to Torah commentaries. The four major Bible commentators—Rashi, Ibn Ezra, Nachmanides, and Seforno—had radically different approaches to scripture. They were the products of their respective times. Yet objections to Rashi's interpretations by later commentators were based on clear, coherent thinking, not on emotion or a preconceived agenda."

I got up from my desk and took my daughter on a virtual tour of both my Judaic and general library. The Tanach, the Talmud, the Mishneh Torah, the Shulchan Aruch, and my volumes of midrashim were my most precious Judaica possessions. In addition, I also cherished my books on Jewish and general history and on Jewish and general philosophy, as well as my collection of Jewish, American, and world literature. From the days I began rabbinic school, I acquired over one thousand books and am still counting.

"As you can see, Bracha, while my quantity of books is rather modest by rabbinic standards, it is still formidable. One of them is an old edition of *Pirkei Avot*, which was originally owned by my grandfather. As you know, Bracha, it is a section from the Talmud which focuses on Jewish values rather than ritual. My grandfather gave it to a student when he was a Hebrew teacher in Kiev. That student became an elderly Hebrew teacher himself as well as a refusenik. He gave *Pirkei Avot* to me for fear that his apartment would be raided and that this valuable work will be confiscated. I smuggled it out of the former Soviet Union, and it is currently one of my most treasured possessions. Someday, you will inherit it as well as most of this library.

"I like to look at social issues from every conceivable point of view. I like to walk in the shoes of other people and try to see their world view from their perspective. Perhaps the author who assumes the role of the devil's advocate may have an insight that I haven't considered.

"Doubting is good for the human soul. Living with uncertainty is part of the human condition. The basic definition of a fanatic is the person who is 100 percent certain of every issue 100 percent of the time.

"My library is where conflicting ideas such as critical race theory and eugenics coexist. My library is where I can hold the Holy Bible under one arm and Darwin's *Origin of the Species* under the other arm. My library is where the open marketplace of ideas goes to live.

"My library is where social awareness is embraced. My library is a counterculture and the determined enemy of groupthink. My library holds the individual human mind sacrosanct. My library embraces bold viewpoints that challenge the fads and mores of contemporary society. Ralph Waldo Emerson in his famous essay, 'Self-Reliance,' wrote, 'To believe your own thought, to believe that what is true for you in your private heart is true for all…That is genius.'

"That's the beauty of democracy, both in America and Israel. Despite the atrocities and tragedies that have taken place in both countries, past and present, due to bad behavior, there is still vigorous discussion, debate, and national self-criticism. This sort of thing is nonexistent in authoritarian dictatorships.

"Do you remember me telling you about the strip search that took place thirty years ago at the Leningrad airport? I was initially stopped because one of the customs agents found a cassette tape in my belongings, played it, and heard snippets from a Russian television show. When Yuri, the chief customs official, looked at the Hebrew books that I was taking out the country, he went ballistic! He astutely noticed that I didn't come out with the same Hebrew books that I brought into the former Soviet Union. As he was convinced that I distributed Hebrew books to Jewish dissidents, he searched my naked body thoroughly and looked up my *tuchus* [rectum] for possible addresses. My Hebrew books promoted a Jewish worldview, which did not conform to Communist dogma. Original ideas and alternative perspectives are the most lethal weapons that can be launched against totalitarian governments."

"Really, Daddy, you really seem to be on your soapbox today!"

"When I am passionate about something, I have that tendency. But now, my sermon is finished. What I am really trying to say is that you must absorb all the information that you have been given and make your own decisions. And remember, Torah is not confined to books and lectures. Go out into the world. Look at the facts on the ground. You will find Torah in every human activity."

Bracha replied, "As a matter of fact, I am visiting the Knesset tomorrow. I will be attending a hearing on garbage removal in East Jerusalem."

"My point exactly. Even garbage removal has moral implications."

"Indeed, it does. I am looking forward to your visit in a few weeks."

"Mommy and I can hardly wait. I am personally looking forward to visiting the Arab quarter in East Jerusalem and to going on the Breaking the Silence tour."

"You will definitely see facts on the ground, as you call it."

"Have a blessed evening, Bracha. *Lila Tov.*"

"Love you. Lila Tov."

Chapter 7

THE GUARDED GATE

Give me your tired, your poor,
Your huddled masses yearning to breathe free,
The wretched refuse of your teeming shore.
Send these, the homeless, tempest-tossed, to me:
I lift my lamp beside the golden door.

—Emma Lazarus

Wide open and unguarded stand our gates,
And through them presses a wild motley throng—
Men from the Volga and the Tartar steppes,
Featureless figures of the Hoang-Ho,
Malayan, Scythian, Teuton, Kelt, and Slav,
Flying the Old World's poverty and scorn;
These bringing with them unknown gods and rites,
Those, tiger passions, here to stretch their claws.
In street and alley what strange tongues are loud,
Accents of menace alien to our air,
Voices that once the Tower of Babel knew!
O Liberty, white Goddess! Is it well
To leave the gates unguarded?

—Thomas Bailey Aldrich

God gathered the dust of the first human from the four corners of the world-red, black, white, and green. Red is the blood, black is the innards and green for the body. Why from the four corners of the earth? So that if one comes from the east to the west and arrives at the end of his life as he neared departing from the world, it will not be said to him, "This land is not the dust of your body, it's of mine. Go back to where you were created." Rather, every place that a person walks, from there he was created and from there he will return.

—Yalkut Shimoni

Considering that the people during the Second Temple did not perform the sinful acts of idol worship, forbidden sexual relations and bloodshed that were performed in the First Temple, why was the Second Temple destroyed? It was destroyed because that there was baseless hatred during that period. This comes to teach you that the sin of baseless hatred is equivalent to the three severe transgressions: Idol worship, forbidden sexual relations and bloodshed.

—Yoma 9b

I

Jerusalem
February 13, 2014

For many weeks, Bracha absorbed many historical tidbits and was exposed to much theorizing about the Zionist dream. At the

Knesset, she would be exposed to the present-day world and see facts on the ground.

Bracha was not new to the Knesset. She saw it many times from the bus window during her regular commutes to the Edmund J. Safra campus of Hebrew University in Givat Ram. Several weeks ago, she went on a tour of the building.

The three Chagall tapestries impressed her the most. It portrays the Jews in Jerusalem and the Jewish Temple. King David is playing the harp. In the background is the Ark of the Covenant and on the left, the Israeli flag with the Star of David and "Israel" written in Hebrew. The joyful tapestry emphasizes the centrality of Jerusalem throughout Jewish history.

The central tapestry depicts various biblical themes such as the binding of Isaac, Jacob's wrestling with the angel, the exodus from Egypt, the golden calf, and Moses receiving the Ten Commandments. More recent historical events such as pogroms, the burning of homes, and depictions of the Holocaust were also woven into this tapestry. Chagall even included the wandering Jew with a sack on his back.

The right tapestry depicts Isaiah's messianic vision of the future:

> And the wolf shall dwell with the lamb, and the leopard shall lie down with the kid; and the calf and the young lion and the fatling shall graze together; and a little child shall lead them.

This beautiful picture of peace and tranquility and a world without conflict was certainly far removed from reality, thought Bracha.

Bracha and her immediate supervisor, Miriam Saltzman, as well as two dozen other individuals, were ushered into one of the conference rooms. Some of them included several high-ranking officials representing the sanitation department which ultimately operated under the Jerusalem Municipality. The last person to enter was a member of the Knesset, Adi Kohl, who represented the party *Yesh Atid*. She was a rising star in the Israeli political landscape.

Yesh Atid could be translated as "There is a future." Founded by Yair Lapid, it won a surprising 19 of the 120 Knesset seats in the election held on January 22, 2013. Adi Koll was one of the victors. The party's focus was primarily on civil life—education, housing, health, transportation, and policing. It sought equality in education, the reduction of poverty, and the pursuit of better relations between Jews and Palestinians.

Yesh Atid's platform suited the thirty-six-year-old politician's temperament. After receiving her bachelor's degree in law at Hebrew University, she continued her studies at Columbia University where she received her juris doctor's degree. Throughout her life, she considered herself a social activist.

As part of her practical training, Bracha was asked to give a presentation concerning the abysmal state of garbage removal in East Jerusalem. Much fact gathering and preparation went on behind the scenes. Adi Koll was eager to hear what she had to say.

Bracha spoke in almost perfect Hebrew. She began her presentation with statistics: "About 12.5 percent of the streets of Tel Aviv and Haifa were considered very dirty. They contained fifty items of garbage for every hundred meters. Turning to the disparity between East Jerusalem and West Jerusalem, she pointed out that while 37 percent of Jerusalemites live in the east, they received 10 percent of the work of the sanitation employees, 7 percent of the dumpsters, and 6 percent of the garbage disposal routes. As a result, dumpsters were overflowing, and mounds of garbage accumulated in the streets and on the sides of roads and caused a stench.

"The situation was even worse in the neighborhoods on the far side of the separation barrier, where according to the comptroller, the municipality allocated miniscule sums for sanitation. These neighborhoods have also been eliminated from the Environmental Projection Ministry's program to improve the sanitation situation in East Jerusalem.

"Even though Palestinian East Jerusalemites pay taxes and constitute over one-third of the city's population, the Palestinian residents have received only 8 percent to 10 percent of the municipal budget."

Then Bracha really stuck in the knife by quoting another set of statistics compiled by the human rights organization, *B'Tselem*. "Entire Palestinian neighborhoods are not connected to a sewage system and do not have paved roads or sidewalks. Almost 90 percent of the sewage pipes, roads, and sidewalks are found in West Jerusalem. West Jerusalem has one thousand public parks while East Jerusalem has forty-five. West Jerusalem has thirty-four swimming pools while East Jerusalem has three. West Jerusalem has twenty-six libraries while East Jerusalem has two. West Jerusalem has 531 sports facilities while East Jerusalem has thirty-three."

Virtually everyone around Bracha, including the officials from the sanitation department, were aware of the elephant in the room. Her supervisor said weeks before the hearing, "The national policy was determined to maintain a Jewish majority in Jerusalem and, indeed, in all of Israel, at all costs. Jabotinsky's Iron Wall remains in effect to this very day. A two-state solution, although personally advocated by Adi Koll, was not in the cards at the present time. Outright expulsion of the Palestinian population or a mass transfer of Palestinians to Arab lands would cause a major firestorm, both within and outside of Israel, and would be politically costly. However, if poor municipal services could encourage a sizeable population of Palestinians to leave the country, the national agenda could be achieved in a less painful way."

Adi Koll was a smart cookie. She was not at all surprised by Bracha's presentation. She screamed at the officials like a *chaleria*: "How can you people allow East Jerusalem to be covered in *shmutz* [filth]? Most of the residents are hardworking people who pay taxes and who are entitled to live in dignity. Do we expect them to earn their daily bread and raise their children while living in a pigsty?"

Adi Koll reminded the municipal officials that substandard living conditions and poverty go hand in hand. She threw out some statistics of her own by pointing out that 75 percent of East Jerusalemites live below the poverty line, compared with 29 percent of Jews and 52 percent of Arabs in the rest of the country. In East Jerusalem, 81 percent of the children live in poverty. As a woman who promoted equal education for all, she also pointed out the continued disparity between the education of Jewish children and Palestinian children.

She ended her tirade by saying, "How can you so-called leaders sleep at night? How can you live with yourselves?"

Almost no comment from the municipal officials. They were not about to publicly admit that all this nonsense had backing in high places. They looked back at the young fireball from *Yesh Atid* with downcast eyes, almost like Lassie. There was a vague promise to reassess the situation, make some improvements, and get back to Adi Koll at a future meeting. Stonewalling at its finest.

Bracha whispered to Miriam Saltzman, "Do you think that this session is going to make any difference in the long run?"

"Probably not," responded Miriam. "But we are not absolved from continuing to push our cause. I'll tell you something, Bracha. If we continue to tolerate second-class citizenship in a Jewish state, *yesh atid* [there is a future] will degenerate to *ayn atid* [there is no future]."

After the session, Adi Koll walked toward Bracha.

Miriam said, "It seems that you made an impression."

"Why would a member of the Knesset be interested in me?"

"Having contacts with political leaders and forging alliances are important. In the end, Knesset members are public servants. They are paid to serve the people of Israel regardless of their background. Never forget that."

"*Tov Me-od*, Bracha. Very good. I detected an American accent."

"I grew up in New York."

"I lived in New York for a few years. I got my juris doctor at Columbia University. Great school."

"I will be studying law soon. Human rights law."

"*Zeh Yotsei min ha klal*—that's extraordinary! Do you want to practice human rights law in Israel?"

"I think so."

"In Israel, human rights activists are often regarded as malevolent fifth columnists who are out to destroy Israel."

"I am passionate about defending the underdog."

"Israel needs idealists like you. I hope that we can become friends in the future."

While Bracha found it flattering to have gained a new contact, she found the session to be rather depressing. This was not the Israel that she was taught to love back in North America.

II

New York
February 14, 2014

My appointment with Amelia and family was for 4:00 p.m. School would be finished for the day, and I would be able to meet with everyone, including the two daughters who were of school age.

The architecture of the Northern Manhattan Episcopal Church could be best described as Gothic. To enter this rather massive building, I climbed a few outside steps, went through a set of heavy, brown doors, passed through a small foyer which contained various brochures on small tables, and entered the sanctuary.

The cavernous sanctuary was rather dark and contained hundreds of fixed pews. This place must be quite busy on Sunday mornings. Across from the large, elaborate pulpit was the church office. Father Lorenzo Burgos was sitting behind one of the desks. He was speaking in rapid Spanish on his cell phone. When he saw me, he quickly terminated the conversation and gave me his undivided attention. Although we only met for the first time a few days ago, he embraced me and greeted me as a long-lost brother.

"Welcome, Rabbi! I was on the phone with our local congressman."

"Are you on such intimate terms with him that he has your cell phone number and you have his?"

"Of course. We have a Latino congressman and a Latino family in our church. It's a big deal. Having a family in sanctuary has ramifications beyond our local community. Political support from high places is essential."

"Wow!"

"Rabbi, never be afraid to speak your mind to political officials. They are paid to serve us. They are paid to put up with our shit."

"True."

"I suppose you want to speak with Amelia and her children. We have a faithful congregant, Isabel, who spends a lot of time with them. She is practically Amelia's second mother and the children's second grandmother. She will serve as your translator."

"Let's get at it."

*****

Next to the church office was another room. Father Burgos knocked on the door, and we were invited to enter. What was once the church library was converted into a mini suite consisting of a tiny reception area/kitchenette and a very cramped bedroom. The makeshift bedroom consisted of two bunk beds designed for four people as well as closet space.

In the reception room, the entire family was present. Father Burgos first introduced me to my interpreter, Isabel, who greeted me warmly. Afterward, he introduced me to Amelia, who was seated. She was a beautiful woman with long black hair running down her entire back and perhaps the prettiest dark eyes in all of Guatemala. Her daughters, Dulcina and Danita, who stood on each side of her, were beautiful as well. Her son, Dani, who was pleasingly plump, initially hid behind the chair. Feeling claustrophobic from his surroundings and being fearful of strangers in general, he came from behind the chair, stared at me menacingly, and gave out a loud grunt. Amelia gave him a jab in the shoulder, and he moved to the makeshift bedroom.

"Sorry," said Amelia.

"That's okay," I replied. "If I was three years old and had to suddenly leave the comforts of home, I wouldn't be happy either."

Amelia was delighted to meet me but was quite agitated as well. She was trying to deal with her children after they returned from school and to be a good hostess at the same time.

Father Burgos proclaimed, "This is Rabbi Levin. He is my brother."

Amelia responded, "He doesn't look anything like you."

Father Burgos made a remark in Spanish, which made Amelia laugh.

I added in English, which Isabel translated to Spanish, "Brotherhood knows no ethnic boundaries."

Father Burgos, who wore many hats and balanced many balls as the spiritual leader of the church, said, "I'll leave you to it. Let's stay in touch, Rabbi."

*****

Although I had done my homework and knew something about Amelia's background, I invited her to tell her story in her own words and share whatever she believed to be important.

"I grew up in Dolores, Guatemala, not far from the border with Mexico, in a landscape known for Mayan ruins scattered through the deep green forest. But while aesthetically beautiful, the area was desperately poor, with few jobs.

"In 2004, I left Guatemala, travelled to Monterrey, Mexico, and crossed into Texas. I came to America in part because of Guatemala's high crime rate and because I was afraid of the paramilitary group that had been trying unsuccessfully to recruit one of my brothers. These groups do not accept no for an answer. They would readily kill people and those related to them if they did not comply with their demands.

"I was detained at the US-Mexico border in 2004. None of the federal agents gave me a credible fear interview, the first step in the process of applying for asylum. All I received was a nasty cold, a result of the freezing detention center, and an English-language notice to appear in immigration court. I had almost no English, and I was very clueless at the time. Fearing deportation and unaware that I could apply for asylum, I headed north again, first joining my sister in Maryland and then settling in New York. What I did not know was the judge back in Texas issued a deportation order four months after I left for Maryland.

"I held several under-the-table jobs, such as working at a dry cleaner and a factory that manufactured guitar and cello strings. I paid taxes as well.

"In 2012, I was in a car accident, and immigration authorities rediscovered me. I checked in regularly as required while seeking some way to stay in the United States. Then came the famous appointment when I was told to come back with a one-way ticket to Guatemala.

"I had two weeks to decide what I was going to do. My children were growing up safe and happy here. Back in Guatemala, one of my cousins had been murdered. Therefore, returning as a family to Guatemala was out of the question. I did not want to return by myself and leave my children either. Therefore, I fled with Dulcina, Danita, and Dani to this church with the help of the New Sanctuary Coalition, an interfaith group that helps immigrants.

"The move from Long Island happened quickly, in a matter of days. The children and I were uprooting our lives. We packed clothes, toys, and the pet fish. The New Sanctuary Coalition searched for an appropriate church and found this one. They procured sleeping bags and other necessities. They connected us with lawyers as well."

I sat quietly and took everything in and made a few notes. The eldest child, Dulcina, began to warm up to me and contributed to the conversation.

"When we got to the church, we were astonished that the church was kind of big and looked kind of scary. The ladies that worked there, including Isabel, showed us our mini suite. Their concern for us made us happy, but within an hour of our arrival, our father returned to Long Island. In these uncertain times, he wanted to keep his construction job at all costs.

"He said to Danita and me, 'I want the two of you to be brave. Listen to your mother and take care of your little brother. It's tough to leave your comfortable home and to live under these conditions. Try to live as normal a life as possible. Go to school. Do your homework. Get involved in activities after school is finished. It will make the days pass better. In the meantime, we'll find occasions to bring you back to Long Island for some weekends and holidays.'

"After my father spoke, I got emotional and began to cry. My mother told me that I am sensitive by nature. During the first night, we slept on the floor of the bedroom with our sleeping bags. The first days were difficult, and I cried a lot because I missed my dad. I was super sad. I often wished that I was back in Long Island with my dad."

Amelia continued, "In the days and weeks that followed, I and the congregation members transformed the space, installing bunk beds and elevating the library's books, *The Pentagon Papers*, *The Final Speeches of Malcolm X*, to the highest shelves to make room for the family's belongings. Volunteers stockpiled the adjacent reception room with teas and cereals, liters of water and bunches of bananas, a bag of freshly picked red delicious apples and two lone Kohlrabies, a seemingly extraterrestrial variety of cabbage. A neighborhood group organized a system to deliver hot meals every afternoon—tilapia and roasted potatoes, rice and stewed beans and grilled beef, rotisserie chicken, and cooked carrots and hard-boiled eggs. A Salvadoran woman began coming to paint my nails. An older Jewish woman washes the family's laundry. We even get visits from various church groups.

"While everyone had been nice to me and I have found community in my new home, I still long to return to Long Island with my family. During the day when my daughters are in school and Dani is asleep, I will often spend hours looking though old photos of my life before the church.

"I have left the church only a handful of times. Once, I required an emergency root canal. Another time, I slipped out to the church parking lot to feel the winter's first snowfall. I rarely see direct sunlight, and I have never been inside my daughters' new elementary school."

Danita, the more outgoing daughter, chimed in, "There are times when I would like to go to the park and play ball with my mother. But I am always reminded that ICE has its eyes on this church. She could easily be snatched up, be put in detention, and be deported to Guatemala."

Dulcina, the sensitive daughter, said, "I am tired of being paraded before reporters and cameras. I can't understand why ICE is so cruel to my mother. She may be undocumented, but she obeys the law. She paid taxes. Why can't ICE leave our family alone?

"My three-year-old brother has lots of tantrums. He is used to having a large space to play in. He doesn't understand what's taking place or why he must live the way that we do. My brother and sister and I only want to have a normal childhood. It's just not fair!" Tears started rolling down Dulcina's cheeks.

At that moment, Amelia began to get more emotional. She continued, "I believe, I don't know, but I imagine I've been sick psychologically. Being enclosed, I feel like I can't breathe. I feel like I'm not breathing anymore. I want to scream. I want to feel free, to not have a single preoccupation." At that point, Amelia completely burst into tears.

I lightly placed my right hand on Amelia's shoulder to give a modicum of comfort. I responded, "Seeing your family living under these conditions tears me up inside. It brings back traumatic memories. When I visited the former Soviet Union over thirty years ago, I witnessed a mathematician and his family living in poverty for no other reason than they were Jews. I saw the terror in his face as he was hiding a Hebrew book lest he be discovered and arrested. He feared the KGB like you fear ICE. Their two sons, who were poorly nourished, could not go to school for fear of being physically attacked by their schoolmates simply because they were Jews. The Soviet Union was a totalitarian country with a long history of anti-Semitism. In America, we are supposed to be a democracy which embraces diversity. We are supposed to be better than this.

"Back then, there was little that I could do other than distribute gifts from the West and give some encouragement. Here, I can do a lot more."

At that point, Amelia and I completely embraced, and we both shed some tears. I didn't expect her family's plight to conjure up such sad memories and to have the effect that it did on me.

I continued, "I plan to visit you and your children regularly. There are members of my congregation who are eager to provide meals and other types of services. I will be organizing an interfaith vigil in this church on March 8, three weeks from Saturday. It will have a Jewish flavor, but other faith communities will participate as well. When I return to this church, I'll be bringing back all the love from our community that your heart will be able to hold.

"Because I also live in Long Island, I can easily liaise with the children's father and transport various items or people in both directions. I will leave my cell number with Father Burgos. All he needs to do is call me."

While the visit was emotionally draining, it went better than expected. It put me in a warm and fuzzy mood to lead erev Shabbat services two hours later. Amelia and I embraced one more time. The daughters embraced me as well. Even the interpreter, Isabel, gave me a hug. Isabel and I were destined to become powerful allies in the months which lie ahead.

I shook hands once again with Father Burgos as I walked out of the church. "I have a feeling that our paths will cross frequently," I said. "See you on March 8."

"Goodbye, my brother!"

*****

Long Island
February 18 to 19

On a cold Tuesday morning, I was working from home. I was sitting at the computer and composing my sermons for the upcoming Shabbat services. Out of nowhere, my cell phone rang. The unexpected call came from Father Burgos.

"Hello, my brother!"

"Hello. Great to hear from you!"

"Last Friday, Amelia and her children enjoyed your visit. So did Isabel."

"Really. I was very nervous that day. The visit brought back painful memories from one of my visits to the former Soviet Union in the 1980s. I am glad that I was able to hold it together."

"Perhaps that was why you came across as a caring person."

"Thank you."

"We need a favor from you. When is your next visit to the synagogue?"

"Tomorrow morning. However, it's a short day. I plan to take care of a few administrative details and briefly visit with the sisterhood."

"Here is the situation. As you know, it is President's Week and the New York schools are closed. The children are restless, and they are really missing their father. Marcos would love to bring them home for a few days, but he is working long hours at his construction job and, at present, can't spare the huge amount of time that it would take to drive to and from the city to collect them. He rearranged his schedule so that he can take off Thursday through Sunday and spend a long weekend with Dulcina, Danita, and Dani. I am wondering if you could come to my church in the afternoon and bring them to their house in Long Island."

"Wow," I replied. "This is a huge responsibility. I just met the family properly last Friday. I don't count the two rallies that I attended. They are putting their trust in someone who is practically a stranger."

"You are no stranger to us. I trust you 100 percent. Even more important, Amelia trusts you 100 percent."

"I will do it, but under one condition. I want Isabel to come with me. She speaks Spanish. The children are obviously comfortable with her. She is the grandmother type."

Father Burgos chuckled over the phone. "Consider it done," he said.

"Secondly, I will pick them up at 1:00 p.m. This will enable me to get out of New York City well before rush hour. I strongly recommend that the children have lunch before the trip."

"Consider that done as well."

"Thirdly, I am going to make a small detour which hopefully will not take us too far out of the way from our destination. I want to make a brief stop at the Cold Spring Harbor Laboratory Complex. As we just completed our symposium there about a week ago, perhaps you can provide a brief history to Amelia, Dulcina, and Isabel."

"Will do."

"See you tomorrow."

"Peace be with you, my brother."

*****

As promised, I arrived at the Northern Manhattan Episcopal Church promptly at 1:00 p.m. Father Burgos, Amelia, and the passengers were waiting on the top steps of the entrance to the building.

Dulcina, Danita, and Dani gave their final hugs to their mother. Isabel and I helped them load their suitcases in the trunk of my car. The children piled in three abreast in the back seat. Isabel took her place in the passenger side. Before I reentered the car, I said to Father Burgos, "The next time that we meet will probably be the vigil."

Standing with Amelia, who had mixed emotions about being separated from your children for a few days, Father Burgos waved and wished all of us a good trip.

"See you soon, my brother," he said.

*****

I drove north on Ft. Washington Avenue, turned right on 181st, and eventually merged on the Cross Bronx Expressway. Driving from east to west except on Sunday mornings is like maneuvering in a parking lot. However, when travelling eastward at this time of day, the traffic is normally reasonable. We soon crossed the Whitestone Bridge, travelled down the Cross Island, and eventually entered the Grand Central Parkway. In my effort to make everyone feel as comfortable as possible, I explained the route carefully as I went along.

Isabel said, "A brilliant idea to leave at one. The traffic is not bad at all."

I replied, "If we would have left two or three hours later, the situation would have been totally different. There is method to my madness. I am staying on the Grand Central for as long as possible. We won't have to worry about trucks and commercial vehicles, which are forbidden on all parkways."

While Dulcina, Danita, and Dani did not converse with me directly, they exchanged some words in Spanish with Isabel and chattered quite amicably among themselves. Isabel was briefly on her cell phone with their father. He was curious as to where we were. I communicated our current location and our route to Isabel and gave a ballpark figure as to when we would arrive at the house.

The Grand Central eventually turned into the Northern State. Suddenly, a police car with flashing lights was driving perhaps three hundred yards behind me. My heart was pounding. I took special precautions to stay within the speed limit. Although I haven't had to use my brake lights on the highway, I was almost certain that they were in good working order. There were no visible reasons to explain why my car should be pulled over.

"I hope that we are not his target," I blurted out. "I would rather not explain my passenger list."

Fortunately, the police car moved into the faster lane and sped past me. Someone else was being chased, or there was an emergency down the road. What a relief!

We finally arrived at the Cold Spring Harbor Laboratory complex. I parked just outside the Charles Davenport House. I explained to my passengers, "About one hundred years ago, this complex conducted science experiments to explain the differences between White people who have lived in this country for generations and people who immigrated from other parts of the world. The person who directed these experiments and who this modest building is named after, Dr. Charles Davenport, believed that we could understand the makeup of human beings in the same way that we can understand the makeup of corn and racehorses. He believed that just as we can sort out the best racehorses, the best bulls, and the best pigs from the worst racehorses, the worst bulls, and the worst pigs, we can do the same for men and women."

Dulcina asked, "Did Dr. Davenport believe that some races are better than others?"

I replied, "He certainly did. His findings, based on poor science, were used to prevent undesirable immigrants, especially from Asia and Eastern Europe, from entering the country. It led to the Johnson-Reed Act of 1924. Fortunately, all my grandparents got here earlier. One of my grandmothers got here under the wire in 1922. Unfortunately, many Jews attempting to flee from Adolf Hitler were not allowed to seek sanctuary on our shores. Although this law was repealed in 1965, distrust of immigrants has not disappeared, and immigration is a political football to this very day."

"Now I understand better why ICE is so nasty to my mother," Dulcina replied.

"The Cold Spring Harbor Laboratory had abandoned this thinking a long time ago. It attracts scientists and students from all over the world. However, in the early 1900s, Dr. Davenport and his followers felt that they could scientifically prove that everyone travelling in this car was of lesser quality than the White Anglo-Saxon founders of America. He believed that our country should be more populated by real Americans of good stock and less populated by people like us. In short, that's why we are in the mess that we are in today."

"That's terrible!"

I restarted the car, drove out of the complex, headed for the Seaford-Oyster Bay parkway, and proceeded toward the South Shore. I got off on the Sunrise Highway and drove eastward. Within five minutes, I pulled into a residential area and arrived at the address which was given to me by Father Burgos. I parked my car in the driveway of a small high ranch home. The children recognized it immediately and bolted out of the car.

The front door opened, and Marcos walked toward the car. He was tall, dark, and handsome and could easily have become a movie star in another life. He and his beautiful wife make an excellent pair.

Dani raced toward Marcos, and his father scooped him up. The two daughters were not too far behind. They embraced Marcos from both sides. Dulcina shouted, "Papi!" She and Danita burst into tears. Tears were running down Marcos's cheeks as well. After embracing his children, Marcos also embraced Isabel.

Upon witnessing this scene, I was feeling choked up myself. I then opened the trunk of the car, and everyone pulled out their luggage.

I finally spoke up. "I am sure that all you want to spend a lot of quality family time this weekend, so I will be heading home. Does Isabel have a ride back to the station?"

"I will look after her."

"If there is anything else that I can do for you, please let me know."

Marcos replied, "Thank you for my children. When our situation improves, our families should get together one day for a barbecue."

"I would love that. Eating together promotes friendship."

At that point, we shook hands. I gave a quick hug to Dulcina and Danita.

As my passengers made their way into the house with their luggage, I departed for my home in Long Island.

*****

I returned to the synagogue late Friday morning. I normally check in with the main office before going to my study. Sanford Kantor, who was part of our symposium last week, greeted me warmly.

He said, "Earlier this morning, a Latina woman who said that she belonged to the Northern Manhattan Episcopal Church brought this box. She said that the contents are for you."

"What a surprise! Do you know what's in it?"

"That's for you to find out, Rabbi Levin."

I opened the box and found six pupusas, Latin American flatbread filled with cheese and beans. It was one of Amelia's signature dishes.

III

June 23, 2012
West Bank, Israel

After the afternoon session at the Knesset, Bracha returned to her apartment on Rechov Bezalel. As she sat on her living room sofa and closed her eyes, she reflected on a previous occasion when she experienced facts on the ground. The clock ticked backward, twenty months in the past, to June 23, 2012.

*****

Bracha was deeply engaged in field research for her undergraduate honor's thesis. Part of her research involved attending a protest on the West Bank. As it turned out, her sponsoring professor, Dr. Isadore Lamb, was in Israel and attended the rally with her. They boarded one of six buses carrying Israeli activists, international activists, and some crazy American Jews to join Palestinian protestors from all over the West Bank in a small village known as Susya.

Susya was in the South Hebron Hills. Like most Palestinian villages in the area, the residents lived very simple lives. Their homes were shacks or tents, their ovens were caves, and their schools were trailers. These villages were also not connected to the main power grid or water system in the West Bank, although the illegal settlements surrounding them were. And so international aid organizations often provided them with their basic needs. In the case of Susya, an Israeli organization called COMET-ME had raised enough money to provide the village with energy-producing solar panels. The donations came from Germany.

What was this protest all about? On June 7, just two weeks earlier, the Israeli High Court of Justice issued an interim injunction to stop all construction in the village, and subsequently the Israeli Civil Administration issued an all-encompassing demolition order for the fifty-two structures that comprised the village. Included in this draconian order were solar panels, shacks, ovens, schools, and clinics. Imagine, a demolition of an entire village, hundreds of individuals left homeless and lost.

The idea was to march from the current village of Susya, fifty-two structures built on the villages' historical agricultural land, to the old village of Susya, now closed to the original residents after they were expelled in 1986. What was the official reason? Israeli archeologists found remains of an old synagogue in the village. How does that justify turning people out of their homes? What was the real reason? Creeping annexation.

The march was cut short by percussion grenades and stun grenades. Suddenly, the protestors were surrounded by Israeli soldiers and police, dressed in full riot gear, weapons potentially meant for them. Bracha was terrified. When she heard the loud booming sounds, she stopped walking. She heard orders in Arabic, "All of the small children, back to the village!" She saw a jumbled, confused group of children running back toward their homes.

Bracha saw a large cloud overtake the demonstration. Unsure what it was, Bracha started to walk back and found Professor Lamb watching the demonstration from afar. He was standing atop of a rock, so Bracha climbed up to see how he was doing. But the wind was slowly blowing the cloud toward them, and the professor suddenly felt droplets of tear gas in his eyes. Bracha helped him down from the rock and pulled out his water bottle. He splashed some water into his eyes, dried off, and replaced his glasses. He said, "This reminds me of my Vietnam days. That was the first time I got gassed!"

While the protestors were 100 percent nonviolent, the Israeli soldiers had decided to use tear gas anyway. Bracha wondered what next was in store.

Bracha looked around and found two tiny Palestinian girls quietly staring ahead. She asked if they were okay and if they wanted water. They nodded yes. Immediately after they finished sipping from her water bottle, she began to hear percussion grenades again. The girls attached themselves to either side of Bracha and clasped her hands.

"Shh, it's okay," she said. "They're just loud noises. Don't be afraid." She walked with them, slowly, toward the back of the crowd. The activists were running, but if Bracha learned anything about dealing with children, it's to surround them with calm in situations of fear or stress. When they safely arrived at a low area, far behind the demonstration, they sat down and talked. The girls played with Bracha's camera and tried on her glasses. She asked them a little bit about their lives in the village. And suddenly, her role at this protest became very clear. It was to be with the children. Bracha offered several other children water, comfort, and smiles. She was truly a blessing. As they joked in Arabic, she swallowed the sadness of shielding children from the terror of sound grenades only a few yards away. All of this was a far cry from her childhood in North America.

The demonstration continued for about four hours. At one point, the army pointed skunk water nozzles toward the crowd, but it was mostly for intimidation. They never used them. At another point, a tear gas cannister hit an eighteen-year-old demonstrator in the head, and he was rushed to the hospital. He was okay, needing stitches and not much more. And in the end, the protestors turned around, walking back toward the village. Although they were unable to march all the way to the site of original Susya, the ending felt triumphant. No matter the result, there was something amazing about a group of hundreds of Israelis, Palestinians, and a few internationals gathering to join hands for justice. It felt like the best of her community, the potential of what Israel could be. Imagine it: Israeli Jews known universally as human rights activists, pursuers of justice, lovers of humanity. Expressing Judaism as love for one's neighbor, welcoming the stranger, finding the image of God in each human being. Imagine Israel's potential.

IV

New York
February 22, 2014

On February 2014, I was a man on a mission. After having visited the Grace Afternoon School and after my unsuccessful attempt to persuade our licensing committee to rent space to this venerable organization, I took the case to the congregation itself. I passionately addressed the issue from the pulpit two weeks ago and sent a general e-blast to the congregation.

I reminded my congregants that sixty years after the landmark decision, *Brown v. Board of Education of Topeka*, there was still widespread de facto segregation in the United States. I reminded them that the New York City school system was one of the most segregated school systems in the country with 70 percent of African American and Latino students attending schools in which less than 10 percent of the students were White. Wouldn't it make a great statement on the sixtieth anniversary of *Brown v. Board of Education of Topeka* to not only rent our facilities to Grace Afternoon School but to also use it as a springboard for all kinds of interfaith and interethnic programming? Integration is not just about warehousing non-Jews in our building for money. It's more about bringing diverse people together and fostering meaningful interactions.

I reiterated the same points that I made at the licensing committee meetings. I mentioned the potential of converting the synagogue into a community center which would become a beehive of activity seven days a week. The busier a congregation is, the more attractive it is to potential members.

I mentioned new opportunities for intergenerational programming, interfaith social action projects, interfaith interactions among teenagers, and interfaith adult education. I mentioned the possibilities of interfaith Thanksgiving celebrations and other community events hosted by the congregation.

This Shabbat morning, I gave another "fire and brimstone" sermon. I discussed the importance of supporting the family that is currently receiving sanctuary from the North Manhattan Episcopal Church. I pointed out that the current problems in Guatemala, poverty, illiteracy, and gang violence were rooted in American foreign policy. The CIA deposed a democratically elected government to protect the interests of the United Fruit Company and agrarian reform was reversed. From that time onward, the country was plagued by civil wars and political instability. Combined with our broken immigration system, is there any wonder why we have illegal immigrants from Latin America?

As I have done in many past services, I quoted my favorite biblical verses:

> When a stranger sojourns with you in your land, you shall not do him wrong. You shall treat the stranger who sojourns with you as the native among you, and you shall love him as yourself, for you were strangers in the land of Egypt: I am the Lord your God.

While we are a nation of laws and should fix our federal immigration policies, we should not be vilifying and penalizing migrants and refugees. I concluded my message by advertising my Havdalah vigil at the North Manhattan Episcopal Church, which would take place on March 8 at 7:00 p.m., two weeks from today.

Come Monday, this message would also be e-blasted to the greater congregation.

*****

Apparently, neither sermon went down very well with the Shabbat morning attendees. Shortly after I returned to my study, I was visited by our president, Rolf Samuels. The verbal volleyball match was on.

Rolf said, "As you know, I am always direct, so I'll give it to you straight. I just heard lots of complaints. How many times must I advise you to leave politics out of the pulpit? It's the surest way of alienating congregants. I've seen many rabbis being shown the door for openly expressing their political views."

"What was so political about promoting Grace Afternoon School?"

"First of all, members do not want to hear about de facto segregation in the schools or about *Brown v. Board of Education of Topeka*. It's an open sore in this community. Not all members embrace public education and even send their children to specialized schools in other parts of New York City. Secondly, they feel that negotiations with prospective renters shouldn't be made public. They are conducted behind the scenes by competent lay leaders."

This was a load of rubbish. I responded, "Congregants have the perfect right to choose the appropriate schools for their children. But if there is an opportunity to level the playing field a bit and to provide a loving home for children who have fallen through the cracks of public education, why shouldn't we open our doors and offer a helping hand?

"Furthermore, I agree that the pulpit is no place to discuss specific details of synagogue business, but the truth is that the presence of Grace Afternoon School in our building will impact upon the lives of our entire membership. While there would be growing pains, it's a potential game changer. As a spiritual leader, I feel obligated to point out the benefits and to do all that I can to prevent the congregation from shooting itself in the foot."

"Don't get me wrong, Rabbi. I would like the negotiations to succeed myself. Like you, I also see the big picture. I see the financial benefits. However, there is a lot of push back. Whenever you mention Grace Afternoon School, some congregants go ballistic. These congregants are afraid of being crowded out of the activities that they love, such as rummage sales and monthly Shabbat dinners. If the school is in the building on Saturday morning, they fear major disruption."

"Logistics can easily be worked out. There is lots of low-hanging fruit."

"And that leads to today's sermon. You seem to have a tremendous capacity to upset people."

"Guilty as charged. Isn't it the job of the rabbi to disturb the comfortable?"

"The old-timers, for the most part, do not want to hear about the troubles of the world. Many were refugees themselves and do not want to be reminded of their own plights in the 1930s."

"Whether I speak on so-called safe issues or social issues, politics is unavoidable. Ignoring the outside world is not the political statement that I wish to make. What do you think congregants want to hear?"

"They want the rabbi to focus on the Torah portion of the week and to give a learned discourse. You're a smart man. I have seen you do it many times."

"If the Torah doesn't relate to what's going on in the world, why should anyone take it seriously?"

"This is not a social action congregation."

"And yet we call ourselves Congregation Rodef Tzedek, the congregation which pursues justice."

"I know that you are heavily involved with the refugee family at the Northern Manhattan Episcopal Church. I hope that you are not doing anything illegal. After all, we are a nation of laws."

"Don't even get me started on this subject. Nazi Germany considered itself to be a nation of laws when it passed the Nuremburg Race Laws which disenfranchised and denied civil liberties to German Jewry. The former Soviet Union considered itself to be a nation of laws by firing Jewish professionals for applying to leave the country, by creating red tape to apply for exit visas, and by denying Hebrew teachers the use of Hebrew books. This country violated international laws by intervening in the affairs of Latin American countries, including Guatemala, by creating political instability, and by partially manufacturing the refugee crisis at the borders. Our government hypocritically then turned around and clamped down on so-called illegals. While our system is broken and two wrongs don't make a right, I am not comfortable with the term *a nation of laws*. Under these circumstances, it comes across as sanctimonious.

"Yes, I broke laws by smuggling Hebrew books into the former Soviet Union. Regarding Amelia and her children, I won't be stupid, but I'll do whatever is in my power to make their lives a bit easier. Religion, in the end, is much more than what takes place at services. It's about people.

"There is an elephant in the room. What is it?"

"The elephant in the room is the crescendo of people who believe that you are spending too much time with non-Jews. Congregants, old-timers especially, want a pastoral rabbi who looks after his flock, not a community organizer."

I smiled. "Only a music director and accompanist would use the term *crescendo*. In terms of pastoral work, I do my share of life-cycle events, visits, and phone calls. In terms of my work with non-Jews, it was never my preconceived agenda. It fell into my lap because of our non-Jewish occupants and because of what is going on in our neighborhood. To put it in crude terms, non-Jews pay a large portion of our utilities. It behooves us to treat them respectfully, to cooperate with them on projects, and to form a bond so that they stay here for a long time. To put it in more enlightened terms, good relations between all segments of the community is desirable for its own sake."

"You are a stubborn old goat! It's a quality that I admire in you but find frustrating at the same time."

"I'm simply passionate about certain social issues."

"While I admire your grit, you should take heed. I just don't want these tensions to escalate." With that remark, Rolf Samuels left my office.

Rolf was an intense fellow. Such critical words sting. In the end, I felt confident that he will eventually see the synagogue from my point of view.

At my seminary, one of my teachers told me that if the congregation is not ready to run you out of town, you are not a good rabbi. If the congregation succeeds in running you out of town, you are not a good person. Creative tensions are part of congregational life. I have lived with them throughout my career.

I had an appointment with a couple who wanted to be married in June. The appointment was at 3:00 p.m. After having a tuna wrap and a Diet Coke, I attempted to take a nap but fell into a deeper sleep than I expected.

*****

"You're slumbering on the job. If you were working for me, I should have you sacked! Awake!"

I opened my eyes and saw a tall elderly man standing in front of the door to my study. A truly imposing figure! He spoke with an Oxford accent. He must undoubtedly be English.

"Who are you?"

"Henriques is my name. Basil Henriques."

"The gaffer?"

"That's my normal nickname."

"But you died many years ago."

"I beg to differ with you. You care for immigrant children. You encouraged tons of young people to go to Jewish camps and served on faculty as well. You promote the synagogue as a Jewish center. You promote my ideals. As far as you are concerned, I am very much alive."

"Well, gaffer, not everyone embraces my ideas. There has been plenty of negative feedback."

"It's lonely to have ideas which are far ahead of your time. I was a social worker and an international expert on juvenile delinquency. I didn't want to wait until young people entered my office. I was determined to be proactive. I set up youth clubs to get young immigrant children off the streets. I offered wholesome activities. I sought to transform them into valuable citizens of British society. I sought to inculcate *Brittishkeit* even more than *Yiddishkeit*. Some people, I am afraid, referred to me as a Victorian do-gooder."

"Be that as it may, the president of my congregation just busted my chops. He wanted me to stop riling up the congregation on social issues. He urged me to focus more on individual congregants and less on the greater community. I've got a lot of work to do to persuade Rolf that I have the right priorities for the congregation. We are on the cusp of greatness."

"You'll win him over. Someday he will thank you for what you are trying to accomplish. I watched you from the *Olam ha Ba*, the World to Come. I saw the masterful way that you conducted Simone Da Costa's bat mitzvah and how you twinned her with that unfortunate girl in Leningrad."

"If we had served the Settlement Synagogue at the same time, do you think that we would have worked well together?"

"You were a shy bloke and inexperienced but showed promise. Your heart was in the right place. In time, my wife, Rose, and I would have whipped you into shape. But I think that role was performed admirably by Lillian Goldwasser and other senior lay leaders. They did a jolly good job."

"So how do I overcome all of this opposition?"

"You want to start a revolution overnight. You want to take an institution which, for many years, served as a refuge for countless Holocaust survivors who suffered the atrocities of the non-Jew and immediately convert it into an interfaith community center. You must be more judicious.

"I started my Jewish career by establishing a Boy's Club. A Girl's Club, founded by my wife, was the next logical step. I then founded the Settlement Synagogue because I, like you, believed that social service and religion cannot be separated. From there, Bernhard Baron, a tobacco manufacturer and philanthropist, donated £65,000 toward the purchase of a massive building. Within this one-hundred-room structure were an array of organizations which offered social services that catered to people from the cradle to the grave. The Oxford and

St. Georges Settlement, as we called it, represented the evolution of many baby steps along the way.

"You don't have to start a revolution overnight. Touch individual lives. Help save some lost souls. Inspire congregants with the power of Torah. Initiate new programs. Build on your successes. Perhaps the totality of all these endeavors will be the revolution that you seek.

"In my day, if someone crossed me, I would say, 'Over my dead body!' I don't suggest that you follow my example. I do suggest that you believe in yourself. As Shakespeare would have put it, 'To thine own self be true, and it must follow, as the night the day, thou canst not then be false to any man.'

"I must return to the *Olam ha Ba*. I am scheduled for afternoon tea with some of the old boys from the Settlement Synagogue. I'll send your regards to Sam Kaiser. Isaac, I am expecting good things from you. Don't disappoint me."

I replied, "I won't."

Basil Henriques disappeared in a cloud of smoke.

*****

I woke up from my nap. That was quite a dream. I was flattered that the gaffer chose to visit me from the World to Come. I better heed his words.

It was now 2:30 p.m. Time to get ready for my meeting with the prospective bride and groom.

V

Jerusalem
February 24, 2014

Bracha had just finished Professor Yehezkel's class, the Land of Israel in Biblical Sources, and headed toward the Mt. Scopus bus stop. She would board the bus to the Edmund J. Safra campus, have a light dinner in the cafeteria, and head for the National Library. Shaul Mendelbaum was standing at the entrance to the academic building. He appeared to have the "wrath of the gods" expression on his face.

He said, "I was waiting for you. I know that Professor Yehezkel's class finishes at about this time."

Bracha replied, "You haven't been in class for a couple of weeks."

"I dropped the course. I can't possibly sit in a Bible class where the professor denies that the Tanach was literally written by God."

Bracha had no patience for Shaul's narrow-mindedness. "That's your decision. However, I urge you to consider Ben Zoma's statement in *Pirkei Avot*, the Sayings of the Fathers: *Azeihu Chacham Ha-lomaid mi-kol adam*. Who is wise? He who learns from all men."

Shaul's anger intensified. No woman was going to show him up. He said, "There is nothing that I wish to learn from either Professor Yehezkel or from you. I know all about you. You encourage classmates to go on Breaking the Silence tours of the West Bank. You bring your friends to Arab shops in the Arab quarter of Jerusalem and encourage them to buy from Arab vendors. You work as an intern for Ir Amim, a human rights organization which advocates for Arabs. You learn from an *apikores* who embraces multiple authorship of the Torah."

Bracha recognized Shaul for who he was. Despite his black kipah and tzizit, he was a bully. She refused to cower to him and stood her ground. Although he professed to being Orthodox, she had a good Jewish background in her own right and felt that she knew at least as much Torah if not more than he did.

She responded, "You obviously have been stalking me. It's unbecoming of a Jew who believes in Torah-true Judaism."

"If you like Arabs so much, why don't you suck some Arab cock? Or if that isn't enough for you, perhaps you would like to go all the way and fuck an Arab of your choice."

Shaul really crossed the line, yet Bracha kept her composure. She replied, "Your words are disrespectful, misogynist, and downright obnoxious. I guess that when you follow Jewish law, you are much more interested in what goes into your mouth than what comes out of it."

Shaul spit on the ground and laughed disdainfully. "I don't respect you one bit. *Smolanim* [leftists] like you are destroying our country. My family made Aliyah from Boston last year. We live in

Kiryat Arba, near Hebron. While I live in the dorms on weekdays, I go home for Shabbat every Friday and Saturday. I may not have lived in Israel for very long, but I know that we must cope with terrorism and suicide bombs virtually every day of the week. If that isn't bad enough, we are forced to deal with people like you who supposedly fight for human rights but really give comfort to our enemies. You people make me sick."

"You greatly underestimate my knowledge of Israel. I've been here many times, speak both Hebrew and Arabic, studied in the universities, made numerous connections throughout the country on both sides of the West Bank, worked with human rights organizations, and have become familiar with the basic workings of the government. While I also condone terrorism, it is no excuse for violating the civil rights of Arab Israelis and Palestinians. Even Mizrachi Jews do not often get a fair shake."

"God willing, the Messiah will come and build the Third Temple. When that day comes, we will raze the Al Asqa Mosque and kick all the Arab scum out of Israel."

"Do you really think that the Third Temple will give Israel peace?"

"I do."

Bracha realized the futility of attempting to reason with a fanatic. She will never figure out why he enrolled in a university dedicated to free academic inquiry. Yet she persevered. She replied, "Read Jeremiah 7:4. It states, *Al Tivtechu Lachem el Divrei Hasheker Haichal Adonai, Haichal Adonai, Haichal Adonai Haima.* Do not trust in deceitful words, the temple of the Lord, the temple of the Lord, the temple of the Lord are these.' According to the Talmud, the Second Temple was destroyed because of baseless hatred. If there is still baseless hatred, what chance does the Third Temple have avoiding the fate of the Second Temple?"

"The Messiah will defeat all of our enemies and bring eternal peace to Israel."

"Don't hold your breath," Bracha retorted sarcastically. "I prefer to work with my human rights organization. Our job is to give the Messiah a nudge. Through our work, we will create a more equitable society, a precursor to the Messianic Age."

By that time, Shaul went ballistic. He shouted, "This is heresy. *Mavet l'smolanim!* Death to the leftists!"

By this point, Professor Yehezkel had also exited the academic building and caught the last bit of this nasty verbal exchange.

"*Maspik*, Enough," she said. "This is certainly not a *machloket b'shaim shamayim*—a dialogue for the sake of heaven. I suggest that you both cool off. Unless you are prepared to have a more civil conversation, I suggest that you stay away from each other."

Shaul returned sullenly to his dorm. Bracha continued toward the bus stop. Her interaction with Shaul caused her to miss her bus. The next one would leave in twenty minutes.

Bracha experienced an ugly side of Israel, but she was comforted by the fact that her parents will be visiting her in just a few weeks.

VI

New York
March 8, 2014

A mixed multitude entered the Northern Manhattan Episcopal Church to participate in the vigil for Amelia and her family. Both the Washington Heights Community Church and the Church of the Heights, the Latino group currently using our facilities, agreed to participate in the program. They brought a significant number of people with them. In addition, there was a sizable representation from Father Burgos's congregation. Nonaffiliated residents of the local area also showed up. Anton Muharsky brought some of the faculty and high school students from the Grace Afternoon School. Important players in the sanctuary movement, Father Juan Carlos Ruiz, Ravi Ragbir, and of course, Father Burgos supported me as well. There must have been about two hundred souls altogether. However, we were in a large space which had several hundred seats. To counteract the cathedral complex in which people scatter to all parts of a sanctuary, we politely asked our visitors to sit toward the front. Out of this interfaith and interethnic group of people, we created community.

While my stirring of the pot in Congregation Rodef Tzedek created some drama during the past several weeks, it turned out not to be in vain. Many of the younger members turned up at the vigil. I learned that evening that several families were delivering hot meals to Amelia's family on a regular basis. One member was on a committee that established a schedule for people to sleep overnight in the church. Their role was to see to the needs of the family, especially if there was a medical issue, and with a special phone in their possession, to report suspicious activity. Another member, Sarah, was giving Amelia weekly English lessons while her children were away at school. She had three children of her own, the eldest being born in Mexico. All of them had various levels of Spanish fluency and took it upon themselves to engage Amelia's children in fun activities while the vigil was taking place.

Other attendees included Jean Guberman, the curator of our synagogue art exhibitions; our synagogue vice president, Jane Lieberman; and my fellow activist, Sanford Kantor.

With five minutes to go, Fritz Bernstein entered. I was shocked.

I said to him, "Fritz, I am delighted to see you. Are you up to this? You had major heart surgery after our Kristallnacht program. You were in a coma for a few days and in the hospital for two weeks. This must have been quite an ordeal to come here."

"Rabbi, I had to come. My niece drove me here. When I think of this poor family, I remember the ordeal of many of my acquaintances who were on the *St. Louis* and who participated in the voyage of the damned. I must tell my story. Will you allow me to speak?"

"Of course, I will, Fritz. I have a pretty good idea as to where to put you in the program."

"Thank you, Rabbi Levin."

*****

Before the vigil got under way, we distributed booklets which provided all the readings and music lyrics that would be used. The program was intended to be both interactive and easy to follow.

We began the program with a musical number that was familiar to both English and Spanish speakers, "Guantanamera." Although originally a Cuban love song, "Guantanamera" developed Cuban patriotic overtones. In America, it has been used during anti-war demonstrations, union strikes, marches for an overhaul of the US immigration system, and civil rights for immigrants. In keeping with the gravity of this event, additional words were added to the original Spanish lyrics written by Joseiro Fernandez.

The English lyrics speak of an honest man who comes from where the palm tree grows. Before he dies, he wishes to pour out his poetry from his soul. He tends a white rose in July as in January for the sincere friend who gives him his hand. He tends the white rose despite all the cruelty of the world. He wants to cast his lot with the poor people of this earth. He knows of a great pain among the nameless sorrows; the slavery of man is the world's great trouble. He is a good person who wishes to die in dignity, facing the sun. The honest man pouring out his poetry concludes with the words, "I send you my inspiration as big as a furnace doorway. You hear my song, stay with me, Guantanamera!"

With the aid of a keyboard, several guitars, and stringed instruments, the singing was led by the combined choirs of the Washington Heights Community Church and the Church of the Heights. There were both male and female soloists. Robust singing also came from both the English-speaking and the Spanish-speaking component of the congregation. Everyone felt uplifted and super ready for the next parts of the program.

After our opening song, we proceeded to the readings. Pastor Brenda Corbett read a well-known piece written by Langston Hughes:

> What happens to a dream deferred?
> Does it dry up
> Like a raisin in the sun?
> Or fester like a sore—
> And then run?
> Does it stink like rotten meat?
> Or crust and sugar over—

> Like a syrup sweet?
> Maybe it just sags
> like a heavy load.
> Or does it explode?

We continued with a special prayer for refugees. Pastor Lars Munson read the prayer in English, and Pastor Doreen Williams read the Spanish translation.

> Loving God, our journey through life is long and hard. We cannot make this trip alone; we must walk together on the journey. You promised to send us a helper, your Spirit. Help us to see your Spirit in those you send to journey with us. In the refugee family, seeking safety from violence, let us see your Spirit. In the migrant worker, bringing food to our tables, let us see your Spirit. In the asylum-seeker, seeking justice for himself and his family, let us see your Spirit. In the unaccompanied child, traveling in a dangerous world, let us see your Spirit. Teach us to recognize that as we walk with each other, You are present. Teach us to welcome not only the strangers in our midst but the gifts they bring as well: the invitation to conversion, communion, and solidarity. This is the help you have sent: we are not alone. We are together on the journey, and for this we give you thanks. Amen.
>
> Dios Amoroso, nuestro viaje por la vida es largo y duro. No podemos hacer este recorrido solos; debemos caminar juntos durante el viaje. Prometiste enviarnos un ayudante, tu Espíritu. Ayúdanos a ver tu Espíritu en los que envías a viajar con nosotros. En la familia refugiada, que busca seguridad ante la violencia, Déjanos ver tu

Espíritu. En el trabajador migrante, que trae alimento a nuestras mesas, Déjanos vertu Espíritu. En el solicitante de asilo, que busca justicia para sí y su familia, Déjanos ver tu Espíritu En el niño sin compañía, que viaja solo en un mundo peligroso, Déjanos vertu Espíritu Enséñanos a reconocer que cuando caminamos juntos, *Tú estás presente*. Enséñanos a acoger no sólo al forastero entre nosotros sino también los dones que nos trae: las invitaciones a la conversión, la comunión y la solidaridad. Pues esta es la ayuda que has enviado: no estamos solos. Estamos juntos en el camino, y por esto te damos las gracias. Amén.

Following the readings, I made the following remarks:

"For the Jewish people, the upcoming Sabbath will be Shabbat Zachor—the sabbath of remembrance before the festival of Purim. Synagogues throughout the world will read the following passage from Deuteronomy from their respective Torah scrolls: 'Remember what the Amalekites did to you along the way when you came out of Egypt. When you were weary and worn out, they met you on your journey and attacked all who were lagging; they had no fear of God.' We recall a period of our history when our ancestors were strangers in a strange land and faced hostility among the local populations. Today, Amelia's family and many like her are also strangers in a strange land. They do not deserve to be treated with suspicion and hatred as our ancestors were treated in biblical times. They deserve better. Hence, we are holding our vigil this evening. We will now hear from others within our interethnic community."

Several individuals representing different faith organizations offered words of encouragement to Amelia in English or Spanish. Some presented gifts which were either practical household items or various pieces of artwork. Fritz Bernstein—whose family escaped the tyranny of Nazi Germany, received temporary sanctuary in Cuba, and who were eyewitnesses of the fate of the *St. Louis*—offered the keynote remarks:

> My father, who had a distinguished military career during World War I, was arrested on Kristallnacht and sent to Sachsenhausen in November 1938. He was released after suffering many ordeals. There was no doubt in our minds that we had to leave Germany. Although we eventually wanted to settle in America, we had to reside in Cuba until we got our visas. We arrived in Cuba on April 3, 1939. I was not yet thirteen years old.
>
> Because of the kindness that was shown to me by Cuban children at the time, my heart cries out for Dulcina, Danita, and Dani. Cuba was an exotic country, and I had never met a Black person before. I was astonished when some neighborhood children came to play with me. They were equally amazed by my clothing, speech, and manner. Though we couldn't speak a word to one another, we still formed a bond, and I learned from them. I learned how to open a coconut, peel a mango, and how to tell a ripe fig from one that is not.
>
> You cannot imagine how much these black-skinned, Spanish-speaking children meant to me. They were my first real friends. Jews were marginalized in Nazi Germany. I led a lonely, solitary childhood. But in Cuba, friendship transcended language and skin color.

On May 27, just a few weeks after my family's arrival the *St. Louis* arrived in Havana. Cuban officials revoked most of the landing permits. Only a minimal number of passengers were allowed to disembark. Among the passengers were friends of my mother.

Passengers were caught in a squabble between different corrupt factions in Cuba. The Great Depression also extended to this part of the world, and there was fear that Jewish refugees would compete with indigenous Cubans for scarce jobs. In addition, Nazi agents were sent to Cuba to agitate and orchestrate anti-Semitic demonstrations.

On one of those days in which the *St. Louis* was anchored in the harbor, we communicated with our friends by shouting across the water. With so much pressure being exerted by Jewish organizations, we were expecting to welcome them into our home within a few days. That never happened.

Within a week, the *St. Louis* left the harbor. All of you know the rest of the story. It was quite tragic.

At my bar mitzvah which took place in November 1939, I read a passage from the Torah which aptly described our family's story: "And the Lord said unto Abraham, Get you out of your country and from your kindred and from your father's house." Our tradition portrays Abraham as a sterling example of hospitality. Just as he was a stranger in a strange land, so he received strangers in his own home with graciousness. As slaves in Egypt and as refugees from Nazi-controlled Europe, many Jews know what it is like to escape from tyranny and to be refugees. Should we not display the same empathy and compassion to refugees within our own country?

My story had a happy ending. My family arrived in America in the middle of 1940. Should we not do all that we can to provide the same happy ending for Amelia and her three children?

Many heads were nodding after Fritz Bernstein spoke. We then proceeded to the Havdalah ceremony adapted from the siddur, *Gates of Prayer*. Havdalah is a Jewish ceremony in which we say farewell to the Sabbath, welcome the new week, and make a distinction between the holy and the mundane. Although the sanctuary was already dark, the lights were dimmed a bit further, and white glow sticks were distributed to all the attendees. I then filled a wine glass to overflowing, symbolizing the overflow of God's blessings. I lit the long braided blue and white candle and displayed the spice box.

As the cup of wine was raised, the congregation recited together, "Wine gladdens the heart. In our gladness, we see beyond the ugliness and misery which stain our world. Our eyes open to unnoticed grace, blessings till now unseen, and the promise of goodness we can bring to flower. The sweetness of the wine reminds us of our potential to bring sweetness into the world.

"*Ba-ruch ata, A-do-nai E-lo-he-inu Melech ha-o-lam, bo-rei pe-ri ha-ga-fen.*

"Blessed is Adonai our God, Ruler of the universe, Creator of the fruit of the vine."

I then put down the full goblet of wine and held up the spice box.

"The added soul Shabbat confers is leaving now, and these spices will console us as we are saddened by its departure. They remind us that the six days will pass, and Shabbat will return. And their bouquet will make us yearn with thankful hearts for the sweetness of rest, and the fragrance of growing things, for the clean smell of rain-washed earth and the sad innocence of childhood, and for the dream of a world healed of pain, pure and wholesome as on that first

Shabbat, when God, finding His handiwork good, rested from the work of creation.

"*Ba-ruch ata, A-do-nai E-lo-he-inu Melech ha-o-lam, bo-rei mi-nei ve-sa-mim.*"

"Blessed is Adonai our God, Ruler of the universe, Creator of all spices."

I opened the door of the spice box and smelled the cinnamon and clove that was contained within it. I then passed the box onto some of my congregants who were seated in the first few rows. They would see to it that it would be available to all who wished to partake in this ritual.

I then handed the braided candle to Davida Dubinsky, who was attending the vigil with her mother. I told her that the height in which she held the candle would be the height of her future husband. Davida held it way above her head, at least to the six-foot level! Perhaps she will eventually marry a basketball player!

"The rabbis tell us: As night descended at the end of the world's first Sabbath, Adam feared and wept. Then God showed him how to make fire, and by its light and warmth to dispel the darkness and its terrors. Kindling flame is a symbol of our first labor upon the earth.

"Shabbat departs, and the weekday begins as we kindle fire. And we, who dread the night no more, thank God for the flame by which we turn earth's raw stuff into things of use and beauty.

"The holy lights of Havdalah contrasts sharply with the unholy fires that burned Torah scrolls and sacred Jewish books in Nazi Germany, that obliterated my relatives in Tuchin, Poland, and reduced our ancestors to ashes in the extermination camps.

"The candle's double wick reminds us that all qualities are paired. We have the power to create many different fires, some useful, others baneful. Let us be on guard never to let this gift of fire devour human life, sear cities, and scorch fields, or foul the pure air of heaven, obscuring the very skies. Let the fire we kindle be holy. Let it bring light and warmth to all humanity.

"*Ba-ruch ata, A-do-nai E-lo-he-inu Melech ha-o-lam, bo-rei me-o-rei ha-eish.*

"Blessed is Adonai our God, Ruler of the universe, Creator of the light of fire."

At that point, I held my hands up to the candle and gazed at the reflection of the light on my fingernails. As it was now a new week, we could once again create and make use of light for all our purposes.

We continued with responsive readings. The congregation responded with the words in italics.

>Havdalah is not for the close of Shabbat alone; it is for all the days.
>
>Havdalah means separate yourself from the unholy; strive for holiness.
>
>*Havdalah means separate yourself from fraud and exploitation; be fair and honest with all people.*
>
>Havdalah means separate yourself from indifference to the poor and deprived, the sick and the aged; work to ease their despair and their loneliness.
>
>*Havdalah means separate yourself from hatred and violence; promote peace among people and nations.*
>
>May God give us understanding to reject the unholy and to choose the way of holiness.
>
>*May God who separates the holy from the profane inspire us to perform these acts of Havdalah.*
>
>"Ba-ruch ata, A-do-nai E-lo-he-inu Melech ha-o-lam, ha-mav-dil bein ko-desh le-chol, bein or le-cho-shech, bein yom ha-she-vi-I, le-shei-shet ye-mei ha-ma-a-she, Ba-ruch ata, A-do-nai, ha-mav-dil bein ko-desh le-chol.
>
>"Blessed is Adonai our God, Ruler of the universe, who separates sacred from profane, light from darkness, the seventh day of rest from the six days of labor.
>
>"Blessed is Adonai, who separates the sacred from the profane."

At that point, I poured a drop of wine on a small plate and extinguished the candle. I continued with one more prayer.

"The light is gone, and Shabbat with it, but hope illumines the night for us, who are called prisoners of hope. Amid the reality of a world shrouded in deep darkness, our hope is steadfast and our faith sure. There will come a Shabbat without Havdalah, when the glory of Shabbat, its peace, and its love, will endure forever. Herald of that wonderous Shabbat is Elijah, the Prophet, whom now, in hope and trust, we invoke in song."

Our student cantor, Joe Finkelstein, strummed his guitar and led the singing of *Eliyahu hanavi*.

Ei-li-ya-hu ha-na-vi, Elijah the Prophet
Ei-li-ya-hu ha-tish-bi. Elijah the Tishbite
Ei-li-ya-hu, Ei-li-ya-hu, Elijah, Elijah
Ei-li-ya-hu ha-gil-a-di. Elijah, the Giladite
Bi-me-hei-ra ve-ya-mei-nu, ya-vo May he soon in our days come
e-lei-nu; im ma-shi-ach ben David, to us with the messiah of David.
im ma-shi-ach ben David, with the messiah of David.

I then addressed all the attendees. "In a democracy, one person is a lot of people. Every individual is entitled to live in dignity. Amelia and her family are entitled to live in dignity. Every individual in this sanctuary can make a difference by playing his or her part in building a kinder, gentler society.

"And so we conclude our ceremony with the singing of the special composition written by Barry Manilow and performed by him at the Nobel Peace Prize concert in 2010. When he wrote the song, he was inspired by a dream. He believed that every person should speak out and say what's on his or her mind. One solitary voice singing in the darkness often inspires other voices to join in, and there is a gradual crescendo of music. With every note and with every octave sung, hands are joined, and fears are unlocked. By the end, there are many sopranos, altos, tenors, and bases blended in song, and the message of that one solitary voice is proclaimed loud and clear. Social progress often begins with just one original idea, with just one voice!"

Student Cantor Joe Finkelstein began the song as a solo and was soon joined by a quartet from the Washington Heights Community Church. During the last verse, the combined choirs of the Church of the Heights and the Washington Heights Community Church supported the quartet. After the combined choirs completed the song, the entire congregation, using the printed booklets, belted the lyrics out again. At Northern Manhattan Episcopal Church, one voice gradually became two hundred voices!

Father Burgos was particularly moved by the ceremony. In the presence of this diverse congregation, he warmly embraced me and said, "Rabbi, you are truly my brother." Taking notice of the two hundred glow sticks and quoting Matthew 5:14, he continued, "All of you in this sanctuary are the light of the world. A city built on a hill cannot be hidden. Neither do people light a lamp and put it under a bowl. Instead, they put it on its stand, and it gives light to everyone in the house. In the same way, let your light shine before others, that they may see your good deeds and glorify your Father in heaven."

I responded, "*Shavuah Tov.* A good week, everyone. Feel free to take the glow sticks with you. They will help light your way home."

After the ceremony, I embraced Amelia as well as my colleagues, Ravi Ragbir, Juan Carlos, Fritz Bernstein, Pastor Doreen Williams, Pastor Brenda Corbett, Pastor Antonio Vasquez, Anton and Maria Muharsky, and a few assorted worshippers who were moved by the event. For publicity purposes, Student Cantor Joe Finkelstein, Jane Lieberman, Sanford Kantor, and I participated in a photo-op with Amelia. I gave an interview with a local reporter as well. In these challenging times, events like these need all the publicity that they can get.

I left the church on a spiritual high. I felt confident that we can build that city on the hill, both at Congregation Rodef Tzedek and throughout our local area. All it takes is one voice singing in the darkness, and before long, we will create a great community movement dedicated to *tikkun olam*, repairing our broken society. We can begin this process by welcoming Grace Afternoon School into our building.

Chapter 8

ISAAC AND ISHMAEL

> And Abraham said to God, "If only Ishmael might live under your blessing!"
> As for Ishmael, I have heard you: I will surely bless him; I will make him fruitful and will greatly increase his numbers. He will be the father of twelve rulers, and I will make him into a great nation. But my covenant I will establish with Isaac, whom Sarah will bear to you by this time next year."
>
> —Genesis 17:18, 20–21

Sarah saw that the son whom Hagar the Egyptian had borne to Abraham was mocking, and she said to Abraham, "Get rid of that slave woman and her son, for that woman's son will never share in the inheritance with my son Isaac." The matter distressed Abraham greatly because it concerned his son. But God said to him, "Do not be so distressed about the boy and your slave woman. Listen to whatever Sarah tells you, because it is through Isaac that your offspring will be reckoned. I will make the son of the slave into a nation also, because he is your offspring." Early the next morning Abraham took some food and a skin of water and gave them to Hagar. He set them on her shoulders and then

> sent her off with the boy. She went on her way
> and wandered in the Desert of Beersheba.
>
> —Genesis 20:9–14

> Then Abraham breathed his last and died at a good
> old age, an old man and full of years; and he was
> gathered to his people. His sons Isaac and Ishmael
> buried him in the cave of Machpelah near Mamre,
> in the field of Ephron son of Zohar the Hittite.
>
> —Genesis 25:8–9

I

The West Bank
March 27, 2014

Two weeks after the vigil in the Northern Manhattan Episcopal Church, Tova and I embarked upon a whirlwind trip to Italy and Israel. It was a combination of business and pleasure. The first stop was Milan. While Tova attended an international medical conference, I used the city as a home base for various sightseeing tours. It was my first visit on the European continent since my return to North America nearly three decades ago.

In Israel, Tova was scheduled to give medical lectures at both Hebrew University and Haifa University. The lecture circuit presented a golden opportunity for us to reconnect with our Israeli relatives and to visit with Bracha. Knowing that both of us have been to Israel several times and have seen most of the major sights over the years, she prepared a special itinerary for us.

We arrived, just after midday, at Ben Gurion Airport. We were met by Yehudah and Rivkah, and we drove to the house of Rivkah's younger half sister, Shiri, who also lived in Petah Tikvah. There we were greeted by a large entourage of *mishpocheh* (family). We were treated to a feast consisting of matzo ball soup, chicken schnitzel, raison kugel, Israeli salad, and a nice strudel.

It reminded us of a similar gathering a few years ago when we were visiting our son in Israel. Gregory was participating in the Eisendrath International Exchange. It was a program which enabled high school students from reform synagogues to study in the Holy Land for a semester and still meet their academic requirements in North America. This semester just happened to coincide with Gregory's birthday. Tova, Gregory, and I were treated to the same sumptuous meal with the welcomed addition of a birthday cake. Much fuss was made over Gregory.

North American relatives were deeply treasured, especially if they descended from their cousin and Tova's mother, Mashe. If anyone of them were to find themselves in Mashe's home, they would get the same treatment. My mother-in-law would never consider entertaining out-of-town guests with less than two entrees, two starches, two vegetable servings, and two desserts. In all the years that Tova and I were married, I never left her home hungry.

Yehudah eventually transported us to our hotel in Jerusalem. Bracha greeted us in the lobby.

"Hello, sweetheart!" Tova exclaimed as she wrapped her arms tightly around Bracha. "You look well."

I embraced Bracha as well. "Well, Bracha, although we've had several discussions via Facetime, it's good to finally see you in the flesh."

Bracha replied, "Well, Daddy, we'll have much more to discuss after tomorrow's Breaking the Silence tour. Both of you will see a side of Israel that you probably haven't seen before. Some Israeli soldiers will be breaking the silence by discussing those aspects of policing the West Bank that the Israeli government doesn't want the public to hear. At my Jewish High School, such subjects were taboo."

Tova replied, "I'll be honest. I have serious reservations about this tour. It will undoubtedly be biased."

I retorted, "Nobody in Israel is objective about anything, especially when it comes to the Israeli-Palestinian crisis. Over the years, and on many occasions, I have heard the official government position. I want to hear other voices as well. As I have said many times, Bracha, I look at all sides of an issue and even entertain uncomfortable ideas before passing judgment. You can bet on the fact that I will be taking my handy-dandy notebook and pen and will be recording all my observations. I am not afraid to pose awkward questions to the presenters."

Bracha interjected, "Ask all the questions you want. Just be respectful and have an open mind. Did you tell our cousins what we are doing tomorrow?"

"I prefer to keep politics out of all family relationships. As the Shakespearean character Falstaff once said, 'The better part of valor is discretion.'"

Bracha nodded. "Just a reminder. The tour will begin at 8:30 a.m. and conclude by 3:30 p.m. This will give us plenty of time to get to the special Kabbalat service that I will be taking you."

"Sounds good," said Tova.

March 28

Our tour guide was Moshe Goran. During his stint in Hebron, he had the rank of sergeant and knew this area very well. He escorted our group of fifteen people to our first stop, Kahane Park in *Kiryat Arba*. It was named after Rabbi Meir Kahane, who headed the far-right racist *Kach* Party. At the edge of the park was Dr. Baruch Goldstein's grave, overlooking eastern Hebron. Just twenty years ago, on the actual day of Purim, Goldstein entered a room in the Cave of the Patriarchs that was serving as a mosque, wearing "his army uniform with the insignia of rank, creating the image of a reserve officer on active duty." He then opened fire, killing twenty-nine worshipers and wounding more than 125. Eventually, Goldstein was overcome and beaten to death by survivors of the massacre.

The Purim story, which is found in the Book of Esther, is quite bloodthirsty. In the name of self-defense, in addition to the public hanging of the villain Haman and his ten sons, seventy-five thousand Persians were killed as well. Some revisionist scholars even argued that the carnage was less about self-defense and more about Mordecai fulfilling what King Saul failed to do in his lifetime—to annihilate the descendants of Amalek because of his mistreatment of our ancestors when they were wandering the wilderness. Fast forward to 1994, Goldstein's vile deed reenacted part of the Purim story and was perhaps following in the footsteps of Mordecai.

I was disgusted by Baruch Goldstein's tombstone. It provided much more information than simply his name, the date of his birth, and the date of his death. The wording lauded his vile behavior. At the top of the stone were Hebrew acronyms that said: "Here is buried, the Holy, the Physician, Baruch Kappel Goldstein, Blessed be his holy and righteous memory, May the Lord avenge his blood." Farther down the stone were the explicit words, "Gave his life for the nation of Israel, its Torah and its land—Clean of hands and pure of heart." Finally, at the bottom, it mentioned that on the fourteenth of Adar, corresponding with Purim, he was martyred sanctifying the Lord.

While many extremists have made pilgrimages to this burial site, Baruch Goldstein was a mass murderer, not a martyr. He certainly did not have clean hands and a pure heart. His actions did nothing to enhance Torah or the land of Israel. The first stop at his tombstone set the tone for the rest of the tour.

The second stop was a natural continuation of the first stop, the Cave of Machpelah, the Tomb of the Patriarchs. As a rabbinic student, I visited the Cave of Machpelah and once recited the weekday afternoon service there. In biblical days, Abraham negotiated respectfully with the people of the land and paid the price in full to secure a burial spot for his dear wife, Sarah. Acknowledging that he was a stranger in a strange land, he practiced audacious hospitality toward strangers. He shunned tribalism. His vision transcended preoccupation with his family and community. He pleaded the cause of "the righteous pagan" who might go down with the wicked inhabitants of Sodom and Gomorrah. What bitter irony that in the tomb of our patriarch who loved the stranger, a Jewish fanatic committed mass murder against the other.

*****

The remainder of our tour represented the reenactment of the bitter conflict of the descendants of Abraham's sons, Isaac and Ishmael. Sarah demanded that Abraham get rid of the slave woman, Hagar, and her son so that there wouldn't be the faintest possibility of Ishmael sharing the inheritance with Isaac. While Abraham was distressed, he complied. Early the next morning, Abraham took some food and a skin of water and gave them to Hagar. He set them on her shoulders and then sent her off with the boy. The water supply dried up.

In Hebron, the descendants of Ishmael, the Palestinians, were metaphorically cast out into the desert and literally segregated from the descendants of Isaac, the Israelis. Under Moshe Goran's direction, we proceeded to the city center with many abandoned stores lining its main street. It was one of the busiest commercial areas in the West Bank until the start of the 1990s. Security was the magic word that justified all restrictions. Hence, the Israeli army deemed it necessary to close off most of the area to Palestinian movement. What we saw before our eyes was virtually a ghost town.

Moshe pointed out, "To prevent terrorism at all costs, we keep a tight rein on movement in this area. Even ambulances aren't allowed to pass."

"This is outrageous," replied my wife. "Surely, there are medical emergencies."

"Of course, but the soldiers in charge of the roadblocks don't care. On several occasions, I have spoken up, 'You need to let the ambulance through. It's allowed to pass.' The response that I would invariably get is 'No, the permit isn't here. We won't let the driver pass.' Life-and-death decisions like these are always at the discretion of the soldier at the checkpoint and the commander with him."

"I guess the Palestinians have no recourse."

Moshe laughed. "The Palestinians have no one to turn to. Whether or not an ambulance gets through the roadblocks is totally out of their hands. It's just one of those things that happen to Palestinians. Let's move on."

*****

We arrived at Shuhada Street in the Old City of Hebron. Moshe pointed out, "Shuhada Street, lined with small shops whose owners typically lived upstairs, was once among the busiest market streets in this ancient city. But in 1994, in response to Baruch Goldstein's horrific massacre, the Israel Defense Forces began clamping down on Shuhada Street. They welded shut the street-facing doors of all the homes and shops and, by the time of the Second Intifada in 2000, had turned the bustling thoroughfare into a ghost street on which no one was permitted to set foot. No one, that is, who is Palestinian. Israeli Jews and foreign visitors are free to come and go along the road—to snap photos and make their way to Hebron's three Jewish settler outposts, Beit Hadassah, Beit Romano, and Avraham Avinu. But there is nothing to buy, nothing to see, no reason to tarry. The stores are all closed. The few Palestinians who remain have been barred from the street where they live. If they want to enter their homes, they must do so through back doors, which in many cases involves clambering over rooftops."

One of the members of our group, Ruthie, raised the obvious rhetorical question. "A Jewish extremist was responsible for the carnage. Why is it that the Palestinian community is forced to suffer the consequences? This is an obvious case of blaming the victims."

"Many Israelis believe that the very presence of Palestinians provokes settler violence. Remember what took place in Nazi Germany. When Herschel Grynspan learned that his parents, Sendel and Riva, were expelled from Poland, he plotted to assassinate the German diplomat, Ernst vom Rath, at the German embassy in Paris. After the assassination was completed, the German government responded with a November pogrom, commonly referred to as Kristallnacht. There were extensive damages to businesses. Who was blamed? The Jews. They were required to foot the bill for the clean-up."

"How does this policy enhance Israel's security?"

"It makes the powerful statement to the Palestinians that someone is ruling over them. Don't mess with us. We are in charge. On Shuhada Street, there's a checkpoint where the Palestinians can come in and out, where they're checked. My friends would always strip them, not letting them in even though they had entry permits. Even if there wasn't the slightest possibility of bad behavior, they were still given a hard time. The objective was pure humiliation."

Ruthie persisted, "Tell us about the strip searches that took place at this checkpoint."

"Normally, when a Palestinian wishes to enter through any checkpoint, he shows an ID. The general policy is to do a minimal security check and let him in. If he isn't suspect and if he doesn't express intent to harm or, God forbid, do something, then you don't have to strip him. But because they're Arabs, because they're Palestinians, they are automatically considered to be potential troublemakers. When they arrive, there is a competition among the soldiers of who's the most macho and who carries out the most rigorous security check, who aims his weapon and threatens the most, who shouts the most, and who degrades the most people."

"So mistreatment of Palestinians is part of a pissing contest!"

"*Bediuk!* Precisely. If a Palestinian family is bringing children with them, many soldiers strip the father in front of the kids. The kids see everything, always. People are delayed for hours. Eventually, we get on the two-way radio and run the ID number through. By making the family wait for at least two hours at the checkpoint, we add insult to injury."

"The ultimate in humiliation," replied Ruthie.

*****

We left Shuhada Street and walked through the part of Hebron that was occupied by the Jewish settlers. Everywhere we looked, there was graffiti on the walls. The most common inscriptions were *Mavet l'Aravim* (death to the Arabs) and *Mavet l'smolanim* (death to the leftists).

Bracha remarked, "I guess *Mavet l'smolanim* means people like me. I already had an ugly confrontation on Mt. Scopus."

For the benefit of American visitors, there was a large English poster stating, "There is no such entity as a Palestinian people. Send these people back to the Arab countries where they belong."

After the group observed most of the graffiti, Moshe continued his remarks. He wanted to describe a typical house search.

"We entered a Palestinian home at two o'clock in the morning. The father opened the door for us, in his robe, and the mother and grandmother and two little kids woke up too. The father is kicked in front of the kids, and everybody else moved to one corner. The kids were completely terrified. As we moved from room to room, we opened drawers and closets, threw out all the contents, and literally trashed the house. Nothing was put back in its proper place. In the end, the chaos that we created was to no avail. We were at the house for one hour and found absolutely nothing. The soldier that was with me went nuts. Based on the so-called intelligence that he received, he expected to find weapons."

Another person in the group, Jerry, asked, "Was there any communication between the soldiers and the family whose home you searched?"

Moshe answered, "None. That was just the point. You didn't need words. You can just see the faces of the kids. It's obvious that they hate you, they don't want to see you, and they think that you are the enemy. I was wordless. I had nothing to say to them."

*****

We finally came to *Tel Rumeida*, the last stop on our tour. While most of the site's area is used as an agricultural land, it is also the location of a Palestinian neighborhood and an Israeli settlement. Our guide pointed out that this section of Hebron has had a long history of violent relations between the Jewish settlers and the Palestinian population.

Moshe informed us that under Yitzhak Rabin, the Israeli government proposed closing down the settlement at Tel Rumeida after the Cave of the Patriarchs massacre in 1994. Far-right rabbis moved to block evacuation of the settlements by issuing a halachic ruling against removal of settlements in Eretz Israel. Under tremendous pressure, Prime Minister Rabin was forced to back down. The Deir Al Arba'een mosque, where Palestinians who resided in Hebron had prayed until the mid-1990s, was declared a closed military zone and converted into a synagogue, renamed by settlers *Tomb of Ruth and Jesse*, and thenceforth all access to it by Muslims was forbidden ostensibly for security reasons. During the Al-Aqsa Intifada, which took place in 2000 to 2005, the Jewish settlement came under regular fire from Palestinian militants.

Moshe added, "In 2005, violence against Palestinians in Hebron most frequently originated with the settlement at Tel Rumeida. Of the original five hundred Palestinian families who were living there, only fifty had remained after what the prominent Israeli journalist, Gideon Levy, called a reign of terror. Palestinian cars were torched. There were long curfews and restrictions on Palestinian movements in the area. Palestinian families had difficulty sending their children to school like the local Qurtuba [Cordoba] elementary school whose main entrance was sealed with razor wire by the IDF in 2002, and whose students were subject to settler stoning. As a result, according to one testimony, residents in the Palestinian neighborhood were forced to abandon their homes, and a grocery business and a small hospital were forced to close. Palestinian vehicles were forbidden on Tel Rumeida's streets, and Arab residents could only move in the area on foot.

"Let me say a few words about olive trees. While the settlers believed that the olive trees belonged to them, the fact was that these trees were Roman olive trees, here for some two thousand years, and it wasn't the settler's land. So a decree was issued, and we stationed a *Yasam* unit [Israel Police Special Patrol Unit], and the Yasam saw to it that the Palestinian olive harvest took place."

My wife, Tova, asked, "Were there any violent incidents perpetrated by settlers?"

"Although the Yasam made sure that the Palestinians were able to plow their lands and harvest to the very last olive, there was often theft and vandalism which took place overnight. There was one instance in which the vandals hung up a sign, 'Mohammad is a pig.'

"Stone throwing was a much more serious issue. Palestinian children feared the children of Israeli settlers. Not that they did anything to them, but these children would throw stones at them as they passed by. And their parents would say nothing. You could come to Tel Rumeida any day and see this. It had already become the norm."

Bracha spoke up. "I have spent a lot of time in Israel. I have seen this occur in other parts of the country as well."

Moshe continued, "I know the kids' parents teach them to hate Palestinians. They give them perfect legitimization to throw stones and swear at them. All this messes me up. I often can't figure it out what side I should be on. On the one hand, I am a Jewish soldier and am supposed to be loyal to my own kind. I am supposed to be against the Arabs who are my enemies. On the other hand, the settlers' children are clearly in the wrong. One reason why I am stationed in Hebron is because the settlers harass and scare the Palestinians. Many times, I resent my fellow Jews and then feel guilty because I am one of them."

*****

At Tel Rumeida, Moshe Goran arranged for us to enter a small park where we would have a short question and answer period and meet with one of the Palestinian activists. However, our forward movement came to a halt.

"What's going on?" I asked.

"There's some tension brewing between the settlers and the Palestinians in this neighborhood. It happens from time to time. The security forces are trying to calm things down and make sure that it's safe for us to pass."

"I don't like the sound of it," replied Tova.

Bracha moved forward. To her left, she saw a group of settlers who apparently had their noses out of joint. To her right, she saw a group of Palestinians who were equally sullen. No words needed to be exchanged. The body language expressed it all. The settlers and Palestinians were staring each other down.

On the Palestinian side, Bracha recognized familiar faces. She caught sight of Yousef with his wife and two small daughters. It was one of the Palestinian families she interviewed when she was conducting research for her undergraduate honor's thesis.

As she began to address them in Arabic, Tova whispered to me, "Has Bracha lost her mind? This is an explosive situation."

I replied, "At her young age, she is already a seasoned veteran of this part of the world. I am confident that she won't say or do anything stupid."

Bracha spoke calmly but firmly. "*Salaam*, Yousef! It is wonderful seeing you again. You were so kind to invite me to your home during Ramadan and sharing the *iftar* meal with me. You served generous portions of lentil soup, roasted lamb with oriental rice, and a delightful fruit salad consisting of dates and figs. I was able to wash it all down with orange juice. I know that making ends meet in this neighborhood is tough, but I'll always remember how you made me feel like an honored guest."

"Hospitality is our way," said Youssef. "We were honored to have you spend time with us."

Bracha looked in the other direction and found her Russian-born friend from her Hebrew language course, Svetlana Furman. She seamlessly switched from Arabic to Hebrew.

"*Shalom*, Svetlana! Once again, I would like to thank your family for allowing me to spend the Sabbath with you. I enjoyed the raisin challah, the matzo ball soup, the roast chicken and mashed potatoes, and the tea and cakes afterward. Nothing beats lemon tea from a samovar."

Svetlana replied, "It's great seeing you again, Bracha. I was thinking about the class in which you translated a passage of Maimonides from Arabic to Hebrew. I agree with the belief that we must tend to the body as well as the soul. I agree with the belief that we can't truly be religious without *tikkun olam*—repairing the world."

"My dad is with me. He visited refuseniks in the former Soviet Union, smuggled Hebrew books, and brought many gifts with him from England. The persecution of Jews and the blatant anti-Semitic rhetoric that was spewed out by the nationalist group, Pamyat, disturb him to this very day. He and I also believe in *tikkun olam*."

Svetlana's father spoke up. "Bracha, we consider you part of our family. Someday, we would be honored to welcome both your father and you into our house."

Both the group of settlers and the group of Palestinians lowered their heads in embarrassment.

Amos, one of the influential settlers, concluded that this moment wasn't the best time for picking a fight. "Let's go inside and get ready for Shabbos. The hour is getting late."

Moshe's mouth was wide open with astonishment. His training in terms of Israeli-Palestinian relations was the zero-sum game, winner take all. One side, the Israelis, can only win if the other side, the Palestinians, lose. The notion that the children of Isaac and the children of Ishmael can walk away from a senseless confrontation was alien to him.

Moshe whispered, "Your daughter has guts."

With a smile on my face, I replied, "One giant step forward for humanity. One giant step backward for groupthink."

*****

The group entered the small park and sat on the benches. Moshe encouraged us to ask questions.

Ruthie asked the first question. "Based on all the things that you were required to do, how did it make you feel?"

Moshe responded, "Terrible. Hebron is one of the least popular places that Israeli soldiers want to be stationed. You are caught, as you would say in America, between a rock and a hard place. I would occasionally hear soldiers speak disparagingly about the settlers. They would say, 'These shits are the reason we're here in the first place.' We wish they would get out of here already. On the one hand, you are angry at your own people for being here, at the Jews who live here. On the other hand, you also hate the Arabs because they kill your buddies and give you a hard time. In the end, you hate everyone. It's sometimes tough to determine who is the real enemy. It's a schizophrenic existence.

"I once heard the story of an Israeli officer who was very much against Israeli action in Lebanon back in 1982. However, he had very close relationships with his fellow soldiers. He could not walk out on them. Desertion was out of the question. When he got a forty-eight-hour leave, he went home, visited with his family, demonstrated against the war in Tel Aviv, and returned to Lebanon until he was discharged. Many Israeli soldiers embrace contradictions. Any more questions?"

"I have one," I said.

"*B'vakasha*, please."

"Policing a hostile people is difficult business. It seems to me that it requires sensitivity and diplomacy. Surely, Israeli soldiers are not only trained to perform well on the battlefield but also how to treat the Arab population with dignity. It is written thirty-six times in the Torah about loving the stranger for we were strangers in the land of Egypt. If the Bible is such a critical source of Zionist thinking, how can you justify harassment at checkpoints, home invasions, senseless strip searches, and other violations of basic civil rights?"

Moshe cracked a smile. "A good question. Unfortunately, we live in a world where science and technology has far outstripped the development of religious and political institutions. In Israel, we have all sorts of intelligent people. We have economic intelligence, scientific intelligence, medical intelligence, and of course, military intelligence. However, our country, as is the case in many other countries, is lacking in emotional intelligence. Rabbi Levin, were you in your twenties when you received *semicha* [rabbinic ordination]?"

"Yes."

"When you served your first congregation, did you feel that you had the life experiences and interpersonal skills that were necessary to work with difficult congregants?"

"Absolutely not. Looking back on those times, I was almost clueless. I made many blunders. There were many situations which I could have handled much better."

"It's the same thing in the Israeli Army. The army puts men in their twenties with little or no social skills in charge of a hostile population and expects them to function effectively. This is acceptable because security is the bottom line, not public relations.

"The Arab population, in which there is a high rate of unemployment and poverty, already feels humiliated by what they call the Occupation. Instead of displaying empathy, the immense power that many immature soldiers have over human lives goes to their heads. The macho culture of our society encourages them to compete as to who can strike the most fear in the population that they are supposed to control. Manliness and cruelty become synonymous.

"They are also products of an educational system that teaches them to objectify Arabs and to look upon them as the scum of the earth. Finally, as I have mentioned, the settlers who cause much of the problems also pressure the military to take their side in all cases. As a result, you have the civil rights abuses that I described today. It's a recipe for disaster."

After those grim remarks, there were no further questions.

Moshe continued, "Let me introduce you to the Palestinian activist Issa Amro who is based here in Hebron. He is the cofounder of the grassroots group Youth Against Settlements or YAS. Amro advocates the use of nonviolent resistance and civil disobedience to fight the injustices perpetrated against his people. In 2009, he won the One World Media award for the Shooting Back camera project, which he coordinated in Hebron. The project distributed cameras to Palestinians for the purpose of documenting human rights violations by Israeli soldiers and settlers. In 2010, he was declared Human Rights Defender of the Year in Palestine by the Office of the United Nations High Commissioner for Human Rights. Issa, please describe your work before this group."

"I grew up near Shuhada Street in an area which is now closed to Palestinians. I think that my friend, Moshe, filled you in on the background.

"Two years after the start of the Second Intifada, the Israeli Army declared the Palestine Polytechnic University a closed military zone and sealed off its entrances. At the time, I was in the last year of an engineering degree and decided to oppose the closures. With the participation of other students in the university, I organized actions of nonviolent resistance and civil disobedience for half a year. These actions included protests and demonstrations, moving into classrooms, sit-ins, and having lessons in the presence of Israeli soldiers. The campaign was a success, and the university was reopened in June.

"A few words about Youth Against Settlements. This organization is designed to protest the expansion of illegal settlements and to document human rights violations. Here in Tel Rumeida, the group regularly receives groups of local and international activists, observers, and diplomats to teach them about the reality under occupation. The group further aims at educating young Palestinians in nonviolent resistance through nonviolent action, media, and advocacy work.

"Through resilience campaigns, YAS also helps families suffering from settlements and other occupation activities to remain in their homes. As part of the campaign, YAS has built up and maintains the first kindergarten for Palestinian children in Hebron's H2 area, which is predominately Palestinian.

"One of the main flagship campaigns of YAS is its yearly Open Shuhada Street Campaign, which is implemented both in Palestine and internationally. It calls for an end to closures and restrictions enforced on Hebron's main street."

Bracha, who prided herself on being a community organizer, asked Issa Amro to comment on the use of nonviolence.

"Given the intense feelings of rage among my people, nonviolence is a difficult sell. But given the overwhelming might of the Israeli Army, violence is both futile and counterproductive. Why should we commit suicide? It provides bad publicity and supports the stereotype that Arabs are animals and terrorists.

"Instead, we engage in unarmed warfare. We protest by refusing to carry Israeli-issued IDs, by defying curfews, by blocking roads, by planting trees on sites intended for settlement, by tearing down fences, by staging sit-ins, and by inviting mass arrests to fill to breaking point Israeli jails. Such actions require mass participation, mobilizing women, children, and the elderly—the very groups likely to be excluded by armed struggle.

"Violence, giving into rage, is easy. Nonviolence plays the long game. It requires discipline, cooperation, and perseverance. We send a message that we are willing to stand up for ourselves with nothing but our bodies and hearts.

"We draw upon the teachings of both Martin Luther King and Nelson Mandela and have translated some of their works into Arabic.

The American civil rights movement was big on publicity. It used the news media, especially television, to expose violence against African Americans to the public. The Shooting Back camera project follows the same principle.

"How many of you have heard of Bull Connor?"

Most of us raised our hands.

"On May 2, 1963, thousands of children gathered at Sixteenth Street Baptist Church in Birmingham, Alabama, in place of their parents, who, under Alabama law and social oppression, faced harsh penalties such as loss of their jobs and jail time if they protested the racist and unjust segregation laws of Alabama.

"The authorities had no qualms about cracking down on children. In fact, the Commissioner of Public Safety, Bull Connor, ordered the police to use police dogs, high-pressure fire hoses, and batons to stop the demonstrations. He also ordered them to arrest these children if 'deemed' necessary. Despite this harsh treatment, children still participated in the marches. On May 5, protestors marched to the city jail, where many young people were being held and continued practicing their tactics of nonviolent demonstrations.

"Before the Children's March, federal response was limited to balance federal authority and state rights. The Children's March played a pivotal role in ending legal segregation as the media coverage of the event further brought the plight of Southern African Americans to the national stage. After additional measures were taken, President Kennedy could not avoid the issue. On June 11, 1963, he presented his intentions to establish new federal civil rights legislation which would effectively end segregation in Birmingham.

"Just as nonviolent protest forced the American people to face their demons and eventually led to meaningful change, so it is aimed to compel Israelis to reexamine themselves. It forces Israelis to choose what kind of people they are and creates division and dissent among the oppressor population, weakening its resolve."

I pointed out, "Nonviolence has indeed led to civil rights legislation in our country. However, there is still a long way to go before racial discrimination in all of its forms comes to an end."

Issa Amro ended with the statement, "The same applies here, but it's important that we make a beginning."

"Amen," said all of us.

The tour ended. We boarded the bus to return to Jerusalem. There was just enough time to make it to Kabbalat Shabbat services.

*****

Davening (praying) in Jerusalem is beautiful. There is so much variety that a prayerful Jew can easily choose his or her adventure. Even among Orthodox synagogues, which provide services according to the letter of Jewish law, there is a wide range of styles and customs. The worship community that our daughter chose for us was quite unique.

As we entered the sacred space, we saw an orchestra in the round which consisted of a keyboard, a guitar, and an array of string and wind instruments. We were about to observe *Shabbat Hachodesh*, the sabbath which takes place directly before the Hebrew month of *Nisan*. Nisan is significant because it is the month in which *Pesach*, the Jewish festival of freedom, takes place. To prepare the community for Pesach, the Israeli-born rabbi, Shira Barsch, organized a program in which verses of *Shir ha Shirim* (Song of Songs), which is recited during Pesach, are set to music and dance. In addition to the instrumentalists, there was a corps of dancers, including Rabbi Barsch herself. Everything, of course, was egalitarian. The orchestra, the dancers, and of course, the congregation were represented by males, females, and those who identified themselves as LGBTQ.

It was quite the production. The rabbi explained the liturgy as we went along. Noticing that many of those sitting in the congregation were from North America, some explanations took place in English.

Considering the events that took place earlier today, there was bitter irony. We were attuning our souls to celebrating the liberation from human bondage while only a few hours ago, we were witnessing firsthand the oppression of another people. The Haggadah teaches that we should regard ourselves as if we personally came out of Egypt, yet the oppression of Egypt was being inflicted upon others.

Shir ha Shirim can be classified as Jewish erotica. There is much sexual imagery. It is recited at this time of year because it is a metaphor for God's special love for the children of Israel. But sometimes, one must ask, "Does God love the other as well?" Abraham, who purchased the Cave of Machpelah in Hebron, certainly thought so.

After the musical and dance performance, we then turned to the Kabbalat Shabbat service. The opening psalms, the *Lecha Dodi*, *Mizmor Shir L'Yom ha Shabbat* (Psalm 92), and the evening prayers were completed in about twenty minutes. Those who were observing *Yahrzeits*, the anniversary of the death of a loved one, had the opportunity to recite *Kaddish*.

We got a taxi to drive us to the home of another set of cousins who lived just outside the city. These cousins consisted of Shiri's daughter, her husband, and her two adult children, both young women. When Tova, Bracha, and I arrived, we were warmly welcomed and directed to the dining room table. I was given the honor of chanting the *Kiddush*, the prayer over the wine and the sanctity of the Shabbat Day. Tova recited the blessing over bread. We delved into the traditional sumptuous Friday night meal. And so the peace of Shabbat brought a quiet end to a turbulent and eye-opening day.

II

March 29

I woke up early in the morning to attend the 8:00 a.m. Shabbat service at the Central Yeshurun Synagogue in Jerusalem. When I studied in the Holy City many years ago, I would often *daven* there. The cantor at that time, Asher Heinovitz, was blessed with a beautiful tenor voice and rendered the ancient melodies of our tradition in such an uplifting manner. There was always a full house. Although there was now a new cantor, the worship experience continued to set the perfect tone for the rest of the day. It was slightly longer than the typical Shabbat morning service. As it was *Shabbat Hachodesh*, the *baal koreh*, the designated Torah reader chanted from two scrolls. In the first scroll, a passage was read from the middle of Leviticus, *Parshat Tazria*, which focused on skin ailments and other types of plagues. The second scroll, a passage was read from the book of Exodus to get the worshippers ready for Pesach. While last night's Kabbalat Shabbat service, with its emphasis on music and dance, appealed to the emotions, this Shabbat morning service appealed more to the intellect.

I met Tova and Bracha outside the synagogue building, and we proceeded to walk to the Old City. It was the end of March, and the warmth of late morning was not oppressive. Although I recited many words of prayer, the blanket of Shabbat peace covered Western Jerusalem. Not a single business was in operation. Public buses were in hibernation until sunset. The only buildings that were open were synagogues.

Having connected with my Jewish world, I was ready to enter the Muslim world. Bracha led us to the Muslim Quarter, where the bustling stores and boutiques sharply contrasted with the placid city that was just a few hundred yards behind us. Although this was a Jewish state and Jerusalem officially observed the day of rest, Shabbat laws were not imposed upon the Muslim sector of the population.

We entered a large upscale store. It was filled with expensive, finely crafted furniture and artwork. Bracha introduced Tova and me to Omar, the owner of the store. As I shook hands with him, he warmly greeted Bracha in Arabic like an old familiar friend.

"*Salaam,* Bracha. Wonderful to see you again. Thank you for introducing me to your parents."

I responded, "Bracha appears to be well-known in this store."

"Bracha owns the store!"

"How so?"

Bracha replied, "I bring my friends from Hebrew University all the time and drum up some additional business."

Tova entered the conversation. "Can they afford the merchandise?"

"Probably not. But when their parents come to visit them, they take a very serious look at all the items. I encourage my friends to shop at other Arab-owned stores as well."

"This shop seems to be doing very well for itself."

"Omar also offers online services and ships the merchandise to other countries as well."

Bracha then said to Omar, "I will have to cut short this visit. I want to show my parents lots of other things today."

"You are always welcome here. I hope that your parents enjoy the rest of their trip."

*****

We came to a small outdoor restaurant where we enjoyed *mansaf*. Mansaf is a traditional Jordanian dish made of lamb cooked in a sauce of fermented dried yogurt and served with rice. In the background, we heard what I believed to be the Muslim call to prayer.

Bracha explained, "The Arabic word was *adhan*. It means 'to listen.' The ritual serves as a general statement of shared belief and faith for Muslims, as well as an alert that prayers are about to begin inside the mosque. A second call, known as *iqama*, then summons Muslims to line up for the beginning of the prayers.

"The *muezzin* is a position of honor within the mosque. He is considered a servant of the mosque, selected for his good character and clear, loud voice. As he recites the *adhan*, the *muezzin* usually faces the Kaaba in Mecca. The institution of the *muezzin* position is a long-standing tradition, dating back to the time of Muhammad."

After lunch, we browsed through a few boutiques and then boarded the 218 bus at the local bus station. Our next destination would be Ramallah.

During the bus ride, I noticed heaps of garbage along the way. Sanitation services in the West Bank often left much to be desired.

Bracha whispered to me, "I reported this problem at the Knesset just a few weeks ago. Adi Koll, representing the Yesh Atid party, raised a real stink. Obviously, no progress has been made."

To my knowledge, virtually all the passengers were Palestinians. As I looked upon them and pondered, I did not see terrorists or troublemakers. I did not see backward savages, as portrayed by the earliest Zionists. I saw run-of-the-mill people who were going about their daily business of making a living, struggling to make ends meet, educating their children, and trying to lead decent and peaceful lives. My observations, I am sure, would also apply to most Israelis. Politicians from both the Israeli and Palestinian sides create conflicts. Extremists from both sides incite violence. Maybe, someday, there will be a groundswell of ordinary middle-of-the-road Israelis and Palestinians who will say, "Enough!" On the bus, I felt tension in the air. This tense and often violent status quo cannot continue indefinitely.

Upon arrival, we noticed impressive buildings and an array of swanky stores. Stereotypes of Arab backwardness and dirtiness were instantly exploded. Bracha directed Tova and me to an upscale coffee shop, Star and Bucks. It faced Ramallah's famous Al-Manara Square. The interior was very modern, in fact, more inviting than many of the local Starbucks that I have frequented.

Like the owner of the East Jerusalem store, the proprietor of this coffee shop, Salman, greeted Bracha as an old chum. He was tall, handsome, and rather youthful. A man in his early thirties.

"Salman, I want you to meet my parents."

"Pleased to meet you," replied Tova.

"Any friend of Bracha is a friend of mine. Any family member of Bracha is part of my family. Please order coffee and pastries. It will be on the house."

Not wishing to take advantage of the generosity of Bracha's friend, who was probably working hard to keep this place afloat, I replied, "Your generosity and hospitality are most appreciated, but if you don't mind, we would prefer to pay the price in full."

Salman smiled.

"As you wish," Salman replied. "The final bill will be ₪20 to ₪30. What's ₪20 to ₪30 between me and you?"

We received generous portions and impeccable service.

During our midafternoon snack, Bracha commented, "I get here about once a month. Do you remember my speaking to you about

Anwar? When we were planning our Israeli Children's Literature project, we chose this coffee shop among many others."

When we were finished and I settled my bill, Bracha thanked Salmon. After walking a few more blocks, we returned to the local bus station and boarded the return trip to East Jerusalem.

Toward the end of the trip, two Israeli soldiers boarded the bus. One, I recall, had a very stern face and wore very academic-looking eyeglasses. They checked identification. The incident compelled me to recall a train ride from Luxembourg to West Berlin that I made with classmates from university. The East German officials boarded the train and demanded to see our passports. They were most vigilant in preventing escapees to the free sector of divided Germany. Fortunately, there were no incidents.

When we returned to East Jerusalem, we left the Old City. Shabbat had ended. Commercial life returned to West Jerusalem. We saw two cabs in front of us. Without warning, Bracha got into a rather loud conversation with an Israeli cab driver.

She told us, "This man is rude and disrespectful. We are going in the other cab."

The driver noticed that we were entering the taxi, which was being driven by an Arab. He went ballistic and kicked the tire of his car. In this country, few people have problems expressing their thoughts!"

As we drove through the streets of Jerusalem, Bracha instantly switched to Arabic and engaged the driver in conversation.

The driver, who was rather elderly and had a white beard, smiled. He had a twinkle in his eye. By deliberately choosing to address him in his own language, Bracha displayed great respect for his culture. Our sage, Ben Zoma, once taught that a person who is honored gives honor to others. How much the more so does this apply to honoring the other!

We arrived at the door of an apartment building. We were scheduled to have motzei Shabbat dinner in Jerusalem with yet other Israeli cousins.

III

March 30

Bracha called for me at the hotel at 9:00 a.m. Tova was already en route to the Hadassah University Hospital on Mt. Scopus. Once again, she was giving a lecture on neutropenia, a similar presentation that she had made in St. Petersburg.

"Bracha, I would like to stop for a moment at the nearest Bank Leumi. I would like to cash a $100 traveler's check."

"You use traveler's checks in 2014! Really, Daddy!"

Within five minutes, we arrived at the bank. As usual, I was carrying a briefcase with my handy-dandy notebook and pen. While I approached the teller, my briefcase was standing a few feet away from me. In the time that it took for my traveler's check to be cashed, several people were standing around the briefcase, gesticulating with their fingers and jumping up and down.

Realizing that the cause for all the commotion was my carelessness, I snatched up the briefcase and quickly opened and closed it to calm everyone down. My face blushed with embarrassment. I timidly uttered the word *slicha*, pardon me, and got out of the bank as quickly as possible.

Bracha folded her arms in exasperation and said, "Really, Daddy. This was not one of your smartest moves."

"Agreed."

We moved on to the office of the human rights organization, Ir Amim. Bracha introduced me to her fellow field workers and one of the lawyers who offered pro bono services to the organization. We were received with smiles. She was equally at home in both this office and in Omar's store in East Jerusalem or at Star and Bucks in Ramallah. Whether it be an Israeli milieu or a Palestinian milieu or some combination of the two, she never appeared to lose a step.

Bracha then took me to the office of Miriam Saltzman, her supervisor. She pointed out to me that this was a very busy office.

"The four main areas of concern," she said, "were the political issues of Jerusalem, urban planning, settlements and parks, and the separation barrier. Bracha probably told you about her recent presentation about garbage removal in the Knesset."

"She did indeed. She's a smart young woman. She takes after her mother."

"You should be very proud of her. A native English speaker who is also fluent in Hebrew and Arabic and who can translate documents across the three languages is worth his or her weight in gold. In addition, she is passionate about our mission and thorough in all her work. Adi Koll was impressed with her at the Knesset, and frankly, so am I."

"That was a paid political announcement," replied Bracha.

Everyone laughed.

Although I had been a congregational rabbi for many years, it was easy to get wrapped up in the daily nitty-gritty of pastoral work and administration. Congregational life was often tribal. We have often become immersed in the toys of religion rather than in the real things of religion that matter. At Ir Amim, religious principles were put into practice. There was real commitment to repairing the world.

I responded, "We're separated by the Atlantic Ocean and Mediterranean Sea, but all of us are doing God's work. You work for civil rights and address social issues in Jerusalem while I work for civil rights and address social issues in North America. I feel energized by what I see here."

Miriam responded, "All I can say is that Israel needs an *ashet chayil*, a woman of valor, like your daughter. I hope that she will consider coming back after she completes her law degree. As for you, I wish you much success in your own endeavors in New York."

*****

Bracha and I boarded a cab and made our way to a café. As we entered, Bracha waved merrily to the staff and even some of the regular customers. It soon became obvious that this was yet another establishment in which Bracha Levin was a household name.

"This café is one of the hangout places for *smolanim*. It's a great place to have deep conversations with like-minded people."

"Sounds good to me."

"What were your impressions of the Breaking the Silence tour and our visit to the West Bank?"

"I think of a passage in Genesis. When God promised that Sarah will bear a son and that an everlasting covenant will be established with him and his descendants, Abraham responded, 'If only Ishmael might live under your blessing!' God reassured Abraham that Ishmael will surely be blessed. He will be fruitful and will greatly increase his numbers. He will be the father of twelve rulers and will become a great nation.

"Isaac and Ishmael both had value in Abraham's eyes. Just as there were twelve tribes of Israel, so twelve rulers descended from Ishmael. The moment in which Hagar and Ishmael were cast away into the desert was the beginning of second-class citizenship for the descendants of Ishmael.

"Fast-forward Jewish history. When the Jews first settled in Palestine at the beginning of the twentieth century, there was a real possibility of peaceful Jewish-Arab coexistence. Both Jews and Arabs had skill sets that were mutually beneficial. There was significant interaction. The early settlers purchased land from the local inhabitants. There was extensive use of Arab labor.

"I believed that you learned in one of your classes that organic nationalism, borrowed from Central European thought, was the prevailing ideology of the early Zionist thinkers. The racial stereotypes that the European populations had of Jews were projected upon the local population. The nationalist impulse dictated that Jewish labor was central to the success of the *Yishuv*. Many Arabs lost their jobs and became marginalized. Relationships began to go south.

"The turning point was the Balfour Declaration. Both the Zionists and the Arabs felt that they got a raw deal. As you also probably learned, the Arabs were promised a state of their own if they rebelled against the Ottoman Empire. Instead, Britain and France carved out spheres of influence from Arab lands in the secret Sykes-Picot treaty. The subsequent promise of a Jewish homeland in the Balfour Declaration was the last straw. It meant the establishment of a Jewish state as a proxy for British imperialism. As far as the Jews were concerned, the Balfour Declaration was partially motivated by a desire to keep European Jewish immigrants out of Britain and a desire to garnish the support of world Jewry during World War I. The subsequent White Paper, which emphasized homeland over state and which took Transjordan off the table, was looked upon as a betrayal. And so what we have today and what I briefly saw on Friday were the results of bad decisions made many decades ago. In short, the chickens came to roost."

Nothing that I said was particularly new to Bracha. Yet she posed the question, "So how do we get out of this hell of a mess?"

"Israel has detractors from both ends of the political spectrum and at points in between. The early church fathers argued that the fall of the Second Temple and the loss of national sovereignty in 70 CE was divine punishment for the crucifixion of Jesus Christ. Indeed, the Vatican did not recognize the State of Israel until 1993.

"For the anti-Semitic far right, anti-Zionism is simply the latest frontier of anti-Semitism. During the Spanish Inquisition, Jews were persecuted because of their religion. In Nazi Germany, Jews were denied civil rights and eventually exterminated because they were then believed to be an inferior race incapable of redemption. Today, when Jews want to live in a country of their own in which there would no longer be religious or racial persecution, anti-Semitism extends to the belief that not only are Jews unwelcomed in the countries that they currently reside, neither do they have any right to become a separate nation and to determine their own destiny. It's a classic catch-22!

"I am certainly aware of the BDS movement—boycott, divestment, sanctions. Yet it puzzles me why Israel's presence in the West Bank should get special attention from *smolanim* in Israel and from progressives elsewhere. Ethnic cleansing and racist policies have taken place throughout the world. Even our country is not immune from it."

"Do many wrongs make a right?"

"Of course not. The oppression of one group of people by another group of people is an international problem that can't easily be fixed through economic measures. Nations, including America and Israel, must look into their very souls. It's not enough for leaders and citizens to consider specific policies and laws but also the ideological underpinnings that propagate policies and laws."

"Wishful thinking," Bracha replied.

"Let me give you my theory as to why I think Israel is singled out for BDS. I'll begin with a story."

"You tell plenty of them from the pulpit."

"The British prime minister visited the president of the United States in the White House. He noticed that there were five white telephones and one red telephone.

"The prime minister asked, 'What do you use the red telephone for?'

"The president replied, 'It's a hotline to God.'

"The prime minister asked, 'How much does it cost?'

"The president replied, 'It costs $10,000!'

"The prime minister proceeded to pay the $10,000 and used the red telephone to speak to God.

"A couple of weeks later, the British prime minister visited the Israeli prime minister. He noticed that there were five white telephones and one red telephone.

"The British prime minister asked, 'What do you use the red telephone for?'

"The Israeli prime minister replied, 'It's a hotline to God.'

"The British prime minister asked, 'How much does it cost?'

"The Israeli prime minister replied, 'It costs ₪10.'

"The British prime minister exclaimed, 'What, ₪10! In the United States, it cost me ten thousand dollars!'

"The Israeli Prime minister replied, 'In Israel, it's a local call.'"

Bracha chuckled.

"I think that the world holds Israel up to a higher standard because in that country, people are supposedly closer to God and should behave better. Israel is the land where the holy people of the Bible lived.

"The only problem is that the so-called holy people of the Bible weren't so holy. Rebecca conspired with Jacob to steal Isaac's blessing, which was designated for Esau. As great a leader as Moses was, God chastised him for referring to the children of Israel as rebels and for misleading them into thinking that he could bring forth water from a rock through magic. The judge, Samson, was a cowboy who was motivated by his personal needs than by the welfare of his community. King David couldn't keep it in his pants and had Bathsheba's husband sent to the front lines of war so that he could have her for himself.

"Solomon built the First Temple by levying heavy taxes, especially in terms of labor. Deuteronomy issued a prohibition against multiplying gold, silver, and wives. Solomon violated that prohibition several centuries later. Did God have a crystal ball to predict Solomon's behavior? No, the passage was probably recorded by someone who lived after the time of Solomon to warn of the consequences of Solomon's policies."

"You sound like my Bible professor at Hebrew University. She also embraced the documentary hypothesis," Bracha remarked.

"When Rehoboam assumed power after Solomon's death, he was a youngster with zero maturity and zero emotional intelligence. Because he refused to lighten the tax burdens, there was rebellion, and the kingdom became divided.

"When Naboth refused to sell his vineyard to King Ahab, trumped up charges of treason were levelled against him, and he was executed. King Ahab confiscated the vineyards anyway. In fact, much of the ancient monarchy was governed by greed, corruption, and bloodshed.

"And for that matter, the holy people of America that we were taught to venerate in school were not so holy either. George Washington and Thomas Jefferson owned slaves. Andrew Jackson presided over the removal of Indian tribes. Abraham Lincoln, who signed the Emancipation Proclamation, certainly did not believe in the equality of African Americans. Theodore Roosevelt and Woodrow Wilson espoused the superiority of the Caucasian race. Although Wilson formulated the fourteen points of peace after World War I, he also screened the pro Ku Klux Klan movie *The Birth of a Nation* in the White House and openly praised it. Indeed, he sought to make the world safe for democracy, but was far less willing to make America safe for African American people."

Bracha then posed the question, "Does that mean that Israel should be given a pass for its bad behavior?"

"Absolutely not. I see it this way, Bracha. Israel has been around for almost seventy-six years. It was founded mostly by people with no Western democratic background. They drew upon the nationalistic models and racial theories in their home countries. A few were even attracted to Italian-style fascism.

"While political coalitions are complicated in the Knesset, while religious parties have disproportionate influence on government policy, and while oppression and second-class citizenship is justified in the name of security, it's amazing that there is a working parliamentary system in place. Transfer of power is often chaotic but has never come about through a military coup or a national uprising. As imperfect as the Israeli political system appears to be, it is a freer society than just about every other country in the Middle East.

"While there is plenty of inequality, discrimination, and violation of civil rights, Israel has also opened its doors to persecuted and dislocated Jews, Holocaust survivors, former refuseniks and prisoners of conscience, Ethiopians, and refugees in other parts of the world. Many of them arrived broken in body and spirit, but Israel utilized much of its resources to absorb them into their society.

"On the other hand, look at our country. We have been around for almost 238 years. While the Declaration of Independence, which declared that all men are created equal, was written in 1776, the Emancipation Proclamation freeing slaves in the rebellious states did not take place until ninety years later. *Brown v. Board of Education* was not handed down by the Supreme Court until 1954. Segregation was not outlawed until the mid-1960s. The Voting Rights Act, which gives all American citizens equal right to the ballot box, regardless of race, creed, or color, did not become the law of the land until 1965. Even today, we still have virulent racism, mass incarceration, anti-Semitism, anti-immigrant sentiment, and downright xenophobia. What is our excuse? What kind of a role model are we for younger, less developed democracies? Our country must get its own house in order as well.

"There is still a lot of room for the maturation of Israel's political process. Organic nationalism has characterized Zionism from the beginning. It must eventually evolve into liberal democracy where preoccupation with security must give way to more inclusive human rights and more widespread participation in government."

"This is precisely my point," replied Bracha. "In a Jewish state, the distinction between church and state is blurred. It's totally different from the American political system. As we both know, the theocracies of the biblical monarchy were abysmal failures. Rulers put God in the service of accumulating power.

"Israel is designed, first and foremost, to promote Judaism. There is much concern about maintaining a Jewish majority. Doesn't this lead to second-class citizenship for non-Jews, particularly Arabs? Wouldn't it be better if we had a one-state solution which is jointly run by Jews, Christians, and Arabs?"

"That would be nice. However, given the mood of the country, I am not so sure that it's workable at this time. At present, the Israeli government hasn't done a consistent job of following the commandment of loving the stranger. Given what I have seen in the last two days, what I have read, and what I have heard, I can't imagine that commandment being followed by a potential non-Jewish majority either. It certainly wouldn't be a repetition of the Golden Age of Spain. I feel that the two-state solution is probably more realistic. Much in Israeli society would have to change before the model that you suggest could be implemented.

"I don't believe that a Jewish state is intrinsically evil. I often wonder why a small country, which approximates the area of New Jersey, provokes so much acrimony. Given my experiences as a rabbi in the Diaspora, there is a need for a place in the sun where Jews can determine their own destiny.

"In northern Manhattan, I once attended a forum which addressed the uptick in anti-Semitic incidents in the New York area. Jewish leaders sat down with non-Jewish local leaders. The non-Jewish leaders promised us greater protection and more extensive Holocaust education in the public schools.

"I have spent a fair amount of time in the local precinct. I cultivated good relationships with those in charge of public affairs. I often arranged special police coverage for Jewish holidays and for special interfaith events at the synagogue. I once spoke at a police force roll call and ended with the phrase, 'Let's be careful out there.' In short, I felt like a court Jew.

"Dr. Ruth Westheimer, who spoke at one of our community functions, came up to two officers and said, 'If you protect the rabbi and me at the next public event, I promise you a lifetime of good sex!'"

Bracha laughed. "So what happened afterward?"

"We never had a single anti-Semitic incident at our synagogue!

"The point that I am making is that Jewish security in the Diaspora, even in America, depends upon the generosity of non-Jewish police and non-Jewish officials. This is not the case in Israel."

"That's all very well, but as you admit yourself, Israeli Jews look after their security to the point that it trumps everything else."

"In the ideal Jewish state, Jewish values would govern interpersonal relationships and the relationship between the individual and the state. They would consider all who reside in Israel as being created in God's image and would implement these values through liberal, democratic institutions."

"From your mouth to God's ears. I am dreading Yom Ha'atzmaut, Israel Independence Day. While it's a big deal around here, it's often an occasion for rightwing nationalists to parade and strut through Arab neighborhoods. It's a shitshow. Given the violation of human rights, what is the purpose of celebrating Israel Independence Day?" Given the oppression of minorities in America, what is the point of celebrating the Fourth of July?"

I replied, "In both cases, we are celebrating an ideal. In America, our Founding Fathers who formulated the Declaration of Independence affirmed that all men are created equal and are endowed with the unalienable rights of life, liberty, and the pursuit of happiness. While we have a long way to go to achieve this goal in our society, we must never lose sight of that goal altogether.

"The same thing applies in Israel. As a rabbi, I have never advocated circling the wagons and offering unconditional support for specific government policies. However, I am not prepared to write Israel off and discard her in the dustbin of Jewish history.

"The founders of the Jewish state in its Declaration of Independence affirmed freedom, justice, and peace as envisaged by the prophets of Israel.

They affirmed their commitment to complete equality for all inhabitants irrespective of religion, race, or sex, along with freedom of religion, conscience, language, education, and culture. The Declaration must remind Israelis that they can be better than what they are. Instead of being a holiday of vulgar jingoism, Israel Independence Day should remind Israelis of how short they have fallen from the lofty principles of their founders and encourage them to perform national *teshuvah* [repentance].

"I like Martin Luther King's comparison of the American Declaration of Independence to a promissory note which promises people of all colors the basic human rights endowed by our Creator. He pointed out that America has defaulted on this promissory note insofar as her citizens of color are concerned. The bad check has come back marked 'insufficient funds.' On every Fourth of July and on every Israel Independence Day, American and Israeli citizens alike must be made to realize that they hold the promissory note of equality, freedom, and the right to live in dignity. Will ethnic and religious minorities be able to finally cash the check, or will it come back insufficient funds? That is the challenge of 2014 and beyond. I am an optimist. While there are political problems on both sides of the Atlantic, I am not prepared to bet against either America or Israel."

Tova completed her lecture and met Bracha and I at the hotel. Bracha had personal commitments and would remain in Jerusalem for the rest of Sunday and Monday. Tova and I collected our bags, made our way to the station, and boarded a train to Haifa. We were met by other cousins, Avigdor and Beila, who invited us to dine with them and to stay at their home.

IV

Haifa
March 31

After breakfast, Tova left for Haifa University to give her lectures. I believe that today she was focusing on non-Hodgkin's lymphoma. Avigdor slipped out for a couple of hours to collect groceries. Beila and I remained in the apartment.

Beila took out an old DVD of the film *Sabra*, also known as *Pioneers of Israel*, and offered to show it to me. I was most curious about the depiction of early Zionism in the cinema and accepted Beila's offer. In 1933, it was produced by the great Polish Jewish director Alexander Ford. The film told the story of a group of Jewish immigrants who arrived in Palestine at the beginning of the twentieth century and who were determined to establish a Jewish settlement based upon communal life. It expanded into a polemic work about Jewish-Arab tension, the classical conflict between Occident and Orient.

In *Sabra,* the pioneers bought a piece of land from an Arab sheik and settled close to an Arab village. Although initially welcomed, the enthusiastic young pioneers soon found themselves the victims of Arab irrationality, being blamed for a drought presumably caused by their pioneer witchcraft. The hardships of the idealistic newcomers on a waterless soil were now exacerbated by Arab hostility. Misled by the exploitive sheik who oppressed his own people, the Arabs attacked the Zionist settlers just when the latter found water. The bloodthirsty Arabs, as portrayed by the film, ceased their destruction when they learned that it was the sheik himself who had closed the Arab well. This discovery about the true nature of the greedy Arab leader as opposed to the generous Zionists was blessed by a happy down rush of water, leading to acceptance by the Arabs and to peace and harmony.[1]

Three themes struck me. It represented the newly emerging Jew in Eretz Israel. Incorporating the anti-Semitic rhetoric which pointed to the racial inferiority of Jews to Europeans, the *sabra* hero was portrayed in "Aryan terms" as healthy, tanned, often with blond hair and blue eyes. He was the antithesis to the Diaspora Jew who was weak, sickly, and pale. He was cleansed of all "Jewish" inferiority complexes. In Hebrew, *sabra* literally referred to the cactus plant, common in the area, thorny on the outside and sweet on the inside. Similarly, the portrayal of the Jewish male as confident, proud, and brave, with a mask of cynical toughness in language and manner, as with the *sabra* plant, concealed great sensitivity and tenderness.[2] Regarding the conflict with Arabs, and later in the post-Holocaust context, the robust sabra was portrayed as someone who fights back and resists victimization, who refuses to go like a "sheep to the slaughter." The superior sabra, in effect, rises above the historical inferiority of his Diaspora ancestors.[3]

The narrative, in general, represented a projection unto Arabs, as the new Goyim, the experience of Jews in Europe with the old Goyim (Christians). The Arab accusation against the Jewish immigrants, unjustifiably blamed for bewitching the water, is reminiscent of similar accusations in Europe as during the black plague.[4]

Thirdly, one couldn't help but notice the sharp contrast drawn between the Hebrew settlement and the Arab village. Regarding the Arab village, the film showed primitive people at work while the sheik simply observed. It portrayed an oriental version of feudalism which characterized Europe during the Middle Ages. On the other hand, the settlement was egalitarian, productive, and unified.[5] It conveyed the classic Zionist narrative that the settlers came to a primitive land, devoid of civilization, and made the desert bloom. This narrative incorporated the redeeming of the wasteland and its restoration to fertility, the construction of a new society and the civilizing of the "primitive Arabs."

I understood perfectly why Beila liked the film and was eager to show it to me. A great Zionist propaganda film. That's exactly what Alexander Ford was commissioned to create. I posed the question, "How was this film received back in the day?"

She responded, "The leaders of the Zionist movement received it quite favorably. As for the British under the mandate, not so much. They perceived it as anti-Arab, which it was. As they were trying to keep the peace in Palestine, they felt that a film like that would aggravate Jewish-Arab tensions."

I offered an observation and raised another question. "When the Arabs were getting ready to attack the Jewish settlers, they engaged in a war dance around the fire, raised their swords, proclaimed *Jihad,* and cried, 'Death to the infidels.' It seems to me that they were portrayed like American Indians. Do you really compare Arabs to American Indians?"

"Many Israelis love American Westerns. As far as I am concerned, both Arabs and Indians are primitive savages. Vladimir Jabotinsky based his philosophy of Zionism on how Indian tribes were dealt with in America during the mid-nineteenth century."

"I would have been happier if the film portrayed Arabs as people rather than as stereotypes or as cardboard characters."

"If you lived in this country in 1948 or 1967 or 1973, you would probably think differently. Our survival was precarious. Most Americans have never experienced the inside of a bomb shelter like we have.

"I am aware that the Israeli historian Benny Morris believed that our leaders overestimated the war capabilities of our country in 1948, but that's all hindsight. When a group of Arab states threaten to exterminate your people, there is no choice but to take them seriously. Our determination and self-discipline were the difference between life and death."

As I attempted to empathize with Beila, I realized that her feelings were real, and I did not wish to dispute them. However, I did say, "I am trying to walk in your shoes. As a university student, I was studying in Luxembourg in 1973. When I saw images of the Yom Kippur War projected on Luxembourg TV and had difficulty making out all the commentary in rapid French, I was terrified. I am sure that it wasn't anywhere near what you felt at the time."

"That's absolutely true."

I raised one more question. "The dispute over water as portrayed in the film disturbed me. If the Arabs hadn't come to realize the sheik for who he was, and if there wasn't a gush of water that was shared by all, the film would have ended very badly."

"Water is a valuable and often scarce commodity in the Middle East. The theme of finding water is prevalent in many Israeli films. In the mid-1960s, Israelis and Arabs clashed over water issues. Israel completed its National Water Carrier project, which siphoned water from the Sea of Galilee in 1964. This was unacceptable to the Arab League, who argued that Israel's prosperity was a threat to the entire Arab nation. The Arab states decided to deprive Israel of 35 percent of the National Water Carrier capacity by a diversion of the Jordan River headwaters to the Yarmouk River. A major escalation took place in 1964 when Israel declared it would regard the diversion project as an infringement on its sovereign rights.

"Other clashes took place. The Arab countries eventually abandoned their project. Control of water resources and Israeli military attacks against the diversion effort were considered among the factors which led to the Six-Day War."

I responded, "Water disputes go back to the days of the Bible. Abraham complained to Abimelech about a well of water that Abimelech's servants had seized. But Abimelech said, 'I don't know who has done this. You did not tell me, and I heard about it only today.' So Abraham brought sheep and cattle and gave them to Abimelech, and the two men made a treaty. Abraham set apart seven ewe lambs from the flock, and Abimelech asked Abraham, 'What is the meaning of these seven ewe lambs you have set apart by themselves?' He replied, 'Accept these seven lambs from my hand as a witness that I dug this well.' So that place was called Beersheba, because the two men swore an oath there.

"Abraham was a model of a wise and hardworking person who conducted his business openly and made fair use of appropriate legal protections. In the business of shepherding, access to water was essential. Abraham could not have continued to provide for his animals, workers, and family without it. The fact of Abraham's protection of water rights was therefore important, as well as well as the method by which he secured those rights. While Abraham was determined to protect what was his, he negotiated and settled the dispute with directness and fairness. He respected the leader with whom he had the water dispute. Would that Abraham's example be followed in the twenty-first century."

"The realities of life are totally different than they were in Abraham's time," Beila pointed out. "Abraham had a negotiating partner. Israelis do not. I see no resolution to the Palestinian-Israel conflict. We will fight each other until both sides get tired or until the Palestinians realize that resistance is futile and finally capitulate."

Although I struggled mightily to be a good listener and to avoid judgment, I found myself becoming sermonic. I retorted, "If Israelis like American television and cinema, as you say, let me throw another example at you. In the television series *Star Trek*, a warrior whose face was white on the left side and black on the right side fought against another warrior whose face was black on the left side and white on the right side. They represented two separate nations and continued their conflict on the USS Enterprise. The commander of the ship, Captain James Kirk, chastised the two adversaries and asked rhetorically, 'Is this your last battlefield?' I would pose the same question to the leaders of both Israel and the Palestinians. 'Is this your last battlefield?'

"The two opponents were beamed down to their home planet, which was converted to rubble. Totally oblivious to the consequences of the conflict between their two nations, they continued their struggle, probably to the end of time.

"A crew member asked Captain Kirk, 'Do you suppose that the two men had more than their hate?'

"Kirk responded, 'Yes, but that's all they have left.'

"Jews and Muslims had much positive interaction over the centuries. There was the Golden Age of Spain. Maimonides wrote his famous *Guide for the Perplexed* in Arabic. Is hate all that is left?"

Beila concluded the conversation by simply saying: "We both have strong opinions. We will have to agree to disagree. Jews have done that throughout the ages."

*****

It was midafternoon in Haifa. I hopped into a cab and headed to the apartment of Reuven and Gnessy Zelin, two former refuseniks who I had visited thirty years ago in the former Soviet Union.

Reuven ran the underground ulpan, defied the Soviet authorities, and ended up in a gulag, a labor camp. When I visited them for the second time in 1984, Soviet Jewry was in a very sorry state. They finally realized their dream of settling in the Jewish homeland. I was eager to celebrate with them. However, would Reuven and Gnessy recognize me after thirty years?

When I arrived at the apartment complex, Reuven buzzed me in through the main door. I climbed a flight of stairs, and the door of his apartment swung open. We immediately embraced. He was still tall and well built, but obviously aged over thirty years.

"Reuven, *shalom aleichem!*" (Peace unto you!)

"Isaac, *aleichem shalom!*" (Unto you, peace!)

"Do you recognize me after all this time?"

"Of course, I do. You put on some weight since our last meeting."

"Just a few pounds. That's exactly the comment that I received from Luba Murzhenko when she walked into my synagogue."

"Do you know Luba?"

"Yes. We first met in Kiev. As you know, she and her late husband, Alexey, settled in New York."

"You remember the infamous Leningrad Trials. Alexey was a great man. He can surely be termed a righteous gentile."

Reuven showed me around their spacious apartment. Their living room, which contained a balcony, had a panoramic view of the Mediterranean Ocean. There was no comparison between their current residence and the bleak rooms that they occupied behind the Iron Curtain. He finally directed me to the dining room table.

"Isaac, do you remember my wife, Gnessy?"

"Of course," I responded as Gnessy and I embraced. "Great to see you again, Gnessy."

As she brought in the tea and the coffee cake, we continued our conversation.

"Now that you are living in the land flowing with milk and honey, what are you doing with yourself? Do you have projects?"

"I still run an ulpan in the apartment. I teach mostly Russian immigrants and children of Russian immigrants. I still use the Hebrew grammar book that you managed to smuggle into Leningrad."

"So you have done well for yourself. During the two times that left you in Leningrad, you were totally dejected. You said, 'There is no hope.'"

"I was simply being realistic."

"Then I invited you to look to the Urals which were to the east of you. I said, *'Esa Einai el heharim, mei ayin yavo ezri. Ezri me-im Ha Shem, oseh shamayim v'aretz.* [I lift my eyes toward the mountains, from where does my help come. My help comes from God who makes heaven and earth.]' I predicted that someday, you and I will be sipping Russian tea from a samovar in your Haifa terrace apartment."

"You're a prophet!"

"Look at you now! Congratulations!"

"In the former Soviet Union, our enemy was the KGB. Now it's the Arabs."

Gnessy added, "I won't even enter the same municipal pool as these people. So dirty!"

I responded, "How can you say that? Anti-Semitism was part of Russian culture for centuries. As you know, Pamyat and other extreme Russian nationalists have often used racist diatribes against Russian Jews. Why do you wish to use similar rhetoric against Arabs? Palestinians have also suffered human rights abuses. Just as refuseniks were fired from important jobs and deprived of the means to make a living, so draconian measures have prevented many Palestinians from making a living. Shouldn't we as Jews have compassion?"

Gnessy said curtly, "I have no compassion for these people."

"Why should Arabs be the enemy? You are living quite comfortably in Haifa."

Reuven reentered the conversation and came to the defense of his wife. "In Leningrad, you remember what I once told you. Your world in America was different from our world in the Soviet Union. You lived in a free society while we did not. You were like Martians to us."

"I remember."

"You must understand the situation from my point of view. For months, I languished in the labor camp. Although I had high blood pressure, my diets were salty. The keepers of the labor camp could care less. Food was rationed. Conditions were often unsanitary. We were limited as to how many times we were allowed to urinate. It was an elaborate form of torture.

"Prisoners could work up to fourteen hours a day. Many engaged in hard physical labor in the most extreme climates, such as cutting down trees or mining. Those who mined coal or copper often suffered painful and fatal lung diseases. Political prisoners, such as me, often received harsher treatment than the others. Beatings were commonplace.

"Many prisoners broke down after this type of incarceration. What kept me going during the months that I spent in the labor camp was the belief and the hope that I will someday settle in the Jewish homeland with my family. The dream of *eretz Yisrael* kept me alive! My dream has finally been realized. Now that Gnessy and I are finally here, I will be damned if Arab terrorists or even a potential Arab majority of the population take my country away from me. For me, the first principle is the security of the Jewish state. Gnessy and I, as well as many other former Russian Jews, consistently vote for *Likud*.

"Shall the civil rights of individuals be sacrificed on the altar of security?

"The life of the individual has died. History has killed it. Identity politics is the new reality. People want to belong to a group. Zionism is posited on the concept of the state being greater than the sum of its individual citizens. Without Jewish nationalism, we would have been devoured whole by Russian totalitarianism long ago. In Israel, Jewish nationalism will keep us strong and disciplined and help us to stand up against our enemies."

I argued, "And yet the freedom of the individual to make choices is the prerequisite of living a life of Torah. God did not want to create automatons. The Soviet Union assaulted freedom of religion. The KGB raided your home, confiscated your books, forced you to organize an underground ulpan, and put you in prison. And let me point out that religious rights have also been assaulted in America."

"How so?" asked Reuven quizzically.

"Many years ago, I was a prison chaplain. I was required to conduct weekly Shabbat services and seders for the three levels of security within the same prison complex, for three prisoners in minimum security, for five prisoners in medium security, and for six prisoners in maximum security. No one had the opportunity to pray in a minyan [minimum of ten people for worship], and yet transferring all prisoners to maximum security for services was very doable and, in fact, very easy."

"What did you do?"

"With my full support, the Jewish inmates sued the Department of Corrections. We were defended by a Catholic lawyer. The magistrate listening to the case was African American. A Jewish lawyer was defending the Department of Corrections."

"A Jewish lawyer defending our oppressors. Jewish Kapos! We know their kind during World War II. Who won?"

"The Jewish congregation. The case was ultimately decided by three judges appointed by President Ronald Reagan!"

"Amazing!"

"We know what it's like to be deprived of civil rights in Europe, the former Soviet Union, and even in America. In Israel, the shoe is on the other foot. While I detest terrorism as much as anybody else, the Israeli government is not entitled to create an inferior class of people."

"What of the issue of security?"

"With the building of the separation barrier, with the use of checkpoints, with the building of illegal settlements which are designed to establish facts on the ground and to preclude a final peace settlement, with the use of detention, deportation, and torture, with depriving many Palestinians with the means of making a living, is Israel any more secure as a nation?

"Israel has invested huge funds in security. It accounts for 16 percent of the budget and 9 percent of the Gross National Product. Think about the millions of dollars that have been used to policing the occupied territories. This money obviously could be invested differently, certainly in social services.

"I would argue that the preoccupation with security at the expense of civil rights has made Israel less secure. We give oxygen to the anger of a population who lives without hope. Only yesterday, Israelis went nuts in a bank because my briefcase was more than two feet away from me. I believe that there is a great deal of trauma in this country. The Torah teaches that perpetual national insecurity is the penalty for nonfulfillment of the commandments. Deuteronomy states that the Lord shall smite us with madness and blindness and astonishment of heart. We shall grope at noonday, as the blind gropes in darkness.[6] In modern Israel, however, insecurity does not come directly from God. It is self-inflicted on a national scale.

"What does psychological insecurity look like in 2014? Professor Daniel Bar Tal, a visiting scholar at the Steinhardt Social Research Institute at Brandeis University, wrote that a prolonged experience of fear makes people over sensitive to threatening cues, causes over estimation of dangers and threats, and increases expectations of dangers and threats. Fear leads to adherence to old patterns of thinking, avoidance of risk, uncertainty, and novel situations, and prevents openness to new ideas. Fear manifests itself by initiating a confrontation, even when there is little or nothing to be achieved by doing so.[7]

"Franklin Delano Roosevelt put it more succinctly. He said, 'The only thing we have to fear is fear itself—nameless, unreasoning, unjustified terror which paralyzes needed efforts to convert retreat into advance.' Fear freezes this country in the status quo and prevents leaders from trying something new and perhaps venturing into the unknown. Fear forces Israeli soldiers to pick fights with Palestinian civilians for no good reason. And so we have a dangerous state of paralysis. On the one hand, the Palestinians clamor for greater self-determination of their destiny. On the other hand, the obsession with security has caused Israeli leaders to stick to their party platforms and has prevented them from thinking outside the box and taking risks. The result is a festering and dangerous stalemate that could escalate at any time."

I stopped my diatribe abruptly, and the apartment became silent. I really went over the top this time! Reacting to negative comments about Arabs, I ignored the pain that Reuven and Gnessy experienced in the former Soviet Union and Reuven's harrowing incarceration in the Gulag. Instead, I found myself getting on my soapbox and pontificating to them as if I was thundering from the pulpit.

I suddenly felt ashamed of myself. During Israel's War of Independence, I wasn't born yet. I didn't reside in Israel during the Six-Day War or during the Yom Kippur War. Normally, I embrace all family members regardless of their politics. Yet I presumptuously lectured on Israeli-Palestinian relations to a member of our Israeli family who experienced all the existential threats to Israel from 1948 to the present.

I never lived in a totalitarian state, nor was I harassed by the KGB and sent to a Gulag. What right do I have to become holier-than-thou and to criticize people who have opened their home to me? Thirty years ago, I judged Reuven's friend Gennady Grishin in Leningrad for refusing to serve in the Russian army and risking another jail sentence. In 2014, I was judging Reuven and Gnessy in Haifa. Why didn't I learn my lesson thirty years ago?

While I normally deplore extreme views and strive to walk in the shoes of others, my own intolerance and my personal agenda have gotten the better of me more times than I wish to admit. When that happens, empathy gives way to self-righteousness. A sanctimonious attitude never brings about a meeting of the minds but almost always destroys relationships. This is what I felt was happening to my relationship with Reuven and Gnessy. As it says in Proverbs, "He that troubles his own house shall inherit the wind: and the fool shall be servant to the wise in heart."

I tried to do damage control. After the long silence, I said meekly to Reuven, "Forgive me, I had no right to talk to you and Gnessy in such an aggressive way. While I am passionate about many things, the last thing that I want to do is to hurt the people that I care about."

Reuven replied, "Apology accepted. I am also zealous in my beliefs. Jews love to argue. The expression is 'Two Jews, three opinions.'"

To which I responded, "Verbal arguments are preferable to arguments with fists or guns, but words can also be hurtful as well. For my harsh words, I am sincerely sorry."

He shrugged his shoulders and reiterated Beila's views, which I heard earlier this morning. "This is an intractable conflict. There is no hope for a lasting solution."

"Thirty years ago, you said the same thing about your fate in Leningrad. When we stop hoping, we stop living."

"And what is the basis for your hope?"

"There is no other choice. Either war must be finished, or humanity will be finished. I am no political scientist, but this is what I think. Georg Hegel believed that history always progressed to higher and higher stages. As a good Lutheran, he believed that Christianity was the highest stage of human life. Karl Marx embraced the same concept but contended that communism brought on by the dictatorship of the proletariat was the highest stage. From there, the state would wither away, and material goods would be distributed to each according to his or her needs. You know how well that theory succeeded in the Soviet Union and elsewhere. The journalist John Sullivan, who coined the term *manifest destiny*, believed that democracy was the highest stage of civilization. However, it was restricted to White people only, especially males. I am not so sure that I believe in this concept of history, but if I did, I would say that the highest level of human civilization is a nonracial society where different ethnic groups would no longer have the need or inclination to have a greater piece of the pie than other ethnic groups.

"The prophets Isaiah and Micah were on the right track. They envisaged a world in which God will judge between the nations and will settle disputes for many peoples. They will beat their swords into plowshares and their spears into pruning hooks. Nation will not take up sword against nation, nor will they train for war anymore. Everyone will sit under their own vine and under their own fig tree, and no one will make them afraid, for the Lord Almighty has spoken."

"I am responding to you as your friend, Isaac. What you are saying is a pipe dream! In this fatal optimism, you might be one of the last remnants of the liberal world order. However, in some of your methodology, you are a fighter for our people. In terms of your Jewish heart, it's in the right place. When you return to New York, please kiss Luba for me."

And so my long-awaited reunion with a former refusenik and prisoner of conscience came to an unspectacular end. In the years which followed, my connection with Reuben and Gnessy fizzled out, and I would never meet in person with them ever again.

V

April 1

From the psychological point of view, travelling to Israel was like travelling to the former Soviet Union. There were peaks and valleys. The peaks were experiencing Shabbat in the synagogue and with my family. The valleys were the sights and experiences in the West Bank and my recent conversations with Beila and Reuven. Although living in a free society where Jews are no longer the pawns of non-Jewish rulers or victims of state-sponsored anti-Semitism, they still live with insecurity. Beila was traumatized by the ashes of her Uncle Berl in Tuchin and the unholy flames of war in 1948, 1967, and 1973. Reuven was traumatized by harassment from the KGB and his incarceration in a Soviet labor camp. Both were haunted by ghosts from the past.

I clamored to see another side of Israel, and so I persuaded my wife and daughter to take a tour of the Leo Baeck Educational Center. Beila's daughter, Yael, who vehemently rejected Orthodox Judaism and who was searching for an alternative, was also curious and offered to be our chauffer.

While driving to our destination, I asked Tova how her lectures in Jerusalem and Haifa went.

"I think that they went well," she replied. "I have come to one conclusion. Whether it's in New York, St. Petersburg, Jerusalem, or Haifa, neutropenia and non-Hodgkin's lymphoma claim their share of victims."

The Leo Baeck Educational Center in Haifa was older than the State of Israel itself. It was established in 1938 as a kindergarten for children fleeing prewar Europe and is now considered one of Israel's finest educational institutions. The total enrollment of its elementary, middle, and high schools consisted of 2,400 students. The main campus, the progressive synagogue, and the Community and Sports Center, as well as the seven satellite centers, serve more than thirty-five thousand people who reside in Haifa's most dynamic and mixed neighborhoods.

The Leo Baeck Educational Center was where *Talmud Torah* (the study of Torah) and *Tikkun Olam* (the repair of the world) walked hand in hand. This inclusive culture brought together Jewish and Arab children, youth at risk, Ethiopian Israelis, immigrants from the former Soviet Union, people with special needs, and the elderly. Leo Baeck conducts numerous shared existence activities and social outreach programs in conjunction with Haifa's Arab community. They are aimed at increasing opportunities for frequent and meaningful contact, closing social gaps, and eliminating stereotyping and lack of understanding prevalent among both Jews and Arabs.

I called ahead and requested a tour and a meeting with the director, Dr. Meir Katz. Dr. Katz was anxious to meet with rabbis. He counted on them to bring back stellar reports to their congregations. Donations from North America supported many of the award-winning programs.

The four of us were met by the office manager, Zehava. She took us down the massive hallways and into some of the classrooms. The diverse groups of children pursued a modern curriculum where the lessons of Torah were thoroughly integrated with the secular disciplines of language arts, history, science, and mathematics. Both serious Hebrew and Arabic literature were taught at the high school level, and I learned that the director specialized in Arabic poetry. The general library contained extensive Judaica. The science labs were stocked with modern equipment.

We came to the *Ohel Avraham* (Tent of Abraham) Synagogue. In keeping with the ideals of our patriarch who practiced audacious hospitality, the synagogue sought to provide a spiritual home for the many non-Orthodox and secular Jews who did not fit the traditional mode. It welcomed Jews from the LGBTQ communities, embraced special-needs children, and even provided support for battered housewives and their children. Yael picked up a brochure and read, with great interest, about the wide range of programs that were offered. It was clear to her that this was the place to be.

We entered both the Appelbaum Bet Tefilla (House of Prayer) and the Hugo Gryn Outdoor Synagogue and Gardens, which created a natural environment for the community's spiritual programming. As Tova, Bracha, and Yael reentered the complex, I remained for a few moments. A sanctuary named after one of my teachers filled me with both awe and determination. I spoke aloud, and perhaps Hugo was listening to me in the *Olam ha Ba*.

> A child of Auschwitz, a spiritual leader in Marble Arch,
> A perennial optimist, believing that social progress in on the march.

Teaching Jews and non-Jews through precept and example, a Rabbi for all.

Raising me up from humble beginnings and helping me to walk tall.

O Hugo, I was not your brightest light.

But inspired by your example, I fight for truth and right.

And for justice, I will speak out strong and aloud,

And somewhere in heaven, I will make you proud!

*****

We were directed into the office of Dr. Katz.

"Welcome, Rabbi Levin," he said. "Delighted to meet with your family!"

I looked at Yael and replied, "I think *Ohel Avraham* is about to get a new member."

"Splendid! Splendid!"

Yael, who blushed with embarrassment, spoke up. "I never realized that such a place like this existed in Israel."

"Although I would like to think that we are out there in the Haifa community, we still are a revelation for many, including people who live near us.

"Let me say that the Leo Baeck Educational Center was founded on the principle that all of Israel's citizens are entitled to equal rights and equal opportunities. Our focus is on sharing experiences and loving our neighbors regardless of their religion, mother tongue, race, or cultural background.

"Coexistence is not enough for us at Leo Baeck. We are committed to shared existence. This means more than living side by side and merely tolerating each other. Here in Haifa, we live together. Our commitment to shared existence is evidenced by the multitude of programs that we sponsor as well as by the international peacebuilding programs in which we participate.

"The Cultural Rainbow program is a shared existence program in Arabic and Hebrew that introduces Jewish and Arab kindergartners to multicultural openness, cooperation, and positive communication.

"Every summer, a hundred Jewish and Arab children ages six to eleven come to the Leo Baeck Arab-Jewish Summer Camp for a variety of shared activities, including arts and crafts, theater, sports, music, fields trips, and programs that promote cross-cultural understanding.

"The Interfaith Peace Drums Project pairs Leo Baeck with the Mar Elias School in Ibillin and promotes peace among Jewish, Muslim, and Christian youth in Israel through the medium of music.

"The *Yachad* Program enables Leo Baeck High School students and youth from Yarka, a Druze town situated in the Lower Galilee region, to partake in joint community service activities and cross-cultural events prior to their enlistment in the IDF. One recent activity was a joint visit to wounded Syrian refugee children being treated at the Western Galilee Hospital in Nahariya.

"The Youth Parliament is a leadership development program that trains and empowers Arab and Jewish high school students living in four of the country's mixed Arab-Jewish cities to work together to improve their own lives and the lives of their entire communities.

"The Clore Shared-Existence Center provides low-cost high-quality shared existence enrichment programs, activities, and community-wide multicultural events for Arab and Jewish children, teenagers, and adults.

"While we are unabashedly a progressive Jewish institution, we also understand that we are educating Christian and Muslim children as well. We must also be sensitive to their observances. For instance, Holiday of Holidays is an annual community celebration of Christmas, Chanukah, and Eid al-Adha [Fast of the Sacrifice]."

"So the Leo Baeck Educational Center envisions itself as a counterculture within Israeli society," I remarked.

"Absolutely! More than any other historical event, the Shoah has shaped Israeli identity. In the Israeli mindset, the death of the six million who were like sheep led to the slaughter represented the complete failure of the Diaspora. Thus, the rallying cry in Israel was 'Never again!' The sabra would be a new kind of man, a fighter who would take on the enemy in mortal combat. The date for *Yom ha Shoah* was deliberately set to coincide with the destruction of the Warsaw Ghetto. Two weeks after the Jewish world observes God's liberation of the Hebrews from Egyptian bondage, it would also remember how against all odds, the Jewish fighters in the Warsaw Ghetto attempted to rescue their people from Nazi bondage. This observance would deliberately be followed by *Yom HaZikaron*, remembrance of Israeli soldiers fallen in battle, and then by Israel Independence Day. Greater emphasis was placed on militarism rather than on mourning the six million.

"Consequently, we developed a culture in which all forms of bad behavior were justified in the name of security, whether it be the atrocities of Deir Yassin and the expulsion of thousands of Palestinians in 1948, the military excesses in the twenty-first century, or the overzealous policing of the West Bank.

"As a state that claimed to represent the Holocaust survivors, what the Nazis did to our ancestors in the 1930s and 1940s has been projected unto Palestinian terrorism. In essence, the Palestinians became the new Nazis. With the ascent to power of Menahem Begin and the nationalist right, the inverted equation of Palestinian opposition with the terror of the Nazi state became total. Begin argued that in the Land of Israel, we are condemned to fight with all our soul. Believe me, the alternative is called Auschwitz. We are determined to do everything to prevent another Auschwitz. This ultimately led Israelis to practice on Palestinians that which is fantasized and feared about Palestinians. Thus, during unsettled situations, Israeli settlers may bash in the heads of Arab adolescents or set fire to Arab fields without fear of punishment.[8]

"Just as there is transference, so there is countertransference. Just as the Israelis project Nazi atrocities unto Palestinians, Palestinians also transfer Nazi atrocities unto the Israelis. Palestinians argue that they, too, are victims of Nazism, not only indirectly through the United Nations decision to compensate Jewish victims of World War II with part of Palestine but directly through Israel's use of so-called Nazi tactics and racist violence. Israelis see the comparison as grotesque and a further indication of Palestinian immorality. Only they fail to see that it was the Jewish-Israeli collective that committed the original sin of twisting the memory of the Holocaust to promote a self-serving agenda.[9]

"At the Leo Baeck Educational Center, we are dealing with poisoned people, to use the language of the Holocaust laureate, Aharon Appelfeld. Through our programming, we are offering national family therapy. As you know, we also have programs to deal with domestic violence. Domestic violence is often perpetuated through the generations. Abused children often become abusers themselves. Family therapy attempts to break this vicious cycle. Similarly, we seek to break the vicious circle of Israelis and Palestinians vilifying each other and labelling each other as Nazis. We also seek to reverse the prevailing belief in Israeli culture that all physical and psychological force is justified in the interest of security."

"How do you achieve this?" asked Bracha.

"It's very easy to vilify the other if you never live or interact with the other in daily life. It's very easy to vilify the other if negative stereotypes are constantly expressed through textbooks, literature, television, and even social media. What we do is promote real and meaningful interaction on many levels. In this institution, there is no such thing as trigger phrases or microaggressions. We encourage plain talk. Directness can also be respectful. Students can disagree without being disagreeable. When Arabs and Jews and Druze study together, make music together, live together, and break bread together, negative images disappear. Maybe someday we can break this cycle of hate and violence.

"At Leo Baeck Educational Center, the faculty promotes a healthy style of interactions of which most Israelis are unaccustomed. Yes, we are a counterculture. We are following in the footsteps of one of our former directors, the visionary Rabbi Robert Samuels."

Yael was beaming. She vowed to return.

"I am blown away," I said to Dr. Katz. "There's much to consider."

"Just put in a good word to your congregants and colleagues once you return to New York."

"I have an appointment to see the afternoon program in the Ruth Center. It resembles a Latinx afternoon program that I am trying to bring into my own synagogue."

"Alas, our influence is already being felt! The Ruth Center is housed in one of our satellite campuses. It's located in the Kiryat Sprinzak neighborhood in Western Haifa. You will have only a short drive from the main campus. The husband-wife codirectors, Cassy and Rahel Pereira, are expecting you. They have planned a little surprise."

"We can hardly wait," said Yael.

*****

We finally arrived at the Ruth Center. From what I read in the literature, it was established in 2005 and offers numerous programs for underprivileged youth from first grade through twelfth grade. The Ruth Center is run by a professional and experienced team that works together with the youth division of the main Leo Baeck Education and Community Center. There are also high school graduates who volunteer and do a year of community service before joining the IDF. Perhaps working with a diverse group of children, which includes Arabs and Ethiopians, would provide the emotional intelligence that young people require to do the thankless work of policing the West Bank.

We were directed to a large hall. It was 3:30 p.m., and the afternoon school was about to begin. Children between the ages of six and twelve were marching cheerfully to the main assembly area. We were warmly greeted by Cassy and Rahel.

"Welcome, Rabbi Levin. You brought part of your family with you."

"Indeed, I did. Here is my wife, Tova, my daughter, Bracha, and our local Israeli cousin, Yael."

"As a couple, my dear wife and I represent what the whole population of Israel looks like. My family is from Morocco, and I grew up in Casablanca. My wife's family is from Warsaw. A Sephardic Jew is married to an Ashkenazi Jew. A couple of generations ago, it was almost unheard of in Israel. Nowadays, it's quite common. The children in this room are also from diverse backgrounds."

Rahel chimed in, "Yet we love all of them, and we give them the skills to succeed in life. More specifically, we help the Arab children with their Hebrew so that they can someday land good jobs in Israel and support their families. Many success stories come out of this afternoon school."

Cassy continued, "For the first fifteen minutes or so, we hold an assembly, and we give announcements. As Dr. Katz might have told you, we have a little surprise for you."

In the assembly area, there was a stage. Dramatics and music were an important component of the afternoon program. Cassy introduced me as a rabbi from New York who was interested in their program. He introduced Tova, Bracha, and Yael as well. Suddenly, he asked the children to mount the stage in three rows. At the count of three, they sang "It's a Small World," interspersing both Hebrew and Arabic lyrics. When the children got to the chorus, they sang in Hebrew, Arabic, and even English:

> It's a small world after all.
> *Zeh olam katan me'od*
> *Bledna srira baakilshi*
> It's a small, small world.

Tears ran down my cheeks. After the performance, I exclaimed, *"Yafe Me-od. Very beautiful!"* All four of us and the two directors applauded with great enthusiasm.

After the assembly, the children dispersed to their various classrooms which were assigned according to grade level.

Rahel said to us, "The next hour will be devoted to homework time. It is normally supervised by both the teaching staff and high school volunteers. Some of our volunteers also function as reading buddies and work with some of the children on an individual basis."

"I know all about reading buddies," I said. "I do similar work in New York. Just as you strive to create greater Hebrew fluency among Arab children to make them more productive members of society, so we strive to create greater English fluency among Latinx children to achieve the same purpose."

"Perhaps one of you would like to read to one of our children." Bracha replied, "*Lama Lo.* Why not?"

Rahel directed us to an empty table and two chairs. She then entered one of the classrooms and brought in a pretty Arab girl with long black hair. She must have been about eight years old.

"Bracha, I would like you to meet Farah. Farah, would you like Bracha to read you a story?"

Farah wasn't sure what to make of us, so she remained silent.

Then Bracha whispered a few words of Arabic to her and immediately won her confidence. Then Rahel handed her the children's book entitled *Lo Ra-ev Velo Ohev.* It was the Hebrew version of Dr. Seuss's *Green Eggs and Ham.* It can be literally translated as "I'm Not Hungry and I Don't Like It." Like the central character Sam in the English version, the central character Sheiv is invited to try a food that is new and appears disgusting to him. In the Hebrew version, ham was strategically removed as the book was written for mainly Jewish audiences, and the green substance that Sheiv is invited to try is unnamed.

Bracha and Farah made a deal. Bracha would read the story while Farah would turn the pages. As Bracha read, Farah turned the pages faster and faster to get Bracha to read faster and faster. Back at the Grace Afternoon School, Mia tried to do the same to me!

Bracha's reading beautifully captured the same rhythm as in the original book. When Bracha finished, Farah wanted Bracha to either read the story again or perhaps another book. Unfortunately, Bracha explained in Arabic that we had to move on.

"*Lo, lo, lo.* No, no, no!" shouted Farah. "*Od pa-am.* Once again."

She firmly grabbed Bracha's left arm and tried to hold on to her for dear life. "I love you!" she exclaimed in Arabic.

I felt that the little Latina girl, Anna Leah, who had tried to monopolize me at the Grace Afternoon School, had just been transplanted to Haifa. I remembered the words of esteemed educator Mrs. Evelyn Dister back at my university in Ohio, when I trained for tutoring inner city kids. "No matter where children come from, they are still children."

Rahel was choked up as well. She said to my daughter, "Bracha, you truly are a blessing. You would be welcomed in this afternoon program at any time."

Bracha nodded in appreciation of this compliment.

Bracha gave Farah a hug, and Rahel lovingly escorted her back to her classroom.

Cassy came to us and explained that at about 5:00 p.m., the children would be served a hot meal. Chicken shawarma, rice, and Israeli salad was on the menu for today.

Cassy explained, "The meal is a very important part of our program. Not only does a diverse group of children have an opportunity to break bread together, but sadly, for many of these children at risk, this is the major or maybe the only meal of the day. After the meal, there is either a special program, or we continue with the homework help."

The serving of the afternoon meal was our cue to make our departure. The four of us shook hands with Cassy and Rahel and thanked them for treating us like honored guests. I promised not only to give a glowing report but also to inform them of my progress in getting Grace Afternoon School into our synagogue facility in northern Manhattan. We entertained the possibility of putting a pen pal system into place.

Tova, Bracha, and I were to leave Haifa tomorrow and move on to our next destination. As I rode in the car, I viewed the hills of Haifa gazing upon the waves of the Mediterranean Sea. The same sky which hovers over this picturesque Israeli city is the same sky which hovers over Manhattan. The aspirations and struggles of people are the same in both places.

Robert and Richard Sherman got it right when they wrote the English lyrics of the simple but poignant song I heard this afternoon: "There is just one moon and one golden sun. And a smile means friendship to everyone. Though the mountains divide and the oceans are wide, it's a small world after all."

VI

April 2
Neve Shalom / Wahat al-Salam

Through Bracha's connections in both the Israeli and Palestinian world, she arranged for us to attend a *sulha*. It was to begin in the early evening. These events were always organized during the middle of the week so as not to offend any of the three major religious groups: Jews, Christians, and Muslims.

Sulha is Arabic for "reconciliation." It is related to the Hebrew word *slicha*, which can be loosely translated as "excuse me." Slicha, I spilled my grape juice. Slicha, sorry I bumped into you. Slicha, I completely forgot to call you. Slicha, I left my briefcase unattended in an Israeli bank! That was the most recent example.

In Arab culture, a sulha is a reconciliation between families, a resolution of an escalating conflict. In the *sharia* (Islamic canonical law based on the teachings of the Koran), it is a form of contract—a settlement, if concluded between believers—consisting of an offer and acceptance, binding on personal and community levels, and aimed at ending a conflict and restoring peace. But in this place where the larger conflict is between Israelis and Palestinians, a group of peace activists has claimed the term for the establishment of a wider peace. Each month, a group of Israelis and Palestinians meet as a Jewish-Arab coexistence community to participate in a sulha. The Jewish organizers work each month to bring a group of Palestinians into Israel from the West Bank, obtaining permits, coordinating with the army, and meeting them, if necessary, at checkpoints. When the group finally joins together, there is a bonfire. Guitar. Singing. Blessings. Eating. And finally, dialogue. Harsh, raw talking.

"Well, Isaac, I am sure that you will be in your glory," said Tova. "Throughout your career, you have been a great fan of encounter groups and interfaith gatherings."

"True," I replied. "This evening, we will have both."

Bracha added, "I am skeptical myself. My concern is that it will turn into one big kumbaya organized by a group of well-meaning leftists. I am a person who doesn't like talk without action. Really, Daddy, what is the point of dialogue? Is that going to end the conflict? Reverse racism? Alleviate the suffering of thousands on both sides?"

"I don't overestimate the importance of these types of events, but I don't underestimate them either. Quite frequently, they put people into a special frame of mind and may motivate them to get their hands dirty later. Services are not designed to solve the world's problems, but the mitzvah of *tikkun olam* flows from the fine ethical principles of our liturgy and from the sacred words of the Torah and Haphtarah.

"I am reminded of a joke. How many hippies does it take to change a light bulb? Ten. One to change the bulb and the other nine to share in the experience. Let's share in this experience and reserve judgment later."

The setting immediately caught my attention. The bonfire of reconciliation reminded me of the Havdalah candle and glowsticks that I used in the Northern Manhattan Episcopal Church. What a contrast to the unholy fires of Tuchin and Auschwitz! Along with the bonfire was a small dusty clearing, colorful blue mats, trees all around framing a patch of sky.

Yoav, a young Jewish activist, was the master of ceremonies. With the bonfire in the background, he rephrased a verse written by William Shakespeare:

> O, for a Muse of fire, that would ascend
> The brightest heaven of invention,
> A Jewish-Arab village for a stage, people to sing and dance and speak
> And pursuers of peace to behold the swelling scene!

"The ancient Jewish sage, Hillel, taught us in the *Pirkei Avot*, to be like the disciples of Aaron, loving peace and pursuing peace. If we define peace, *shalom,* as *shalem*—seeking wholeness—then wherever we live, we should seek to become a bridge between different worlds. We can bring awareness to people and situations that may seem to oppose each other on the political, social, or religious level yet resonate together on a deeper, perhaps hidden level.

"My teacher, Rabbi Shlomo Carlebach, always taught that we should wear our *Moshiach*, or Messiah glasses, at all times. That is, to see the world through the eyes of the Messiah, not just to see the world as it is, broken, but how it has the potential to be mended…to see the potential for healing, transformation, and wholeness in every situation."

Yoav was aware of the participants. He noticed that there was a critical mass of young people from America and European countries that had limited experience and knowledge of Israel. He continued in a slightly different path.

"Israel has gotten lots of negative publicity over the years. Many people associate Israel with bloodshed, occupation, and relentless government policies. In Israel, people are dealing with a lot of despair, both on the Palestinian side and on the Israeli side. The government appears to be doing everything it can to avoid peace, and few of us see light at the end of the tunnel.

"The truth of the matter is that Israel is a complex country. It is a country with many different faces. After I completed university in the 1960s, I visited Israel and fell in love. The country is beautiful, but the people are even more beautiful. There's warmth here and an immediacy, a straight-talk ethos. And I had wonderful conversations. I felt wanted. I felt that wherever I went people reached out to me and said, 'You're a Jew. Your place is here.'

"I help to organize the monthly sulha because of my love for Israel and because I want to show my Jewish, Christian, and Muslim brothers and sisters that there is another side to Israel besides what appears in the media. For your information, the Sulha Peace Project is not the only Israeli-Palestinian outreach group in Israel. There are at least sixty other organizations that also do excellent work.

"This evening, we will sing and dance together, pray and bless the food together using our different religious traditions, and most important of all, we will engage in serious dialogue. We will operate in Hebrew, Arabic, and English. We have many translators so that no one will feel left out.

"The most important task is listening. God gave us our subtle hint when he gave us one mouth but two ears. So many of us are so intent on saying what it is we want to say that we forget about listening. Particularly in Israel and Palestine, the level of listening is quite dismal, and people are sort of waiting for you to take a breath so they can leap in and say the next thing they have to say.

"When people are preoccupied with winning, this is the way of the warrior, but it's not the way that peace is made. The deeper experience of listening is about fully being with people when they are talking. I might disagree with you very strongly and still respect you enough to let you finish what you want to say. When people truly listen to each other, it leads to intimacy and closeness between them. The job of the facilitators is to create a space where people feel safe enough to share their personal experiences.

"At sulha, we very much emphasize the importance of listening. The heart of our monthly gathering is the listening circles where we take the Native American technique of using a speaking object, something that has some significance for the facilitator, and only the person holding that object speaks. We don't argue. We really have people deliver themselves to whoever is speaking, to listen from the heart and speak from the heart. We stay away from political arguments because people can argue politically all the time if they want to. But active listening through each other's stories and listening to people talk about their lives and themselves is quite rare. What creates safety enough so that people can express themselves is that we pay attention to each other. And work more from the heart than we do from the head.

"Now that I have laid out the philosophy of sulha, have given you an idea of what will be taking place, and established the ground rules in terms of listening, we can begin the program. Dialoging with the other, dialoging with people who are not your friends and who are, perhaps, your enemies, is a novel experience for many people. Facing the unknown in dialogue is a metaphor for facing the unknown in life. As Rabbi Nahman of Bratslav once said, 'Life is a narrow bridge. The main thing is not to be afraid.'"

The two guitarists—Moti, the Israeli, and Malik, the Palestinian—strummed their guitars and led our group of about one hundred people in song.

> *Kol Ha'olam kulo*
> *Gesher Tsar me'od*
> *Gesher Tsar me'od*
> *Gesher Tsar me'od*
> *Kol Ha'olam kulo*
> *Gesher Tsar me'od*
> *Gesher Tsar me'od.*
> *Veha'ikar—veha'ikar*
> *Lo lefached*
> *lo lefached klal.*
> *Veha'ikar—veha'ikar*
> *lo lefached klal.*

Following our opening group song, we clapped and cheered as a young Dabke dance troupe joined arms and grinned around the bonfire. The Palestinian traditional dance was slightly more intricate than the Israeli *hora*. Israelis and Palestinians together initiated additional dances. They were swaying their hips and flinging their arms in a crazy expression of affirmation.

Afterward, Gabriel Meyer, the son of Rabbi Marshall Meyer and one of the original founders of sulha, sang two songs that he composed himself: The first one was "Global Visa." The lyrics were in English and Spanish. It was a plea for the end of national barriers. It envisioned a world in which ethnic identity is stretched in many ways. The key English words of this song were, "Grammar and passports disappearing from the frame. I'm singing my visa to you, so open your borders to me."

The second song with all English lyrics was "Children of Liberty." This song was about people from diverse groups living as neighbors and sharing dreams of liberty. It beckoned them to display the courage to change the brutal reality of life by standing up for human rights, equality, and dignity.

Then came the listening circle. It began with a series of stories on checkpoints, barriers, and obstacles. Unlike many committee and board meetings that I have attended over the years, there was truly attentive listening. Three Palestinian teenagers, especially, focused on everything that everyone said whether they be Jewish, Christian, or Muslim. Their faces turned to the speakers. They breathed in their words and were deeply serious. Their sight was validating, comforting, beautiful, and inspiring.

Ibtisam, a Palestinian woman living in the Arab Israeli town of Fardis in the Haifa district, spoke of the tragic death of her grandparents in 1948. Despite her grief and bitterness, she expressed her commitment to peace. She stated that she didn't want to leave anger and sadness in her heart. Despite her feelings, dialogue and discussion is preferable to violence. Violence is easy. Mass destruction can take place with one push of a button. Making peace is more difficult and takes decades of work.

Ibtisam compared peace to a tree. After it is planted, it takes twenty years before you can enjoy its fruits and leave to those who come after you. The most important thing is confidence, optimism, and always keeping in mind that tomorrow will be another day.[10]

Yoav offered additional words to the remarks that he made at the beginning of the program. "Once I was hospitalized, and the guy lying next to me in the hospital bed turned out to be a settler, Yossi. My automatic reaction was rejection. I thought we had nothing in common. Then Yossi started telling me about his life, and it turned out he had lost his parents and siblings in a terrorist attack. He was on his way into the army. Then I told him about myself and about sulha. To my amazement, he asked, 'Why don't you invite me to one of your gatherings?' Finally, he came. We asked one of the Palestinians, Ahmed, to spend some time with him one-on-one. Ahmed had spent some time in Israeli prisons and was still limping from the wounds he had suffered when he was arrested. He was very suspicious about talking to a settler. Yossi was also very reluctant. But he agreed. Within ten minutes, they were in deep conversations with each other. They even refused our invitation to participate in the activities because they were just talking, laughing, and sharing cigarettes. At the end of the evening, we asked the Palestinians to get back on the bus because they had a deadline to be back at the roadblocks on the border. Ahmed hugged Yossi and said to him, 'Listen, in a couple of months, you will be a soldier, and you will be standing on the roadblocks, and I will be across the road throwing rocks at you guys. Please take of yourself.' It was so sad to see that they both felt locked into their roles, a future soldier and a potential rock thrower. But a connection had been made between them, and Ahmed was concerned that his new friend Yossi would be hurt. It was quite a magical moment."

The appropriate blessings over the food were recited by representatives of the three faiths. I had the honor of reciting the Jewish blessing over the bread. We then had a simple meal consisting of hummus, rice, and vegetables. Israelis and Palestinians mingled seamlessly and were engaged in much joyful, sometimes tearful, but always animated conversations. Tears came to Bracha's eyes as she watched Israelis and Palestinians sitting together and coming together to feel real love.

Gabriel Meyer made the last remarks. "I was born in Argentina. I grew up in a dictatorship when the military took over the country, so I grew up in a lot of oppression. I was also beaten up by Argentinian police by just being outside after ten at night with my friends when I was a teenager. My father was a human rights activist doing his work because of the prophets of the Bible. These prophets proclaimed the message of love and justice that I was brought up with. And those were the main values that I was instilled with in a summer camp that my father and my mother created, in nature, integrating creativity and culture and the values of love and justice coming from the Jewish people. I grew up in a house which was very open to loving non-Jews and working for them. My father worked with the priests in Argentina, which was unheard of then—a rabbi and a priest working in a shanty town together.[11]

"As peace-loving Jews, Christians, and Muslims, we have the power to make a difference. We must not delegate this power to so-called professionals, whether they be politicians, journalists, or community organizers. On the contrary, we must assume responsibility and attempt to change reality. This is our job as creatures of God."[12]

I asked Bracha, "Do you feel better about this type of event?"

She responded, "For me, the sulha felt like a form of group therapy. I arrived with an amalgamation of pent-up emotions, talked, listened, and felt a release. A sense of hope. A sense of inspiration. I think that others had similar experiences. In an environment of suspicion, tension, hardship, often hatred, the sulha was pure love. People arrived wanting to trust, ready to hold each other, Israeli or Palestinian. Hands were grasped, numbers exchanged, dance steps stamped into earth. And I realized this is humanity. In a place where conflict rages, we human beings can only survive if we hold onto our humanity. Beyond politics, there are smiles and bodies and individuals who shake and hold still in the night breeze. For as many Israelis and Palestinians as this sulha can possibly touch, it is worth it. Because it allows them to feel like people, to be understood and respected simply because they are alive. And while that type of thing is not going to influence politics and coalitions, it will keep this conflict from robbing even more humanity. In the Talmud, we learn that saving one life is like saving an entire world. If the sulha can save with love, if it can light a spark of hope in even one soul, then yes, it is worth it. It is wonderful."

As the Israeli-Palestinian conflict has caused so much suffering and death, the *Sulha* concluded with everyone singing *Shir Lashalom* (Sing for Peace), written by Yaakov Rotblit and set to music by Yair Rosenblum. The guitarists accompanied us. The song was sung entirely in Hebrew. The lyrics beckon us not to focus on the tragedies of the past but to look forward and to pursue peace.

The final words were particularly powerful. In English translation, they appear as follows:

> Lift your eyes with hope
> Not through the rifles' sights
> Sing a song for love

> and not for wars.
> Don't say the day will come
> bring on that day—
> because it is not a dream—
> and in all the city squares
> cheer only for peace!

The words of the Torah tell us that Abraham breathed his last and died at a good ripe age, old and contented, and he was gathered to his people. His sons, Isaac and Ishmael, buried him in the cave of Machpelah near Mamre, in the field of Ephron son of Zohar the Hittite.

Why was Abraham contented in his old age? Perhaps he was contented because he knew before his death that Isaac and Ishmael at last became reconciled with him. Isaac came to terms with his near death at Mt. Moriah, and Ishmael came to terms with his banishment in the wilderness. Perhaps he was contented because he knew before his death that Isaac and Ishmael would cast aside all animosities that they might have had toward one another.

The conflict between the descendants of Isaac and the descendants of Ishmael, which began long before the birth of the Jewish state, continues to rage today. It rages even in Hebron, near the site where Isaac and Ishmael reunited to bury their father. Like Isaac and Ishmael who came before them, they continue to bear past hurts and grievances. Reconciliation with history and with each other remains elusive.

Yet this evening, a mixed multitude of one hundred Israelis and Palestinians came together to mourn their brothers and sisters who did not live to a contented old age like the father of their respective peoples, Abraham. The descendants of Isaac and Ishmael boldly proclaimed that they can't get used to death and will not get used to death. They affirmed that the living must be given a turn. Rather than wait for some distant Messianic Age, they pledged to bring about a new day through human effort. They yearned for the day when Arabs and Jews will share the promised land as equals in life as they have shared it for decades in death.

Never shall I forget that night, my first night at *Sulha*, that transformed my rabbinate and my life.

Never shall I forget that campfire that provided warmth and comfort.

Never shall I forget those flames of reconciliation and hope in which the descendants of Isaac and Ishmael met in loving embrace.

Never shall I forget the sweet faces of people engaged in prayer, in song, and in dialogue.

Never shall I forget the nocturnal silence of Jews and Arabs absorbing the words of our passionate speakers.

Never shall I forget these things, even were I privileged to live for 120 years, the life span of Moses.

Never.

*****

I spent one week in the promised land, a country which could boast of wondrous achievements and which suffered unspeakable tragedies, a country which faces serious challenges but which also has potential for greatness. I had come home again, and there would be much to remember and to write about when I returned to New York.

Part Three

A Dip into the Future

For I dipt into the future,
far as human eye could see,
Saw the Vision of the world, and all
the wonder that would be;
Saw the heavens fill with commerce,
argosies of magic sails,
Pilots of the purple twilight, dropping
down with costly bales;
Heard the heavens fill with shouting,
and there raind a ghastly dew
From the nations airy navies
grappling in the central blue;
Far along the world-wide whisper of
the south-wind rushing warm,
With the standards of the peoples
plunging thro the thunder-storm;
Till the war-drums throbbd, no longer,
and the battle-flags were furled

In the Parliament of man, the
Federation of the world.
There the common sense of most shall
hold a fretful realm in awe,
And the kindly earth shall slumber,
lapt in universal law.

—Alfred Lord Tennyson

Chapter 9
THE EXODUS REVISITED

Therefore, say to the Israelites: "I am the Lord, and I will bring you out from under the yoke of the Egyptians. I will free you from being slaves to them, and I will redeem you with an outstretched arm and with mighty acts of judgment. I will take you as my own people, and I will be your God. Then you will know that I am the Lord your God, who brought you out from under the yoke of the Egyptians. And I will bring you to the land I swore with an outstretched hand to give to Abraham, to Isaac and to Jacob. I will give it to you as a possession. I am the Lord."

—Exodus 6:6–9

In each and every generation a person must view himself as though he personally left Egypt, as it is stated: "And you shall tell your son on that day, saying: It is because of this which the Lord did for me when I came forth out of Egypt" (Exodus 13:8). In every generation, each person must say: "This which the Lord did for me," and not: This which the Lord did for my forefathers.

—The Talmud (Pesachim 116b)

I

New York
April 7, 2014

The week before Pesach was a hectic time at Congregation Rodef Tzedek. The synagogue kitchen was being thoroughly cleansed and changed over for Pesach. This year, I was preparing for two *sederim*, the annual congregational seder which caters mainly, but not exclusively, to the elderly Jewish population in our neighborhood and an interfaith model seder that I would be conducting at the Northern Manhattan Episcopal Church. The model seder was scheduled for Wednesday evening before Pesach. While I planned to focus on the basic rituals, it was especially designed to call special attention to Amelia and her family and to the general plight of immigrants and refugees from Latin America.

My meeting with our president, Rolf Samuels, and our student cantor just concluded. We were working out the logistics of both the congregational seder and the eight days of Pesach services which followed.

In late January, Greg returned to the university campus for the second semester. An hour before the Rodef Tzedek religious school was scheduled to begin, Greg called me from his fraternity house.

"How's it going?" he asked.

"Hectic! Life must be boring now that you are no longer gallivanting around Europe."

"I'm not bored. Whether I am in Germany or the US, I always have an active social life."

"I have no doubt. What are you doing for Pesach?"

"That's why I called you. Some of my Jewish fraternity brothers and I are organizing a seder. So is it correct that it's not customary to drink wine between the first and second glasses of wine, or between the third and fourth glasses, or after the fourth glass, but we can drink as much as we like between the second and third glasses?"

"Correct. The meal takes place between the second and third glasses."

"Good to know. We might drink so much wine that we won't get to the third glass! Hah, hah, hah!"

"Try to restrain yourself, my good man! It would be nice if you could finish the second half of the seder."

"I'll think about it. My job is to prepare the brisket. I'll make it nice. It's all in the presentation."

"In the past, Hillel seders never interested you. I'm glad that you are organizing one on your own."

"Last semester, I visited Sachsenhausen. During the summer, I visited Dachau. During my semester in Israel, the class visited Auschwitz and Birkenau. After seeing all the horrible things in those four concentration camps, I have a more mature appreciation of living in a free society.

"Do you remember my speaking of Johanna, the German girl that I met in my school? Seeing her pain at losing part of her family in Sachsenhausen really got to me. This year, it's important for me to have a seder of some kind, even if it's less formal than the ones that you conducted at home."

"Good to hear!"

I didn't push further. In congregational life, there are often expectations of rabbis' children. As Bracha and Greg are now adults, I prefer to stay low-key and let them find their respective Jewish ways.

"Changing the subject, Daddy, I aced all my courses in Berlin, particularly the classes in German language and Jewish history. If I can keep my grades up for this semester and for next year, it will be a cinch to graduate cum laude. I even have an outside chance at magna cum laude."

"I'm impressed. Speaking of Johanna, are you keeping in touch with her?"

"I'm glad that you asked that question. That's the other great news that I wanted to give you. She is transferring to my school next year. We are looking forward to seeing a lot of each other."

"It seems like the beginning of a beautiful friendship! *Chag Sameach* [happy festival], Greg!"

"Chag Sameach!"

*****

As I turned my attention to the model seder in which I would be calling attention to Amelia's family, to many other refugees like her who are fleeing dangerous, turbulent societies in Latin America, I thought of the seder that I conducted thirty years ago at the Settlement Synagogue. My thoughts at that time were directed toward another family, the Tsivkins of Leningrad, and many others like them who were fleeing anti-Semitism and the iron fist of totalitarianism. My connection with the New Sanctuary Coalition was just an extension of my work with Soviet Jewry. This year, the distance between my world in 1984 and my world in 2014 greatly diminished.

II

London
April 14, 1984

As I held up the "bread of affliction" before the attendees of the seder, I said, "In addition to remembering the needy, let us also be mindful that I will be visiting people who long to be free and who yearn to celebrate Pesach in the Jewish homeland."

I took an extra whole matzah from a separate plate. It was the matzah of hope. Leisel Harrison read the special prayer: "This matzah, which we set aside as a symbol of hope, for the three million Jews of the Soviet Union, reminds us of the indestructible link that exists between us. As we observe this festival of freedom, we know that Soviet Jews are not free to learn of their Jewish past, to hand it down to their children. They cannot learn the language of their ancestors. They cannot teach their children to be the teachers, the rabbis of future generations.

"They can only sit in silence and become invisible. We shall be their voice, and our voices shall be joined by thousands of people of conscience aroused by the wrongs suffered by Soviet Jews. Then shall they know that they have not been forgotten and they that sit in darkness shall yet see great light."

Toward the end of the communal seder at the Settlement Synagogue, we observed the custom of opening the door for Elijah.

Elijah symbolized the Pesach of the future, a messianic time in which there would be an end to all oppression. The hearts of the parents would turn toward the children, and the hearts of the children would turn toward the parents.

At the seder, I commented, "Pesach is a holiday which links past, present, and future. We celebrate Pesach and hold a seder to remind ourselves of our past, how the Egyptians enslaved our ancestors, and how God delivered them from freedom to slavery. We think of the present and remind ourselves that there are many people throughout the world who are still not free. We think of the Cold War and the savage division which continues to exist between East and West. We think of our brothers and sisters in the Soviet Union who cannot practice Judaism the way that we do in London. With Elijah's cup, we think of the Pesach which is yet to come. We think of the Pesach when rabbis such as me no longer are obliged to make the type of trip that I am about to make and deliver materials that Soviet Jews should take for granted."

Upon expressing our yearning for the Pesach of the future, my London congregation concluded the seder by proclaiming in unison, "Next Year in Jerusalem!"

III

New York
April 9, 2014

The model seder at Northern Manhattan Episcopal Church was a very modest affair. It took place in one of the back meeting rooms. It was organized by some of the Jewish members of the New Sanctuary Coalition and a few volunteers from the church. A long table was set up with a nice white tablecloth. The required Pesach items were available in plentiful supply: haggadot, which related the exodus from Egypt and which guided Jews and non-Jews alike through the various seder rituals, the matzot, the wine, the seder plate, the bitter herbs, the charoset, the shank bone, the saltwater, and the cup of Elijah. Assembled at the table were Father Burgos and his wife, Ravi Ragbir and his wife, Father Juan Carlos Ruiz and his wife, Amelia, Dulcina, Danita, Dani, and Isabel. Even Marcos made it in from Long Island. Also present were Kate, Tara, Matthew, Sanford Kantor, and of course, me. A good critical mass.

I went through the major prayers and readings and carefully explained the rituals as I went along. Isabel provided translations in Spanish whenever needed. Specific moments during the seder were particularly emotional.

At the very beginning, when I chanted the extended blessing over the first goblet of wine, I said, "Thirty years ago, I conducted a seder in London, and my thoughts were directed toward the plight of Russian Jews. As it turns out, the English date of that seder and the one I will be doing next Monday night is identical, April 14! The connection between the liberation of our ancestors from Egyptian bondage, the liberation of our Russian brethren from religious persecution, and the liberation of Holocaust survivors from Nazi tyranny is powerful. While Nazi Germany is no more, the Soviet Union has disintegrated, and most Jews who wished to leave there have emigrated, we still have negative attitudes toward non-European immigrants in our own country. We still have refugees hiding in places like Northern Manhattan Episcopal Church.

A few minutes later, we got to the ritual in which I broke the middle matzah into two parts. The larger part was designated as the *Afikomen* and was hidden away. Thirty years ago, I recited a prayer for Soviet Jewry. At this seder, I recited another prayer: "God of all creatures, grant our country, its officials, and its citizens more of your compassion for the plight of immigrants, refugees, and asylum seekers. Soften the hearts of the American people to their situation and help us follow your lead in seeking justice and mercy on their behalf. We pray for an end to the wars, the poverty and human rights abuses that drive desperate people to become refugees in the first place. Teach us to welcome not only the strangers in our midst but the gifts they bring to our country as well. This is the help you have sent: we are not alone. We are together on the journey, and for this we give you thanks. Amen."

In recounting the narrative, we arrived at the iconic verse, "In each and every generation, a person is obligated to regard himself as though he actually left Egypt."

I explained to the group, "Maimonides, a famous Jewish teacher in the eleventh century, wanted to change the wording. He felt that it should read, 'In each and every generation, we should act as if we were leaving Egypt.' The traditional explanation is that the exodus from Egypt is 'acted out' by eating the appropriate foods and performing the required rituals associated with Pesach. I would like to take it one step further. We 'act out' the Pesach story by working to end oppression within our own society. Remembrance is not enough. If my own people continue to oppress others even after observing Pesach, they have not really learned the moral lessons of the holiday. Action must flow from remembrance. Former victims of oppression must not tolerate the oppression of others."

Father Burgos entered the conversation. "This is what I have been preaching all along. Faith without good works is empty. Men and women of religion must get their hands dirty. They must get involved in politics. They must take a stand. Silence is also a political statement. Nonaction is the same as forming an alliance with the oppressor."

After the first part of the seder, we enjoyed the dinner. The light meal that was prepared consisted of baked chicken, boiled potatoes, carrots, and raisin kugel for dessert. While the adults were finishing, the children searched for the *Afikomen*, which I hid in their living space. Dulcina found it quite quickly. I rewarded all three of them for participating in the search by giving out age-appropriate books.

In our abridged seder, we soon arrived at the popular ritual of opening the door for Elijah. Danita opened the door of the room that all of us were in. Thirty years ago, I focused on the messianic day when all Russian Jews would be permitted to leave their country, and for many, the next year might be in Jerusalem. This year, the focus would be a better life for immigrants and refugees. Instead of presuming to know what freedom meant to those seated around the table, I asked a general question, "What does liberation from oppression mean to you?"

Amelia answered, "Being able to move around in the outside world without the fear of being arrested. Being able to work again. For Dani, it would mean being able to play with his Micky Mouse teddy bear and sleeping in his own bed at home."

Danita answered, "It would mean going to my old school in Long Island and playing with my old friends."

Dulcina, the sensitive one, answered, "It would mean that the American government stops going after Mommy."

Ravi Ragbir answered, "It would mean the end of harassment from ICE. I know the meaning of *detention, incarceration,* and *near deportation.*"

Juan Carlos answered, "It would mean the end of my searching for churches for all those seeking sanctuary. It would mean the end of many Latinos living in the shadows."

Father Burgos answered, "It would mean the appreciation of the contribution that immigrants make to this country and the beginning of a more civil society. It would mean a time in which people get involved and not leave social progress to the politicians."

Finally, Marcos answered, "According to our lawyer, Amelia and I believe that we are on our way toward a proper asylum hearing. I believe that we meet all the criteria. As you know, I am in the construction business. When this ordeal is over, I am going to build a very fine home for our family with a nice swimming pool for our children. As hardworking immigrants from Guatemala, we look forward to the day when we will reap the fruits of the American dream. Rabbi Levin, I hope that your family and my family will become neighbors on Long Island and that we will get together frequently."

"Amen," I replied. "Someday, your family will proclaim the famous words, 'Free at last! Free at last! Thank God, Almighty, we're free at last!'"

IV

Moshav Mata, Israel
April 14-15, 2014

Around noontime, Shmuel Sassoon and Bracha boarded the 292 bus which took them from the Central Bus Station of Jerusalem to *Moshav Mata*. It was about a thirty-five-minute bus ride. The name *Mata* is the Hebrew word for plant. It was derived from Ezekiel 34:29:

> And I will raise up for them a plant of renown, and they shall be no more consumed with hunger in the land, neither bear the shame of the heathen anymore.

The village was established in 1950 by immigrants from Yemen on land that had formerly belonged to the depopulated Palestinian villages of Allar and Khirbat al-Tannur. The founders were later joined by more immigrants from North Africa. Moshav Mata was established as a haven for North African Jews leaving Muslim lands for a more prosperous life.

As the population of the moshav was only several hundred, the area was relatively small, and most places were within walking distance. Upon arrival in Mata, Shmuel and Bracha made their way to the Sassoon home. They were eagerly greeted by the entire family, Shmuel's parents and two younger sisters. The father's name was Ofer. The mother, Fariya, embraced Bracha immediately.

The house consisted of a living room, a dining room, a smallish kitchen, three bedrooms, and one full bathroom. Shmuel gave up his bedroom and volunteered to sleep on the pull-out living room sofa for the night. His bedroom was allocated to Bracha.

As the deadline for eating leavened products had already passed, Fariya offered Bracha water and various kinds of fruits to tide her over until the seder, which wouldn't begin until after sundown. Shmuel's sisters, Hana and Leilah, were much younger than him, eight and ten years old respectively. Bracha went out with them to the backyard to the swing set. Hana and Leila got on each of the two swings and Bracha pushed both girls. After they got tired of the swings, they had a little chat, and Bracha told them of her North American background. They were quite animated and excited to be entertaining a visitor who came from a different country.

Near sunset, the men recited both the weekday afternoon and festival evening services at the local synagogue. Afterward, it was time for the seder to begin. It took place at a communal hall where about eighty people from the moshav got together. While the group was predominately dark-skinned Yemenites, one of the women was married to a tall blond Ashkenazi man. Yet he seemed to fit in with the group seamlessly. Shmuel sat with his family, and Bracha sat next to Shmuel.

Although Bracha knew the Haggadah thoroughly, had presided over many seders in the past, and was fluent in Hebrew, she found this seder to be challenging. The melodies were totally African, totally different than what Bracha had ever experienced. The leader of the seder went through the Haggadah at blinding speed, and it was a constant challenge for Bracha to keep her place. Whenever she felt lost, there were always many Black fingers ready to point her in the right direction. Yet while the seder appeared foreign on the surface, it was the same Haggadah, and she was still celebrating the same Pesach with Jews. Bracha welcomed the new experience and took everything in her stride.

When it came to the Pesach meal, even the food was different. In her Ashkenazi home, she was used to brisket, chicken, potato kugel, tzimmes, and matzo ball soup. Here she had a big bowl of soup with rice. Unlike Ashkenazi seders, the eating of rice was the staple diet of Yemenite seders. In the *Shulchan Aruch*, edited by the Sephardi rabbi and scholar Joseph Karo, rice was permitted for Jews coming from Spain and Portugal.

All the haggadot in Europe and North America conclude with the phrase, "Next Year in Jerusalem." This Haggadah said, "Next Year in Jerusalem, the built city." This, of course, implied the building of the Third Temple. For Bracha, this "built city" meant the building up of inclusion and civil rights so that Jerusalem could truly be the city of all peoples. Nevertheless, unlike all previous years, Bracha was not simply praying about being in Jerusalem at some distant time. She was really living in Jerusalem, and the seder was as close to Jerusalem as one could possibly get.

The beautiful and exotic seder concluded at a reasonable hour. Bracha easily fell asleep back at the Sassoon home. Pesach observance would resume tomorrow morning.

*****

Bracha joined Shmuel and his father for Pesach morning services at the Yemenite synagogue. They were conducted in a traditional manner, so men and women sat separately. Ofer and Shmuel joined the men while Bracha joined the women. Men and women prayed on one level and were separated by a cloth *mechitza* (partition) down the middle of the synagogue. Although Bracha was an egalitarian Jew to the core and preferred mixed seating, this arrangement worked out for her as she could participate fully in the praying.

Like last night's seder, the melodies were African and foreign to Bracha's ears. Also, like last night, the *davening* was quite rapid. Fortunately, as a product of day school education through twelfth grade, she knew the festival morning service very well and successfully kept up.

The Torah service was extraordinary as it was the first time that Bracha experienced readings from a circular Torah scroll. Moreover, after each Torah verse was chanted, the Aramaic translation was read by the *meturgeman* (translator). Many centuries ago, when Jewish communities thrived in Babylonia, the spoken language was Aramaic. In fact, the predominant language of the Babylonian Talmud was Aramaic. In 2014, the spoken language at the moshav was Hebrew, and so the Aramaic translation was purely ceremonial and followed a tradition within the Yemenite community. In Talmudic days, the meturgeman translated from a language that was not generally used to a language that everyone understood. In 2014, it was the exact opposite. The meturgeman translated from a language that is also spoken in the streets to a language that is only used for religious purposes, i.e., prayer and wedding documents. After services, the worshippers returned to the Sassoon residence for a family Pesach lunch.

Later in the afternoon, Shmuel and Bracha walked through the town and visited various homes along the way. As the walk proceeded, they became increasingly comfortable with each other. They soon walked hand in hand.

At each stop, Shmuel would introduce Bracha to a different family, some small and some quite large. What they all seemed to have in common was their unconditional acceptance of Bracha. Her western background and her social activism appeared to captivate them. It was obvious that Shmuel was Moshav Mata's "favorite son." Few Yemenites in this moshav had attained higher education. Yet Shmuel's neighbors were puffing up their chests with pride that Shmuel would someday receive his doctorate in mathematics from Hebrew University.

By the end of the day, the Yom Tov (holy day) came to an end. Upon sunset, evening prayers were recited. The entire Sassoon family walked Bracha to the bus stop, where she would catch the 292 bus headed to Jerusalem.

Bracha was overwhelmed by the last twenty-four hours. She said to them, "We come from different parts of the world. We have different backgrounds. We have different customs. We eat different foods. Yet we are one people."

Ofer replied, "Our skin tones may be different, but all of us are Jews. We are you and you are us. Perhaps someday, you will make aliyah and make Israel your permanent home."

Bracha sighed. "Most of my family is in North America."

Shmuel retorted, "In Israel, you will always have family. I consider you as part of my extended family."

Fariya continued, "When you get back to the United States, please remember us. Don't forget your way home."

"I never will."

"You will always be welcomed in Moshav Mata," said Ofer.

"Next year in Jerusalem," the last words of the Haggadah, was the rallying cry for Soviet Jews many years ago. Perhaps someday, it will become a reality for Bracha as well.

Chapter 10

THE THREE RABBIS

Blessed are You, Lord our God, and God of our ancestors
God of Abraham, God of Isaac, and God of Jacob
The great, mighty, and awesome God, God most high
Who bestows loving kindness and goodness
and who creates everything
Who remembers the good deeds of the Patriarchs
And who will lovingly bring a redeemer to their
children's children for the sake of His name
King, Helper, Redeemer, and Shield
Blessed are you Adonai, Shield of Abraham.
—The Jewish Prayerbook

A man must not depend on the work of his ancestors. If a man does not do good in this world, he cannot fall back on the merit of his fathers. No man will eat in the Time-to-Come of his father's works, but only of his own.

—Midrash Tehillim

Rav says: All the ends of days that were calculated for the coming of the Messiah have passed, and the matter depends only upon repentance and good deeds.

—Sanhedrin 97a

I

New York City
May 1, 2014

At Congregation Rodef Tzedek, we were looking forward to our annual Israel Independence Day service. In addition to the normal Friday night liturgy, we would light the traditional seven candles of the candelabra that are described in the Torah. The lighting was accompanied by readings pertaining to the history, the ideals, and the values of the Jewish state. In lieu of a sermon, we arranged for a medley of best loved Israeli melodies, rendered by a Klezmer band. Rolf Samuels, who continued his dual role as synagogue president and musical director, utilized his extensive contacts in the New York area and made all the arrangements.

I was putting the finishing touches on the text of the service when the phone of my office study rang. The call came from Anton Muharsky, who had desperation in his voice.

"Isaac, can you help us out? We had a fire in the church basement."

I was saddened but not shocked. I had a bad feeling that something like that would happen sooner or later in the space that Grace Afternoon School was renting.

"None of the children or staff were hurt, but there was some damage to the walls, and the kitchen has become inoperable. Everything is being covered by insurance, but the church will have to make some repairs over the next few months. The children have nowhere to go."

I replied, "We have provided emergency use to various church groups in the past. As we have precedents, I think that we might be able to swing this. I will do my best to arrange an emergency meeting of the licensing committee within the next few days."

"Much obliged," said Anton. "You are a lifesaver!"

*****

The committee met the following Monday after our celebration of Israel Independence Day. It was the same cast of characters. In addition, Fritz Bernstein, who participated in November's Kristallnacht service and who recently pleaded for embracing Amelia's family, and Rolf Samuels, were also in attendance.

Like the other discussions concerning the Grace Afternoon School, the conversation began along the same lines. Even though the children of Rodef Tzedek and Grace had gotten together and developed friendships, the same arguments about the organization wanting too much space and intruding on synagogue programming were trotted out once again. Fritz and Rolf kept quiet.

Dena Schwartz once again complained about the peacefulness of Shabbat worship being disturbed by the mentoring program.

Mendel Kornblum shook his head, took a deep breath, and said, "I just don't know. I just don't know."

Jane Lieberman suggested, "It's getting late. Maybe we should table this for next month!"

"Not so fast!" shouted Fritz. "We can't put this off to the next meeting. The Grace Afternoon School has an emergency on its hands. Didn't our observance of the seventy-fifth anniversary of Kristallnacht last November or our recent observance of Yom ha Shoah [Holocaust Remembrance Day] mean anything to you? When Kristallnacht marked the beginning of the end for European Jewry, not one country, including America, wanted Jewish refugees. The *St. Louis* was turned away from American shores in 1939. And now you want to turn away mostly Dominican children who have nowhere to go after school, even if their stay would most likely be temporary. This is appalling!

"When my family came to New York as immigrants, we rebuilt our lives from broken glass. We must have a hand in rebuilding the lives of newer immigrants. This synagogue is Congregation Rodef Tzedek! We pursue justice. Justice, justice, we shall pursue."

"I will go further," added Rolf. "I am prepared to sign a contract with Grace Afternoon School even if it's not approved by this committee."

"You can't subvert our committee structure," replied Mendel, who was totally flabbergasted.

"I was never stopped from doing such things in the past. We are talking ourselves out of doing the right thing."

Monroe Morgenstern entered the fray. "There have been church groups in the past who have had to abruptly leave their accommodations, and we have never turned them out. Why is Grace Afternoon School any different?"

Mendel replied, "They have a much bigger operation than our other tenants."

"For a few months, we can inconvenience ourselves. If we had a fire in our own building, I know for a fact that the church down the street wouldn't wait for us to ask for help. The two ministers, Doreen and Brenda, would already have a plan in place as to what rooms to give us."

"That's true." Mendel nodded. "The shoe could just as easily be on the other foot. Closing our doors to people in dire circumstances is not the Jewish way." The others seated around the table nodded.

"Let's rent this space to them for three months with a definite end point. If Grace Afternoon School needs a bit more time or if this arrangement seems to work for everybody, we can provide an extension."

Jane Lieberman replied, "I think that we can all agree to an emergency rental. If there is no further business, the meeting is adjourned."

At last, the congregation took ownership over my vision. The challenge was to make it work. The devil is always in the details.

I called Anton after the meeting and relayed the happy news.

II

I returned to my Long Island home and retired for the evening.
"Good night, Tova," I said.
"Good night, sweety," she replied.
From the point I nodded off to sleep, my subconscious mind took over.

*****

I was in the synagogue sanctuary. I had just finished my practice reading of the weekly Torah portion and was rolling and dressing the scroll before returning it to the Holy Ark. At that point, Maureen, our office assistant, came up the stairs and said, "An elderly man wants to see you. I have no idea who he is, but he says that he knows you. He read your name on our outdoor placard."

"Invite him into the sanctuary," I replied. "Please put him on our special chair lift and press the magic button."

"Will do."

As I stood at the top of the stairs to greet him, it was none other than Grandpa Abe! He looked just as I remembered him only one week before we received the news that he had died in his sleep at the nursing home.

"Papa!" I exclaimed. "Is it really you?"

"Isaac?"

"That's me! It's been a long time—over forty-five years."

We embraced. I asked him how he got here. He replied that he turned in for the night at the nursing home and suddenly found himself on Fort Washington Avenue in New York.

"You've grown up and became an adult since I last saw you. So you became a rabbi. I was intrigued by the sign."

"Yes, I did."

"Big mistake. I hoped for better things from you. You had a great mind for mathematics. You could have been an accountant or an actuary. You also had the gift of the gab. You could have become a lawyer."

"I wanted a profession where I could make a real difference in the world."

"You might make a difference, but how can you support a family? I also had *s'micha* [rabbinic ordination] back in the old country. I was an *illui*, a genius in Talmud. I gave private lessons to Jewish boys in Russia. I even taught the violinist Yasha Heifetz. I earned just enough to meet the bare necessities."

"It's different in America. I am not rich, but I earn a decent living."

Grandpa Abe looked at our gorgeous stained-glass windows, the ornate roof, and the *Bima* with the *ner tamid* (eternal light) and the Holy Ark.

"You obviously did well for yourself. You worship in a beautiful sanctuary that has a touch of the Old World. I am not sure that I like it. He quoted 1 Samuel 16:7 by heart: "The LORD does not look at the things people look at. People look at the outward appearance, but the LORD looks at the heart."

Grandpa Abe was obviously in a cranky mood. He resented having his sleep disturbed. On the spectrum of showiness, my synagogue ranks near the bottom.

"Papa, let's not quarrel. I don't have half your knowledge, but I taught Torah to the best of my ability, served congregations for almost thirty-four years, engaged in interfaith work, was a presence in the wider community, comforted the disturbed, and disturbed the comfortable."

"I bet you had to report to hundreds of *am ha-aratzim* [ignoramuses in Jewish matters] who do not know the Hebrew letter, *aleph* from the Hebrew letter, *bet*, but who are quite willing to tell you how to do your job."

"It's true, but I have no regrets."

"I couldn't do your work, even in America. I do not suffer fools gladly."

"Oh, Papa, who knows how much time is left to spend together? As a teenager, I yearned for the day when we could study the sacred texts together as two mature adults."

"So you want to study texts. Here's one for you."

Grandpa quoted the first chapter of *Pirkei Avot*. "Moses received the Torah at Sinai and transmitted it to Joshua, Joshua to the elders, and the elders to the prophets, and the prophets to the Men of the Great Assembly. They said three things: Be deliberate in judgment. Raise many disciples and make a fence round the Torah.

"If you follow all of chapter 1 into chapter 2, you have the chain of Jewish tradition from Moses to the supposed editor of the Mishnah, Judah ha Nasi. So what is the purpose of introducing *Pikei Avoth* by giving the chain of tradition at the very beginning?"

I responded, "To show that the rabbis did not cook up their ethical teachings from the tops of their heads but that everything is ultimately connected to the Torah received by Moses."

"Precisely! Let's apply this to your situation. I received Torah from the yeshivah in Kiev. In your youth, I transmitted some of it to you. You have undoubtedly transmitted it to many others. Unlike me, you are patient and deliberate in judgment, not only of law but of people as well. You probably raised many disciples. You have done your best to prevent Torah from diminishing on your watch."

"When I visited the former Soviet Union, one of your former students gave me a version of *Pirkei Avot* that you once owned before you immigrated to America. When I read it, I feel that you are still part of me even though you are now in the *Olam ha Ba*. For one day in 1981, I walked the same streets of Kiev as you did and taught Torah as you did."

Grandpa Abe was dumfounded by this revelation. "So my collection of *Pirkei Avot* ended up in your hands, and you have also taught in the old country. It gives me *nachas* [gratification]. Even now, I know you well."

Maureen came up the stairs. "There's someone else who wants to see you. He's a much younger man, probably in his thirties. He was also intrigued by your name on the placard. Rabbi Levin, you are popular today!"

The man who walked the stairs was about six feet tall and of medium build. Although he had a dark complexion, he had many familiar family features, including the high forehead that both Grandpa Abe and I had in common.

"How did you get here?" I asked.

"A cloud of fog surrounded me, and I found myself standing on Fort Washington Avenue and staring at your name on the placard. Are you my grandfather?"

I thought to myself, *That's quite a feat. Neither of my adult children are married, and I know of no pregnancies at this time.*

"Who are you, and how do you know me?"

"I am Jacob. I believe that I am your grandson. I only knew you as a small child. I was born in Israel. My father, Shmuel Sassoon, is a

Yemenite mathematics professor at Hebrew University. My mother, Bracha, is an immigration lawyer. After starting her career representing undocumented immigrants from Latin America, she made aliyah and now works with Jews, Christians, and Muslims, both Israelis and Palestinians. She is quite a fireball who has great influence in the Knesset. She even has the ear of the Israeli prime minister."

"I'm not surprised," I replied. "She's probably giving the prime minister an earful!"

"My mother is so thorough in her paperwork that she kills a lot of trees along the way. For her, the annual JNF appeals and tree planting in Israel on Tu B'Shevat, Jewish Arbor Day, have special relevance."

"What do you do for a living?"

"Like the two of you, I am also a rabbi. I was ordained at Hebrew Union College in Jerusalem. My official name is Rabbi Jacob Levin Sassoon, but most people refer to me as Rabbi Jacob or Rabbi Yaakov. I also have a PhD in Jewish education and am currently the CEO of the Leo Baeck Educational Center in Haifa."

"Your English is fluent. Where did you get your education?"

"Mostly in Israel. I earned my doctorate at Gratz College in Philadelphia."

"So you had to navigate through the GRE tests."

"My mother said that if you can read the English language, you can ace any standardized American test. She was right!"

"Did you come across Uncle Greg?"

"Oh, Uncle Greg. He rose to the tippy top of his consultancy organization, made a good chunk of money, and owns a rambling mansion in Westchester County. He founded a high-end restaurant in New York City which specializes in presentation. On the second story is a cooking school."

"Has he visited you in Israel?"

"Uncle Greg comes here frequently. He took me on my very first bar hop. He's a favorite among Israeli bartenders! He also became a philanthropist and has given tons of money to the Leo Baeck Educational Center. As a visitor, he puts on the best Purim parties. There is food galore, some of which comes from his recipe book, and the Carmel wine is flowing. The children adore him!

"Uncle Greg was named after Georges Garel, who hid Jewish children and smuggled some of them outside of German-controlled France. I guess that was not part of Greg's calling."

"I would like to correct you, if I may. There are more ways to save children than physical deliverance. With his money and with his support, he has saved Israeli and Arab children from ignorance and bigotry. Maybe it comes from the semester he spent in Germany and his visits to Auschwitz, Birkenau, Dachau, and Sachsenhausen. Greg is not particularly interested in Judaism per se, and you will rarely find him in the synagogue. But he cares deeply about Jews."

"What are you doing now?"

"I am travelling to other Israeli cities, notably Tel Aviv and Jerusalem, and am trying to set up other schools based on the Leo Baeck Educational Center model. Jewish learning and tikkun olam, repairing our world go hand in hand. A Jewish state and democracy are compatible. I am a rabbi for Jews, Christians, and Muslims alike. All of Israel hungers for Torah! The entire world needs Torah!

"Educating a new generation, with emphasis on coexistence and cooperation, is the key. I have read Jewish history books written by Jewish scholars from all points of the political spectrum. One characteristic is common to all of them—the lack of empathy! Right-wing history books focus on violent acts of Arabs and gloss over Israeli atrocities while Left-wing history books focus on Israeli atrocities and gloss over violent acts of Arabs. All Arabs are branded as terrorists. All Zionists are branded as usurpers engaged in ethnic cleansing and erasure of Arab culture. The truth is not so simple. *Shoah* must be taken seriously by Arabs, and *Nakba* must be taken seriously by Israelis.

"I have a strong network with both Israeli and Arab educators. We are striving to replace textbooks which have perpetuated stereotypes for generations and to replace them with textbooks that provide a more balanced approach to the Israeli-Palestinian conflict. The book *Side by Side* accomplishes this goal by juxtaposing Israeli and Arab readings of history and taking both Israelis and Arabs out of their respective comfort zones. If there is Jewish-Muslim cooperation in the education field, it could easily spill over into many other areas as well. Perhaps the totality of all this cooperation is overall peace in the Middle East, God-willing!

"Simply bringing Israeli youth to the Polish camps is counterproductive. It reinforces the Zionist agenda by sending a message that non-Jews are our enemies. It encourages Israeli youth to project their trauma unto Arabs.

"During the summer break, I am organizing multidimensional journeys which emphasize hope and trust. Groups of Israeli students, Jews and Arabs, will visit Spain—Aragon, Castile, and Andalusia. They will become familiar with the Golden Age when Islam and Judaism had mutually beneficial relationships. Each one of them will see and understand that there was a time of spiritual alternatives to military service, suicide bombing, and terror. From Spain, they will travel to Germany and Eastern Europe and study the Shoah in its full European context. They will visit immigrant Muslim concentrations in the heart of Europe where a new European Islam is attempting to exist. From there, they will return home to Israel and tour the confrontational history of Jews and Arabs. In the end, they will sit down to draw their own conclusions of this historic journey. I am certain that they will come away with the belief that racism and violence does not have to be the inevitable reality."

"So like the Jacob of the Bible, you have engaged in a bit of God-wrestling yourself."

"I wrestle with bigotry, ignorance, and narrow-mindedness among both Israelis and Arabs. Maybe someday, I will truly become Israel."

Grandpa Abe responded, "Well, Isaac, your grandson is following in your footsteps just as you have walked in my footsteps. Perhaps you have raised up disciples after all!"

At that point, another figure suddenly appeared in the sanctuary—a man with white hair, a long white beard, and a holy face.

"Who are you?" I asked.

"I am the Messiah," he replied.

"That's about what I would expect. My grandfather reappears from the dead. My grandson, who in 2014 hasn't been born yet, appears out of the blue. And now the Messiah."

"A pretty neat trick." The Messiah chuckled. "Your grandfather was a bit of a challenge. I took him out of the nursing home just before he was scheduled to die, dressed him in appropriate clothes, and brought him to your synagogue."

"If you really are what you say you are, why don't you simply put an end to all the calamity which exists on our planet? Why do you trouble a person like me?"

"Empowerment, my boy! That's the problem with this world. Men and women expect a strong man to step in and solve all their problems. Charismatic leaders have existed throughout the beginning of time. If they fail to deliver the goods, they become yesterday's news. Alternatively, such leaders often deliver the goods at the expense of curtailing civil liberties or by pointing to the other as the source of all the community's woes. Change is only meaningful if ordinary people are empowered and take ownership of the problems which plague humanity. That's why I am troubling you."

"Why did you take my grandfather and my grandson out of their time streams and bring them here? I'm not supposed to meet Grandpa Abe as an adult, nor do I see any grandchildren on the horizon."

"You need some motivation and, quite frankly, a swift kick in the butt! Is not a man the total of his past, present, and future identities? Isaac, you have been given a once-in-a-lifetime gift, an opportunity to interact with your grandfather and a window unto the future. The Holy One, blessed be He, has reserved this gift for you! Don't squander it!"

"I suppose your taking Basil Henriques out of his time stream was part of the general plan as well. Isn't all this a bit unorthodox?"

"It was also approved by the Holy One, blessed be He. We live in unorthodox times. People like me must think outside the box, so to speak. Can I count on you?"

"Here's a news flash, O holy Messiah. I am not a *lamed vavnick*. I am not among the thirty-six righteous men sent to bring holiness to our world. I am not the greatest prodigy that ever came out of my seminary. I would never have been voted as the most likely to succeed. I am not an *illui* like my grandfather, Abraham, nor am I a mover and shaker like my grandson, Jacob. I am an introvert that prefers to work quietly behind the scenes."

"What makes you think that the Holy One, blessed be He, expects you to be a *lamed-vavnick?* What makes you think that God expects you to be a genius or a person that turns the world upside down? God expects you to live up to the potential that is within you!"

"And what specifically what do you think God expects of me?"

"You are a connector. You, Isaac, are the link which connects your grandfather, Abraham, and your grandson, Jacob."

Grandpa Abe added, "Without you, this great scholarship that the entire family thinks I have would have ended up in the dustbin of history. I didn't have the courage to seriously apply my knowledge. You took whatever you learned from me, what you have learned from the seminary, and what you have taught yourself and have applied it to your community work."

Jacob continued, "From the stories that my mother told me, your work with African Americans, Latinx, and Muslims inspired her to do the work that she does, which in turn inspired me to shake up the education system and be a big shit disturber in Israel."

The Messiah reentered the conversation. "Isaac, did you not connect Simone from the west and Sanna from the east so many years ago? The heavenly ledger also shows that you brought many young people to Jewish camp, influenced many to enter Jewish professions, and mentored student rabbis and student cantors? Who else could bring a diverse group of clergy and teachers to a remote Long Island town, which was once the center of pseudoscientific bigotry, to eat, drink, study, and pray together? You have made a difference in this world, but you still have much to do. There is much potential in you. So don't give me this business that you are not up to the job!"

"I've gotten a lot of pushback. So many of my congregants seem so tribal. They refuse to see the big picture."

"Did I ever suggest that being a spiritual leader in the twenty-first century is easy? It's often a lonely life. Many people have little desire to see a big picture. The vision of many congregants does not extend beyond the latest synagogue dinner. Many are preoccupied with pet projects and parochial interests. Many see their place of worship as a fortress, as an escape from the harsh realities of the outside world. They expect people like you to condemn sin but to avoid controversy and to avoid offending anyone."

"What is a spiritual leader supposed to do?"

"Follow the wise words of Dr. Kent M. Keith, who once wrote, 'The biggest men and women with the biggest ideas can be shot down by the smallest men and women with the smallest minds. Think big anyway.'

"Abraham, Isaac, and Jacob, it's time to say your goodbyes."

"Papa," I cried. "I lost you so many years ago. I can't bear to lose you again."

"My dear Isaac, I am not afraid of returning to my time stream. I am not afraid of death. Now I know that I have two able replacements that will put into practice what I didn't accomplish during my lifetime. Just remember these words.

> When life's career reaches your height
> In vigor, substance your rightful share
> In quiet meditation, in a dreamy night,
> Papa's memories you may cherish to care.

"Grandfather," said Jacob. "If I report this meeting to the faculty and students of the Leo Baeck Educational Center, I am sure that I will be committed to a mental institution. Nevertheless, I will internalize this rich legacy that you passed on to me, and it will inspire me to make Israel a better place. Let's shake on it. Let's have a group hug!"

Grandpa Abe who came before me, Jacob who will come after me, and I shook hands and embraced one final time.

"Splendid chaps, all three of you," said the Messiah. "Now I must say farewell myself."

"Will I see you again?" I asked.

The Messiah replied, "One day I shall come back. Until then, continue the good fight even when you stumble or face criticism. Just go forward in all your beliefs and prove to me that I am not mistaken in mine. Goodbye, Isaac. Goodbye, my friend."

Grandpa Abe, Jacob, and the Messiah then disappeared in a cloud of smoke.

*****

I woke up from my dream. Jacob had his encounter with the divine so many centuries ago. I had my own last night. Surely God was in this bedroom, and I was not aware of it.

"Sweety," said Tova. "You tossed and turned all night."

"I had this insane dream in which I met my grandfather, our future grandson, and the Messiah. Great changes were in store for the Israeli educational system. The Jewish State was on the cusp of achieving everlasting peace between the Jewish and Arab populations."

"From your mouth to God's ears."

I replied with Theodor Herzl words: "*Im tirtsu, ayn zo aggada. If you wish it, it is not a dream.*"

Chapter II
The New City on a Hill

Thank God for kids, there's magic for a while
A special kind of sunshine in a smile
Do you ever stop to think or wonder why?
The nearest thing to heaven is a child

—Edward Futch

And the old shall dream dreams, and
the youth shall see visions,
And our hopes shall rise up to the sky.
We must live for today; we must
build for tomorrow.
Give us time, give us strength, give us life.

—Debbie Friedman

I

Washington, DC
May 17, 1954

Chief Justice Earl Warren had butterflies in his stomach as he got ready to render the Supreme Court's decision on *Brown v. Board of Education of Topeka*. In 1951, the issue of segregated schools came before the highest court of the land. The NAACP was doing a frontal assault on various Jim Crow laws at the time. The team of lawyers was now seeking to overturn the landmark case *Plessy v. Ferguson*, which was decided in 1896. The Supreme Court at that time held that the Fourteenth Amendment of the Constitution, which prevented states from enforcing any law which shall abridge the privileges or immunities of American citizens, did not prevent segregated institutions provided that the facilities were equal. The NAACP dared to question the principle of "separate but equal."

Under the leadership of Chief Justice Fred Vinson, who was the chief stumbling block, the case appeared to be dead in the water. Other justices, such as Felix Frankfurter and Robert H. Jackson, disapproved of segregation but also disapproved of judicial activism. Justice Tom C. Clark also believed that the states should work the problem out on their own. Justice Stanley F. Reed believed that the cultural assimilation of Blacks was incomplete and that they were actually better off with segregated schools.

In September 1953, fate turned its huge hand. Chief Justice Fred Vinson suddenly died of a heart attack, and President Dwight Eisenhower nominated Earl Warren as the new chief justice. It was a curious appointment. While Earl Warren had been a practicing lawyer and had much government experience, he had not spent one day on the bench. He took on the mantle of leadership at a critical moment of American history.

Chief Justice Earl Warren could count on the support of William O. Douglas, Hugo Black, Harold Hitz Burton, and Sherman Minton. Together, the five of them would have made up the required majority. Earl Warren's goals were much higher. He wanted a unanimous decision! If the Supreme Court's verdict on *Brown v. Board of Education of Topeka* passed, he imagined many government and school officials folding their arms, grimacing their faces, and reiterating the words of President Andrew Jackson: "The Supreme Court made its decision. Let them enforce it." By seeking a unanimous decision and avoiding even a single dissension, the Court might avoid massive Southern resistance.

Earl Warren convened a meeting of the justices and presented to them the simple argument that the only reason to sustain segregation was an honest belief in the inferiority of Negroes. He further submitted that the court must overrule *Plessy* to maintain its legitimacy as an institution of liberty. The final vote was 9-0.

After taking a deep breath, Chief Justice Earl Warren uttered the following words:

> In approaching this problem, we cannot turn the clock back to 1896 when Plessy v. Ferguson was written. We must consider public education in the light of its full development and its present place in American life throughout the Nation. Only in this way can it be determined if segregation in public schools deprives these plaintiffs of the equal protection of the laws.
>
> To separate children from others of similar age and qualifications solely because of their race generates a feeling of inferiority as to their status in the community that may affect their hearts and minds in a way unlikely to be undone.
>
> We conclude that in the field of public education the doctrine of "Separate but equal" has no place. Separate educational facilities are inherently unequal.

II

New York City
May 19, 2014

The Grace Afternoon School had moved into our building, lock, stock, and barrel. The office space and classrooms were all in place. Chairs were set up facing the stage in preparation for our opening assembly. Tables were also set up for snacks and the kitchen, manned by both the Grace staff and Congregation Rodef Tzedek teenagers, was humming along. Our bilingual custodian, William Ramirez, did much of the heavy lifting and was quite excited. The children would arrive at around 3:00 p.m.

In preparation for our newest tenant, I voluntarily moved my study to the second floor. The room that I vacated was converted to a multipurpose room. It could be used for both classes and meetings. It had the advantage of having a built-in air-condition unit. I referred to the place as the situation room.

And a situation room it was. The same group of clergy people that accompanied me to Cold Spring Harbor was now assembled around the table. I wanted a large cross-section of the northern Manhattan community to take ownership of this program. The most vocal, of course, were those colleagues who were also using the building: Sanford Kantor, Anton Muharsky, Pastor Renjiro Suzuki, and Pastor Antonio Vasquez. It was a golden opportunity for Pastor Antonio. He was best qualified to meet the pastoral needs of the Latinx families entering the facility. Perhaps some of them will join and support his growing congregation.

In the situation room, I made it clear that I wasn't interested in simply warehousing a group of children for revenue. In fact, I also said that I do not want to be viewed as the landlord. We would be full partners in building something special. The money that we received from organizations using our facilities would be looked upon by me as reimbursement for use of the building and for the normal wear and tear.

We were outdoing ourselves in coming up with potential programs. On Wednesdays, for instance, we would arrange the logistics so that some of our children would interact with the elderly members of our sisterhood. Most of the sisterhood members were European immigrants many decades ago. Many of the parents of the children came to the United States as immigrants from the Dominican Republic. A definite area of commonality.

Anton Muharsky inquired as to the possibility of some of our retired members and some of our high school students seeking community service credit serving as reading buddies.

I responded, "Of course. Now that I am here, it will be even easier for me to continue as a reading buddy myself. We might even have a few idealistic members who could serve as mentors on Saturday mornings as well."

Pastor Antonio Vasquez suggested that we have a Monday evening forum for teenagers from his congregation, from Grace Afternoon School, and from Rodef Tzedek to get together to discuss the social issues of the day.

Sanford Kantor was enthusiastic and said, "Rodef Tzedek will provide the pizza, the salad, and the apple juice."

"Count my congregation in as well," said Pastor Renjiro Suzuki.

Sanford continued, "Perhaps we can get a mixed group of teenagers to work in the Hebrew Union College soup kitchen. It would be a social action project with a social component was well."

Pastor Renjiro continued, "If we put our minds together, we can do all sorts of joint social action projects."

I said, "For instance, we can join forces in the annual rummage sale. In this way, we can expand our network and serve an even larger cross section of the community."

Anton observed, "If other organizations see us doing our own thing so successfully, they'll want to get in on the action. This building will be rocking from dawn to night seven days a week. Nothing succeeds like success."

"That would be tremendous," I said. "It's been my goal for a long time. Let's include the possibility of a weekly adult education night. Professionals from the four organizations using the building would offer classes, and we would have guest speakers. It would provide a great opportunity to learn more about each other's religious traditions."

"I propose that we meet regularly as we now have a nice juicy project to keep us busy for a long time. In August, we should reconvene and plan an interfaith Thanksgiving program in November. Given our discussion in Cold Spring Harbor and America's track record with Native Americans, it probably won't be a celebration about what happened at Plymouth Rock. It will more likely be a celebration of multiculturalism and the wonderful opportunity for diverse groups to pray and sing together. Thankfulness is a universal religious value."

"Amen," said the Lutheran minister, Lars Munson.

Anton tried to conclude things. "We could go on forever and ever. We will obviously think of new projects as we go long. But now, it's time to meet the children for the first time and hold our opening assembly."

***

We left the situation room and entered the social hall. Chairs were already set up on the stage where all of us would sit together during the proceedings. Before we ascended the stage, three additional people joined us: our representative on the New York Assembly, Anita De La Cruz, and our councilman representing the Tenth District, Bernard Rodriguez, and our synagogue president, Rolf Samuels.

Anita De La Cruz and Bernard Rodriguez were delighted to be making public appearances for a happy event. Too often, they are called upon to appear during crises. Too often, they have appeared in gatherings in the park across the street, to speak whenever racism or anti-Semitism reared their ugly heads.

Anita De La Cruz was a pretty but unpretentious young woman. I once had a one-to-one meeting with her in her office and was incredibly impressed by her intelligence and sensitivity to community issues. She embraced me immediately and told me, "Good job! This will benefit northern Manhattan!"

Meeting Anita De La Cruz at public gatherings was always a treat. She gave the best hugs!

Bernard Rodriguez was a tall handsome man. The relocation of the Grace Afternoon School and the willingness of so many clergy to take an interest made him ecstatic. He was once a teacher himself. He worked behind the scenes and helped both Rodef Tzedek and Grace to get special grants. He had been a true friend to us for years!

The proceedings were about to get under way, and Rolf Samuels said to me, "Perhaps I have been too hard on you. I am often so wrapped up in my music and keeping the synagogue afloat that I sometimes miss what's right in front of me. The Grace Afternoon School and the clergy alliance you helped to build will truly benefit us. Only you with your ability to interact with non-Jewish leaders could pull this off."

"Thank you, Rolf. Much appreciated."

Before Rolf took his seat, he greeted both Anita and Bernard. When I saw Rolf and Bernard shaking hands and exchanging pleasantries, I smiled. It truly warmed my heart.

The assembly opened with brief remarks from Anita De La Cruz, Bernard Rodriguez, and Anton Muharsky. Rolf Samuels extended greetings as the lay representative of the congregation.

I was now up to bat, so to speak. Maria Muharsky stood next to me to offer the simultaneous Spanish translation as I went along.

"I would like to welcome the children and staff of Grace Afternoon School to our synagogue. As I have said to all our tenants when they convened for the first time, I hope that you will make our home your home. Over the past few months, you have gotten to know me, and I have gotten to know you. Rodef Tzedek may seem strange to you at first, but in time, your school and our congregation will become very comfortable with each other.

"Today, our congregation has been formally transformed into a community center which is under the bubble. It will be a community center which will offer protection against the harsh realities of the world. We are a place where all of you will feel safe, cherished, and loved. We are a place that will provide lots of kind words and plenty of hugs."

Pastor Renjiro interjected, "When this man gives hugs, he really gives real hugs!" The rest of the group on the stage chuckled.

"There is a saying that it takes a village to educate a child. Our village consists of the congregations that use this building, my colleagues sitting on this stage, as well as other interested parties in northern Manhattan. The mayor of this village is your very own, Anton Muharsky. My office is upstairs. To make this transition as smooth as possible, both students and teachers are invited to reach out to me. I will do my best to provide aid in any way that I can. I believe that I speak for my colleagues as well.

"To the children of Grace Afternoon School, I can truly say that this entire village is here for you. I would like to paraphrase a poem that is special to me.

> We didn't give you the gift of life, but in our hearts,
> we know The love we feel is deep and real, as if it

had been so. For us to have each other is like a dream come true!

No, we didn't give you the gift of life. Life gave us the gift of you.

"Today, Grace Afternoon School has officially crossed Broadway. For too long, Broadway has been a psychological barrier in northern Manhattan. Together, we will break this barrier. Children, your energy and your enthusiasm are your gift to all of us. We hope to give back by providing a wonderful learning environment.

"This auspicious day is taking place on virtually the sixtieth anniversary of the Supreme Court's verdict on the landmark case *Brown v. Board of Education of Topeka*. The decision declared that 'in the field of education, the doctrine of separate, but equal has no place. Separate educational facilities are inherently unequal.'

"For sixty years, communities have found ways to get around this ruling. We only know it too well in New York. But in this place, this type of thinking goes to die! However, as a product of public schools, I know that integration is not simply about lumping people from different backgrounds together. It is about people of different backgrounds appreciating one another's gifts and working together to achieve a common goal. That's what we will achieve in this newly formed community center.

"Bennett Park, which is just across the street, is the highest spot in New York City. In this community center, we will become a new city on a hill. A city on a hill is not a form of religious or national exceptionalism as it was in the days of the Puritans, but a city on a hill which generates multicultural exceptionalism. We will be an example to the rest of New York City. The eyes of fellow New Yorkers will be upon us. Their hopes and prayers will be with us. Yet there is the knowledge that the war against tribalism and bigotry is still to be won.

"In Jewish schools, it is customary to serve apples and honey on the first day of classes. It symbolizes the sweetness of Jewish learning. In a few moments, all the children will be served apples and honey to go along with the normal snacks of which they are accustomed. May their days in this building be filled with only sweetness."

After my rather prolonged words of welcome, the high school volunteers as well as Davida came out of the kitchen to serve apples and honey and juice to the children from the Grace Afternoon School.

I went around to the various tables to greet them more individually.

Samantha, the old soul, asked me, "Will this be our forever home?"

"Time will only tell. I hope so," I replied.

Joel then came up to me with a Bible. He expected me to read to him as I did on the other side of Broadway.

"Please use your words, Joel."

He opened the book to the creation story. "As this is my first time in this building, I thought that we would restart with the very first story."

And so I read, "In the beginning…"

I recalled the verse from Matthew, which I saw in the main hall of Grace Afternoon School's former location, and which will forever serve as the mission statement: "Let the little children come to me, and do not hinder them, for the kingdom of heaven belongs to such as these."

III

Haifa
May 21, 2022

At the Ruth Center, Cassy was conducting the daily assembly of the afternoon school.

"*Talmidim*, students. I just received an email from Rabbi Levin. I am sure that you all remember his visit only a few weeks ago. Let me read the letter.

"Dear Cassy and Rahel,

"I promised to keep you up to date as to the progress of the Grace Afternoon School. On Monday, we formally welcomed their staff and children into our building. We hope to be more than a place which is renting out space. Like the Leo Baeck Educational Center, we hope to be a multicultural community center in which many religious faiths and many religious cultures work for the greater welfare of our wider community in Northern Manhattan.

"Your model, which brings Jews and Arabs together in both educational and social settings, is an inspiration to me. Like you, we emphasize tikkun olam. After all, we are *Rodfei Tzedek*, pursuers of justice. If I achieve half as much success in New York as you have done in Haifa, I will consider myself a very successful spiritual leader.

"L'shalom, Yitzchak."

Cassy continued, "You have no idea how much receiving a letter like this from a sister community means to me. It is good to know that our influence is not only felt in Israel but throughout our worldwide progressive movement. Perhaps we can arrange some correspondence between the children of our two schools. Jews and Muslims interact frequently around here, but how many of you have met children whose parents come from Latin America? It will be a new experience."

The students nodded approvingly.

"We have given student concerts in the New York area before. Perhaps we can reach out to this congregation."

Simultaneously, the children burst out in song:

> It's a small world after all.
> *Zeh olam katan me'od.*
> *Bledna srira baakilshi.*
> It's a small, small world.

***

THE SECRET OF REDEMPTION

Jerusalem
June 2014

Bracha and Anwar shared coffee and pastry for perhaps the last time at Aroma Espresso. They reflected on the many times that they broke bread together in this special café. They would often sit there for hours to discuss their research on the treatment of Arabs in Israeli textbooks and in children's literature. Their strategizing as to how to approach their project often gave way to conversations about their personal lives and their dreams. That would soon come to an end as Bracha would soon be returning to the United States and begin law school.

Anwar asked, "Are you excited about this new chapter in your life?"

Bracha responded, "Nervous as well. I will be spending three intense years. It will involve reading volumes of technical material, writing papers, and participating in clinics. My time will not be own."

"What type of law will you be studying?"

"Human rights law."

"Human rights are dirty words in Israel," remarked Anwar. "Many Israelis associate it with pro-Arab sensibilities and leftwing agitation against the Occupation. I wouldn't mention that term when you are interrogated by Israeli officials at Ben Gurion Airport. You will set off alarm bells. You could be detained."

"Thirty years ago, my dad got strip searched at Leningrad Airport because a customs official found a Russian language recording on a cassette tape. If the incident happened today, he would have ended up in prison or a labor camp."

"Will you have a specialty?"

"I'm especially interested in immigration law and Indian law. There is a need for immigration law, both in America and Israel. I would like to come back to Israel and work with Palestinians. I believe that my Arabic is fluent enough to function properly."

"Palestinians need all the help that they can get in terms of immigration law. They have relatively few advocates in Israel."

"What will you be doing next year, Anwar?"

"I will continue my work on my master's degree in education. And then, perhaps later, I will find a nice man and get married."

"Good luck to you. I must go home and finish my packing."

"I know that you will soon be immersed in American life and in your studies. Whatever you do, do not forget Jerusalem. Do not forget me!"

Bracha responded, quoting from Psalm 137, "If I forget you, O Jerusalem, let my right hand forget her cunning. If I do not remember you, let my tongue cleave to the roof of my mouth if I prefer not Jerusalem above my chief joy. As for you, Anwar, we have developed a special bond. I will never forget you, and I will never forget what many Palestinian families experience daily."

Anwar commented, "It's 2014. We can communicate by computer! In the meantime, may Allah be with you always."

Bracha and Anwar warmly embraced for the longest amount of time and then went their separate ways. Perhaps their paths would cross again.

Chapter 12

Two Dreams Realized

Hold fast to dreams
For if dreams die
Life is a broken-winged bird
That cannot fly.

Hold fast to dreams
For when dreams go
Life is a barren field
Frozen with snow.

—Langston Hughes

I

New York
May 29, 2014

I arrived at Kennedy Airport about thirty minutes after Simone Da Costa's plane landed. By this time, she probably collected her belongings, was going through passport control, and handing in her customs declaration. As I was standing in the waiting area of Terminal 4, my heart was thumping with excitement. I had been waiting for this reunion for many years. The last time that I saw Simone in London was in 1988.

My overseas guest finally came out with her bags.

We embraced. "Long time no see! Thank you for travelling such a long distance to participate in Davida's bat mitzvah. How was your flight from London?"

"Very smooth!"

We proceeded to my car, which was parked just outside the terminal. I laughed when Simone tried to enter my car from the driver's side. "You're in America now," I said.

It was a forty-five-minute drive to our home in Long Island. Simone was impressed with how residential this area was. It reminded her of her neighborhood in Barkingside, which was an eastern suburb of London.

She said, "If my plane hadn't landed at JFK, I would have never thought that I was in New York."

I responded, "You'll surely see the real New York when you come to my synagogue on Saturday."

May 31, 2014

In addition to Davida's family and friends, members of the congregation and other visitors also poured into the sanctuary. About fifteen minutes before the service, an entourage of the Russian community took their places in the back few rows. Among them were Luba Murzhenko, her daughters, and one of her nieces. I made a point of going up to her and giving her a big hug and a kiss as well.

I told her, "I recently saw Reuven Zelin in Haifa. He sends his best. He asked me to kiss you on his behalf."

Luba smiled. Although he lived in Leningrad and she lived in Kiev, she certainly had heard of him through her late husband's connections.

In addition to the Russian contingent, Anton and Maria and many students from the Grace Afternoon School took their places in the balcony. The program was already in full force in our building. In lieu of the usual Saturday mentoring program, the school elected to attend the service and expose the children to a real live bat mitzvah. The children knew Davida well from her volunteer work. They were here to root for her. One afternoon, I had also explained the special significance of a Russian American girl celebrating her special day on the thirtieth anniversary of the twinning of Simone Da Costa and Sanna Tsivkin. Everyone from Grace Afternoon School was excited!

Between the blasts from the past, taking the form of Luba and Simone, and our newest tenants, taking the form of Grace Afternoon School, all my yesterdays and all my hopes and aspirations for the future came together to visit me in the precious present!

The first part of the service was very straightforward. Student Cantor Joe Finkelstein led the singing and was accompanied by Rolf Samuels. I led the praying.

The worship experience became more intense when we reached the Torah service. First, Davida's parents presented her with her tallit. Davida was in her glory. Normally, she was a casual dresser, but today she was wearing a pretty light blue dress. Very tasteful!

Afterward, Simone, the ark openers, and the Torah dressers joined us on the *Bima*. When I took out the Torah, I handed it to Simone, who then handed it to Davida. It represented the passing of Torah from a former student that I taught thirty years ago to my current student. During the procession, Davida walked with the Torah and was followed by Simone, by various family members, and, of course, by me as well.

The Torah scroll was eventually undressed, and Davida read through the Torah portion like a pro. She chanted the same description of the Nazirite as Simone did in 1984 on the other side of the pond. Her rendering of the Haphtarah narrative on the birth of Samson was equally impeccable.

After the readings and after the scroll was put on a stand, it was time for Davida to begin her speech. Saddened by Russia's annexation of the Crimea only a few months ago, her remarks attempted to connect the Torah portion to both the current situation and to her special identity as a Russian American Jewish woman.

> The end of the Torah portion focuses on the priestly blessings, when Aaron and his sons are commanded to bless the whole community of Israel:
> May God bless you and protect you. May God shine His countenance upon you and give

you grace. May God raise His countenance towards you and give you peace.

The first blessing refers to material prosperity. The second blessing refers to the continuous presence of God in one's life. The third blessing refers to the beauty of inner peace. Of the three blessings, inner peace is the hardest to achieve. During the Refusenik period, back in the 1980s, it was even harder to achieve this peace when so many of our brothers and sisters were separated by thousands of miles and ruthless laws from the rest of the Jewish world.

I consider myself a proud descendant of those who had to overcome those miles and laws to join the Hevrah and become part of the free world. Those who had to raise themselves to carry their own tabernacle, and never forget their identity. Those who were hated and discriminated against, and yet found and made their way to the priestly blessings. Those who lived in the former Soviet Union. Almost thirty years ago, some extraordinary thing happened, which later influenced me to choose *Parshat Naso* for my bat mitzvah. In 1984, Rabbi Levin made what seemed to be impossible come true. With *Parshat Naso*, he twinned the bat mitzvah of an English girl, Simone Da Costa, with the bat mitzvah of a Russian girl, Sanna Tsivkin. The perestroika and glasnost movement barely got under way in the Soviet Union, but thanks to Rabbi Levin, it took full course in the life of Sanna Tsivkin, and allowed the Jewish girl from Leningrad to join the great world of the international Jewish community. Thousands of other Soviet Jewish teens had no such opportunity. My parents were among them. They could not attend synagogues, because that could lead to expulsion from the mandatory youth organization of Komsomol, as well as from their colleges. Many of their friends were not admitted to colleges or workplaces of their choice because they were Jews. They were surrounded by refuseniks, who were neither allowed by the Soviet government to live decent lives, nor to emigrate. I looked at my parents' photos from 1984. I saw bright-eyed teens with funky hairstyles, and self-made clothes, imitating their peers from the free western world. The world they would join just several years later. The world that would open the doors for their freedom, and their spiritual and material blessings, which were impossible in their homeland. The world of the beauty of inner peace.

    I was lucky to have been born in this world. I feel myself to be a proud American, as well as a proud resident of one of the most amazing and diverse communities of the city dubbed the center of the world. I am proud to have friends of so many cultural backgrounds, who enhance my life with their knowledge and experience. Unlike those Soviet teens, I have the benefits of the priestly blessings. I can travel the world. I can participate in many extracurricular activities and pursue my passions. I can support my community by all the goodness of volunteering that I have been, and always will be doing. Rabbi Levin's awesome endeavor came full circle. Today is a personal milestone, as I become the first female in my family to celebrate a traditional bat mitzvah, and to read from the Torah.

    For many years, the membership of this congregation has consisted largely of Holocaust survivors who also suffered from anti-Semitism on the other side of the Atlantic. And so, I would like to mark this special day by commemorating a beautiful young man named Rudy Seidman, who perished in the Holocaust at the age of thirteen, never getting a chance to enjoy his bar mitzvah, to enjoy his adulthood, this beautiful world, and beautiful life. This is for the dear brother of my dear mentor, our own Mr. Alfred Seidman.

I will keep striving to achieve the beauty and harmony of the inner peace. As I enter the doors of my adulthood, and become a daughter of the commandment, I am thinking of striving to lead a "priestly life." I will try to bring the blessing of beauty and harmony with my art, whether I would teach it to children or participate in international projects. I will try to use my knowledge and experience to mend the bond between the two great nations of Russia and America, the bonds which had undergone so many changes and harsh tests of time. Any Jew should look beyond the Yiddishkeit and see how and where the help is needed; that would be the greatness and beauty of a true Jewish soul. With the independence movement evolving in my father's native Ukraine, and people having died for their country's freedom from Putin's Russia, I am proud to know that many Ukrainian Jews, despite the threat of traditional anti-Semitism, raised their heads and stood together with their Ukrainian compatriots against the totalitarianism imposed by Moscow, and for the unification with the European Union. We have witnessed Russia's invasion into the sovereign state of Ukraine, and along with the whole progressive humanity we must rise against it, or the history may repeat itself yet again... Let us remember Hitler's Anschluss of Austria. No one spoke then...

Having dumped over $51 billion into the lavish show-off Olympics, the Russian government lets millions of elderly citizens, weak and sick people perish in utter poverty. Nowadays, the Russian kleptocratic government is turning the wheel of history back to the Soviet trends of an authoritarian regime. The freedom of speech is being suffocated and any opposition is crushed. The corruption of the authorities is immeasurable and sexual minorities are bashed with impunity. All of this can be compared to Nazism. At any given time, the Russian government could turn back to the old Soviet policy of anti-Semitism, and the teens of the 2020s would face the same fate as their parents and grandparents did under the Communist regime.

And if there would be anything I could do to extend the priestly blessings to the keepers of modern Russia's tabernacle, and to any oppressed society there, I would strive to help rise above the limits set by authorities, to help reach the beauty of inner peace, theirs, and mind.

After that profound message, Davida's mother, Larissa, offered a few words of her own. Facing Davida, she addressed her in Russian. Although she was overcome with emotion and broke down in tears in the middle of her spiel, she got through her speech. She ended with a special blessing:

Baruch she-p'tarani mei'anshah she-lazot. Blessed be the One who has made our daughter responsible for herself. Into our hands, O God, You have placed your Torah, to be held high by parents and children, and taught by one generation to the next. Whatever has befallen us, our people have remained steadfast in loyalty to the Torah. It was carried into exile in the arms of parents that their children might not be deprived of their birthright. And now, we pray that you, Davida, may always be worthy of this inheritance. Take its teaching into your heart, and in turn pass it on to your children and those who come after you. May you be a faithful Jew, searching for wisdom and truth, working for justice and peace. May the one who has always been our guide inspire you to bring honor to our family and to the house of Israel. Amen.

To the surprise of the congregation, I introduced Simone Da Costa, the Englishwoman who participated in the twinning thirty years ago and who was able to be with us today. Simone came up to the *Bima* and also made some comments.

Davida, it is a great honor to finally meet you. I don't feel that I am addressing a young teenager. I feel that I am addressing a grown woman. The way that you carried yourself and the way that you spoke showed great maturity.

It's hard to remember everything that took place thirty years ago, but I can tell you this. We have two things in common. We both shared a common teacher, Rabbi Levin, who was quite demanding.

Secondly, we are both connected to the former Soviet Union. I was twinned with Sanna Tsivkin, who suffered some of the bad experiences that your parents suffered, and with whom I had the pleasure of reconnecting via Skype some time ago.

There is one big difference. During my bat mitzvah at the Settlement Synagogue, there was an empty chair with a tallit draped over it. It symbolized the reality that Sanna could not celebrate her own bat mitzvah, nor share in my celebration. When I called her in Leningrad, an operator listened to our entire telephone conversation.

Here in New York, there is no empty chair with a tallit draped over it. You can wear a tallit. You can read from the Torah. You can celebrate with family and friends. You can express your Judaism openly.

If there is a lesson to be learned from this day, it is to value your freedom. Do not squander it. Never be satisfied with mediocrity. Use your God-given talents to benefit society. I wish you much success for the future.

At that point, I came up to speak.

Congratulations to you, Davida, for becoming a daughter of the commandment and taking your place in the community of Israel. Both your reading of Torah and Haphtarah and your thoughtful message blew me away. It was the product of incredibly hard work and perseverance. As the first female bat mitzvah of your family, which would have never taken place during the refusenik era, all your relatives must be ecstatic. They come to Congregation Rodef Tzedek from Russia with love.

As another connection between Simone's bat mitzvah in 1984 and yours in 2014, I am displaying the same doll dressed in Ukrainian costume that I displayed thirty years ago. Back in the old country, the doll was used to warm the teapot. I keep it for only display purposes. The name of this doll is Alanna. She symbolized the refusenik child who could not receive a Jewish education and had to hide her Jewish identity while she was still living in the Soviet Union. Fortunately, in New York, as a Russian American Jew, you can proclaim your Jewish identity loud and clear and thrive in our community.

The following words are attributed to the Baal Shem Tov. "Forgetfulness leads to exile, but remembrance is the secret of redemption." I partially agree with him, but I would argue that remembrance is not enough. *Pamyat* is the Russian word for memory. It is also the name for a fanatically nationalist and anti-Semitic organization in Russia. It makes negative use of memory and classical Jewish stereotypes to spew out their venom.

While memory is important in Judaism and is featured in the Haggadah, memory often creates bitterness. People often draw the wrong conclusions from their memories. Alcoholism is often passed on through the generations. Spouse and child abuse is often passed on through the generations. Racism is often transmitted through the generations. Oppressed people are often obsessed with seeking revenge against their oppressors. Alternatively, they often project the pain afflicted by their oppressors unto other peoples and oppress them in turn.

The most important mitzvah in our tradition is to love the stranger because our people were strangers in the land of Egypt. It is repeated in the Torah thirty-six times for emphasis. The psychology behind this commandment is profound. God delivered our ancestors from Egypt and was also aware that they would face many formidable enemies as they enter the promised land. Instead of projecting what was done to them unto people outside of their community, they are to embrace the other and to welcome them as equals. It's an important lesson for Holocaust survivors. It's an important lesson for those who became victims of Soviet oppression.

Thus, remembrance must be accompanied by *tikkun olam*, repairing our broken world. Given your wide spectrum of friends in our great multicultural neighborhood and your long track record of volunteerism in both the Jewish and wider communities, I believe that as a Jewish adult, you will balance remembrance with social action.

We hope that you will continue your Jewish studies in our Hebrew High School and continue to be involved in our community. May you evolve from a bat mitzvah, a daughter of the commandment, to a *baalat mitzvah*, a master of the commandment, and become an invaluable asset to our North Manhattan community.

I then laid my hands upon Davida. Student Cantor Joe Finkelstein chanted the priestly blessing in Hebrew as it appeared in the Torah scroll and as was quoted in English in Davida's Dvar Torah.

I recited the English translation. Although Davida and I are not normally demonstrative people, we got caught up in the emotion of the moment and warmly hugged each other.

There was a musical interval. Just as the Settlement Synagogue's organist, Jacob Walsh, played an excerpt from Tchaikovsky's sixth symphony, the *Pathetique*, our organist, Rolf Samuels, played the same melody today.

Sanford Kantor then came up to the *Bima*. In his usual style, not only did he congratulate Davida, he also collected positive comments from friends, family, and fellow students and read them before the congregation. He then presented Davida with the Gunther Plaut

Chumash with commentaries and the relatively new reform siddur, *Mishkan T'filah*.

At that point, the congregation hurled candy at Davida while the congregation sang "Seman Tov! Mazel Tov!"

After the closing hymn and my closing benediction, Rolf Samuels played another Tchaikovsky piece that was also played by Jacob Walsh, the opening bars of the *Serenade for Strings*.

Thirty years ago, two girls spoke on the telephone from their respective sides of the Iron Curtain and held loving hands across a war-torn continent. The ballad of east and west was bittersweet.

This Shabbat morning, east and west met face-to-face in joyous celebration.

II

Jerusalem
December 24, 2018

On a rather chilly Monday morning, with the Western Wall in the background, Esther became bat mitzvah and took her place as a young woman in the community of Israel. Esther was the daughter of Sanna Tsivkin and the granddaughter of Vladimir and Irina Tsivkin.

Somehow, the Torah portion, *Parshat Shemot*, was *bashert*, destined to be. Esther chanted the same verses from Exodus that I quoted four years ago at the Cold Spring Harbor symposium: "And Pharaoh said unto his people, 'Behold, the people of the children of Israel are more and mightier than we: Come on, let us deal wisely with them; lest they multiply.'"

Pharaoh's legacy has been played out throughout world history. In America, it played out in the form of the Johnson-Reed Act of 1924 and has remained just beneath the surface ever since. In the former Soviet Union, it played out in the form of racist propaganda spewed out by state-supported anti-Semitism. All of this caused anguish and suffering for Esther's mother and grandparents.

Immediately after Esther completed the reading from the scroll, the three generations of Esther's family joined hands and danced around the large table containing the Torah. They joyfully sang "Seman Tov! Mazel Tov!" Coming to Jerusalem to celebrate the bat mitzvah of a granddaughter was a dream come true for ex-refuseniks Vladimir and Irina. This unabashed merrymaking represented the ultimate triumph of Torah over Soviet-style oppression!

This confident young woman represented a new generation. Esther was the new Jew in Israel who chose to put the ghosts of the past in the rearview mirror. When delivering her commentary on her Torah portion, she put a much more positive spin by focusing on courage. She cited the bravery of the midwives for refusing to drown newborn Hebrew sons and for sparing the life of Moses. She cited the bravery of Moses's sister, Miriam. When the Pharaoh's daughter found baby Moses floating in the basket down the Nile, she wanted to keep him. Miriam judiciously offered to serve as the wet nurse so Moses's mother would be able to keep tabs on him. Esther also cited the great risks that Moses took in serving as an intermediary between the powerful Pharaoh and the children of Israel.

Moses's actions were particularly significant. When confronting the Pharaoh time and again, he spoke truth to power. He demanded that he "let his people go," or there would be grave consequences. The consequences, of course, were the ten plagues.

Esther concluded her speech by emphasizing that Jews are responsible for one another and for the welfare of society in general. People need to get involved when there is injustice, become intermediaries, and speak truth to power if necessary. As a daughter of the commandment, she promised to answer that call.

Just as Larissa offered a prayer and words of wisdom to her daughter, Davida, nearly four years ago in New York, so did the parents of Esther. They said together:

> *Baruch she-p'tarani mei'anshah she-lazot.* Blessed be the One who has made our daughter responsible for herself. May the voices of the generations of our people move through you and may the God of our ancestors be your God as well. May you know that there is a people and a

rich heritage to which you belong and from that sacred place, you are connected to all who dwell on the earth. May the stories of our people be upon your heart and the grace of Torah rhyme and dance in your soul.

The rabbi who officiated at the ceremony congratulated Esther on her wonderful achievement and her entire family for reaching this special milestone. In her comments, she made the following remarks:

> Esther, your Torah portion is the origin narrative of Jewish history. Throughout the ages, Jewish people have been at the mercy of leaders who "did not know Joseph." They ignored the contributions that Jews have made to their countries and were quick to hold them up as scapegoats for their internal problems. To satisfy the masses or to consolidate power, they were equally willing to persecute them, to torture or murder them, to insist upon conversion, or to resort to outright expulsion. It happened in Spain and was later applied to native Americans in the New World. It happened in Nazi Germany. It happened in the former Soviet Union.
>
> Yes, Moses spoke truth to power. So did the biblical prophets that came centuries after him. They did not hesitate to chastise their leaders for their immorality, for their bloodshed, and for their corruption. They did not hesitate to point out the inequality which existed in society.
>
> In your Dvar Torah, Esther, you affirmed your eagerness to become an intermediary and to speak truth to power when necessary. The *megillah*, which is read on Purim, described the heroism of Esther. She risked her life by seeking an audience with King Ahasuerus. If he didn't raise

the royal scepter and didn't welcome her to his court, she could be put to death. Esther spoke truth to power by exposing Haman's evil plot against Persian Jewry. She served as an intermediary between King Ahasuerus and her people by pleading for their lives. To take your place in the community of Israel sometimes means having the courage to speak out whenever there is injustice. This is what it means for Jews to be responsible for one another.

Your grandparents followed the examples of both Moses and the prophets. In their own special way, they spoke truth to power. They refused to live under harsh conditions in the former Soviet Union. They refused to be subjected to the anti-Semitic propaganda of *Pamyat*. They took steps to leave the country, even at the risk of losing their jobs and being callously treated by government officials.

Intermediaries played a role in their campaign. Your grandmother, Irina, spent months touring the United States and speaking to local Soviet Jewry chapters.

Intermediaries also played a critical role in your grandparents' ultimate departure from the Soviet Union. They were well known by politicians in the houses of Congress and in the hallways of Parliament. The most prominent intermediary was Senator Frank Lautenberg. Indeed, the Lautenberg Amendment of 1990 facilitated the emigration of Soviet Jews by relaxing stringent standards for refugee status and by granting immigrant status to those who could show religious persecution in their native lands.

Because of the courage of Vladimir and Irina, we are all able to celebrate this morning.

> Back in the 1980s, traveling to Jerusalem was but a pipedream in the former Soviet Union. Today it is a reality. As the Haggadah might put it, "Thirty years ago, your grandparents and mother were slaves to totalitarian tyranny. Today, they are free people." You are a free woman living in America. And so we can say with great joy, "This year in Jerusalem."
>
> Blessed are you, Adonai our God, the ruler of the universe, who has kept your family alive, has sustained them, and has helped them to reach this season.

The rabbi handed the Torah scroll to Esther, and there was more intergenerational singing and dancing.

Afterward, Esther recited the words of Edmond Fleg, a Jewish French writer, thinker, novelist, essayist, and playwright of the twentieth century.

> I am a Jew because my faith demands of me no abdication of the mind.
>
> I am a Jew because my faith requires of me all the devotion of my heart.
>
> I am a Jew because, in every place where suffering weeps, the Jew weeps.
>
> I am a Jew because at every time when despair cries out, the Jew hopes.
>
> I am a Jew because the word of the people of Israel is the oldest and the newest.
>
> I am a Jew because the promise of Israel is the universal promise.
>
> I am a Jew because, for Israel, the world is not completed; we are completing it.
>
> I am a Jew because, for Israel, humanity is not created; we are creating it.

The ceremony concluded with the singing of "Yerushalayim Shel Zahav" (Jerusalem of Gold), written by Naomi Shemer. Irina sang the first verse as a solo.

> *Avir harim tzalul kayayin v'rei-ach oranim*
> *Nisa b'ruach haarbayim im kol paamonim.*
> *U'tardeimat ilan va-even sh'vuyah bachalomah*
> *Ha-ir asher badad yoshevet uv'libah chomah.*

> (The mountain air is clear as wine and the fragrance of pine is carried in the evening breeze with the sound of bells.
> In the slumber of tree and stone, captive within her dream, is the city which sits deserted, and the wall at its heart.)

Everyone at the bat mitzvah ceremony joined in the chorus.

> *Y'rushalayim shel Zahav*
> *V'shel n'choshet v'shel or*
> *Halo l'chol shirayich ani kinor.*

> (Jerusalem of gold, of bronze, and of light, am I not a harp for all your songs.)

The b'not mitzvah of Davida in New York and Esther in Jerusalem are etched in my memory to this very day. They accomplished in 2014 and 2018, respectively, what could not have been considered in the 1980s. And so the tale of two dreams comes to a happy ending. Martin Luther King Jr. was right. "The arc of the moral universe is long, but it truly bends toward justice."

Epilogue

And once again the scene was changed
New earth there seemed to be
I saw the holy city beside the tideless sea
The light of God was on the streets
The gates are opened wide
And all who would might enter
And no one was denied
No need of moon or stars by night
Or sun to shine by day
It was the new Jerusalem
That would not pass away

—Frederic Weatherly

Long Island, New York
June 2, 2014

    I picked up Simone Da Costa at the Merrick train station. She spent the morning in New York City with Larissa and Davida. We loaded her luggage in the trunk of my car, and we drove off to JFK Airport. With moderate traffic, I expected a thirty-minute ride at most.

"So tell me about your visit. Did you have a nice lunch?"

"Yes, indeed. They took me to one of the most touristy spots in New York—the Statue of Liberty! As we stood underneath Lady Liberty, who lifted her lamp beside the Golden Door, Larissa described how she was among those huddled masses yearning to breathe free."

I replied, "As were the Tsivkin family, first Vladimir and then his wife and daughter. As were my grandparents almost a century ago. My maternal grandmother kissed the ground when she entered Ellis Island."

Simone continued, "God intervened and helped both families and thousands of others to find their way to America. Perhaps not through an outstretched arm and great wonders but through Gorbachev's more liberal policies, friends in high places, sheer luck, or some combination of the three. Human perseverance brought about the great wonders."

"While I made a life for myself in New York, I reflected fondly on my former life in Great Britain. It was a less aggressive place than America. Most people had manners. Whenever I watch the last night of the Proms on YouTube, listen to the rendering of 'Land of Hope and Glory,' and see the throngs in the Royal Albert Hall waving their union jacks, I get a lump in my throat."

Simone smiled. Perhaps she thought I was being a little bit corny or mawkish.

"One of the highlights of my nine-year stint in Great Britain was my visit to the House of Lords. In my capacity as a representative from the Assembly of Rabbis, an arm of the former Reform Synagogues of Great Britain, I witnessed the launching of Martin Gilbert's official biography of Winston Church. His grandson, Winston Churchill III, made some comments of his own.

"As I walked through the Parliament Building, powerful words from the venerable prime minister echoed within those walls:

> And even if, which I do not for a moment believe, this island or a large part of it were subjugated and starving, our Empire beyond the seas, armed and guarded by the British Fleet, would carry on the struggle, until in God's good time, the New World, with all its power and might, steps forth to the rescue and liberation of the old.

"The so-called Old World, so many years ago, stepped forth and came to the rescue of me. I was a shy, insecure young man back then. If it weren't for the hospitality, the support, and the encouragement from friends, teachers, and even congregants, I am not sure if I would have made it.

"Someday, I will return. By offering rabbinic services to underserved communities, such as teaching or officiating during the High Holy Days, I will repay all the kindness that was thrown my way."

"I hope that you can make it happen. You won't recognize the old neighborhood where you lived in South Ilford, nor some parts of London. Many changes. I'd be delighted to give you a tour. You'll have to get used to our glorious city all over again."

"May that happen *bimheira uvyameinu*, speedily and in our days."

We arrived at Terminal 4. As we got out of the car and removed the bags from the trunk, I said, "Simone, it was great having you here. Not only because of your contribution to Davida's bat mitzvah but also because it was an opportunity to renew my friendship with you."

"I feel the same," she responded.

"Give my love to your parents."

"I will."

After we briefly embraced, Simone made her way to the terminal. I made my way back to Long Island.

*****

En route to my residence, I made a detour and proceeded to Jones Beach. It was early evening, and many of the sunbathers had returned to their homes for dinner. After parking my car, I removed my shoes and socks and walked across the sand toward the ocean. In a secluded spot, I stopped and sighed and reflected. I tried to process the events of the past several months.

O Lord, in a world so rich and lovely and plentiful for all, can't your children find anything better to do than to grab a disproportionate share of your gifts to satisfy their naked greed? Animosity toward the other first appeared in the Cain and Abel narrative and continues to the present. Throughout history, beginning with the formulation of the great chain of being, human beings have categorized themselves into superior and inferior species. Human beings have negatively branded those who do not share their preferred ethnic background, have usurped wealth and power at the expense of others, and have taken steps to maintain supremacy for their privileged group.

In the movie *West Side Story*, two star-crossed lovers, a Pole and a Puerto Rican, gazed passionately at each other on opposite sides of a fire escape grate. Perhaps Anton and Maria experienced the same in their youth.

Thirty years ago, Katarina and I, children of the Cold War who grew up on opposites of the Iron Curtain, held hands in Paris and Cambridge. Simone and Sanna held hands on opposite sides of the Berlin Wall. More recently, Bracha and Anwar held hands with the separation barrier at their backs. The children of Congregation Rodef Tzedek held hands with the children of Grace Afternoon School within the invisible walls of Broadway.

On June 12, 1997, President Reagan once said, "Mr. Gorbachev, tear down this wall." Other walls must be torn down as well. In New York, its residents must cross Broadway. In Jerusalem, Israelis and Palestinians must freely cross the separation barrier. Maybe someday it will come down and become an anachronism like the Berlin Wall.

It's time to build bridges instead. Hatred and distrust of the other creates walls. Only love can build a bridge.

When will this vicious cycle of coveting wealth and power, of stoking the flames of culture wars and fanatic partisanship, of engaging in name-calling, ethnic cleansing, and violence come to an end? Perhaps it will take the coming of the Messiah. Perhaps it will never come. All is left is to bring about a Messianic Age through human endeavor.

It is 2014. I know this. Unless the vicious cycle of us and them is broken, humanity will not move an inch.

My efforts to soften the blows of segregated schools and of hostility to Latin America immigrants have not changed the overall picture in America. Bracha's work with Ir Amim has not changed the overall picture in Israel. But they are beginnings. As the Talmud states, "All beginnings are hard. We are not required to finish our work, but we are not free to desist from it."

I look toward the east and face Jerusalem. Many centuries ago, Abraham immigrated to the promised land to build a middle-of-the-road community. It would become a community that would depart from the lawlessness of the generation of Noah when everyone did what was right in their own eyes. It would also become a community which would depart from the artificial unity of the generation of Babel, when everyone spoke the same language and was of the same mind. Abraham's community would reject the two extremes of anarchy and organic nationalism. Rather, it would be a shining example to the rest of the known world, and through Abraham, the nations of the world would be blessed.

Centuries later, after the loss of nationhood, our people scattered throughout the four corners of our planet. My ancestors made their homes in Europe and North America. Two of my great aunts, who I had never met, were massacred by the pogroms in Russia. Two of my great-grandparents died during the Bolshevik Revolution. My wife's great-uncle, Berl Valdman, and his family in Tuchin were burnt to ashes to avoid capture by the Nazis. One cousin, Georges Garel, worked in the French Resistance and kept European children out of Nazi concentration camps. Other relatives made it to Ellis Island to pursue the promise of America. Sadly, anti-Semitism persisted even in the free societies of the United States and Canada.

One of our own, Bracha, will soon return to the birthplace of our people and will rejoin our Israeli cousins. From the ashes of Berl Valdman, Bracha will help build the New Jerusalem. May she play a major role in recreating Abraham's world and developing the type of society which God had imagined all along. O Bracha Shulamith, may the blessing of peace become the herald of the dawn of a new day.

This New Jerusalem would be built, not by establishing the Third Temple, not by restoring the antiquated sacrificial system, and not by excluding a large section of the population. The New Jerusalem, both in theory and in practice, would once again become a city that would embrace the world's three great religions—Judaism,

Christianity, and Islam—and would be tolerant of all others. The New Jerusalem would emphasize inclusiveness, hospitality, civil rights, equal opportunities for all, and peaceful coexistence with the surrounding neighbors.

The New Jerusalem does not have to be confined to one geographic location. The New Jerusalem can be rebuilt with chariots of fire in England's green and pleasant land. The New Jerusalem can be rebuilt within the rich diversity of New York City. In any part of the world where people continuously strive for a society in which human rights come not from the generosity of the state but from God, there we will find the New Jerusalem.

In building this New Jerusalem, a wondrous thing takes place. One voice crying out for justice in the darkness can soon become a duet. From the duet emerges a quartet. The quartet expands into a choir. From the choir, a full-blown political movement comes about. From one voice singing in the darkness, from the crescendo of music filling our troubled planet, from the expansion of remembrance to the loving embrace of the other emerges the secret of redemption.

Notes

Notes to Chapter 1

1. "Interview with Professor Ben Zion Dinur," *Maariv*, June 1967.
2. Benny Morris, *Righteous Victims*, pp. 9–10.
3. "Interview with Professor Ben Zion Dinur," *Maariv*, June 1967.
4. Ben Zion Dinur, *Israel and the Diaspora*, p. 7.
5. Benjamin Netanyahu, *A Durable Peace*, p. 29.
6. Max Nordau, "Speech to the First Zionist Congress," in *A Zionist Reader*, ed. Arthur Hertzberg, pp. 240–241.

Notes to Chapter 5

1. Maimonides, *Guide for the Perplexed, III:27*.
2. Arye Gelblum, *Haaretz*, April 22, 1949.
3. Abba Eban, *Voice of Israel* (New York, 1957).

Notes to Chapter 6

1. Steven J. Gould, *The Mismeasure of Man* (W. W. Norton and Company, 1996), p. 102, quoted by Ann Gibson Winfield, *Eugenics Education in America* (New York: Peter Lang Publishing, 2007), p. 47.
2. Ibid.
3. Benjamin Palmer, *Our Historic Mission, an Address Delivered before the Eunomian and Phi-Mu Societies of La Grange College, July 7, 1858* (New Orleans: True Witness Office, 1859), pp. 4–5.
4. G. T. Gillespie, "A Christian View of Segregation" (Greenwood: Association of Citizens' Councils of Mississippi, 1954), p. 9.
5. Ibid., pp. 4, 11.
6. Joshua Levinson, "The Travels and Travails of Abraham," in *Jews and Journeys*, edited by Joshua Levinson and Orit Bashkin (Philadelphia: University of Pennsylvania Press, 2021), p. 34.
7. William H. Tucker, *The Science and Politics of Racial Research* (Urbana: University of Illinois Press, 1994), p. 10, quoted by Ann Gibson Winfield, *Eugenics Education in America* (New York: Peter Lang Publishing, 2007), p. 46.

8. John Marshall, *Cherokee Nation v. Georgia, 30 U.S. 1 (1831)*, quoted by Jed S. Rakoff, *Why the Innocent Plead Guilty and the Guilty Go Free* (Farrar, Strauss, and Giroux, 2021), p. 151.
9. Treaty with the Cherokee, 1835, in Kappler, 2, pp. 439–449.
10. Sami Adwan, Dan Bar-On, and Eyal Naveh, *Side by Side*, p. 5.
11. Ibid., p. 7.
12. Ilan Pappe, *Ten Myths about Israel* (New York: Verso, 2017), p. 6.
13. John L. O'Sullivan, "The Course of Civilization," *United States Magazine and Democratic Review* 6, no. 21 (September 1839): pp. 208–211.
14. John L. O'Sullivan, "European Views of American Democracy," *United States Magazine and Democratic Review* 2, no. 8 (July 1838): pp. 352–353.
15. Albert J. Beveridge, *The Meanings of the Times and Other Speeches* (Indianapolis: The Bobbs-Merill Co., 1908), pp. 118–43.
16. Thomas C. Leonard, *Illiberal Reformers* (Princeton University Press, 2016), p. 4.
17. Ibid., p. 21.
18. Woodrow Wilson, *The New Freedom* (New York: Doubleday, Page & Co, 1918), pp. 47–48, quoted in Thomas C. Leonard, *Illiberal Reformers* (Princeton University Press, 2016), p. 101.
19. Edwin Black, *The War against the Weak* (Washington, DC, 2003), p. 39. Also in John H. Noyes, *Essays on Scientific Propagation* (Oneida, NY: Oneida Community, 1872), section 2, section 15.
20. Charles Benedict Davenport, *Heredity in Relation to Eugenics* (New York: Henry Holt and Company, 1911), p. 4.
21. Ibid., p. 216.
22. Ibid., p. 183; Max Reichler, *Jewish Eugenics* (New York: Bloch Publishing Company, 1916), pp. 8–9.
23. Edwin Black, *The War against the Weak* (Washington, DC, 2003), p. 38.
24. Daniel Okrent, *The Guarded Gate* (New York: Simon and Schuster, 2019), pp. 130–131.
25. Edwin Black, *The War against the Weak* (Washington, DC, 2003), p. 100.
26. Ibid.
27. Theodore Roosevelt, "Americanism," from *Fear God and Take Your Own Part* (New York: George H. Doran, 2016), pp. 154–156.
28. Edwin Black, *The War against the Weak* (Washington, DC, 2003), p. 269.
29. Ibid., p. 270.
30. Ibid., pp. 284–285.
31. Madison Grant, *The Passing of the Great Race* (Pantianos Classics, 1916), p. 12.
32. Erika Lee, *America for Americans* (New York: Basic Books, 2019), p. 118.
33. Ibid., p. 139.
34. Daniel Okrent, *The Guarded Gate* (New York: Simon and Schuser, 2019), p. 277.
35. Ibid., p. 278.
36. Erika Lee, *America for Americans* (New York: Basic Books, 2019), p. 142.

37 Ibid., p. 143.
38 Ibid. Also found in James Q. Whitman, *Hitler's American Model: The United States and the Making of Nazi Race Law* (Princeton, NJ: Princeton University Press, 2017) pp. 12, 46–47.
39 Ibid., p. 145.
40 Ibid., pp. 225.
41 Ibid., pp. 248–249.
42 Ibid., p. 249.
43 Ibid., p. 279.
44 Ibid., pp. 279–280.
45 Ibid., p. 283.
46 Ibid., pp. 283–284.
47 Samuel P. Huntington, *Who Are We* (New York: Simon and Schuster, 2004), p. 256.
48 Zeev Sternhell, *The Founding Myths of Israel* (Princeton University Press, 1998), pp. 10–11.
49 Ibid., p. 8.
50 Aaron David Gordon, "Self-Criticism, 1916," in *Writings* 1:353, quoted by Zeev Sternhell, *The Founding Myths of Israel* (Princeton University Press, 1998), p. 53.
51 Aaron David Gordon, "A Clarification," pp. 182–183, quoted by Zeev Sternhell, *The Founding Myths of Israel* (Princeton University Press, 1998), p. 53.
52 Aaron David Gordon, "The Congress," in *Writings* 1:193, quoted by Zeev Sternhell, *The Founding Myths of Israel* (Princeton University Press, 1998), p. 54.
53 Aaron David Gordon, "Letters to the Diaspora" (1921) in *Writings* 1:542–543, quoted by Zeev Sternhell, *The Founding Myths of Israel* (Princeton University Press, 1998), pp. 10–11, pp. 52–53.
54 Arthur Ruppin, *Tagebuch*, quoted by Etan Bloom, *Arthur Ruppin and the Production of Pre-Israeli Culture* (Leiden: Koninklijke Brill NV, 2011), p. 66.
55 Jabotinsky in Bilski Ben Hur 1993, p. 132, quoted by Tom Segev in *One Palestine* (Picador, 2001), p. 151; also quoted and rephrased by Raphael Falk, *Zionism and the Biology of Jews* (Springer International Publishing, 2017), p. 100.
56 Arthur Ruppin, *Relation of the Jews*, p. 109, quoted by Etan Bloom, *Arthur Ruppin and the Production of Pre-Israeli Culture* (Leiden: Koninklijke Brill NV, 2011), p. 97.
57 Eliyahu ben Chorin, *The Middle East: Crossroads of History* (New York: WW Norton & Company, 1943), pp. 230–231, quoted by Nur Masalha, *Imperial Israel and the Palestinians* (Pluto Press, 2000), p. 61.
58 Protocol of the Zionist Executive Committee (November 14, 1934), quoted by Etan Bloom, *Arthur Ruppin and the Production of Pre-Israeli Culture* (Leiden: Koninklijke Brill NV, 2011), p. 104.
59 Arthur Ruppin, *Sociology of the Jews*, II, 29, quoted by Etan Bloom, *Arthur Ruppin and the Production of Pre-Israeli Culture* (Leiden: Koninklijke Brill NV, 2011), p. 93.

60. Etan Bloom, *Arthur Ruppin and the Production of Pre-Israeli Culture* (Leiden: Koninklijke Brill NV, 2011), pp. 99–101.
61. Arye Gelblum, *Haaretz*, April 22, 1949.
62. Ella Shohat, *On the Arab-Jew, Palestine, and Other Displacements* (London: Pluto Press, 2017), p. 56.
63. Ibid., p. 57.
64. Ibid., p. 58.
65. Ibid.
66. Ibid., pp. 58–59.
67. Ibid., p. 115.
68. Ibid., p. 56.
69. Etan Bloom, *Arthur Ruppin and the Production of Pre-Israeli Culture* (Leiden: Koninklijke Brill NV, 2011), p. 342.
70. Ibid., p. 340.
71. Arthur Ruppin, *Jews in the Modern World*, pp. 256–257, quoted in Etan Bloom, *Arthur Ruppin and the Production of Pre-Israeli Culture* (Leiden: Koninklijke Brill NV, 2011), p. 344.
72. James 2:14–16.

Notes on Chapter 8

1. Ella Shohat, *Israel Cinema* (New York: IB Taurus and Company, 2010), p. 35; Ronit Lentin, *Israel and the Daughters of the Shoah* (New York: Berghan Books, 2000), p. 198.
2. Ibid., p. 37.
3. Ibid.
4. Ibid., p. 45.
5. Ibid., p. 40.
6. Deuteronomy 28:28.
7. Bar Tal, "Why Does Fear," p. 604, quoted in Alice Rothchild, *Broken Promises, Broken Dreams* (London and New York: Pluto Press, 2010), pp. 48–49.
8. Henry Wasserman, "Nationalizing the Memory of the Six Million," *Politica*, no. 8: 6–7, quoted in Ronit Lentin, *Israel and the Daughters of the Shoah* (New York: Berghan Books, 2000), p. 123.
9. Ibid.
10. Marc Gopin, *Bridges Across and Impossible Divide* (New York: Oxford University Press, 2012), p. 34.
11. Ibid., p. 101.
12. Ibid., p. 110.

About the Author

Rabbi Jeffrey Gale was born in St. Louis, Missouri. Upon graduation from University City High School, he attended Miami University in Oxford, Ohio. He majored in political science and spent his junior year at the European Study Centre in Luxembourg. Upon graduating cum laude in 1975, he moved to London, England.

After ordination, Rabbi Gale served the Southend and District Reform Synagogue and the Settlement Synagogue. While in England, he served on the reform movement's music committee and on the Soviet Jewry committee. His visits to the Soviet Union in the early 1980s to teach and comfort refuseniks were highlights of his rabbinate in London. Rabbi Gale returned to North America in 1984 and served congregations in Jackson, Michigan, Winnipeg, Manitoba, and Regina, Saskatchewan. From 1998 to 2022, he served three congregations in the New York area—Wantagh, Washington Heights, and Flushing. Rabbi Gale is currently retired. Throughout his career, community relations, interfaith programming, and social causes such as civil rights and immigration are very dear to his heart.

Rabbi Gale is married to Dr. Tsiporah Shore, the associate director of the Bone Marrow Transplant Unit at New York Presbyterian Hospital, and has two adult children, Leanne and Joshua.

Milton Keynes UK
Ingram Content Group UK Ltd.
UKHW040631091123
432260UK00002B/104